GLORIA

GLORIA

Bentley Little

Cemetery Dance Publications
Baltimore
2025

Cemetery Dance Publications
132-B Industry Lane, Unit #7
Forest Hill, MD 21050
http://www.cemeterydance.com

Trade Paperback Edition Printing

ISBN: 978-1-964780-18-4

ONE

Gloria Jaymes had not expected to see her mother again, but immediately following the funeral, her dead mom showed up at the house. For some reason, she looked not the way she had when she died, but the way she had in the 1980s, when Gloria was a child. She was wearing one of those big-shouldered, bold-colored jackets, a bright blue thing over a white blouse with large black polka dots. Her makeup was garish as well—thick red lipstick, high purple eyeshadow—and her hair was blonder than Gloria ever recalled it being, so teased and sprayed that it made the head beneath it look somehow too small.

Gloria did not remember the fashions of the Eighties as being quite so hideous, although that was a strange and frivolous thought to be having when her dead mother was standing in the doorway, waiting to be let in. She glanced back at the guests (or mourners, as they should probably be called), milling about in the living room, dining room and kitchen. The house, she realized, still looked much the same as it had in the 1980s. The sofa and loveseat in the living room had been switched out a couple of times since then, although the replacements had always had the same rough cloth texture and the same off-white color scheme, but the remaining furniture, the tables and lamps and bookcase—and even the books *on* the bookcase—were the same ones she'd grown up with. The only part of the house that was substantially different than it had been during her childhood was her own bedroom, which her mother turned into an "office," once Gloria had moved out.

In the living room, her husband and sons were standing awkwardly next to the fireplace, forced to speak with people they barely knew. Not their forte. Her Aunt Ruth and Cousin Kate were handling all of the food, bringing out drinks from the kitchen and coordinating the potluck dishes on the dining room table. None of them were looking in her direction.

"May I come in?" her mother asked.

Flummoxed, Gloria nodded. It occurred to her that vampires were supposed to have to ask in order to enter a house for the first time. That could explain how she was here, even though she had just been buried. But her mother had not asked the question in the intimidating way a monster would; she had done so in the annoyed sarcastic manner she adopted whenever her daughter was not doing something she wanted her to do. Still, Gloria waited a moment, and when her mother did not bite her neck or start attacking the guests (mourners!), Gloria closed the door behind her.

Amidst all of the black and somber gray, her mother's gaudy wardrobe seemed rude, vulgar and entirely inappropriate. No one commented on it, however. Benjamin and the boys welcomed her in, several people nodded hello, and Kate handed her a paper plate, leading her over to the food table.

No one recognized who she was.

How is that possible? Gloria wondered. Maxine from across the street, her mother's best friend since before Gloria was born, was here, as were old friends from work and from church, not to mention Aunt Ruth and Cousin Kate. They'd all known her mother at that age (and Aunt Ruth was her own sister!). How could they not recognize her? Could this version of her mother have been so superseded in everyone's minds by the frumpy elderly woman of later years that it had rendered her earlier self unidentifiable?

"Mom!" Gloria said, approaching.

Her mother turned toward her. As did everyone else. She saw the looks on all of their faces: shock, sadness, pity. Benjamin hurried over. Like the rest of them, he clearly thought that grief had addled her mind, that stress had taken its toll and she had somehow gotten confused, making her forget that her mother had died. He put his arms around her, and she was about to tell him the truth, when she saw her mom looking directly at her and slowly shaking her head.

For the first time, Gloria felt the emotion that she should have felt from the beginning: fear. She looked away, peering into Benjamin's worried face, then glanced back. Her mother was scooping up a plate of tuna casserole.

"It's okay," Benjamin said. "It's all right."

She glanced over his shoulder at the boys. Both Bradley and Lucas looked frightened. Everyone else was purposely turned away, embarrassed for her.

"Sorry," she said. "Habit. I just..." She trailed off, not knowing where to go from there.

"Why don't you go and lie down?" Benjamin suggested. "Get some rest. We'll take care of things out here."

Maybe she would. Her head hurt, and she was tired of nodding politely and accepting condolences. She wanted all of this to be over, and maybe if she went into the bedroom and took a nap, everyone would be gone by the time she woke up, and she could avoid the lengthy goodbyes that she knew were coming.

And, hopefully, her mother would be gone.

"I think I will," she told Benjamin. "Wake me up when people start to leave."

"I will," he said, but she could tell from his tone of voice that he had no intention of doing any such thing, and for that she was grateful. Gloria retired to the guest room—she was not up to sleeping in her mother's bed—and closed the door behind her before stretching out on the twin bed in the corner.

She was unable to sleep, however. Her most fervent wish at this moment was that she would doze for a half hour and awaken to find that this childhood version of her mother was gone. She might never know why or how her mom had appeared, but that would be okay. As long as she was not here, Gloria would be satisfied.

But was that reasonable to expect? Looking at it from a practical point of view, where did her mother have to go? This was her home. Would she simply vacate the premises, going out with the rest of the crowd, to...what? Wander the streets? It seemed far more likely that Gloria would wake up to find that her mother was back in *her* bedroom, lying down on her bed, or even cleaning the house after the guests' (mourners') departure. The probability that she would leave in the same manner that she had arrived was, to Gloria's way of thinking, mighty slim.

She awoke in a darkened room, unaware that she had even fallen asleep. She had no memory of getting drowsy and drifting off. Her last memory was of mentally cataloguing the possible outcomes of her mother's reappearance, which probably meant that sleep had overcome her instantly, as with a person administered anesthesia before surgery. With the stress she'd been under, such a response was perfectly natural and to be expected, but it was still disconcerting, and Gloria sat up in bed, wondering if everyone had left.

Where was her mother?

That was the real question. Her hope was that the entire incident had been a consequence of her overworked, overtired, overburdened brain and that it had never occurred, but through the partially open bedroom doorway, she heard the distinct and unmistakable cadence of her mother's voice speaking with Benjamin and the boys. It was a voice from the past, a younger version that she had forgotten but that came roaring back from some distant part of her memory banks. All of a sudden, Gloria wasn't sure she remembered her mother's *older* voice, the one she'd lived with for the past decade, the one she'd heard just five days ago in the hospital.

She remained in place for a moment, eavesdropping. The four of them were talking about dinner. Gloria was sure there was plenty of food left over, but Bradley was complaining that he wanted Taco Bell, while Lucas chimed in that he wanted Del Taco.

Her mother laughed, an unexpectedly loud and inappropriately raucous laugh that she remembered from her childhood, and for the first time since her mother had returned, Gloria felt a twinge of sadness. "Homemade tacos are better than any fast food," her mother said. "And healthier, too! I'll make you my famous ground turkey tacos with pico de gallo."

"Thank you, Nora," Benjamin said. "We really appreciate it."

Had her mother revealed her identity, Gloria wondered, or had Benjamin figured out who she was? Because now Benjamin not only knew her name, but she was seemingly integrated into the family in a way no stranger could ever be in so short amount of time.

Gloria got out of bed. Shouldn't her family have been more frightened? Her husband's mother-in-law, the children's dead grandmother, had come back to life as a younger version of herself. Didn't that deserve more of a reaction than passive acceptance? Now wide awake, she made her way out to the kitchen. All four of them were standing in the center of the room, in front of the sink, her husband and sons on the left side, facing her mother on the right.

Benjamin saw her the moment she stepped through the doorway. "How are you feeling?" he asked.

"Feeling? I'm feeling fine."

"I just meant, after your outburst—"

"Outburst?" she said, annoyed, as always, by his condescension. "I didn't have an outburst. I was just—"

Her mother had turned to look at her and, as before, she met Gloria's gaze with those heavily made-up eyes, shaking her overly coiffed head.

So Benjamin and the boys didn't know who she was.

Was it reflex, the naturally submissive response of a child to a parent's directive, or was it something else that caused Gloria to break off in mid-sentence? Either way, she dropped her defensive posture and Benjamin chose not to further engage. "Nora here has kindly volunteered to cook us dinner," he said, switching subjects. "I wasn't sure when you were going to wake up, and knew you wouldn't be in the mood to cook when you did, so when she offered to stay over and make us tacos, I took her up on it. I know there are still a lot of potluck leftovers," he added quickly, "but Nora's already wrapped them up and put them away, and besides, you know the boys don't like casseroles. I figured *we* could eat them for lunch ourselves over the next few days and give the kids something else."

Gloria nodded in acquiescence, although she didn't really care about the food. What concerned her was the fact that Benjamin did not recognize his mother-in-law (the boys she could understand). Gloria wasn't the only one who could see her, but apparently she was the only one who knew who she was. What did that mean? The idea that her family would so readily invite a stranger—a bizarrely retro-looking stranger—into their lives was also disconcerting. They were not that kind of people, not ordinarily, and it made her wonder whether her mother was able to exert some sort of influence over Benjamin and the boys.

What would her mother do after dinner? she wondered. The woman had no home. *This* was her home. Or, rather, it had been. Was she planning to move back in? Was that her intent? Or was she going to move on after cooking the food? Gloria doubted that her mother had any money, and she definitely didn't have any credit cards because Benjamin had, sensibly, cancelled them upon her death. Would she end up wandering the streets, homeless? Or would she try to get a job and find her own place, at an extended-stay motel? Although, thinking realistically, her mother should not be able to *get* a job because she had no Social Security number or valid ID.

Gloria's headache had returned. She watched her mother walk over and open the refrigerator door, and something about the visual angle jogged her memory. She suddenly remembered seeing her mother in this exact same outfit before, with the same big teased hair. It had been at JCPenney's, and Gloria had been in the toy department, trying to find a present for her friend Celia's birthday. Her mom had stood there, making suggestions which Gloria ignored. She was looking for the latest Jem figure because she liked the commercial and the song that said Jem was "Truly Outrageous." Her mother had no doubt worn the same outfit numerous other times, but for some reason, that moment stuck in Gloria's memory, and it gave the woman before her a more concrete and tangible presence. This was *actually* her mother. She had known that intellectually, but now she felt it, and she wanted more than anything else for the two of them to have the chance to talk.

She thought of the look her mother had twice given her, the subtle shake of her head, and knew that if they had a real conversation, they would have to do so out of earshot of the rest of the family.

Benjamin was ushering the boys and her out of the kitchen. The dining room table had been cleared of food while she'd been asleep, and used paper plates and plastic cups had been dumped in an open black garbage sack next to the breakfront. "It was a nice service," he told her. "Everyone said so. They all wanted me to let you know how much your mom will be missed."

Gloria almost had to smile at that. She glanced back into the kitchen, where her mother was grabbing something out of one of the cupboards. *Beans*, she thought. Her mother always put a layer of refried beans beneath the ground turkey in her tacos. She turned to Benjamin. "Could you take the kids into the back room and get a game out of the closet and play with them for awhile? I'd like to talk to...Nora...alone."

"Sure," he said.

Who did he think the woman was? Gloria had no idea, and at this moment didn't care. She just wanted some time alone to talk to her mother. Bradley and Lucas were herded into the back room—"Connect Four!" Bradley said. "Monopoly!" Lucas countered—and Gloria steeled herself before walking back into the kitchen.

"Mom?" she said.

"Yes?" The bright lips smiled radiantly. Gloria expected there to be some sort of giveaway, dead eyes, perhaps, but the entire face was vivacious and engaged and looked just the way her mother's features had when Gloria was a little girl.

"Is it really you?"

Her mother's loud laugh again. "Of course, it's me!"

"How?"

A look of consternation flitted across her mother's face, and to Gloria the effort seemed studied, theatrical, put on for her benefit. But was that really true? Or was she merely seeing what she wanted to see? Because the feeling of insincerity lasted only a few seconds before her mother appeared to her to be genuinely puzzled. "I don't really know," she said.

"But you do know that you died. You had a heart attack here at home last Monday, and then a few days later, at the hospital, you had some kind of embolism and died. We just buried you today."

Her mother was frowning. "It seems like I know that? But I don't remember it."

"What's the last thing you do remember? Because somehow you look like you did when I was little. You're even wearing the same clothes."

"I don't know." Gloria heard the slightest trace of frustration in her mother's voice. "I understand that I'm younger than I should be. But I still know all about Benjamin and Bradley and Lucas. I'm still *me*."

"Are you?"

"Yes! There's just...some things missing."

"What things?"

"I don't know. I only know I feel different."

It was their old conversational rhythm, and they'd fallen into it naturally. She missed her mother, Gloria realized. She hadn't really had time to miss her, but not talking to her for even less than a week had left Gloria feeling surprisingly bereft, something she had not noticed until this moment. Their exchange brought home to her just how reliant she was on her mom, how she sought her mother's advice or approval on everything from major life choices to simple household decisions, despite the fact that she now had a family of her own. She had never stopped being her mother's child, and she wondered if that dynamic held true for everyone. Benjamin's mom had died when he was a teenager, so the tether had been broken early, but in her case, that break had not happened until now.

And suddenly it had been rescinded.

It was comforting to talk to her mother again, yet at the same time there was a reticence on her part because...her mother was dead. This person, this childhood version of her mom, might or might not be who she claimed, and Gloria was expending far too much effort in trying to decode subliminal signals and spot subtle discrepancies in order to figure out which. She took a deep breath and said what she was thinking. "Are you my mother? *You*? Not another you or some version of you, but *you*?"

"Of course."

Gloria sighed. "So how's this going to work? Do you plan on living here? I mean, it *is* your house. But how are we going to explain that to people? What are we going to say? And what about *our* relationship? Are we just going to pick up where we left off? I mean, for the past few years, I've been more of a caregiver than anything else; you were so old, and had so many problems. Now you're as young as I am. What are we going to do?"

Her mother smiled. She took Gloria's hand and patted it, in the same way she'd always done. "Why don't we just play things by ear and see how it goes."

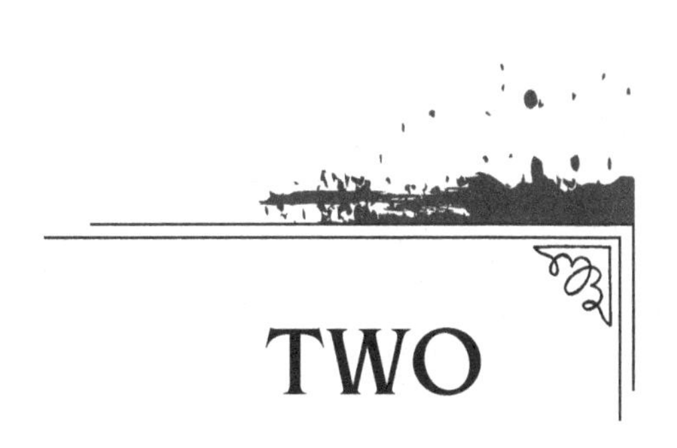

TWO

A month later, Gloria was marveling at how easily and seamlessly her mother had integrated herself into their lives. She had indeed stayed in the house, and though Benjamin had originally wanted to sell it after her death ("What do we need with two houses in the same city?"), he seemed to have forgotten all about that notion. He also seemed to have forgotten his backup plan of renting it out, because her mother was somehow living there without paying a dime.

But she was definitely earning her keep. Now that she was young and well enough to do so, she was babysitting her grandchildren after school, which took a huge strain off Gloria and Benjamin, who hadn't had an actual vacation in several years because their vacation hours had been nickled-and-dimed to death as one, then another, would take off work early or go to work late in order to take care of the boys' needs. Invariably, after coming over to babysit, her mother would tidy up the house as well, for which Gloria was grateful. She'd also been bringing them food. "It's too hard to cook for one person," she said the first time she brought over a pot of stew, and she'd continued to make more than she needed for lunches and dinners, favoring them with the surfeit. Gloria had always appreciated her mother's cooking—as had Benjamin—and since she didn't particularly like preparing meals herself, the leftovers were a godsend.

In a way, her mother's return had also helped her relationship with Benjamin, or, at least, increased her appreciation of him. Because the truth was, over the past few years, they had been gradually drifting apart. It was nothing so obvious or specific as differing interests or changing feelings. And neither of them had found anyone else. In fact, at its core, it probably had a lot to do with her mother. Ever since her mother had gotten sick, Gloria had had to shift her focus from Benjamin and the boys to the needs of her ailing parent. Her husband understood this, at least intellectually, but the reality of it meant that she was more tired, more distracted, more physically and emotionally unavailable. And, Gloria had to admit, spending so much time with her mother had, by a kind of osmosis, influenced her opinions, leading her to see things from her mother's point of view. Since her mom had never really taken to Benjamin, this meant that she herself had started to look at him with a jaundiced eye. She'd begun to grow slightly disappointed with him, with his maddening evenhandedness, with his stodgy plodding approach to everything.

She'd thought, when she originally met him, that Benjamin had been a pianist. It seemed foolish and impossible to believe now—he didn't even like music all that much!—but the first time she'd ever laid eyes on him, in the dermatologist's office where she was a receptionist and he was a new patient, he'd checked in with her and then sat there on the utilitarian chair opposite her window with his hands on his legs, doing that thing where he was tapping on his pants, each of his fingers randomly moving up and down. It looked like he was playing an invisible piano as he absently glanced around the waiting room, and she assumed that he was mentally practicing, going over in his mind a difficult piece that he would perform at some future date. He was actually just doing the finger exercises that a previous doctor had told him to do because of incipient carpal tunnel syndrome, and perhaps if she had known that, Gloria might not have been so susceptible to him. But he came by again the next week, still playing air piano while he waited, and since it was almost lunchtime and there were no other patients, the two of them started talking, both of them disappointed when the nurse opened the door and called him into the back. They talked even more when he returned the following week, and even more the week after that, and on his last visit, he asked her out and she said yes.

Would she have done so if she'd known at the time that he was not a pianist but a computer programmer? It was hard to say. She might well have, but going forward her expectations would have been different, and they might not have ended up where they did.

But it was all good now, as the kids said. Her mother's arrival as a younger, more energetic woman had freed up time for Gloria and Benjamin to be with each other, and they'd discovered that they were still compatible, something that had been by no means certain two months ago. No, he wasn't the most exciting person in the world, but neither was she, and if their marriage wasn't one of the world's great romances, it was nice and comfortable. They'd even taken to kissing each other and saying "I love you" before going to bed each night, something they had not done since the first years of their marriage, and regular lovemaking, which had been intermittent at best, was back from hiatus.

Benjamin was a good man, and he cared about her, and both of them loved the boys. What more could a person ask for in life?

Still, despite all of the positive changes that had come about as a result of her mother's return, Gloria felt uneasy about the woman. She had *died*. Now she was back and roughly the same age as Gloria herself. She also seemed to be getting money from somewhere, since she was able to buy groceries and had purchased an entirely new wardrobe. The 1980s style of her initial reappearance was gone, but the clothes left in the closet, in addition to fitting the more matronly figure of her mother's later years, were of an old-lady style that no longer suited her. So she'd gone out and, somehow, managed to buy herself an entirely new, more modern and appropriate wardrobe. Gloria was not sure how this was possible. Was her mother tapping into some hidden cache of funds that no one else had known about? Was she secretly selling off household items? Was someone else providing her with cash?

This last possibility was the most disturbing, and though Gloria did not want to think about it, it was the one idea that remained floating in the back of her mind.

Disconcertingly, her mother and Maxine were no longer friends. True, they were no longer the same age, but they had lived across the street from each other and had been closer than sisters for literally decades, so Gloria was shocked when she went over one day to check in, and her mother said, "Boy, that Maxine's a bitch, isn't she?"

"Maxine's your best friend!" Gloria responded.

"*Was* my best friend," her mother corrected.

"Why? What happened?"

"Nothing happened. I just woke up, and now I see her for what she really is."

I just woke up.

That might be the most accurate description of what had happened, Gloria thought, but her mother hadn't meant it in that sense. The reference had been to having her eyes opened in regard to her old friend's character, and while, in the past, Gloria would have automatically taken her mother's side in any disagreement, she now felt more kinship with Maxine, and after leaving, she walked across the street to get Maxine's side of the story.

"Oh, that woman is just maddening," her old neighbor fumed. "I know you and your husband probably need the rent money, but I swear, if it was me, I'd just evict her. Your mother would be appalled that such a person was living in her house and cooking in her kitchen and sleeping in her bed. Who is this Nora anyway? Where did she come from? I tell you, Gloria, I don't trust her. If I were you, I'd take a full inventory of all your mom's belongings just to make sure everything's still there when she leaves."

The fact that, even after close contact and personal interaction, Maxine still did not recognize her old friend made Gloria feel uneasy. Why was she the only one to recognize her mother? Even Aunt Ruth and Cousin Kate had had no idea who the anachronistic woman at the post-funeral gathering had been. Kate lived a couple of hours away, but Aunt Ruth was still close by, and Gloria could have easily invited her over to meet with "Nora." She did not, however, and Gloria was not sure if her reluctance to do so was because she was afraid Ruth would not recognize her sister or because she was afraid she would.

Gloria nodded sympathetically as Maxine aired her complaints.

"All I did was try to talk to her, welcome her to the neighborhood." Maxine leaned forward. "And do you know what she called me? 'A meddling cunt!' Can you believe it? Have you ever heard such a thing? What kind of woman says something like that? Your mother and I were friends for forty years, and I guarantee you that she would not put up with that kind of talk! I'm not blaming you, you understand. I know that you and Benjamin need the extra income. But to my mind, that kind of behavior is totally unacceptable. Totally unacceptable!" Her eyes were wet. "And the fact that that woman's living in your mother's house?" She wiped an escaped tear. "I don't know what all!"

After that, Gloria was sure Maxine spied on her each time she came over for a visit, which was why she preferred to have her mother come over to *their* house (and she didn't know *what* Maxine thought about this "Nora" being allowed to drive her mother's car).

Despite all of the uncomfortable weirdness, however, her mother's renewed presence in their lives had freed up more family time, allowing them to go places and do things on the weekends for the first time in a long while.

And, strangely, the boys seemed to love her. Gloria found this particularly baffling. Neither Bradley nor Lucas had ever had much of an emotional connection with their grandmother, which was understandable since she had been sick for a good portion of their lives. But they adored this woman whom they called "Miss Nora." They asked their parents if she could stay and eat with them each time she cooked food for the family, and when Gloria got off work early on the Friday before Presidents' Day and picked up the boys from school, telling them that they didn't need a babysitter that afternoon, she could see the disappointment in their faces.

Benjamin even brought it up one time when Bradley and Lucas were in bed and asleep. It was her turn to do the dishes, and she was rinsing out the cups when he came into the kitchen. Apparently, the boys had asked him if Miss Nora could come with them on their Spring Break trip to Disneyland. "Don't get me wrong," he said. "Nora's a wonderful woman. Really. There's not a bad thing I can say about her. She's been, as my mom might have said, a 'blessing.'"

"But..." Gloria prompted.

"But don't you think Brad and Luke are maybe a little too close to her, a little too dependent?"

Brad and Luke. She didn't like it when he shortened their sons' names. For someone who insisted that everyone always pronounce all three syllables of "Benjamin," he was very lax and disrespectful when it came to the two syllables of "Bradley" and "Lucas." But this wasn't the time to get into that discussion again, because she knew exactly what he was talking about. She'd felt it, too, and while she'd wondered if it wasn't just some sort of maternal jealousy on her part, the fact that Benjamin had noticed the same thing meant that her feelings had some validity. It would be understandable if the boys had known she was their grandmother, but they didn't. To them, she was just a nice lady who watched them after school and sometimes made the family meals or helped their mom with grocery shopping. The attachment they'd formed to her was far out of proportion to what it should have been.

Then again, maybe they could *sense* the familial connection even if they didn't consciously recognize it.

Gloria finished rinsing and wiped her hands on a dishtowel, turning toward Benjamin. "You're right," she said. "And I don't want to encourage it, but I don't want to discourage it, either."

"Me neither. I'm not saying anything like that. I'm just saying that... Well, I guess I'm saying that I don't think we should invite her to family outings like trips to Disneyland."

"Of course not," Gloria agreed.

"Good." That seemed to be all he had come in here to say, and as he left the kitchen Gloria wasn't quite sure why he had made the effort. It suddenly occurred to her that her mother might have lobbied to go along on the Disneyland excursion, putting the idea in the kids' heads, and she wondered how her mother was going to react upon discovering she was not invited.

As it turned out, there was no reaction, at least not that Gloria heard, so perhaps it really was the boys' idea after all.

Losing her mother and, to a lesser extent, getting her mother back, had caused Gloria to reflect on her own children. At the moment, they were completely dependent on her. She woke them up in the morning, made them breakfast, packed their lunches, drove them to school, helped them with their homework, made their dinner, put them to bed. She was the buffer between them and the outside world, and if any problem arose, they would call "Mommy!" and she would deal with it. But already she could see changes to that dynamic. Bradley, nine, one year older than his brother, was starting to question some of her instructions and talking back. He was becoming more independent, something that would eventually spread to his brother. Soon, too soon, she would no longer be at the center of their world. The thought made her sad, and she wondered if her mother had felt like this when she herself started pulling away.

The day at Disneyland was wonderful. As always, they woke up early. Their house in Brea was only fifteen minutes away—a half-hour if there was traffic and the lights on Harbor Boulevard went against them—and Disneyland didn't open until eight, but it took them awhile to dress and eat breakfast, and parking was always a problem. Indeed, when they arrived at seven-thirty, there was already a long line waiting for the tram from the Donald Duck parking structure to the front gate, and they made it just as the gates were opening.

Benjamin and the boys had their itinerary all planned out, heading first to the most popular rides, and Gloria, who didn't really care, followed along. Bradley was braver than Lucas, and there were rides he would go on that his brother would not, so Gloria and Lucas became partners for the day, heading to alternate attractions when Benjamin and Bradley went on thrill rides, sitting together on those that the whole family rode.

In The Haunted Mansion, the "doom buggy" in which she and Lucas sat glided past a ballroom filled with ghosts. One of them, a woman, was blowing out the candles on a birthday cake, and the mundane act put Gloria in mind of her mother, who, at this moment, was probably in her kitchen cooking herself lunch.

What *was* her mother?

It was a question that was always there, in the back of her mind, although at certain moments, like these, it pushed its way to the front. Her mother might not be a ghost, but she was...something. She had come back from the dead, and was alive again, nearly forty years younger.

Why didn't that frighten Gloria more?

She wasn't sure. But if she wasn't as frightened as she should have been, neither did she feel the love that she should have felt for her mother. There was a distance between them, an emotional remove that Gloria did not understand but accepted. She had no idea what her mother might be experiencing or if the woman was able to experience any emotions at all now. Despite the radical uniqueness of their situation, the two of them did not talk openly and honestly about anything important; their conversations were always practical and superficial, as though her mother really *were* just some new acquaintance named Nora.

Open House was coming up at school. Ordinarily, both Bradley and Lucas were excited for their parents to see what had been going on in their classrooms, showing off their artwork and displayed projects, but this year, Bradley did not seem to want them to attend. Nevertheless, all four of them visited first Lucas' class then Bradley's, and Gloria's fear that Bradley might not be doing well turned out to be unfounded. His reluctance stemmed more from a sort of peer pressure, which she discovered when she saw two young toughs wandering through the room without their parents and snickering at those students whose parents did attend. Benjamin noticed, too, and in the car on the way back he warned Bradley to stay away from those boys.

"I do," Bradley said defensively.

"And don't let them get to you. They're the *last* people whose opinions you should care about. Kids like that usually end up in jail. Either that or they'll grow up to be bums. You may take their opinions seriously now, but believe me, when you see them pushing their shopping carts and muttering about aliens, all you'll want to do is get away from them."

Both Bradley and Lucas laughed.

Gloria smiled. Benjamin was good that way. He knew how to make a point in a humorous manner. It was a technique she needed to learn. When she tried to tell the boys something, it was a lecture rather than a conversation. Benjamin had the ability to talk *with* them not *at* them, and those were the lessons that tended to stick.

There was nothing less romantic than Open House night. The kids were still hyped up when they came home, and all of them smelled of fruit punch and Chips Ahoy cookies. But once the kids were in bed and asleep, and they were in their own bed, things turned amorous. With everything going on, it had been awhile, and when Benjamin entered her, Gloria thought he felt bigger. For those first few seconds, she was stretched so tight it was almost painful, but as they got into it, the sensation became more pleasurable, and pretty soon it was wonderful. They would have to do this more often, she decided.

After, instead of rolling over and going to sleep, they talked.

"Do you remember that goofy guy I used to work with when we first started going out?" he asked, turning on the pillow to face her. "Melvin?"

Gloria laughed. "I forgot about him!"

"Remember how, whenever I had car problems and you picked me up at work, he would try to invite himself along on our date?"

She giggled. "Oh, yeah. And we always had to scramble and try to think up some reason why he couldn't come?"

"Well, didn't you think that one kid's dad tonight kind of looked like Melvin? An older Melvin, I mean."

"Which dad?"

"The one who kind of stayed in the back of the room and kept staring at the bulletin board with the ecology stuff?"

"Kind of," she admitted.

"I wonder whatever happened to Melvin," Benjamin mused.

"He doesn't work there anymore?"

"No, he moved on years ago. I think he got a job..." He shook his head. "I don't remember." Benjamin was silent for a moment. "Isn't it weird how people you know kind of drift away? They may not be friends or family, they may even be annoying, like Melvin, but they're a part of your life, and then...things kind of move on, and they're not there. One day you look up, and you think your life has stayed the same, but you suddenly realize that, even though you haven't gone anywhere or done anything different, everything around you has totally changed."

The conversation had taken a melancholy turn, and Gloria said nothing, not wanting to follow this direction. The happy afterglow she had felt faded.

"You know," Benjamin said, "I was thinking about Nora."

Gloria tensed up.

"I feel like I know her from somewhere. She seems real familiar, and it's, like, on the tip of my tongue—or the tip of my brain, really—but I can't remember where we met before. You know what I'm talking about?"

Here was her chance to come clean. And for a brief moment she actually considered it. But the truth was so crazy that there was no way Benjamin would believe her, so she just shook her head. "I'm getting tired," she said. "Why don't we go to sleep."

At work the next day, Benjamin's words came back to her. When she'd first started working at the dermatologist's office, the practice had consisted of old Dr. Gorshin and young Dr. Lee. Dr. Gorshin had long since retired, handing over the entire practice to his partner, and now Dr. Lee was almost as old as Dr. Gorshin had been then. At the time, she had been the ingénue, and the two nurses, one clerk and two assistants had all been older than she was. But the oldest nurse, Guyla, had retired with Dr. Gorshin, not to be replaced, and the other nurse, Susie, had eventually transferred over to Beverly Hospital. The clerk, Pam, had been fired for stealing, her position not filled, and Eve, one of the assistants, had moved back to Minnesota, replaced with Hong, who was younger than Gloria. The other assistant, Beth, had quit last year, unhappy with her hours and pay.

Benjamin was right, Gloria realized. She hadn't moved, but the world around her had changed, and now, except for Dr. Lee, she had been here longer than anyone and was the oldest person in the office.

Although, to save money, she usually brought her lunch to work (and, indeed, had a container of leftover pasta in the small office fridge right now that she'd intended to microwave), Gloria decided to mix things up today, climb out of her rut, and go elsewhere to eat. She had an hour break, and ended up driving almost to Yorba Linda before she found something that looked appealing: an independent fast-casual place called Fresh Garden. Sitting at the tables in the restaurant, alone, in groups or in pairs, were other workers on their lunch hour, most of them women. Before today, such a sight would have made her feel right at home, as though these were her peers and she fit in with them. But now she recognized that she was older than most of the women here, that the view she had of herself was probably a decade behind reality.

She ordered a spinach wrap and a passion fruit iced tea, sitting alone at an empty table for two near the window.

"Excuse me, is this seat taken?"

Gloria looked up from her food to see a tall bearded man holding a lunch tray on which he was balancing a bottle of Evian and a sizeable salad. She hesitated, not knowing what to say, not wanting a stranger to sit with her but not wanting to seem rude either. She glanced around the restaurant, hoping to find an alternative seat to suggest. To her surprise, there were plenty of open spaces; she'd assumed he'd approached her because all of the other tables were taken.

The man laughed. "You don't recognize me, do you, Gloria?"

She shook her head. "I'm sorry, I—" And then it came to her. She tilted her head, changing her viewing angle, trying to imagine him without the beard. "Bobby Perez?"

He grinned. "The one and only. Mind if I sit down?"

"No," she said. "Go ahead."

Back in high school, back in junior high, even, she had had a big crush on Bobby, although she had never admitted it to anyone. He hadn't been the obvious choice for a schoolgirl infatuation. He wasn't on any sports teams, he wasn't on the student council, he wasn't hugely popular. He was just a regular guy. But something about him had always appealed to her, and the semester that he had sat next to her in Economics, her grades had gone down because she'd spent so much time looking over at him to see if he was looking at her. Even now his presence caused her to blush.

He sat. "So what are you doing these days?" he asked.

"I'm married," she said, wiggling the fingers of her left hand to show him her ring. "Two boys: Bradley and Lucas. I work in a dermatologist's office in Brea. My husband's a computer programmer, works for Automated Interface."

"Happy?" he asked.

She smiled. "Very." She took a sip of her iced tea, childishly not wanting to eat in front of him. "Obviously you haven't left the area. Unless you're just here for a visit."

"No, I live in Yorba Linda. Married, also." He held up his hand to show his ring. "No kids. Yet." He chuckled. "My wife's younger than I am."

He looked young himself, Gloria noticed. Certainly younger than she and Benjamin did. She suddenly felt self-conscious.

"I own my own business. Perez Pool Supplies. Over on Imperial past Rose. It's in the Stater Brothers shopping center, next to the Goodwill." He picked up a forkful of salad. "You wouldn't happen to have a pool would you?"

"With two little boys?" She smiled. "Definitely not."

He ate easily, and Gloria felt comfortable enough to start eating herself. They reminisced about old times—neither of them were in touch with anyone from high school—but, unfortunately, after finishing her wrap, she had to head back to work. She didn't feel it would be appropriate to give him her phone number or email, and he didn't ask or offer to give her his, so they parted awkwardly, each saying that it had been nice to run into the other before saying goodbye.

That night, Benjamin informed the family that next month he was going to have to go on a weekend business trip to a coding convention in Phoenix. It was his first business trip ever, the first time either of them would be spending a night away from the kids, and while such an event might be commonplace for a lot of people, it was a big deal to them. Gloria could tell from the way he picked at his food that he was not happy about leaving the boys for two days, and she tried to cheer him up by telling him that maybe he'd been invited because some sort of promotion was in the works.

"Nah," he said. "Everyone's going. It's mandatory. Has nothing to do with any promotion."

The kids did not seem as unenthusiastic about it as he did.

"Can you bring us back a present?" Lucas asked.

"A souvenir?" Bradley said.

Benjamin smiled at them. "Sure."

"You could send us a postcard," Lucas suggested.

Bradley looked at his brother with pity. "He'll be back before the postcard even gets here."

"I don't care. Then we can read it together."

"Done," Benjamin told him.

On the Friday he flew to Phoenix, Gloria went in late to work so she could drive him to the airport. He was flying out of Orange County, which meant that it was closer than LA or Ontario, and while he could have taken a Lyft, Uber or even the airport shuttle, Gloria wanted to see him off. She asked her mother to come over and watch the boys for an hour before taking them to school, and Benjamin kissed both Bradley and Lucas on the forehead, telling them to be good and listen to Mommy. Bradley wiped off the kiss, obviously feeling too old for such sentiment, but Lucas left his kiss intact and gave his dad a big hug before letting him go.

There was work traffic on the freeway, but they'd anticipated that and left home with plenty of time to spare. Gloria had never dropped Benjamin off at the airport before—whenever they'd flown, they'd gone together—and she was surprised to learn that TSA rules were so strictly enforced that she could not even go into the airport with him; she was required to simply drop him off and leave. She'd been planning to sit with him until the boarding call came, then watch through the windows as his plane took off. Instead, they said a rushed goodbye, he grabbed his single carry-on bag from the back seat, and then she was driving away.

He called her at work to tell her that he'd arrived safely, then called home that night to talk to the boys. They were excited to hear from him, wanting to know all about the plane flight and asking if he'd bought them any presents yet. Benjamin told Gloria that there'd been a change in the schedule of events. A required seminar that had been planned for this evening had been moved to Sunday afternoon. Originally, he was to have come home Sunday on a two o'clock plane, but he and everyone else from their company had had to trade in their tickets for a later flight, and now he wouldn't be setting down in Orange County until six-thirty. "But you don't have to pick me up," he told her. "I'm hitching a ride with Dang and Nick."

"Are you sure?" she asked. "I could—"

"It's Sunday night. Brad and Luke need to go to bed early and get ready for school on Monday. Besides, you need to make them dinner."

"Bradley and Lucas," Gloria said.

"What?"

"Never mind."

He was right, Gloria knew. She could have pushed, insisting that she pick him up, but the next day *was* a school day, and the truth was that she did not feel entirely comfortable having her mother come over to babysit the boys. As irrational and superstitious as it might be, she didn't mind her mother watching Bradley and Lucas after school (in fact Gloria was grateful), but the idea of her coming over and spending time alone with them at night made her feel uneasy.

"I'll call you tomorrow," Benjamin said. "Love you."

"Love you, too."

Both boys giggled.

Benjamin did call the next day, late in the afternoon, just before he was about to leave the hotel for the airport. Gloria asked if he was going to eat an early dinner in Phoenix or get something with his coworkers on the way home, but he told her to just save him some leftovers. He'd eat when he got back.

By her calculation, he should be home around seven-thirty, unless someone else in the carpool got dropped off first. For dinner, she made chicken and rosemary potatoes, one of everyone's favorites, and one that could easily and quickly be reheated. After dinner, she let the boys have control of the television, and they watched one of the *How to Train Your Dragon* movies on some kids' channel.

It was a surprise when six-thirty came and went and Benjamin didn't call, but there was probably a reason. When Gloria still hadn't heard from him by seven-thirty, however, she began to worry.

Where was he? Why was he so late? Whatever else might be said about Benjamin, he was reliably punctual, particularly with anything that involved the boys. Right now, for example, he knew that they were waiting up for him, and even if the plane had been delayed, he should have called to tell Gloria to put them to bed, that he would see them in the morning. Unless phone calls were not allowed from planes. She had no idea what the rules and regulations were these days, and while it seemed farfetched, there was a possibility that Benjamin was not able to call and let them know there was a delay.

"When's Daddy coming home?" Bradley whined, not for the first time.

"I don't know," she told him, an unfortunate hint of annoyance creeping into her voice.

And then the phone rang.

THREE

Benjamin did not return after his funeral. Gloria kept expecting him to do so, and for the first few weeks, she was constantly looking out the window or jumping up expectantly every time she heard an unfamiliar sound, opening the front door ten times a day because she thought someone might be there. But he did not come back, and as the realization sunk in that he was really gone, the spark of hope that had helped keep her going began to fade. Oh, she did what she had to do, at home and at work, but her actions were perfunctory, automatic, propelled by duty with no thought or feeling behind them. At night, more often than not, she cried herself to sleep, and though she would eventually have to change the sheets, she had not yet done so because his pillow still contained a faint trace scent of his hair gel.

Why had her mother come back and not Benjamin? Was it the difference in age? Was it where they had died? When they had died? Was it because he had perished in a plane crash and she had passed away in the hospital? Because her mother had left behind a body and Benjamin only...pieces? She might never know the reason, but the question gnawed at her.

Beginning the morning after Gloria had received the news, when she'd needed someone to watch the kids while she tended to all of the necessary arrangements, her mother had been very helpful and sympathetic. Just like...a real mother. She basically moved in with them, took over household duties, did the cooking and cleaning, made sure that the boys got to school on time and that Gloria made it to work. On a practical level, Gloria was grateful for the assistance, and it even felt kind of good to have her mother be there for her emotionally, no matter how disconcerting it was to interact with someone young who should have been old. But Gloria never felt entirely comfortable around the woman, and once, when she awoke in the middle of the night and heard movement in the guest room, she found herself wondering if her mother ever slept. Did she still *have* to sleep, or was she always awake?

Gloria had a hard time falling back to sleep herself after that.

Part of her kept hoping that her mother would turn into Benjamin. After all, she was still not sure exactly what her mother *was*. She might be real, a reincarnation or resurrection of the woman who had died, or she might be some *thing* that was impersonating a younger version of her mother. If that was the case, that *thing* could easily morph into her husband, and Gloria vowed that if that happened, she would accept it gratefully and ask no further questions. She just wanted him back.

But it didn't happen, and each morning when she awoke and heard her mother in the kitchen preparing breakfast, another small part of her died.

She forced herself to remain strong for the boys, although they did not seem as devastated as she thought they should be. Bradley, especially, had been very close to his father, and while both he and his brother had sobbed upon hearing the news, and had cried their way through the funeral, they were now almost back to normal. Perhaps that was just the nature of children, she thought, but while she envied the boys having such a survival mechanism, part of her resented them for it as well. Their *Daddy* had died, and Benjamin deserved a longer and deeper grieving than they seemed able to give.

On the one month anniversary of the plane crash, Gloria arrived home from work feeling especially low. All day long, she had sat behind her receptionist's window staring out at the waiting room where she had first met Benjamin. It hadn't helped that there'd been only one patient that afternoon, which had given her far too much time to think. But she put on a happy face, or the happiest face she could muster, before walking into the house. Bradley and Lucas were at opposite ends of the dining room table doing homework, Bradley filling out a math worksheet, Lucas coloring a map of Europe. She said hello to each, checked on the work they were doing, then went into the kitchen where her mother was making meatloaf.

She'd always hated her mother's meatloaf.

Gloria walked over to the refrigerator, where she got out and popped open a can of Dr. Pepper. She preferred cans to plastic bottles because the slightly metallic taste made her drink less. "Mom?" she said. "Didn't we used to heat up Dr. Pepper at Christmastime? Or was that Coke?" She knew very well that during the holidays of her childhood, her mother would fill up a crockpot with Dr. Pepper, cutting up lemon slices and putting them into the soft drink, letting it warm all day, but she had taken to quizzing her mother about minutiae from the past, trying to trip her up. So far, her mother had passed every single test.

"Hot Dr. Pepper with lemon slices!" her mother said. "I'd forgotten all about that! Do you want me to heat some up for the boys? I bet they'd love it."

"No, that's okay," Gloria said. "We don't like them to have sugary drinks."

We.

She still thought in terms of "we" when now there was just "I." But it was not easy to jettison an entire life, especially one that had been shattered and permanently redirected during the course of a single phone call. She sat down at the kitchen table. It felt as though there were something she needed to say to her mother, but she couldn't seem to figure out what it was.

Gloria felt her mother's hand on her bare arm. "Do you want to run away?"

She jerked her head up, startled. "What? No!"

"It's not unusual. There were many times that I wanted to run away, just leave you and your father and start over again someplace new."

"Well, you've certainly started over again," Gloria said bitterly.

"It's perfectly normal, wanting a fresh start someplace where you're not known. You can do it if you want to. I'll take care of the boys."

Gloria felt an unwelcome tingle caress her spine. "No," she said. "I'd never leave the boys. I've never even *thought* about leaving the boys."

Her mother patted her arm, an old lady thing to do, though they looked almost the same age. "Sure, sure."

That was a warning sign, Gloria thought. But of what she was not exactly sure.

The next morning, when she awoke, before she got the kids up for school, Gloria pulled on her bathrobe and walked into the kitchen, where her mother was putting out boxes of cereal: Cheerios, Apple Jacks and Honey Bunches of Oats. "I think maybe you should go home today," Gloria said.

Her mother looked surprised. "Whatever for?"

"Don't get me wrong. I'm grateful for all your help since...since it happened. But I think it's time the boys and I got back into a normal routine. This isn't just a temporary situation; it's our life now. And we need to get used to it. Besides, I'm sure you'd like to get back to your own place, sleep in your own bed."

Did she sleep?

Her mother smiled. "Oh, don't worry about me. I *like* being here with you, with Bradley and Lucas, with my family."

"It's time for you to go," Gloria said firmly. "I'll still need you to watch them after school, but I don't think you should live here anymore."

Their eyes met, and for the first time since her mother had come back, Gloria saw something in those eyes that she did not recognize. But as quickly as it had arrived, it was gone, and her mother was smiling at her sympathetically. "Of course. I understand. Whatever you want, dear."

Dear.

Her mother never called her "dear."

The house actually did seem emptier with her mother gone. In a way, her presence had served to distract from Benjamin's absence, and now that she was back at her own home the house felt the way it had when Benjamin was on his business trip, like someone was missing. This time, however, it was permanent, and Gloria found herself talking too much, in a too cheerful, too outgoing manner, as part of a futile attempt to mask the hole at the heart of their family. After a few days, the strain of such an effort became too much for her, and she switched to a different tack, turning on the television while they ate, not putting on the news as Benjamin would have, but instead allowing the boys to watch cartoons.

Weekends, Gloria found, were the worst. Weekdays were busy enough that all three of them were kept occupied, but when Saturday morning rolled around, she awoke to face two full days filled with unscheduled hours. There *were* chores to be done, her own plus the work that Benjamin used to do, which was now spread between the three of them. But that still left a lot of free time, and she started to look for weekend events, taking the boys to free festivals, to museums, on guided nature walks, to parades and historical remembrances. Such community involvement did not come naturally to her, and though activities filled up the hours, the fact that she had to participate in activities at all ironically made Benjamin's loss feel that much more acute.

Alone in bed one Sunday night, after spending the day with Bradley and Lucas at a kite-flying exhibition on the sand at Huntington Beach, Gloria scrolled through her phone and saw that Benjamin had had a dentist appointment scheduled for tomorrow. She'd tied up all of the loose ends that a death entailed, completing all of the paperwork. All of the billing accounts were now in her name only, and she had gone through Benjamin's phone and consulted the calendar in the kitchen to make sure that all meetings and appointments were cancelled. But she had not deleted the entries on her own scheduler, and now, here at ten o'clock tomorrow morning, was a listing for Dr. Lu, Benjamin's dentist. She remembered clearly when he had made that appointment, just before the convention in Phoenix. He'd been eating ice cream with the boys, and one of his teeth in the back had hurt. His instinct was to let it go, but she'd told him that he had to have it checked out. The dentist could have easily seen him the following week—the office always left open slots in the schedule for emergencies—but he'd told them he was busy, it wasn't really an emergency anyway, and they'd given him an appointment over a month out.

She recalled perfectly the expression on his face when the ice cream had touched his sensitive tooth, the way he'd flinched in pain.

That tooth pain, she realized, was long gone. It no longer existed.

Neither did Benjamin.

Pulling her pillow over her face, she sobbed herself to sleep.

She woke up late the next morning, having accidentally shut off the alarm after resetting the clock following a short power outage yesterday, and had to rush to get Bradley and Lucas off to school. In the process, she forgot to pack herself a lunch, something she did not realize until twelve o'clock rolled around, and soon afterward, she found herself driving east on Imperial Highway.

After her initial visit, Gloria had not returned to Fresh Garden, though she had liked the restaurant. It was true that she usually brought her own food from home in order to save money, but a couple of times she had gone out to buy lunch, and in each instance she had purposely driven in the opposite direction. Could it have been that she was afraid of running into Bobby Perez again? That was possible, although perhaps *afraid* was the wrong word. Still, there seemed something disloyal to her about making an intentional effort to see her onetime crush again. A random encounter was one thing, but if she returned to a place where she knew he sometimes ate, might it not seem as though she was...interested?

Particularly after Benjamin's death (she still had a hard time thinking about it in such blunt terms), the thought of going to that restaurant for lunch felt wrong. Yet here she was, less than two months after his funeral, driving toward Yorba Linda. Gloria told herself that she was only going out to eat because she'd been in too much of a hurry to pack her lunch—which was true—but she could have easily driven home, or gone to Chipotle or Carl's Jr. or something much closer to the office.

Instead, she told herself that she craved a healthy wrap and drove to Fresh Garden.

Bobby was there, as a part of her had known—

hoped?

—he would be. Was this a restaurant he'd always frequented, or had he only been coming here since their meeting in hopes of seeing her again? Gloria found herself wishing for the latter, though she knew that was wrong. He was seated alone at the same table for two they had shared, and while she noticed him immediately upon entering, she pretended she did not and walked up to the counter to place her order. By the time she had picked up her food, Bobby had spotted her and was waving her over. Acting as though this was the sort of casual encounter that happened to her all the time, Gloria took her tray over to his table.

"Fancy meeting you here," he said as she sat down. It had the feel of a rehearsed line, and she wondered how long he had been waiting for a chance to use it.

"Hi," she said simply.

Now that she was here, Gloria wished she hadn't come. Benjamin had *died* since the last time she'd spoken to Bobby, and while he knew nothing of it, that life shattering event hung between them, and she had no idea of how to even broach such a momentous subject.

Why *had* she come here today?

This had been a mistake, and Gloria was about to tell Bobby that she only had a half-hour for lunch today and needed to get back to work. She was going to take her Mediterranean wrap back to the counter and get it to go; she had only stopped by to say hello. Then he smiled at her and said, "It's nice to see you again," and Gloria put her tray on the table and took a seat.

Could she really be thinking of moving on so soon after Benjamin's death? No. At least, not consciously. There was no way she could possibly be that shallow. Yet here she was, with the person on whom she'd had a crush in high school, and they were chatting lightly about their jobs, and she did not even mention the death of her husband.

"I never told you this," Bobby said, twisting the cap back on his water bottle, "but when we were in Economics back in high school, I used to think you kind of liked me. It always seemed like you were looking at me in class, and I actually thought about asking you to prom." He laughed. "But I wasn't brave enough."

Gloria felt a rush of panic.

"I don't mean to embarrass you," he said quickly. "It was a long time ago, and I just..."

She nodded nervously, looking down at her plate.

"Did you go to prom?" he asked.

She shook her head. "You?"

"No." He smiled at her. "So maybe it would've worked out."

Gloria did not like where this was going, and she stood, gathering her plate, fork, napkin and cup, piling everything on her tray, preparing to take it over to the trash can. "I'd better go," she said. "I need to get back. I was a few minutes late last time," she lied, "and Dr. Lee wasn't happy."

Bobby nodded, following her to the trash can. He dumped his garbage into the receptacle, placing his tray on top of hers on the shelf above. "Well..." he said.

"Goodbye," she told him.

"Maybe we could meet again. Next week? I mean, we both have to eat."

"I don't..."

"I'm sorry," he said. "I don't know why I brought that up, that stuff about high school. I wasn't coming on to you. Honest." He tapped his forehead. "Sometimes, I just think of things and blurt them out, instead of thinking before I speak. Look, I'm happily married, I love my wife, I wasn't trying to make this into anything it isn't, I just... I like having lunch with you. Like I said, I'm not really in contact with anyone from the old days, and I know we weren't really friends back then, and maybe this is just a pathetic attempt to recapture my youth, but seeing you makes me...feel good."

Gloria laughed. "Wow."

"Pathetic, I know. But really, seriously, I have no ulterior motive."

Gloria thought for a moment, and while she knew she should say no, she found herself nodding. "Okay. Next week. Same time, same place."

Bobby held up his hands. "I'm not going to say 'it's a date.' I'll just say...See you then."

"See you then."

Gloria was smiling as she walked out to her car. She'd smiled very little since receiving the phone call about the plane, and she felt guilty for smiling now. Benjamin was dead, for God's sake. Killed in one of the most horrible ways possible. There hadn't even been a body to put in the empty coffin, only clothes and keepsakes. Still, he wasn't a saint. She'd succumbed to the temptation that everyone had to mythologize the dead, but as she got into the car, a memory came to her of Benjamin lecturing her because she had let the car's gas tank fall to below a fourth of a tank without filling up. He had given her the silent treatment all the way to the gas station and had not spoken to her until the tank was once again full. She'd almost forgotten about *that* Benjamin, the rigid, literal-minded plodder.

Two of the afternoon's patients had called to reschedule their appointments, which meant that Gloria had plenty of free time between one-thirty and three, and while she usually caught up on billing, bookkeeping or administrative work during down periods, today she found herself in front of her computer Googling "Bobby Perez." She was not sure what she expected to find, told herself that she was not hoping to see a photo of him and was only checking up to see if he had lied to her in any way, if he was, say, a convicted felon rather than the owner of an innocent pool supply business. But she was not prepared for what she discovered.

Bobby Perez had died five years ago, killed in a hit-and-run accident by a drunk driver.

Gloria sucked in her breath. She thought for a moment that this might be *another* Bobby Perez—it wasn't such an unusual name here in Southern California—but the obituary from the *Yorba Linda Gazette* included a photograph, and it was definitely him. Apparently, he had been coming back from lunch, driving through an intersection, when a drunk driver being chased by police ran the red light and slammed into Bobby's Toyota pickup. The impact had crushed the small truck's driver's side door, and without side airbags, the crumpled metal had pierced Bobby's body and nearly severed his arm. He died from blood loss as one police officer attempted emergency rescue procedures while another officer called for an ambulance. According to the article, a memorial service had been scheduled for friends and family on the following

Saturday at St. Mary's Church, with burial to follow at Yorba Linda Cemetery.

Stunned, Gloria reread the article.

Coming back from lunch.

She needed time to absorb this.

She said nothing to anyone. That evening when she got home, Gloria thanked her mother for watching the boys and for starting dinner, then helped Bradley with his math while Lucas drew a picture and wrote a short entry for the weekly journal that was due each Friday. After homework was done, the three of them watched TV together until it was time for the boys to go to bed.

The next day, during her lunch hour, Gloria drove directly to her mother's house, questions swirling in her brain, questions that had kept her up all night. Using her key to let herself in, she found her mother sitting alone at the kitchen table, staring blankly at the wall, an empty coffee cup in front of her. Gloria pulled up a chair on the opposite side of the table and faced the woman.

"What are you?" she asked.

Her mother looked at her innocently. "What do you mean? I'm your mother."

"You know what I'm talking about." Gloria took a deep breath. "That first day, when you came back and you were younger and wearing those Eighties clothes—"

Her mother laughed. "Weren't they ugly?"

"—I called you 'Mom,' and you shook your head. You didn't want me to tell anyone who you were. And I didn't. I *still* haven't, although God knows why."

Her mother's eyes narrowed. "Get to your point."

"What are you hiding? How come I'm the only one who knows who you are? Even Maxine and Aunt Ruth don't recognize you." Gloria leaned forward. "What are you? What the hell is going on?"

"I told you."

"No, you didn't."

"I don't know." Her mother stood, obviously agitated. She walked over to the sink, looked out the window, walked back again. "I told you, I'm me. I just feel...a little different. Like maybe I'm not *quite* myself. Of course I know what happened to me, but I don't know how or why. I don't remember any white light or any sort of afterlife. I was old, and then I closed my eyes, and I wasn't. I was dying, and then I was alive. That's it."

"That's *not* it," Gloria insisted. "Because sometimes you do things—like shaking your head so I won't tell anyone who you are, or calling me 'dear,' or asking if I want to abandon my kids—that aren't like you at all. Sometimes you seem like you, and sometimes you seem like someone who's been sent to...I don't know." She ran an exasperated hand through her hair. Taking a deep breath, she asked the questions she really wanted to ask: "Did you know ahead of time that Benjamin's plane was going to crash? Did you have any advance warning? Were you involved with it somehow?"

Her mother seemed truly offended. "Is that what you think?"

"I! Don't! Know!"

"I don't either." Her mother sat down again. "Like I said, sometimes, I feel different. And sometimes it seems like I might know more than I should, but it's like when you think of an actor and you can't remember his name. You can see his face, but the name is just out of reach. That's how I feel sometimes. Like there's knowledge I have but I just can't access it."

"See? Right there!" Gloria said. "'Access it.' That's a phrase you've never used in your life!"

"I've changed. I admit it. But...I'm still me."

"You still didn't answer—"

"I knew nothing about Benjamin's plane. It was as big a surprise to me as it was to you." She put her hand lightly on top of Gloria's, but Gloria pulled away.

Gloria thought for a moment. "I've met another one of you. A guy who died and came back."

"Oh?" Her mother seemed suspiciously uninterested.

"I knew him in high school."

"What's his name?"

"Bobby Perez."

"I don't remember any Bobby Perez."

"You didn't know him. He was...in one of my classes. But I ran into him at lunch one day, and when I Googled him, I found out that he'd died five years ago."

"Why were you looking him up?"

"That's not the point! I now know two people who have died and come back to life. How many more of you are there? Are you everywhere? Is this happening to everyone? Or is it just me?"

"I don't know any more about it than you do."

"Bull *shit*, Mom!"

Gloria instantly regretted calling her "Mom," but it was too late to take it back, and she stood, walking over to the sink. Picking up a dry glass from the rack, she turned on the tap, filling the glass with water. Her mouth was dry, and she drank it all. Turning, she saw that her mother had not moved. "Why don't you want me to tell people who you are? Why are you keeping it a secret?"

"Do you want to hear it again? It's the same answer—I don't know."

"You don't get along with Maxine anymore. Have you called Aunt Ruth?"

"No."

'Why not? You two were close."

"And now we aren't."

Gloria put down the glass and moved back over to the table. "Why?" She shoved her face close to her mother's, looking for...what? Some sign that she wasn't who she claimed to be? Some indication that her skin wasn't really skin? That her features had been artificially molded?

She saw none of that.

She even recognized a small freckle near the bottom edge of her mother's right eye.

"We just aren't," her mother said, not explaining further.

"I'm out of here," Gloria announced. "I'm heading back to work."

"I'll pick up the kids from school," her mother said. She smiled calmly, and since Gloria didn't have a retort and the boys needed someone to watch them, she left without saying another word.

Did she trust her mother with Bradley and Lucas? She did for some reason, although she couldn't say why. Later that afternoon, however, during downtime at the doctor's office, she looked online for afterschool daycare options. No, Gloria didn't think her mother would harm the boys, but even though she had very little extra money and even though she might have to cut back elsewhere, she decided she would feel more comfortable if someone else was taking care of her children between the time school let out and the time she came home.

She discovered that a Presbyterian church across the street from Ben Franklin Elementary offered, for a reasonable price, an after-school program that not only supplied daycare and kept the kids until six o'clock, but provided tutors to help with homework. She vowed to stop by after work, check the place out and, if it seemed decent, sign the boys up.

Which she did.

They couldn't start until next week—the program's quota was full, and it was only because two sisters were moving to San Jose that places for Bradley and Lucas had opened up—so Gloria said nothing to either the boys or her mother. Bradley *might* be able to keep a secret, but Lucas definitely couldn't, and she didn't want to give her mother any advance warning in case...

In case what?

Gloria didn't know, but she also didn't want to find out.

The next day, curiosity brought her back to Fresh Garden at lunch. Of course, Bobby was there, and she walked immediately up to his table, not ordering anything.

"I know," she told him.

"Know what?" His feigned ignorance was disingenuous. Behind those eyes, she saw wariness and calculation.

"How did you continue your business after you died?" she asked. "I assume all of your customers, and whatever employees you have, knew about the accident. What did you tell them? How did you explain it?"

Gloria could see him thinking, weighing the options, deciding what or what not to say to her. Eventually, he said in a flat voice, "I don't know what you're talking about."

It was a strangely subdued reaction from a person who had just been asked how he'd navigated coming back from the dead. If she'd put those questions to any ordinary individual, he or she would probably say she was crazy and back away. Bobby remained in place, looking at her calmly.

Gloria thought about telling him the truth, telling him that the same thing had happened with her mother, but she decided to keep that to herself. "I saw an article about your accident," she told him. "Your arm was nearly severed, and you died on the scene."

He took a sip of his iced tea. "That never happened."

She looked at him carefully. Bobby had not come back younger, as her mother had. He looked good for his age, so maybe he'd shaved off a few years, but he wasn't a teenager or anything. How did that work? she wondered.

"There's a lot of fake stuff on the internet," he said.

"It's an article from your Yorba Linda newspaper. It quotes officers who were on the scene. How much do you want to bet that if I went over to the police department or the fire department, they would have a record of that accident and have you listed as dead?"

Bobby shrugged. "It must've been someone else."

"You're going to stick with that, are you? What about your wife? She has to know what happened."

"Nothing did happen." He took a bite of salad. "Sit down. Order something."

She was getting nowhere. "I know what you are," she said and, turning, walked away.

Gloria did not realize until she got into her car that her hands were shaking. Was it fear? Anger? She was not sure what she felt, but her emotions were running high, and she sat there until she had calmed down, before finally driving back toward Brea. Stopping off at an In-N-Out on the way, she bought herself a cheeseburger, some fries and a milkshake, then pigged out on her unhealthy lunch in the car before returning to work.

Driving home after five, Gloria was still thinking about her mother and Bobby Perez. Her mind had been occupied by nothing else all afternoon, and she had come to realize that even if she told someone what was going on, no one would believe her. Not that she had anyone *to* tell. Gloria hadn't really seen anyone since Benjamin's funeral. She rationalized that it was because she was so busy with her newly imposed life as a single mother—everything was on her shoulders now—and that was definitely part of it, but she also hadn't felt like talking to anyone. The truth was that she didn't want to answer questions, didn't want to be the object of pity, didn't want to be reminded of what she had lost.

Paula was the one friend who could be counted on to keep things superficial, and it was Paula she called that night after she put the boys to bed. She was feeling alone and lonely and wanted to reconnect, wanted to get out of her own head and just talk to someone who could take her mind off...dead people. It felt weird and awkward to be dialing her friend's number since she hadn't done so in such a long time (Paula hadn't called her, either. Did she still *want* to keep in touch?), and the palm of her hand was sweaty on the phone as the first ring sounded. But then her friend picked up, Gloria said hi, and everything was fine. There was no heavy discussion, and after a few generic comments on both their parts, Paula was off on a typical tangent.

"You know," she said, "I was getting gas today, at that place that used to be ARCO on Brea Boulevard? and I just started thinking about how much things have changed since I was a kid. I guess it's because I saw this show on PBS the other night called *Things That Aren't There Anymore.* It was hosted by Ralph Story. Remember Ralph Story? He used to do features on Channel Two? Anyway, I was just thinking that when I was little, when we were on vacation, my dad used to get maps from gas stations. I started wondering if gas stations still had maps. I know Triple A still does, but with everyone using GPS and MapQuest and GoogleMaps and what have you, I thought maybe gas stations stopped carrying them. The weird thing is, though, I didn't go in to check. It's one of those stations that still does have a little store and not just one of those booths, but I was paying at the pump and didn't go in. Now I wish I had."

Gloria smiled. Same old Paula.

"I started thinking of other things that changed when I wasn't looking. Like, when did rip *tides* become rip *currents*? When did Cape Kennedy become Cape Canaveral? You know what I mean?"

"I do," Gloria said.

Like when did my dead mother become a much younger 'Nora'?

"Hey, Glo?" Paula offered, her voice suddenly more serious, "I'm sorry I haven't called you since the funeral. Benjamin was a really good guy. But, you know, it's kind of weird when someone dies who isn't that old. It's hard to know how to act or what to say. I'm not really good at that."

"It's okay," Gloria reassured her.

"You coping?"

"The best I can."

"Good." Then, thankfully, the subject was over. "You know who I saw the other day?" Paula asked. "Remember Tu? That real serious Vietnamese chick who was in our book club?"

"You mean, like, ten years ago?"

"Yeah. I saw her at Panera, you know the one in the shopping center where the cheap theater used to be? and she's gotten real fat. I wouldn't've even recognized her, but she recognized me, which made me feel good. You know how she used to be all stuck up and phony and pretentious because she was going for her PhD? Well, get this. She's working at a nail salon! Can you believe it? She used to look down on me because I was a mere clerk working at Barnes and Noble. But she got pregnant from that boyfriend of hers, who dumped her when he found out, and then she had twins! She had to drop out of school and now she's working at a nail salon to make ends meet. How the mighty have fallen. We're going to have lunch next week. Want to come along?"

Gloria stayed on the phone for over an hour, doing more listening than talking, which was how conversations always went with Paula, but she hung up feeling better. Eating lunch with Bobby Perez might have been her first failed attempt to get back in the world, but talking to Paula actually seemed to get her part of the way there. Or was at least a step in the right direction.

Then it all went south.

Sitting down on the bed and taking off her slippers, she realized that she needed to clip her toenails. But the nail clipper was not in the drawer of her nightstand, where she usually kept it, and she tried to remember where she had put it last. She walked into the bathroom and opened the top drawer, sorting through hair brushes, tweezers, a box of Q-Tips, old tubes of Neosporin and Benadryl, and a small pair of scissors. There was still no sign of her nail clippers, so she pulled the drawer out farther—

—and saw Benjamin's comb.

A feeling of emptiness pierced her heart. It happened to her at least once a week, stumbling across remnants of her old life, artifacts that Benjamin had left behind and she had not thought to donate or discard, and, every time, those discoveries were a shock. She was instantly filled with sadness, a feeling of loss so acute and unbearable that if it were not for the fact she was responsible for two boys, she did not know what she might have done.

Gloria picked up the comb. The last person to have held it was Benjamin. He had used it to comb his hair, and she was mortified to realize that she could not remember the last time he had gotten a haircut. Had his hair been short or long when he died? She'd always preferred it long, but he usually got it clipped very short each time he went to the barber because that was the way the other programmers at his work wore it.

He'd always been such a sheep, she thought, such an unimaginative by-the-book kind of man. She had deserved better, and if she'd known what he had been like from the beginning, if she had known what would happen to him ahead of time, she probably wouldn't have married him in the first place. Gloria threw the comb into the wastepaper basket and continued looking until she found her nail clippers in *another* drawer, next to the extra boxes of toothpaste and extra rolls of dental floss, where she must have distractedly put it.

But by the time she had walked back out to the bed and started to clip her toenails, guilt had set in. How dare she criticize Benjamin after he had been killed so horribly? What kind of person was she? He was—he *had* been—a nice man, a good provider, a loving father. It was the "loving father" appellation that got to her, as her mind latched on to the fact that if she had not met and married Benjamin, Bradley and Lucas would never have been born.

The tears came then. She suddenly felt overwhelmed.

"Mommy?" Bradley stood in the bedroom doorway. He looked worried.

Gloria wiped her eyes, trying to smile. "Yes?"

"Why are you crying?"

She shook her head.

"Are you sad? Are you thinking about Daddy?"

Gloria started sobbing. She couldn't help it, and she knew it must be frightening to Bradley, but she lurched across the carpet, took him in her arms, hugging him tightly, holding him close, and then both of them were crying.

"I—miss—him," Bradley managed to get out. "I—miss—Daddy."

At last, she thought. *At last.*

FOUR

Saturday.

Bradley and Lucas were out. Bradley's friend Chris Alvarez's mother had called earlier in the week, inviting Bradley to come with their family to Railroad Days in Fullerton. Chris' mother knew what had happened—everyone did—and thought it might do Bradley good to have a day out. Both Bradley and Chris were big train fans, and in addition to touring a real engine and other train cars, including Bradley's favorite, the caboose, the kids would be able to look at elaborate setups of various model trains. Gloria had said gratefully that indeed it would be good for her son and had thanked Mrs. Alvarez for her thoughtfulness. Meanwhile, Lucas had been asked on a playdate by his friend Brian's mother, who had told Gloria that she would be taking them to Craig Park and then, afterward, to McDonald's for lunch.

So Gloria was on her own. She thought about cleaning the house, thought about shopping, thought about calling Paula again and inviting herself over, but eventually decided to confront her mother again. She had no idea what she would confront her mother *about*, but things had been left unresolved, and more than ever Gloria felt a need to get to the bottom of *what* exactly was going on. She had been far too complacent about her mother's resurrection until now. What should have horrified her or filled her with awe she had simply taken in stride. This was momentous. This was the stuff of religious prophecy or supernatural fiction.

And it was happening to her.

So why didn't it feel as earth-shakingly historic as it should have? How had it merely become a part of her everyday life?

There was an unfamiliar car in her mother's driveway when she arrived, an old-style Trans-Am. To Gloria's knowledge, no one outside of their family had visited her mother since she'd...come back. But someone was definitely there now, and Gloria wondered who it was. It couldn't be someone from her mother's previous life—she seemed to have jettisoned everything from *before*—but Gloria couldn't for the life of her figure out where she might have met someone else.

Something about that car in the driveway made Gloria uneasy, and instead of parking behind the vehicle or by the curb in front of the house, she pulled into Maxine's driveway across the street. It had been at least a month since she'd even seen their old neighbor, and she wasn't sure what their status was, but Maxine came out of the house before Gloria had even gotten out of the car, and Gloria could tell from the expression on the old lady's face that her visit was very welcome. "Gloria!" Maxine exclaimed, giving her a hug. "How good of you to drop by! How are you? How's your husband and your two darling boys? Oh, I miss your mother more every day!"

She didn't know about Benjamin.

Gloria didn't feel like explaining what had happened, was not sure she could even get through the story without breaking down, so she put on a smile and said, "Fine. Everyone's fine."

"Oh, that's good. Would you like to come in and have some coffee?"

"I would love to," Gloria told her. She knew from past visits that, unlike her mother, who drank coffee with guests at her kitchen table, the more formal Maxine liked to socialize in what she called "the front room." Gloria, in fact, was counting on that, since the whole reason she had come over here was to spy on her mother's house through the window.

Moments later, they were both settled on different couches, Gloria having purposely chosen the one that faced the street. "So, have you had any other run-ins with...our tenant?" she asked.

Maxine sighed. "That woman. She's a monster. I just avoid her, although I'm sure she's causing problems for other people. I notice that you've had to go over there quite often to talk to her." Maxine fixed Gloria with a direct stare, awaiting confirmation.

She *had* been keeping track.

"Yes," Gloria said. "And I suppose we'll sell the place eventually, but, honestly, I can't bring myself to do it right now. And we need the money, so we need a tenant."

"Your mother didn't have life insurance?" Maxine pretended to look puzzled. "I thought for sure she told me once that if she died, you and Benjamin would be set."

Her mother and Maxine were such old friends that they'd shared everything, but Gloria didn't want to go into the details of her mother's life insurance right now. Besides, it wasn't as much as Maxine seemed to think, and though everything had been settled, the insurance company hadn't even sent her the check yet.

"We haven't gotten the insurance money," Gloria said simply.

Maxine was curious. "Problems?"

"No," Gloria said. "The wheels just turn slowly."

Maxine sighed again and turned to look out the window at the house across the street. "Have you thought of evicting her and renting it out someone else?"

"We have," Gloria lied, "but there are so many rules and regulations that it's almost impossible to kick someone out unless they've practically committed a crime."

Maxine leaned forward. "You know, the other day I went out for my morning walk, and I found *feces* on my walkway. *Human* feces."

Gloria was not sure she had ever heard anyone say the word "feces" before. But, beyond that, it seemed she was insinuating that Gloria's mother had defecated in her front yard. "That seems like something teenagers would do," Gloria said.

"There are no teenagers on this street. No kids at all. It's just us old people, except for your new tenant. And while I was washing it off with the hose, I looked across the street and saw that woman standing on her porch and *watching* me. She was smiling!" Maxine sat back as if that proved everything.

Gloria had to admit that, as weird as it was, she couldn't automatically dismiss the idea that her mother had, in some sort of bizarre escalation of an inexplicable feud, gone to the bathroom in the middle of the night on her ex-friend Maxine's walkway. But any reply she might have made to that unspoken assertion was pushed aside as, across the street, a man came out of her mother's house and walked over to the Trans-Am parked in the driveway.

Bobby Perez.

Gloria immediately forgot about Maxine and whatever the woman had last said. All of her attention was on the scene across the street, and she watched Bobby get into what was evidently his car, back out and speed away, driving far too fast for such a residential street.

Three days ago, her mother had sat in her kitchen and sworn that she had no idea who Bobby Perez was. Now, here he was, leaving her house after a secretive meeting.

What had they talked about?

Her?

Gloria shivered, feeling cold. This was wrong. She could feel it in her bones. But who could she tell about it? The police? Someone in local government or state government or the federal government? Who would believe a wild story about a get-together between two dead people who had come back to life? And what if someone in authority did believe her? Who would have jurisdiction over such a thing? And what would they do? Exhume her mother's and Bobby Perez's bodies to see if they were still in their coffins?

What if the bodies were still there?

What if they weren't?

Her head hurt from all the possibilities. Maxine was watching her oddly from the opposite couch, and Gloria excused herself, explaining that she didn't feel well. "I'll come back and visit when I'm not under the weather," she said. "It was so nice to see you again."

"You, too," Maxine said. "And I hope you'll give some thought to evicting that horrible woman. If you need me to swear to anything or verify what she's done, I'm always here."

"Thank you," Gloria said sincerely. Something occurred to her. "And if you see anything weird over there, anything I should know about, write it down. Times, dates, everything. You have my number if you need it, right?"

Maxine nodded firmly. "It's in my book."

"Okay, then. I'll see you soon. And thanks for the coffee and your hospitality."

"You know you're always welcome. Your mother was my best friend, and I've known you since you were born. I consider you a member of the family."

"Me, too," Gloria said. Saying goodbye once again, she walked outside. For a brief moment, she considered walking across the street to her mother's house, but the sight of Bobby Perez had thrown her off balance, and she found that she was *afraid* to go over there. She was afraid to be alone with her mother. Driving out of the neighborhood the way she had come, Gloria did not look at her childhood home, not wanting to know if she was being watched through one of the front windows.

Once back at her own house, she called her Aunt Ruth. Something, some vague sense of dread, had kept her from getting the two sisters together until now, but even though Aunt Ruth had not recognized the woman who'd shown up after the funeral, Gloria decided that the time had come for them to meet again. If anyone would know her mother, it would be her own sister.

"I was wondering if you could come over for lunch tomorrow," Gloria said, following some chitchat about how she and the boys were holding up.

"After church?"

Gloria had forgotten how religious Aunt Ruth was. There'd been the hint of a rebuke in her aunt's question, but Gloria chose to ignore it and simply said. "Yes."

"I would not be able to make it until one. Services end at noon—"

"That would be fine," Gloria said.

There was a bit of an awkward pause. "Is there a *reason* you're inviting me over? Not that you need a reason," she added quickly. "And of course I love to see you, Brad and Luke."

Bradley and Lucas, Gloria almost said, but she held her tongue.

"No," she lied. "No reason." Gloria understood why she would ask. Other than the two recent funerals, the last time she had seen her aunt was Christmas. In fact, the *only* time she ordinarily saw her aunt was Christmas.

"Then I will be there with bells on," Aunt Ruth said. Gloria had no idea what that meant, but she was pleased that she'd been able to put her plan in motion and hung up feeling satisfied. The only question was: how was she going to get the two sisters together? Gloria didn't want to invite her mother over, so that left going to her house, and she was not at all sure she would be able to convince Aunt Ruth to go along. Maybe if she made up a story about having to go back and check on some item that her mother had wanted Ruth to have...

What to do with the boys, though? She couldn't very well call up Brian's and Chris' parents and ask them to take Lucas and Bradley for another day. There might be a couple of other moms she *could* call, but Gloria didn't know them as well and would feel as though she were intruding. Should she take the boys with her? That seemed unwise. Who knew how things were going to go? And she definitely didn't want them to hear that their grandmother had returned from the grave; they'd both have nightmares for a year. If only Benjamin's dad hadn't moved to Florida. He could have babysat the kids.

Eventually, she decided to ask her next door neighbor, Cecily Yang, to watch Bradley and Lucas. She and Benjamin had always been friendly with the Yangs, if not close, but knowing everything Gloria had been going through, Cecily had volunteered to watch the boys if Gloria had ever needed help, and she decided that this was the time to take her neighbor up on the offer.

"We don't even know them," Bradley whined, when told the news.

"You've met them. And Mr. and Mrs. Yang are very nice."

"But what are we going to do over there? They don't have any toys!"

"How do you know they don't have any toys?"

"They don't have any kids," Bradley reasoned. "And grownups don't play with toys."

"Well, I'll be gone just for a little while," Gloria said. "I'm taking Aunt Ruth somewhere, and it's boring, and it's not for kids. You and Lucas can bring your own toys to the Yangs, and as soon as I get back, I'll pick you up. Or you could watch TV," she said brightly. "I'm sure Mr. and Mrs. Yang will let you watch what you want on TV."

"They'll probably make us watch the news." Bradley pouted.

Gloria laughed. "I'll tell them you can watch cartoons. Or you could even bring your own DVD. Scooby-Doo or SpongeBob or whatever you want."

It turned out, when she took the boys over the next day, that Mrs. Yang had just baked a batch of peanut butter cookies, which they could smell as soon as the door opened, and which flabbergasted both Bradley and Lucas. Gloria had never baked cookies and seldom even bought them. The idea that a woman without children would make cookies just for herself and her husband was a revelation to both kids, and when Mrs. Yang suggested that the two grab themselves a handful while they were still warm, Bradley and Lucas were sold. They ran into the kitchen.

"Thank you," Gloria said sincerely.

Cicely smiled. "It's no problem at all."

"I should be back in an hour or so, and then I'll take them off your hands."

"No need to rush," her neighbor said. "We'll be fine."

After returning home, going to the bathroom and locking up the house, Gloria drove to Aunt Ruth's, having convinced her aunt that it would be better if she picked her up. She knew it would be easier to hijack her aunt if she were already in the car, and that's exactly what she did. "We need to stop by Mom's house first," Gloria said. "There's something I need you to see."

"The will's already been—"

"Oh, this has nothing to do with the will," Gloria said, mock cheerfully. "It's something else entirely." She quickly changed the subject. "How's Kate doing?"

"Oh, Kate," Aunt Ruth sighed, and, as Gloria knew she would, her aunt spent the rest of the drive lamenting her daughter's poor taste in boyfriends and terrible career choices.

Then they were there.

It was the house in which Gloria had grown up, but just since yesterday, the ranch-style home had taken on a darker aura. She knew it was all in her mind, but to Gloria the low-slung structure looked like the top half of a distorted head, with the peeling shake roof its hair, the wide-set windows its eyes, the front door its nose. The mouth would be buried beneath the ground, and in Gloria's conception it was smiling malevolently.

"What are we here for again?" Aunt Ruth asked as they got out of the car.

Gloria did not answer but led the way up the walk to the door. She knocked, pounding the wooden door more forcefully than she'd intended. Inside, her stomach was churning.

Her mother opened the door. "Gloria," she said, surprised. And, looking over her shoulder, "I see you brought Ru—…a guest."

Aunt Ruth stepped forward. "Hello. My name's Ruth."

Her mother smiled. "Nora. Glad to meet you, Ruth."

Gloria couldn't take it anymore. "You don't recognize her?" she asked.

Her aunt shook her head. "No. Am I supposed to?"

"That's my mom!"

"What?" Gloria could hear the confusion in her aunt's voice.

"It's my mom! Your sister!"

"No it's not," Aunt Ruth said flatly.

"Do you remember what she looked like when I was little, in the nineteen-eighties?"

"What are you talking about?" Aunt Ruth stared at her as though she was crazy, and Gloria wondered for a second if maybe she *was*. Then she saw the look her mother was giving her and knew with utter certainty that she was not.

"I know this sounds insane, but hear me out. Remember after the funeral, here, when everyone came over? A woman showed up dressed in bright Eighties clothes? That was her! I recognized her instantly, but—"

"I think I know my own sister." Aunt Ruth's voice was hard and serious. "And Nora is dead. I was with her in the hospital. I saw her body. So did you. I don't know why you're trying to torture me with this…blasphemy, but I do not appreciate it. I do not appreciate it at all."

Gloria focused on her mother's face and saw the sly smile slowly spread. It was the same sort of smile she'd imagined the house having beneath the earth. Her mother seemed to possess some sort of superpower, the ability to hide in plain sight even from those who knew her well, and that frightened Gloria more than anything else.

Moments later, she left with Aunt Ruth. They hadn't had lunch, the ostensible reason for the visit, and Gloria offered her aunt a meal at the restaurant of her choice, but the older woman shook her head primly at the suggestion and said that she had to be getting home. Gloria knew that wasn't true. Nevertheless, she drove her aunt back, and they said a strained goodbye. The boys at least had had a good time, as short as their visit had been, and Gloria thanked the confused Cecily as she picked up the boys a mere half-hour after she'd dropped them off. To make up for everything, she let Lucas pick where he wanted to eat lunch, and they went to Del Taco, though neither boy ate much since they'd filled up on Mrs. Yang's peanut butter cookies.

Gloria avoided her mother after that. Bradley and Lucas started with the afterschool program on Monday, so she didn't need her mom to babysit anymore, and, despite earlier offering to take the boys from her—

Do you want to run away?

—there was no indication that her mother actually cared about seeing her grandsons at all, since she made no effort to contact them. To Bradley and Lucas, she'd been "Miss Nora," their babysitter, and while they missed her for the first few days and asked over and over again why she didn't watch them anymore, the afterschool program quickly mitigated their sense of loss. And the fact that several of their friends were in the program, as well, made the transition even easier. A week later, they seemed happier than they had been before.

But if Gloria wasn't in contact with her mother, that did not mean that the woman was not on her mind. In fact, eating her lunch at work each day, she often found herself wondering if Bobby Perez was still having salad at his window-side table in Fresh Garden. And in between patients, when she'd caught up on her officework, Gloria would invariably start thinking about what her mother might be doing at that moment.

What *did* she do all day? Gloria wondered. She didn't have a job, credit cards or a bank account. Where was the money coming from to buy groceries, household items and her ever-expanding wardrobe? Was she somehow getting it from Bobby Perez? Gloria was half-tempted to evict her mother from the house and sell it, since, legally, the woman was dead and the house now belonged to her, but fear or inertia or a combination of both kept her from acting on the impulse.

In a delayed reaction, perhaps, to Benjamin's death, it was becoming increasingly hard for Gloria to sleep through the night. For some time, she had been going to bed around eight, shortly after Bradley and Lucas, finding the house far too empty in the evenings. But recently, she'd begun awakening sometime between midnight and two. At first, she tried falling back asleep again, but after several nights staring up at the ceiling, wide awake she found herself getting out of bed and trying to catch up on household chores, things she'd let slide or things that Benjamin had previously taken care of, thinking that if she was going to be awake anyway, she might as well use the time wisely. Her secret hope had been that she would tire herself out and be able to fall asleep again, but that did not happen. She did, however, clean out the junk drawer next to the refrigerator, and, climbing on chairs, move items down from the top shelves of the kitchen cupboards, where only Benjamin had been able to reach, to lower locations where she could easily access them.

Gradually, between weekend work and these clandestine nighttime efforts, the house was being remade in her own image, and traces of Benjamin were disappearing. Pictures from their wedding, pictures of him with her, pictures of him with the kids, a Sears portrait of the entire family and other photographic testaments to his life were still displayed throughout the house, but already the sound of his voice was fading in her mind, and Gloria knew, objectively, that the boys, Lucas in particular, had been so young when they'd lost their father that their memories of him would become faint enough that their recollection of him would be determined more by the stories she told them than by their own personal experiences. The thought depressed her.

One Friday night, Gloria was dead asleep and might have actually made it all the way to morning, but motherly instinct sensed the presence of one of her boys, and immediately she was wide awake, sitting up in bed and with one smooth movement turning on her bedstand lamp.

"Mommy?" Lucas was standing in the doorway in his shorty pajamas. "I'm scared."

She was instantly out of bed and hugging him. "What's the matter, sweetie?"

"I had a bad dream."

"It's all right. Mommy's here." She gave him an Eskimo kiss, rubbing her nose against his.

"I was dreaming about Miss Nora. She snuck into my room and was trying to *eat* me. She had big sharp teeth, and she already ate Bradley. His bed was all bloody and just his skeleton was there."

Gloria was horrified. Where could Lucas have come up with an idea so gruesome? She and Benjamin had always been very strict about what they let the kids watch, and she had no clue what could possibly have made her little boy think of something so violent (although, as reprehensible as it might be, a small secret part of her was glad that his adoration of "Miss Nora" had turned to fear. She thought the reaction far more fitting).

Lucas' lip trembled, the way it always did before he started to cry. "Can I sleep in your bed? I'm scared."

She took his hand. "Come on." Leading Lucas to the bed, she tucked him in on Benjamin's side and gave him a kiss on the forehead.

“Nighty night.” She almost said, *Sweet dreams*, but decided it was better not to mention dreams at all right now.

Lucas turned to her as she got in on the other side of the bed. In the yellow light of the lamp, she could see the worry on his face. “I didn’t know it was a dream at first. I thought it was real.”

“It wasn’t,” Gloria said. “Now go to sleep.”

She shut off the lamp, hoping she sounded more certain than she felt.

FIVE

Her mother's life insurance money arrived a week before the boys' summer vacation and was a lot more than Gloria had been led to believe it would be. She was not sure how she had gotten the numbers so seriously wrong, but between her mother and Bobby Perez, between Benjamin's plane crash and the sudden responsibilities of being a single mom, Gloria was forced to admit that, lately, she had been a bit scatterbrained.

The actual amount was $250,000. Combined with the small amount of money still in the joint bank account she'd shared with her mother, and Benjamin's life insurance, which had been paid much more promptly, Gloria now had well over half a million dollars in the bank. Such a figure was almost impossible to comprehend, and with it came relief and a sense of economic security she had never experienced before.

She took a half-day off work to deal with financial matters, speaking with a very helpful woman at the bank who laid out several options. Not knowing anything about investing and inherently distrusting the vagaries of the stock market, Gloria opted to keep her money in the bank, putting some of it in short-term CDs, some in long-term CDs, some in a money market account and the remainder in her regular checking and savings. It was the first time off she had taken since Benjamin's death, and that in itself had been a rare occurrence, something she had not even had to do for her mother, who had conveniently died on a weekend, but Gloria made the mistake of telling Dr. Lee the real reason for her absence this time rather than claiming she was sick, and she noted the look of disapproval on his face.

He was unusually brusque with her for the next several days, as if harboring some lingering resentment, although Gloria did not understand how that could be the case. It seemed to her that he should have been nicer than usual, more understanding, given that she had lost both her mother and her husband in so short a span of time. Yet he showed her no sympathy, and Friday afternoon when he caught her talking to Paula on the phone while sitting at her desk, even though she was technically on break, he ordered her to hang up.

The next Wednesday, Dr. Lee placed two small piles of papers on her desk. There was no accompanying note, but she knew the drill: file the ones on the left, shred those on the right. Luckily for her, the shredder was broken, since, still mentally distracted by all that was going on in her life, Gloria inadvertently filed the wrong group. When he found out, the doctor gave her a lecture in front of the staff, and Gloria caught Hong, Elaine and the new nurse, Amie, giggling. At five o'clock, as always, she waited for everyone to leave, then turned off her computer, made sure the rest of the equipment had been shut down, turned off all the lights except the two they left on for security purposes, picked up her purse and got ready to leave. Only this time, before switching on the alarm, she scrawled a quick message on office stationary, informing Dr. Lee that this had been her last day.

And, as easy as that, she quit the only job she had had since graduating from college.

Driving home, Gloria felt liberated. On the radio, all of the music seemed happy. She called Paula that night to tell her what she'd done, and while her friend was surprised, she was supportive. "I always thought you should have been more than a secretary."

"Assistant," Gloria corrected her.

"Whatever. You can do better. You have your degree, right?"

"In Art History. Which is why I worked in a dermatologist's office." Reality was starting to set in.

"It doesn't matter. I'm sure you'll be able to find something. You have education in one field, years of experience in another. It shows your range. It's like my brother. You know, Elliot? He's a manager at the county's vector control office, but he got his degree in English. Which is weird, because before he transferred to Cal State Long Beach, he went to Cerritos College, where he got his AA in Computer Science..."

The next day, Gloria attended two graduation ceremonies—Lucas' for third grade at one o'clock, and Bradley's for fourth grade at two. She was not sure if she had said anything to her mother about the date, so she kept nervously watching the twin doorways on opposing sides of the multipurpose room, but, fortunately, her mother never showed up. After school, Gloria and the boys went with a group of other kids and parents to Chuck E. Cheese for the remainder of the afternoon. The three of them celebrated that evening at home with an extra-large pepperoni pizza and two Redbox movies—one chosen by Bradley, one by Lucas.

School ended, oddly, on a Thursday instead of a Friday, and since Gloria had quit her job, they all had the next day free. It was a strange sensation, not having to go to work, and on impulse, she got out the suitcases and announced to the boys that they were going on vacation. They looked at each other, wide-eyed and open-mouthed, like characters in a movie, and the sight made her laugh.

"Where are we going?" Bradley asked excitedly.

"The Grand Canyon?" It was the only vacation Lucas could remember taking.

"You'll see," she told them. "Let's pack some clothes, then maybe some books or games or things for you to do in the car."

"Is it far away?" Bradley asked.

"You'll see." She had no destination in mind, but she packed enough clothes for a week, made sure the boys had a similar amount of clothing, and brought along an ice chest filled with Sparklett's water bottles, and a grocery bag filled with Pringles and other snacks. *Prinkles*, Lucas always called the potato chips, and Gloria had stopped correcting him because she knew that she would miss his cute mispronunciation once he started saying the word right.

She drove first to the bank, where she got $200 out of the ATM, then to the cheapo gas station Benjamin preferred, where she filled up the car's tank. Driving past the park then past Brea Mall, she pulled onto the Orange Freeway, northbound. She still had no idea where she was headed, but in the middle of withdrawing money from the ATM, Gloria had decided that she and the boys were going to start over with a new life in a new town, and while she said nothing to them about it, she intended to drive up to Northern California or maybe Oregon or Washington, until she found a place where there would be no more mothers or high school crushes come back to life, a small town far away from the city, far away from the dead.

The rush hour was over, but the freeway was still crowded—Southern California freeways were *always* crowded—and it was nearly two hours later before they were able to leave the metropolitan area behind. Gloria had brought no maps and had not looked up where to go on her phone because she did not *know* where they were going. Living and working in Orange County, she was not that familiar with the L.A. freeway system, but she just kept going north, and eventually they were on a highway heading through the mountains into the desert. Suburbs gave way to small towns, until somewhere along the line, the traffic thinned out so much that the only vehicles on the road ahead of them were two pickups, one old, one new.

GLORIA

Several hours into her escape, Gloria began having second thoughts. Was she really willing to completely disrupt her children's lives and make them start over in a new city at a new school where they knew no one? She hadn't done any of the things you were supposed to do when you moved. She hadn't had her mail stopped or cancelled her newspaper or had her water and electricity shut off. She hadn't even bothered to clean out the refrigerator, which meant that if they were gone for any length of time, the food in there would spoil. What was she thinking? A person couldn't just go off willy nilly and abandon her life without making proper preparations.

But she had, and the truth was that she did not feel bad about it. Oh, logically, she might be able to dissect the ways in which she was behaving foolishly and irresponsibly, but in her heart Gloria did not honestly believe that she was doing anything wrong. To the contrary, this felt more right than anything in a long time. Besides, she told herself, there were plenty of people who pulled up stakes and started over again because they were unemployed and evicted. Somehow they were able to move west or east or north or south, find jobs and, practically penniless, begin new lives in a fresh location. Certainly she could do the same with half a million dollars in the bank.

Bradley and Lucas had gone through the gamut of emotions since getting into the car this morning: excitement at going somewhere new, frustration at being stuck in traffic, anger with each other over the usual brotherly disagreements, happiness that she let them play games on her phone, boredom over how long the trip was taking. They stopped for lunch at a Subway in smog-shrouded Bakersfield, a city much uglier than she'd expected it to be, and before starting off again, went into a Barnes and Noble across the street from the eatery, where she allowed each of them to pick out something to read in the car. Bradley chose the two Lemony Snicket books he did not yet have, Lucas a trio of Goosebumps, and they were both quiet and happy for at least the first half of the afternoon.

They spent the night at a Days Inn outside of Sacramento. Gloria still did not feel they had gotten far enough away, so tomorrow they were going to continue onward. Bradley and Lucas were in good spirits—they'd gotten a chance to swim in the hotel's pool, and the room's cable TV had both Cartoon Network and Nickelodeon—but she knew they would not be happy spending another day in the car (Lucas had already asked when they were going home), so, in bed, she scrolled through her phone, looking for touristy things to do that were in the general direction they were headed. Fortunately, there were lakes and redwoods and historic forts, spaced roughly an hour apart, so, hopefully, tomorrow would be a little easier.

All three of them fell asleep early, the TV still on, and when Gloria awoke, she heard the *Good Morning America* theme, and saw that the boys were wide awake, staring at her.

"Bradley said we should let you sleep," Lucas explained. "But we wanted you to wake up."

"What's the checkout time?" Bradley asked.

"I don't know," she told him, "but we're leaving after breakfast anyway."

Bradley and Lucas looked at each other.

"What is it?"

"Can we swim before we go?" Bradley asked. "It's a heated pool."

"*Please*?" Lucas begged.

Gloria smiled. She glanced over at the clock on the nightstand between the two beds. It was five after seven. "Okay. We'll go down and have breakfast, then you can swim for a half-hour, then you come back and take a shower, and we'll pack and go."

"An hour?" Bradley pressed.

"A half-hour."

"What if we eat fast?"

"A half-hour. We have a lot of places to go today." She saw their faces fall. "You want to see the redwoods, don't you?" They brightened up. "Put on your bathing suits and a shirt, and we'll go straight to the pool after we eat."

The hotel offered a free continental breakfast. When Gloria was growing up, that meant coffee, orange juice and a Danish from some table in the lobby, but here they had an entire breakfast room with steam trays filled with bacon, sausage and scrambled eggs, as well as a variety of hot and cold cereals, and bread and bagels that could be toasted. There was even fresh fruit and a hot chocolate machine. The room was big enough for several round tables, but only two of them were occupied at the moment: one by a boisterous family of four, their platters piled high with food, the other by a sullen-looking teenage girl sitting alone with a paper cup of coffee in front of her. It was seven-twenty in the morning, and the girl was on her phone, texting, oblivious to everyone else around her. How did people spend so much time on their phones? Gloria wondered. When she was a teenager, in the days before cellphones, her mom used to lecture her about tying up the line when she gossiped with her friends about school or boys or music or whatever. And that had only been in the afternoons or during prime time. Back then, it had been considered rude to call anyone before ten in the morning, and if a telephone ever rang after nine at night, it could only be some sort of emergency. Yet here this girl was, typing a message to someone at a time when many people were still asleep. Were the thoughts of this teenager really so important that sharing them couldn't wait until a reasonable hour?

Gloria ushered Bradley and Lucas over to the food, helping them pick out what to eat, then walked with them over to a table, where she sat them down before getting her own breakfast. On a television mounted to the wall, the *Today* show was on. Gloria had not seen it in several years, and realized as she bit into her multi-grain toast that she did not recognize either of the two hosts. *Everything changes*, she thought again, *and usually not for the better.* She remembered, as a student at Cal State Fullerton, learning from a professor that one of her father's favorite musicians, Tim Weisberg, was a graduate of the school. Her dad had been excited when she told him, and he broke out a bunch of old albums, the covers featuring various versions of a happy hippie with a big bushy mustache holding a flute. A couple of years ago, vacationing in Morro Bay, Lucas so young that Benjamin was carrying him as they walked from store to store in the quaint downtown, Gloria had seen a more recent Tim Weisberg CD in a small book and music shop. On the cover was a short-haired, clean-shaven man with a tight smile and a pinched narrow face, not the loose, long-haired guy with the broad easy grin that she remembered, and she'd put the CD back, feeling sad.

Thinking about her father made her wonder what he would have thought about what had happened to her mother. What would he have done? How would he have reacted?

She wished he was still alive.

Did she wish he would come back?

No, Gloria decided quickly. She did not.

She allowed the boys to swim after breakfast, ignoring the advice her mother had always given her that you shouldn't swim until an hour after eating. They were the only ones in the pool this early, and they were having such a good time that she let them stay a little longer than originally intended. It was after nine-thirty before they were finally on the road, and mentally she scratched off a couple of planned stops. Not a problem, as it turned out, because the pool time had put both boys in a good mood that lasted through the rest of the morning.

Farmland gave way to forest. The tenor of the land was different today. Maybe it was her mood, maybe these smaller towns had genuinely escaped the influence of the bigger cities to the south, but she finally felt that she was getting closer to what she was seeking. Acting on instinct, she pulled off the highway onto a side road, where a green sign informed her that ten miles ahead was the town of Glad. She drove through Glad, which was little more than a gas station, café and a handful of houses, and continued on, the route passing through low hills and then taller mountains.

Either they drove through the mountains or came back out on the same side further north—the road was so winding it was hard to tell—but they were soon in a rolling landscape where hilly towns were separated by swaths of alternating woods and fields. An hour after what would have ordinarily been their lunchtime, Gloria saw a road sign announcing two towns up ahead: the comically named Hicksville, 16 miles away, and Longbranch, 45 miles.

"I'm hungry!" Lucas whined. "When are we going to eat?"

"And when are we going to the redwoods?" Bradley asked. "You said we were going to the redwoods!"

"I told you, we decided to go a different way. The redwoods were on the other highway. And we'll eat as soon as we find someplace."

Gloria was getting hungry herself, and Hicksville, as it happened, was much bigger than she'd expected. For the past few hours, the communities they'd passed through had been more hamlets or villages than towns, but Hicksville had an honest-to-God main street (called, of course, Main Street), and not only were there three gas stations, a small shopping center, two grocery stores and a motel, but several eating establishments, ranging from a burger stand to what looked like a pretty nice Italian restaurant.

"Lunch!" Lucas called out. "It's about time!"

Gloria laughed. "Okay, who wants what?"

They settled, as they often did, on Mexican food. La Cocina was a small eatery located next to a laundromat, and since it was nearly one-thirty and the lunch hour was over, they were the only customers. The chef was also the waiter and, Gloria assumed, the owner. He brought over a basket of chips and a bowl of salsa, then three glasses of water, before passing out menus. "My name's Ricardo," he said in friendly, lightly accented English. "I haven't seen you here before."

"We're from California!" Lucas announced.

"We're still in California," Gloria told him.

"We're from Brea!"

"Oh?" Ricardo said, smiling. "Where's that?"

"It's close to Disneyland," Bradley offered, and Gloria was surprised at how mature he sounded.

"We came up here for the redwoods!" Lucas said.

Ricardo chuckled. "That's the *only* reason anyone comes up this way." He turned to Gloria. "Are you heading to the state park?"

"We have no specific plans," she admitted. "Beyond finally eating lunch."

"Well, I may be biased, but as far as I'm concerned, everything here is good." He started back toward the kitchen. "Give me a shout when you decide what you want."

Gloria liked Ricardo, and she liked his restaurant. And after they ate their lunch and walked back outside, and she looked around the town and saw an exposed section of granite cliff on the otherwise wooded hillside that sat at the end of Main Street, saw a red brick fire station next to a log cabin beauty salon, she decided that she liked Hicksville, too.

Here, she decided. They would stop here.

Holding the boys' hands, Gloria walked up the sidewalk to the next intersection. But where would they live? She did not want to stay in a motel. That was fine for a night or two, but if they were going to relocate, they would have to find a real place to live. In old movies, arrivals in an unfamiliar town usually stayed at a boarding house. But she didn't know if boarding houses even existed anymore. If they did, they probably didn't allow children. Not that she would want to room with a bunch of strangers anyway. No, they needed their own place. An apartment, maybe.

Were there apartments in Hicksville?

A rental house, then.

"The car's back there," Lucas said, pulling on her arm.

"I know," she told him, "but let's stroll around a little bit, walk off our chub." The phrase always made her boys laugh, which was why she used it. Sure enough, they started giggling. Bradley pushed his stomach out as they turned the corner, and Lucas patted it. He then patted her stomach, and Gloria smiled, pushing his hand away.

Beyond Main Street, Hicksville deteriorated quickly. They passed a tire shop that was little more than a dirt lot on which stacks of used tires were piled, the whole operation surrounded by dull chainlink. A hyperactive Pit bull came running up from somewhere, barking angrily and following them along the other side of the fence. Across the street, a dark gnarled man was burning trash in a metal barrel set in his weedy front yard. In the center of the roadway, a boy about Bradley's age walked past with his dad. Both were wearing camouflage and both were carrying rifles.

Who was she kidding? Gloria thought. They didn't belong here. Bradley and Lucas would be eaten alive in a school filled with kids like these. Her entire idea had been stupid, a shallow fantasy based on a faulty premise. Despite the way they were depicted in movies, small towns weren't quaint communities populated by engagingly eccentric people all happily tolerant of each others' quirky differences. More often than not, they were economically disadvantaged regions whose hard-living residents were being devastated by the opioid crisis.

She suddenly felt tired, the only thought on her mind the endless hours of driving ahead of her as she returned them to Southern California.

"Mommy." Bradley was pulling on her sleeve.

She looked down at him. "What?"

"That man."

They had moved past the tire yard and were walking in front of an unfenced vacant lot. At the rear of the lot was a line of tall trees, and in front of the trees stood a small wooden shed only slightly larger than an outhouse. A man was walking toward them on a dirt pathway leading to the sidewalk from the shed, waving. It looked as though he was trying to flag them down.

"I think he wants to talk to us," Bradley whispered.

Gloria stopped, still holding on to her boys' hands. Indeed, the man was approaching rapidly, a purposeful look on his face. An older white man with short salt-and-pepper hair and a gray Sam Elliott mustache, he was dressed incongruously in a blue business suit. Instinct told her to get away from here as quickly as possible, but the man clearly wanted to speak with her, and she waited as he walked up.

"Mommy..." Bradley said worriedly.

"It's okay," she assured him.

The man stepped onto the sidewalk. He was not smiling, but neither did he appear angry or upset. His expression was blandly neutral. "Gloria Jaymes?" he asked.

She was too shocked at hearing her name to even respond.

He offered her his hand. "We've been waiting for you."

TWO

ONE

We've been waiting for you.

What did that mean?

Who was *we*?

Gloria held tightly on to Bradley and Lucas, refusing to take the man's extended hand. She was more frightened than she could ever remember being, but instead of leaving, instead of running away, instead of hurrying quickly back to the car and taking off, she remained rooted in place. She was vaguely aware that the street was more crowded than it had been, that a small group of residents had walked up, but it was as if she had been hypnotized into immobility. She simply stood there, saying nothing, staring at the man before her.

How did he know her name? Had she met him before? Gloria looked at him more closely. Perhaps he did look familiar. His distinguishing feature was the mustache, and she could not remember meeting someone with one so full, but she thought that the large nose above that gray hair and the thin mouth below it looked somewhat recognizable.

Or not.

She was probably just looking for a logical reason to explain something that might not have one.

"Come," the man said.

She should have said, "No," and walked away, but, inexplicably, Gloria found herself following him back up the narrow dirt path toward the shed at the rear of the vacant lot, still holding her sons' hands. She had no idea why she was being so compliant, especially in a strange area of a strange town so far away from home, but somehow she felt in no physical danger, and, in truth, she wanted to know how it was possible that this man and whoever else was with him—

We've been waiting for you.

—knew who she was.

And why they were waiting for her.

Up close, the shed was more homemade and ramshackle than it had appeared from afar. Seeing it from the vantage point of the sidewalk, Gloria had assumed it was one of those prefab structures she'd seen displayed in front of Lowe's or Home Depot, but now she could tell that it was constructed of mismatched boards taken secondhand from other locations and coated with red and white paint that was starting to fade and chip.

The man pulled on a wooden handle, and the door to the shed opened. He stepped aside, motioning for her to enter. "After you," he said.

Gloria shook her head. "I'm not going in there."

For the first time, the hint of a smile played over the man's lips. "I'll go in first."

He stepped into the shed, and Gloria heard his footsteps on the wooden floor. It was dark within, and the sun was shining on the western side of the shed rather than on the doorway, which faced north, so she could not see what was inside.

"Come on," the man said.

No. She drew the line at that, especially with her children in tow.

But she was curious about what was in the small building.

Gloria let go of her sons' hands. "Stay right there," she told them. "Don't move." She stepped forward, placing one hand on the edge of the open door, the other on the doorframe, leaning in until she could see the interior.

It was a shrine.

To her.

The peachfuzz hair on the back of her neck bristled as she stared at a giant framed portrait of herself mounted on the back wall. Other pictures, drawings and photos of her were hung, posted or tacked-up on the sides. The shed was larger than it had originally appeared—it was narrow in width but went back farther than she would have imagined—yet, still, the single room was small. In its center was a raised section of flooring, and on that rectangular area, two men were kneeling, looking toward her with expressions of awe. Next to them stood the man who had led her here.

"Wh-what is this?"

The man smiled slightly. "Gloria." He spoke her name as though she had said something endearingly foolish.

She'd had enough, but turning away, intending to take her sons, walk back to the car and get the hell out of here, she found that the boys were nowhere in sight.

Her heart skipped a beat. "Bradley?" she called. "Lucas?" Gloria's eyes scanned the small assemblage lining the edge of the property but saw only adults, no sign of her boys. "*Bradley*!" she called again. "*Lucas*!"

"Where are my kids?" she demanded. Fury coursed through her. Her fists were clenched, her eyes blazing, as she advanced on the gathered crowd, and her shouts could probably be heard all the way back at La Cocina. "Where are my boys? What have you done with them? *Bradley*!" she screamed at the top of her lungs. "*Lucas*!"

Behind her, from the doorway of the shed, the man with the mustache spoke. "There *is* no Bradley. Or Lucas."

"What are you talking about, you crazy son of a bitch?" She was shouting so loud that her throat hurt.

"You have no children," he said calmly.

"*Bradley*! *Lucas*!"

She swiveled to face him. He had already started toward her, and behind him, emerging from the doorway of the shed, were the two men who had been kneeling inside. Owen Portis and Charles Wister.

How did she know their names?

Gloria's head was spinning. What in God's name was going on?

"Just wait," the man with the mustache said, glancing back at them.

Russell. His name was Russell.

Gloria started running. "Bradley! Lucas!"

"No!" Russell shouted after her. "Stop!"

THREE

ONE

Sometimes Gloria thought: *It would have been nice to be born into a small family.*

She didn't really believe that, wasn't sure why she even entertained the notion, but on hectic holidays like this, the Fourth of July, when her sisters and her brother and all of their families came over to her house, when she spent almost the entire week prior holed up in the kitchen and Benjamin missed most of the holiday itself slaving away over the barbecue in the back yard, Gloria couldn't help thinking that it would be a relief to take a year off, to just spend the day together watching the *Twilight Zone* marathon or going to the beach or out to a movie, without dozens of relatives in tow.

If she and Benjamin had had kids of their own, she might have felt differently. Not that she didn't love her nieces and nephews—she did, of course—but it became overwhelming to have so *many* of them running in and out of the house all day, and after everyone left, there was always damage to tally up. *Once*, she thought, just once, it would be nice to celebrate a holiday at someone else's place, to be able to show up as a guest and leave when it was convenient, and not have to stay to the bitter end and clean up afterward. But Janine's house was in a newer development and had no front *or* backyard, Myra and her kids now lived in a duplex after the divorce, and Paul's gated community frowned on such gatherings; Gloria was not even sure if his authoritarian homeowners' association allowed barbecues.

Janine walked into the kitchen with an empty mixing bowl. "Out of salsa!" she announced. "Do you have any more? It's a hot seller."

Gloria had spent half of last night making that salsa from scratch, from a recipe given to her by her friend Lupe, but she should have known that her family would just chug it down, oblivious to not only the authenticity of its taste but the amount of work that went into it. She might as well have bought a gallon of the most Americanized crap available at Costco and poured it into the bowl. "Sorry," she said. "That's all I made."

She purposely stressed the fact that she'd prepared it herself, but, as usual, the remark flew right over Janine's head. "I'll check the cupboard," her sister said. "Maybe you have something in there."

There was a small jar of artisanal bean dip that one of her co-workers had given her as a thank-you present at the end of the last exhibit, but before Gloria could say, "Leave that, please. I'm saving it," Janine had already plucked it from the shelf.

"This'll do!" And she was off.

Discouraged, Gloria moved over to the sink and looked out the window at the back yard. Whit and Kenny, Paul's sons, her two oldest nephews, were conspiring together about something as they stood next to the corner of the fence. Whit kept glancing over at Myra's daughters, running in circles around the avocado tree, and Gloria knew that didn't bode well. The last time they were here, over Easter, the boys had convinced their younger cousin Lizzie to sprinkle some dirt in her sister Linda's lemonade. All of them had gotten in big trouble, and Paul and Myra had ended up getting mad at each other over their children's behavior and leaving early. If she wanted to prevent a similar incident from happening today, Gloria was going to have to nip this in the bud.

She walked outside. Paul and Janine's husband Sadeen were next to the barbecue, talking to Benjamin. Myra and Janine were at the picnic table, arranging the chips and dip with their usual combination of cooperation and competition. She glanced over at her nephews, now whispering and giggling, their plan obviously coming together. She could walk over there and try to distract them, offer them some food, recruit them for some type of chore, but it would be awkward and obvious and probably wouldn't work. Where was her brother's wife, Danielle? She'd be able to defuse the situation without taking offense, the way Paul undoubtedly would.

"Excuse me."

Gloria moved aside as Danielle came out of the house behind her. She must have been in the bathroom.

"Danielle," Gloria said, touching her sister-in-law's arm.

"Oh, do you need some help?"

"No, no." Over Danielle's shoulder, she saw Whit and Kenny start toward the avocado tree. Gloria pretended to frown as she looked in that direction. "What are the boys doing?"

Danielle turned, saw the giggling boys making their way toward their cousins, and instantly understood the situation. "Uh-oh." She strode purposefully across the yard to intercept them.

Crisis avoided.

Gloria moved over to the picnic table, where Janine and Myra were now silently eating snacks, each of them no doubt feeling slighted by something the other had said. It was strange, Gloria thought, how the dynamics of their childhood had not changed a single bit, even after they grew into adults, even after their parents had died. They were still the same people they'd always been, and she wondered if their personalities had been set in stone from the second they were born, if their interactions with each other would have followed the same pattern no matter where they'd grown up or what had happened in their lives. Being the youngest, she had always gotten along with both of her sisters, but Janine and Myra always seemed to be on the defensive with each other, ever ready to be offended by a casual comment or an innocent question perceived to have a double meaning.

Gloria sat down at the picnic table, taking a tortilla chip out of the bowl and using it to scoop up some of the bean dip. It was *really* good, and she wished her sister had not found it, so that she and Benjamin could have had it to themselves. That would teach her to procrastinate; she should have eaten it a month ago.

Whit and Kenny, obviously dissuaded by their mother from going through with whatever they'd planned, came running up. Each grabbed a handful of chips before taking off again. They were going to run out of chips if Benjamin didn't hurry up and grill the chicken, Gloria thought. She should have bought a few extra bags, but her calculations hadn't taken into account how much all of the kids seemed to have grown since Easter.

"So what about Ben's job?" Janine asked. "Are they still talking layoffs?"

"Benjamin," Gloria said.

Janine rolled her eyes, shared a look with Myra. "*Benjamin.* So are they still laying people off?"

"Looks like he survived this round," Gloria told them. "We'll see what happens at the end of the year. That company's heartless. They always seem to slash and burn right before the holidays."

"May they rot in hell," Myra said.

It turned out not to be a bad Fourth of July when all was said and done. Paul, as always, brought a box of illegal fireworks he'd purchased on one of his business trips to New Mexico, and the kids ran around with sparklers, while Paul set off a series of increasingly large fountains. Everyone got a box of charcoal snakes to take home, and Gloria heard Whit tell Kenny that he was going to sell individual snakes for a quarter each to friends of his at school and make a fortune. The night ended with them all standing in the center of the back yard, looking up at the sky and watching the city fireworks display originating from the nearby high school stadium.

"Well," Benjamin said after everyone left, "no pouting, no fights, no one stalking off. All in all, I'd say that was a success."

She punched his arm. "As if your family's any better."

"The difference is: even if my family lived in California, I wouldn't invite them—and even if I did invite them, they wouldn't come."

It was sort of a joke, but it was true, nevertheless, and although Gloria smiled, she felt sad for her husband. She vowed to herself that she'd give him some good sex tonight.

Hand in hand, the two of them walked back into the house.

TWO

By lunchtime the next day, Gloria had fielded calls from both Myra and Janine, each of them complaining about something the other had said, slights that weren't really slights but that had magnified in both of their minds overnight. It was par for the course, and she wouldn't have thought anything of it, but casual, seemingly unrelated side mentions by them about Paul, concerns that something… wasn't…quite…right, made Gloria wonder. Myra thought it might be trouble in the marriage (she had never liked Danielle), while Janine speculated that there could be problems at work. Gloria had not noticed anything off about him herself, but she trusted her sisters' instincts, and she wondered if she should call her brother under some pretext or other and conduct a fact-finding mission.

How had it come to pass that she was the responsible one in the family, the one who held (or at least tried to hold) them all together? She was younger than Myra by three years, than Janine by five, than Paul by seven. Growing up, Paul had been so much older and so far ahead of her that they might as well have lived in different worlds.

Benjamin was definitely part of it. He was one of those people who'd been born an adult, and his presence automatically granted her a dependability that she might not have been able to manage on her own.

She told Benjamin about her sisters' concerns, but he waved them off. "Paul seemed fine," he said. "I was with him almost the entire time and didn't notice anything."

Benjamin was a good man and a loving husband, but he wasn't the most emotionally perceptive person in the world, so later that afternoon, she gave Paul a call. Her ostensible reason was to tell him how much everyone had enjoyed his fireworks, but she could tell he was distracted, and her antenna went up. Not having to tiptoe around him like her sisters, Gloria just came right out with it. "What's wrong, Paul?"

"Nothing. What are you talking about?"

"Come on. You know I know you better than that."

He sighed. "You can't say anything to anyone. Especially Myra or Janine."

"Okay."

"I'm swearing you to secrecy."

"What is it?" she asked.

There was a second of silence. "I saw Dad."

What the hell? Gloria frowned. Was her brother having some sort of breakdown? Was he on drugs? She cleared her throat. "What do you mean, you saw Dad?"

"I saw him."

She wasn't sure how she was supposed to respond to that. Was he claiming to have seen a ghost? Was he claiming...what? That their father was still alive?

"Where? How? What did he look like? Was he old or did he look like...he did?"

"I knew you wouldn't believe me."

"I didn't say that."

"I can hear it in your voice."

"I'm just trying to figure out what happened."

"You want to know what happened? I took the boys to Disneyland the other day. We were waiting in line for the Indiana Jones ride, and the Jungle Cruise went by. The guide told the riders to wave to us, and they did, and one of them was Dad."

Gloria was relieved. "It's probably just someone who looked like him—"

"It was him," Paul insisted. "He was looking right at me while he was waving. And he was smiling. And he kept waving and smiling at me even after everyone else stopped, even as the boat moved past us. I took the boys out of line, and we went over to the Jungle Cruise. I waited there for five boats to come in, but he wasn't on any of them."

"Because it wasn't him. Probably for that moment, from that angle, it looked a little bit like him."

"I saw him again," Paul said quietly. "And it *was* him. We were walking toward Toon Town to go on the Roger Rabbit ride, and someone called my name. My *full* name. I recognized the way he said it instantly, and I looked down at the Storybook Land canal boats, and there he was, just like before, smiling at me and waving. 'Who's that man?' Kenny asked me. I told him I didn't know, and I hurried them toward Toon Town, but...I was scared, Glore. He looked exactly the same way he did when we were little. *Exactly.*"

She didn't know what to say to that.

He sighed again. "Don't tell Myra or Janine. Promise me. They'll just get all worked up and...who knows? Janine'll think it's a *sign* of some kind, and Myra will try to find a way to get me committed." He let out a small humorless laugh. "But I'm telling you, Glore. He was there and he was real. The boys are witnesses."

"So..." She didn't want to believe him, but she kind of did. "...is he a ghost or a zombie or..."

"He's just him. He's definitely not a ghost. And he acts like a regular person, not a zombie. Even if things like that *did* exist."

"Then maybe he didn't really die."

"We went to the funeral."

He had a point.

"*Why* do you think you saw him? Was he stalking you? Have you seen him since?"

"I haven't. But that doesn't mean he isn't around."

Gloria shivered. "Maybe I should keep my eyes open."

"Maybe you should."

"And maybe we *should* tell Myra and Janine."

There was a pause. "Go ahead if you think they'll believe you. Personally, I don't even think I should've told you."

"I'm glad you did."

She imagined she could hear his shrug over the phone. "I wouldn't tell Benjamin, either. Not unless something else happens."

"Like what?"

Another sigh. "I don't know."

Gloria hung up, less worried now about Paul and more worried about what Paul had seen. Because, she had to admit, she did believe him. She didn't know how it was possible or what it meant, but she could tell from the strength of his conviction that Paul honestly thought he had seen their father, and now she thought he had, too.

Did that mean her dad could be visiting her?

The idea was terrifying. She'd been eighteen when the heart attack had taken him, and of course she'd been sad, traumatized even. But she hadn't known him as well as she should have, and while he'd been there for her entire childhood, there'd always been a distance. Her dad had been a private man, certainly not warm and cuddly, and it had been clear to all of them that Paul was his favorite child. He'd always seemed slightly perplexed by his girls, and they in turn had gravitated toward their mother. So there was no real sense of anticipation or excitement in the prospect of seeing him again, only a cold knot of fear in the pit of her stomach. She had not known her father as a person, and she definitely did not know or want to encounter whatever he was now.

Gloria walked over to the window, pulling the curtains aside and peeking out, all the while thinking about how out of character this was for her. Like the rest of her family, she was not religious, and she did not believe in the supernatural or paranormal. She did not even have any interest in the subject; as far as she was concerned, the Travel Channel had become unwatchable since shifting from travel and food shows to ghost hunting programs. Yet here she was, checking out their front yard to make sure her dead dad was not lurking about somewhere, trying to spy on her.

"What are you doing?"

She dropped the curtain as Benjamin came into the living room. "Nothing."

"I heard you on the phone. Who was it?"

"No one."

He looked at her. "It had to be *someone*."

"All right. I called Paul."

"And?"

She debated whether or not to tell him, but the deliberation was short. There was no way Benjamin would believe any part of Paul's story, and if he sensed that she was swayed by it in any way, he would put on his look of disapproval and launch into a lecture about her gullibility. Gloria didn't want to deal with that right now, so she simply answered, "He's fine."

"Your sisters were seeing things that weren't there."

"I guess so."

He nodded, satisfied. "Told you."

Apparently, Benjamin had come into the living room to grab the newspaper from the coffee table before taking it with him into the bathroom, and he sorted through the sections until he found the sports pages. Gloria waited until he had left the room, then walked out to the front yard. She acted casual, telling herself that all she wanted to do was check out her flowers and make sure they didn't need to be watered, but she was thinking about what Paul had told her, and she walked past her potted geraniums, past her roses and chrysanthemums, all the way out to the sidewalk. She looked up and down the street. She was not sure what she'd expected—her Dad hiding behind a bush or sitting in a car, spying on her?—but, thankfully, there was nothing suspicious, nothing out of the ordinary.

Her eye was distracted by a man halfway up the block mowing his lawn. A little boy, probably his son, was riding his tricycle back and forth along the sidewalk, obviously under strict rules not to venture farther than the boundaries of their house. He would peddle furiously past where his dad was mowing, then come to a quick halt just before the neighbors' driveway, turning around. The scene made her realize, in a way she really hadn't before, that she and Benjamin were actual suburbanites, the "Pleasant Valley Sunday" kind. They lived in a neighborhood of upper middle-class tract homes, they had two cars parked in their two-car garage, they shopped at Whole Foods, they watched Netflix. It was an uncomfortable realization because that was not the way she thought of herself. In her mind, she was a free-spirited type, creative and imaginative. Bohemian. Benjamin might have a genetic tendency toward fuddyduddiness, but she kept him at least slightly on the cool side of straight, her artistic mien lending him Alternative credibility. At least, that's what she'd thought. But she saw now that both she and Benjamin belonged here in suburbia, not just because it was conveniently located for both of their jobs, but because, socially and temperamentally, this was where they were most comfortable. They fit in with their neighbors, with the neighborhood, with the lifestyle, and while that probably should have made her feel depressed, the fact that it didn't, the fact that she felt only a vague and transitory sense of discomfiture, proved just how true it was.

Gloria walked back into the house. As a computer science professor at UC Brea, Benjamin had the entire summer off, a perk she envied him. Her own job as a public relations officer at the Orange County

Museum of Art offered far less vacation time, and she had taken off only two days for the Fourth of July, turning it into a four-day weekend. Her big vacation would be in mid-August, when they were planning a week-long trip up north to visit Yosemite and Gold Rush country. Which meant that tomorrow it was back to work.

She wished they'd planned something for this holiday, even if was just a staycation to Laguna Beach or a quick trip to San Diego.

Gloria headed into the kitchen, taking a Snapple out of the refrigerator. Thank God they still had Diet Raspberry; over the past few years, the Snapple company's goal seemed to have been to eliminate all of the flavors that she liked. There was a package of leftover cookies on the counter from yesterday. She'd told the kids to take them home, not wanting to deal with the temptation, but their parents had all refused—kids were apparently supposed to have only healthy snacks these days—and now the Chips Ahoy were calling to her. Thankfully, they didn't go with diet raspberry iced tea, and she'd already opened the bottle, so those little fat-delivery systems would have to wait until later.

After finishing the bottle, she had to go to the bathroom. Was Benjamin still in there? The toilet in the master bath was clogged up and Benjamin still hadn't fixed it yet—it had been clogged for two days now; household repairs were not his strong suit, or hers, either—so they both had to use the one in the hall. She poked her head through the kitchen doorway. "Hurry up in there! I have to go, too!"

Gloria heard the toilet flush, felt water rushing through the pipes beneath the floor, and put her empty bottle down on the kitchen counter, walking into the hallway just as the bathroom door opened.

Her father stepped out.

Paul had been right. Their dad looked just as he had when they'd been young. She had not remembered him in such detail—all the old photos from their childhood were in albums parceled out between the four of them, and hers were buried somewhere amidst the junk in the hall closet—but seeing him now brought everything instantly back. He was smiling at her, just as Paul said he had at him, and while it was the same smile she remembered from the times he'd praised her school projects or she'd scored a soccer goal, in this context, coming out of her bathroom where Benjamin was supposed to have been, that smile was terrifying.

"Gloria Jean," he said, his smile widening.

She ran out of the house.

There was no thinking; she acted entirely on instinct. Before he could say another word, before he could advance a step closer, she was through the kitchen and out the back door. For a brief second, she worried that she had trapped herself, but then she saw that Benjamin had left the side gate unlocked, and she ran out of the back yard, through her little herb garden on the side of the house, and into the wide open freedom of the front. The sidewalk, the street, the neighborhood, the *world* was in front of her, and she ran into it as fast as she could, seeing in her mind her dad's unnerving smile, wanting only to put as much space between him and herself as possible.

Where was Benjamin? What had happened to her husband? That was her most pressing concern, and she could come up with no answer, could imagine no possible scenario in which what had just occurred might actually happen.

Gloria's pace slowed. Breathing heavily, her heart pounding almost painfully in her chest, she stopped running at the end of the block. She definitely needed to exercise more. She looked back down the street toward their house. What was she going to do? Call the police? Call Paul? Find a neighbor to accompany her back inside? She wasn't about to return to that house by herself, but she knew how these things usually worked, and she expected that, when she returned, there would be no sign of her dad, and Benjamin would be calmly sitting there watching TV or eating a snack or reading a book—

Her father stepped onto the sidewalk and began walking in her direction, smiling and waving.

A bolt of panic shot through her, and she took off again, energized by fear. Her purse was at home with her cell phone in it, so she couldn't call for help. All she could do was race away, and she did so at a speed she had not even attempted since high school. She turned right at the cross street, Fuchsia, knowing that it connected with Imperial Highway two blocks up. Across the street was a shopping center, and Gloria knew that if she could get there, she would be safe. Or at least there would be witnesses. Either way, there was safety in numbers, and she should be able to convince someone to call 911.

"Gloria!"

The voice was right behind her, and she screamed—

How could he have gotten so far so fast?

—as she whirled around to face him. Her plan was to kick him in the crotch as hard as she could, not knowing if it would even work. But then she saw that it was Benjamin, and her tensed leg muscles froze instead of following through with her strike. She should have recognized his voice, and it was an indication of how rattled she was that she hadn't. For it was indeed Benjamin, and he was out of breath from running to catch up with her, and there was no sign of her dad behind him.

Her head was spinning. What had just happened? Had she suffered some kind of break with reality? Had she imagined what she'd seen, influenced by what Paul had told her? Or...

Or what?

Because there really was no other explanation.

"I saw my dad!" Gloria blurted out. "Paul saw him, too. At Disneyland when he took the boys. I saw him when he came out of the bathroom. I thought it was you, but it wasn't, and I ran away, and he came after me."

Her recounting of events was almost incoherent and probably made sense to no one other than herself. She expected Benjamin to hug her and tell her everything was all right and offer vague reassurances, but instead he stood there looking stunned and said, "How did I get here?"

The question made her blood run cold. Everything *wasn't* all right. Something was very wrong, and she tried to speak, but her mouth was dry and she ended up coughing instead.

"I was in the bathroom," he said, almost as though talking to himself, "and then I was here."

She looked at him. Could he have been...possessed? Was that what had happened, her dad temporarily taking over her husband's body, transforming it into his own? It made as much sense as anything else at this point, and Gloria maintained a distance between herself and Benjamin, afraid he might suddenly switch back. But then he looked at her with hurt, confused eyes, the same eyes she'd awakened to in the hospital after her lumpectomy. It was him, completely him, and they fell into each others' open arms. He hugged her tightly. "What happened?" he said.

"I don't know," Gloria admitted.

"I should go to the hospital and get checked out."

"No," she said. "Don't do that."

"Why not?"

And she told him what she'd seen.

THREE

It did not happen again—*had it happened at all?*—and Gloria ended up describing everything to Paul. Shortly afterward, their sisters found out as well, although Gloria was not sure if it was Paul or herself who spilled the beans. Myra, of course, thought she and Paul were playing a joke on her. She was offended and pouted, and no one heard from her for a week. Janine believed that *they* believed, which, in a way, was worse, because Janine thought it was all nonsense. As kids, they had grown up without religion, their parents insisting that such superstitions were merely a ruse to convince unhappy people that their suffering was noble and that they would be rewarded for it after they died. To this day, none of them attended church, although Paul's wife, who had grown up Methodist, did take their children to services on Easter and Christmas. So, to Janine, the entire situation seemed delusional, maybe even the result of mental illness, and she not-so-subtly asked when she called if Gloria were under stress or self-medicating or having headaches or experiencing *other* hallucinations.

Hallucinations.

Could it have been a hallucination? Gloria wondered. It had seemed so real, so matter-of-fact, but then what did she know about such things? In movies, hallucinations were always spectral and wavery, but maybe in real life they seemed just as solid as everything else.

Then she remembered that at Disneyland, Kenny had seen and heard the man, too, not just Paul, and that reassured her that she was not crazy, not imagining things, that it really had happened.

Whether through overhearing adult conversations or because their parents had just come out and told them, all of the kids in the family eventually found out, and when Janine, desperate for a babysitter on Saturday night, dropped her kids off at Gloria's so that she and Sadeen could attend a party thrown by Sadeen's boss that, hopefully, would result in career advancement, Cherie, the oldest girl, asked, wide-eyed, "Did you really see Grandpa's ghost?" Gloria didn't know what to say. Her impulse was to tell the truth, but she knew it would frighten the girls, and she didn't want to deal with the fallout, which would undoubtedly be one of her sister's angry lectures, so instead she changed the subject.

"Who wants ice cream?"

Benjamin, to Gloria's complete surprise, seemed to believe her. Maybe it was a case of mental self-preservation, maybe he just didn't want to confront the possibility that he (and she) might have a brain tumor or some kind of cognitive degeneration, but whatever the reason, they analyzed both of their recollections as though the event had indeed occurred.

"I have another theory," Benjamin said as they sat at the breakfast table the next morning, going over the situation for the hundredth time.

She sipped her coffee. "Hit me with it."

"*He* didn't come back from the dead. *You* crossed over. Just for a minute or two, and I don't know how it happened, but you left this... plane, or whatever you want to call it, the world of the living, and you phased into the world of the dead. That's where he lives."

"In our exact same house, with our exact same furniture? And our same neighbors with the same cars and lawns and everything?" She shook her head. "It doesn't add up. Besides, where were *you*? Even if that did happen to me, everything would have been the same for you. I just would've been gone. You wouldn't have zapped out of the bathroom onto the street, all confused."

He sighed. "You're right."

Gloria patted his hand. "But it was *something*," she said.

It had been a long time since Gloria had talked about their parents with her brother and sisters. Part of it might have been the non-religious thing—their mom and dad were gone and that was the end of it—but a bigger part was simply the emotional dynamics of their family. They weren't really ones for nostalgia, and despite their geographical closeness, they weren't emotional sharers. The four of them had probably talked more about their parents in the past two weeks than they had in all the years since their deaths, and she was surprised to discover how little their memories synced up. They'd grown up in the same household, but somehow their experiences had all been different. It was like that story of the blind men and the elephant. She, Paul, Myra and Janine each had individual takes on their mom and, especially, their dad, and even comparing and combining those different perspectives did not paint a complete portrait.

Gloria, for example, remembered her father as a strict but fair man, somewhat distant, not that involved in family matters, more of a big-picture guy, a throwback to the times when dads brought home the bacon and moms took care of the household and child-rearing. To Paul, however, he'd been a tyrant, a demanding bully never satisfied by anything his only son did. Janine, to Gloria's surprise, found him "creepy" and too affectionate and said that even as a little girl she felt uncomfortable being alone with him. Myra, on the other hand, admired him greatly and thought he had been immensely supportive of her.

Which was the real version of their father? All of them, perhaps. Or none of them. A child's perceptions of his or her parents was at once more intimate than those of adult friends and family, and at the same time more limited.

Why was he appearing, though? What did he want? And why only to Paul and herself? Unless, Gloria thought, he *was* lurking around the periphery of her sisters' lives as well, and they simply hadn't noticed.

She thought of the way he had smiled and waved at her, and shivered.

Curious, Gloria broke out one of the old photo albums, looking for a picture of her dad. Opening it to the first page, she saw her class photo from second grade. She paused for a moment to look it over, surprised to realize that she recognized almost no one. The photo had been taken in the classroom, with all of the students sitting at their desks, and their teacher, Ms. Patricks, standing next to the blackboard. Gloria easily found herself, and Emma Showalter, her best friend in first, second and third grades. Here and there were other faces she recognized, but the vast majority of the class she did not remember at all. Wasn't that funny? She recalled bringing the photo home, and specifically remembered her dad telling her to write down everyone's name on the back. He'd seemed annoyed that the names weren't printed on the picture, as they had been every other year. Gloria had laughed and told him that she didn't need to write down anyone's name. She knew them all and certainly wouldn't forget them.

But she had. Her dad had been right, and her eyes focused on a cute little boy in the front row and she tried to remember his name, his voice, who his friends had been, anything about him, but absolutely nothing came to mind. It made her feel melancholy, wondering how people who had been an important part of her everyday life had ended up being completely forgotten by her.

Was the boy's name Bradley? Gloria thought. For some reason, that name was stuck in her head. And she associated it with the name Lucas. *Could that have been one of his friends?*

There was no way she would ever know, and she turned the page, still looking for a photo of her father.

And there he was.

Chillingly, he was wearing the same shirt and pants he'd been wearing upon coming out of the bathroom in Benjamin's stead. The picture had been taken on one of their vacation trips—it looked like Yosemite—and in it he was standing next to her mother, a waterfall behind them. They were both smiling, but whereas her mom's smile looked natural and happy, her dad's seemed a little too big, a little too forced, a little *too*. Maybe she was reading more into the picture than was there, bringing to it the baggage of recent events, but Gloria didn't think so. There was something unnerving about not only her dad's smile but the way he stared into the camera. He seemed to be looking through the picture and out at her, almost as though he had known at the time what would happen all these years later. Paul must have taken the photo—he was the oldest and a boy, and these sorts of duties usually fell to him—so it was possible that that was who the hard flat stare was aimed at, but Gloria could not shake the feeling that the look on her dad's face was directed specifically toward her.

"Glore?"

She jumped at the sound of her husband's voice.

Her involuntary reaction made him laugh, but his laughter died quickly when he saw what she was looking at.

"That's exactly what he looked like," she said. "Same clothes and everything."

"Maybe you did imagine it, then. Maybe you subconsciously remembered that picture—"

"Did you imagine disappearing from the bathroom and reappearing on the sidewalk in front of me?" Gloria shook her head. "We've been through this before."

"You're right," Benjamin told her. "But it can't be good to keep obsessing about it. Nothing's happened since. Maybe nothing will happen ever again. I just think we need to move on."

She understood why he said that: he was frightened. He might even be right. But she wasn't sure she could put it all aside so easily—even if she wanted to. Still, Gloria nodded in agreement, and closed the photo album.

"What say we bail on this and do something fun?" Benjamin asked her. "I have that Golden Spoon card filled up. Free frozen yogurt."

Gloria laughed. "Okay," she said.

That night, she dreamed that she saw her father's face in the mirror instead of her own while she was brushing her teeth, and in the morning she made sure to brush while Benjamin was taking a shower so as not to be alone in the bathroom.

At work, there wasn't much to do. The museum was closed, as a new exhibit was being installed, and she'd contacted all of the local press the previous week, sent out e-invites for the opening reception to Orange County's movers and shakers, and mailed out flyers to members and longtime supporters. She answered some emails, sent out some other emails, sorted through the physical mail that had been piling up for the past week, and chatted with Sidhil Paramanengerhan and Francis L., the curators of the new exhibit. But mostly, she thought about her father, wondering if he had known that Paul and his sons would be at Disneyland that day, wondering if he would show up here at the museum sometime, pretending to be a regular patron.

Arriving home, her neck was stiff from stress. Benjamin was lounging on the back patio reading a book, a half-empty glass of iced tea on the small table next to him. He looked up at the sound of the sliding glass door as Gloria came out to join him.

"Myra called earlier today," he informed her. "She wanted to know if the girls could stay overnight on Saturday. I told her you'd call her back."

"Did she say why?"

He raised his eyebrows and grinned. "A date, apparently."

"*Overnight?*"

"Maybe she expects to get lucky."

Gloria grimaced. There was nothing ickier than thinking about her siblings' sex lives.

"Come on. They're good kids."

"I know that. It's just..." She shook her head. "Remember what happened with Cliff? Myra goes off half-cocked—"

"Interesting phrase."

"—on these things." Gloria hit his shoulder. "She ends up getting her self-esteem stomped all to hell, and I'm the one who has to nurse her through it. You know she won't confide in Paul, and she and Janine are like oil and water. One of them always ends up getting offended and walking off in a huff."

"Look, we don't know the details here. All she's asking is if the girls can stay over."

"Of course they can," Gloria said. "But—"

"But what? Give her a call."

She could tell he had already tuned out—Benjamin's tolerance for family drama was next to nonexistent—so she gave up talking to him and phoned Myra, letting her sister know that she would be happy to have the girls over.

On Saturday afternoon, Myra dropped the girls off early, shortly after three o'clock. She was almost giddy as she unloaded their small Hello Kitty suitcases, and Gloria could not remember the last time she had seen her sister so excited.

Maybe she expects to get lucky.

Gloria knew she should be happy for Myra, but in her sister's case, this level of enthusiasm was usually not a good thing. Gloria had to resist the temptation to warn and lecture, a move that would have invariably had her sister stalking off, taking the girls, and either cancelling her date and resenting Gloria for God-knew-how-long, or pawning them off on Janine or Paul, undoubtedly ending up in some intra-family quarrel. It was a lose-lose situation, so she held her tongue, feigned support, and waited until her sister had gone before allowing herself to breathe normally.

Lizzie and Linda were full of questions. Myra, stupidly, had made no effort to disguise her date from the girls, who were now wondering if they were going to have a stepfather. Or a *father*, Gloria thought, since their real dad, Myra's ex-husband, could not seem to be bothered with even the most rudimentary parental duties. Which was why the girls were staying here tonight.

Gloria, uncomfortable with the subject, tried to distract the girls by offering them a snack, but they weren't to be dissuaded. "Do you know where Mommy met him?" Lizzie asked.

"We don't even know his name!" Linda piped up.

"I don't either," Gloria said firmly. "Your mother hasn't told me anything about it. I'm sure when she's ready to, she will."

"How did you and Uncle Benjamin meet?" Lizzie asked. She was at an age when everything about dating and marriage seemed romantic.

"We met in college," Gloria said.

"Where did Mommy and my dad meet?"

In a bar, she thought. *Your mommy was a new, naïve waitress, and your dad was a smooth talker who took her home.* But she lied and said, "I'm not sure."

Linda nodded, as if this satisfied her, and reached for the box of tomato-basil Wheat Thins that Gloria had taken out, but Lizzie still wanted to know more. "How old was Mommy when she met my dad?" she asked.

Instead of answering, Gloria called out in a singsong voice, "Uncle Benjamin!" She smiled at the girls. "We have Netflix." She knew Myra couldn't afford Netflix. "Why don't you help your uncle pick out a movie?"

Benjamin walked into the kitchen and, excited, the girls followed him out.

Gloria breathed a sigh of relief. Idly, she grabbed a handful of Wheat Thins for herself. Her niece's questions made her think about when she and Benjamin had first started going out. At the time, she had actually been dating someone else, a factoid that she conveniently tended to leave out when telling the story of their courtship. He'd been a boy from her high school, and up until the time she met Benjamin, she'd assumed that the two of them would end up getting married. Owen Portis was his name, and he was a skinny, introverted, genuinely creative kid. She'd known him forever, and the two of them had been on the same wavelength in almost every respect. They hated the same things, loved the same things, and were both passionate about modern art. Unlike the poseurs she met in college, who talked a good game and dressed as if "art student" was a cosplay role, Owen didn't pontificate about his preferences or wear trendy clothes; the time he did not spend with her or in class, he spent painting. He was who he was.

Then she met Benjamin, who had swept her off her feet. Tall, good-looking, with the intoxicating confidence of someone two years older, he was a teacher's assistant, and was actually allowed to conduct computer science courses. Next to him, Owen seemed like an immature kid, and Gloria, never one for confrontation, simply stopped seeing Owen or taking his calls. In a supreme act of passive-aggressive cruelty, she brought Benjamin to the art department's end-of-semester show, which she knew Owen would attend since he had two pieces on display. They saw each other but did not speak, and her heart broke as she saw on his open face the pain she had caused him. By the beginning of the next academic year, he had transferred to another college.

It had been a long time since she'd thought of Owen, and she wondered what had become of him. She assumed he was married by now, but it was hard to imagine him with kids. It was hard even to imagine him as an adult. In her mind, he was still the same quiet, pale boy she had known, and she wondered if he had gained weight or lost his hair. Would she be able to recognize him if she saw him again?

Would he be able to recognize her?

Gloria *had* gained weight. She was by no means fat but did have decidedly more meat on her bones than she had in college. Her hair was short now instead of long, and her clothes were those of an adult female professional rather than an adolescent girl. Would she still look this way if she had remained with Owen? Gloria wasn't sure, but the idea that her very appearance might be different if the two of them had stayed together made her wonder what her life would be like if they had not broken up, if she had never met Benjamin. In her mind, she would still have the same job, working for the museum, but would be living with Owen in a smaller, funkier home somewhere in Laguna Beach. One room would be their shared studio, and they would work there, side by side or in alternate shifts, taking breaks to walk along the beach hand-in-hand.

Was Owen even an artist? In her mind he was, but she had no idea if that was true. Gloria realized that it would take only a few seconds to Google the name "Owen Portis" and discover exactly where he was now and what he was doing, but the truth was that she didn't really want to know. It would depress her to learn that he now worked some cubicle job for a large corporation, or was stuck behind a desk answering the public's phone calls for a local government agency. No, it was better to leave her fantasies intact, and, not wanting to follow this line of thought, she left the kitchen to find the girls and help them choose their movie.

She and Benjamin made love quietly that night, while Lizzie and Linda were asleep in the guest room. Ordinarily, Gloria did not like to have sex while other people were in the house—she tended to be loud, for one thing—but she'd been in the mood tonight, and she was the one who initiated the encounter. She managed not to scream or cry out, although at one point she was forced to bite Benjamin's shoulder, and after they finished, she put on a nightgown and went in to check on the girls. They were asleep, Lizzie flat on her stomach atop her blanket,

Linda curled into a fetal position beneath hers. Both, oddly enough were snoring. They were not snoring loudly, merely making small piglet noises. Gloria found that very cute, and she stood there for a moment, watching them sleep. Was she feeling maternal? Perhaps. Did that mean she was now thinking about having kids herself? Gloria wouldn't go that far, but she had to admit that she wasn't as adamantly opposed to the idea as she had been in the past.

Returning to the bedroom, she tried to interest Benjamin in another round, but he was spent and unable to get hard again, and after fifteen minutes of trying, she gave up, kissed him goodnight and rolled over to go to sleep.

She dreamed that her dad was in the guest room, that he had killed and eaten the girls and was lying on Lizzie's bed, wide awake, staring up at the ceiling, smiling to himself and waiting for Gloria to come in.

FOUR

She ended up Googling Owen.

Gloria was not quite sure why. She was happy in her marriage, and if confronted with the same choice would instantly choose Benjamin again. But a part of her was curious and wanted to know what had become of her first boyfriend.

Owen, it turned out, *was* an artist, and he *did* live in Laguna Beach. He had not made the sort of mark on the art world that would have put him on the radar of the museum—which was why she was unfamiliar with his work—but he had his own small gallery in one of the touristy quarters of the city, and he had exhibited numerous times at the Festival of the Arts that coincided with the famed Pageant of the Masters. He was also married.

To a man.

That was a surprise. Gloria had never even suspected that Owen might be gay. Or bi, for that matter. He'd certainly been vigorously loving in his relationship with her, and she did not believe that any of that had been feigned.

The man Owen had married was named Charles Wister, and apparently he owned a downtown boutique and was also a Laguna

Beach city councilman. Images of both men were displayed on the search engine, and Gloria was surprised to find that Owen was more handsome than she recalled. He was obviously one of those men who had grown into his looks, and she found it ironic that Benjamin, who had initially seemed so dashing, was now much less striking than Owen. His husband was quite good looking as well, for that matter. Their lifestyle clearly agreed with them.

One of the entries had the address and phone number of Owen's gallery, and on impulse, she dialed the number. A man answered on the first ring. She almost hung up, but at the last second found courage from somewhere within her and answered the greeting "Good morning. Nightshade Gallery" with "Hello. May I speak to Owen Portis?"

"This is Owen," the man said. His voice was not what she remembered and definitely not what she would have expected based on the photos she'd seen. This grown-up Owen sounded *old.* Old and humorless. Gloria decided that she didn't like this voice.

She must have taken too long to respond. "May I *help* you?" Owen said, clearly irritated.

"This is Gloria," she said. "Gloria Jaymes. I used to be Gloria Hiller."

Silence on the other end of the line.

"I work for the Orange County Museum of Art now, and I saw recently that you have your own gallery." She'd only intended to tell him where she worked and let him know that she'd recently found out where he was, but, too late, she realized that he might think she was calling to invite him to submit his work to the museum. "I'm only a P.R.O. I just publicize events and exhibits. But...look at you. You did it. You're a real artist."

There was a long pause.

"Owen?"

"You ruined my life," he said bitterly.

The response shocked her. She'd been prepared for awkwardness, maybe even criticism for the cowardly and callous way she'd dumped him, but his blatant hostility surprised her. She'd ruined his life? How was that possible? He was gay. If they had stayed together, he would have ruined *her* life when he came out. It was pure luck that she'd bailed out of the relationship first. But he seemed to have built her up in his mind as a monster. Apparently, even after all these years, the hurt he'd felt at the time had not abated. She remembered that about him, the way he held grudges. Now that her memories were becoming clearer, she recalled his narcissistic self-absorption, his steely lack of forgiveness even for the smallest slight.

"Sorry to bother you," she said, and hung up. Her hands were shaking, and there was a queasy feeling deep in her stomach.

Benjamin walked into the room just at that moment, and she had never been so glad to see him. If she had not known it before (*and she had, hadn't she?*), Gloria knew now, absolutely and definitively, that she had made the right choice in picking Benjamin over Owen. Still, the phone call left her feeling as though she had lost part of herself.

Benjamin sensed her mood. "What's wrong?" he asked.

"Remember Owen?" she said. "Owen Portis?"

He frowned, thinking. "Can't say that I do."

"The boy I was dating when I met you?"

He seemed surprised. "You were dating someone else when we met? You never told me that."

"I did, too. I told you at the time. We talked about it. We even talked about it after. I brought it up many times."

"Huh," he said. "Don't remember."

"How can you not remember?"

"It was a long time ago," he pointed out. "Do *you* remember everything that was happening back when we first met?"

As a matter of fact, she did. For the most part. There were gaps, no doubt, unimportant things that her brain had decided to remove in order to make room for new information. But on the whole, her memory of those days was as clear to her as her memory of last week.

The elasticity of time, she thought.

Gloria wasn't sure where she'd first encountered that phrase, but the truth of it had never seemed more evident. She remembered that, as a young teen, two years between album releases, or between movies and their sequels, had seemed an eternity. Now, waiting five years for something seemed like the blink of an eye. In the same way, the years that had passed since she'd last seen Owen seemed like nothing to her, while to Benjamin it had been a lifetime ago. Objectively, he was probably more correct, but that was why time was elastic. It changed, stretching differently for different people.

"So what about this Owen?" Benjamin asked.

"Nothing," she lied.

He looked at her strangely but didn't push it. Not wanting him to get the wrong idea, she said, "I just found out he was gay."

Benjamin laughed.

She wanted to tell him it wasn't funny, but that would entail a deeper dive into the topic, something she was not in the mood for right now. Gloria forced herself to smile. "Weird world, huh?"

That night, in bed, Benjamin brought up the idea of The Beach House again. It was something her sisters had been trying to arrange for the past three summers, although Paul, when first presented with the idea, had said simply, "I'm out." Gloria had declined as well, but Benjamin had been intrigued by the thought of staying in a rental house by the beach and, along with Myra and Janine, had refused to let the possibility die.

The reason her sisters were so sold on The Beach House was because when they were little, a wealthy friend of their dad's had rented a house on Balboa Island for a week in the summer. Unfortunately, the man's entire family had come down with some sort of illness (none of them could remember exactly what the illness had been. Gloria thought it had been the flu, Paul food poisoning, Janine chicken pox, while Myra refused to even venture a guess). It had been too late to back out—the full price would have to be paid whether they stayed or not—so their dad's friend had invited Gloria's family to go in their stead. It had been an amazing experience, easily the best and most memorable vacation of their childhoods, one that they all treasured, and it was perhaps only natural when Janine and her family spent a day at the beach a few summers back and overheard the family on the next blanket over talking about renting a beach house for a week, that she started researching home rental prices. As might be expected, the prices were exorbitant, but Janine calculated that if they all chipped in and got a three-bedroom house for a week, the kids sleeping on the floor, one couple taking a roll-out couch, they could get away with five-hundred apiece.

Paul thought that would be a nightmare, and Gloria said there was no way she would pay five-hundred dollars to share a bathroom and sleep on a couch—the most obvious outcome since she and Benjamin were the only ones without kids—but Benjamin's proposal of renting a smaller, cheaper house, everyone chipping in, and each family staying for two or three days won the approval of Myra, as well as Janine and Sadeen. So it came up again every summer. Not wanting to be the Scrooge of the group, Gloria had to keep thinking of practical, realistic reasons why such a scheme was impractical. The most obvious one was the real one: wanting to save her limited time off for her vacation in August, Gloria would have to continue working, so it wouldn't be worth the money just to sleep in another bed at night when she couldn't enjoy the beach during the day (unless she and Benjamin took Saturday and Sunday as their days, which Janine was expressly against because Sadeen still had to work, also, and only had weekends off—and *they* had kids).

So it was a stalemate.

This year, however, Benjamin said Sadeen was taking time off mid-week, and both Janine and Myra had agreed to let Gloria and Benjamin have the weekend. "Let's do it," Benjamin said. "Janine said she found a place available the first week of August, two weeks before we go to Yosemite. It's small, one bedroom, one bathroom, small kitchenette, but it's on Balboa Peninsula, and is right on the beach. Within walking distance of the ferry and the Fun Zone."

Gloria was tempted.

Benjamin could sense that she was wavering. Quickly, he grabbed his phone from the nightstand. "Janine emailed me pictures. Check it out." He scrolled through a Newport realtor's photos of a cute one-story clapboard house. The exterior was white, with large windows. A view through one of those windows showed an expanse of sand stretching to the ocean, where breaking waves fronted a setting sun. The interior of the house showed functional furniture and wall hangings with a nautical theme. Gloria had to admit that it looked appealing.

"Our share for the weekend is literally less than our one-night stay in Yosemite. And it would be fun!" He scrolled back to the ocean view. "That's what we would see each morning."

"The sun's setting," Gloria pointed out.

"Each evening, then. We could lounge around, drinking wine, watching the sun set. Doesn't that sound nice?"

"All right," she said impulsively. "Let's do it."

Over the next few days, Gloria warmed to the idea. She had agreed on the spur of the moment, more to keep Benjamin happy than anything else, but she found that she was actually looking forward to spending a couple of days by the beach. She recalled the week her family had stayed on Balboa Island, the trips on the ferry, the way they had swum in the bay, the times she and Paul had fished off the public pier, the way her dad had sent the kids to downtown Balboa in the mornings to pick up a newspaper. Fond memories all, memories of a simple small-town life that they had lived for one week and never again.

Myra and Janine were on the phone with her several times a day, tag-teaming her. They were both so excited about renting the beach house that Gloria didn't understand why the two of them hadn't gone in together earlier to make it happen. Sure, it was expensive, and Myra obviously wouldn't have been able to contribute as much (they'd even had to pare her contribution for the upcoming week), but Janine and Sadeen could have easily swung it by themselves.

Janine had always been miserly, though.

It was Myra's idea that all of them should come by for a barbecue lunch on the first day, even Paul if he wanted to. Gloria wasn't that thrilled with the idea since it would eat into her and Benjamin's time and, as usual, she would have to act as host, but Benjamin happily and instantly agreed, so on the first Saturday in August, they found themselves meeting with her sisters and their families at the realtor's office to pick up the key, then convoying to the house. It was as cute in real life as it had been in pictures, but with so many people, its smallness was emphasized, and Gloria ended up sending all the kids to play in the water and their parents out to supervise them, just so she could get lunch ready. Paul had declined to come, which was just as well; there would have been no room for him or his family.

It was clear that her sisters planned to stay all day, maybe even through the evening, but after lunch Gloria put her foot down and politely but firmly told everyone that it was time to go.

"We practically just got here!" Myra complained.

"And you'll be back in a few days," Gloria told her. "Right now, Benjamin and I need a little privacy." She met her sister's eyes, making it clear what she was hinting, and Myra turned away, embarrassed.

All of the guests were gone within the hour, and though there was still a lot of cleaning up to do, both she and Benjamin agreed it could wait until later. Locking up the house, they strolled along the crowded sidewalk that ran in front of the row of homes facing the beach, with bicyclists and skaters swerving around them. Eventually, they reached the pier, walking onto it, past amateur fishermen casting their lines over the side, until they reached the end. Gloria looked back at the shore, surprised to see how far they'd come. In the water, a group of wet-suited swimmers were being dropped off by a boat, the first of them beginning to swim toward the beach.

"Lifeguard training," Benjamin guessed.

Gloria nodded. "You're probably right."

They remained by the railing, watching the scene around them, the swimmers all ultimately reaching the shore, an elderly Vietnamese man next to them pulling in a fairly large fish that he unhooked and dropped into a plastic bucket half-filled with water. They ambled back down the pier, checking out the little tourist shops that lined the short street in front of the Balboa Pavilion. A sign on a kiosk announced whale watching tours every hour, and Benjamin remarked that it might be fun to go on one.

"Let's do it," Gloria said. "Tomorrow morning."

So they went up to the kiosk and made reservations for a nine a.m. excursion.

On the way back to the rental house, Gloria's cell phone started ringing, and she pulled it out of the oversized beach bag she was carrying to answer. "Hello?"

"Glore?" It was Paul, and he sounded panicked.

"Paul?"

"We don't have time!" he said, speaking so rapidly that he almost ran out of breath. "It's Dad! He was here!"

"What?"

"I talked to him, and you've got to get out of there!"

"I don't unders—"

"He's on his way! He's going to kill Benjamin!"

FIVE

Gloria stood unmoving in the center of the sidewalk as pedestrians swirled around her. A shirtless jogger ran past, huffing and puffing.

"What is it?" Benjamin asked.

She didn't know what to tell him. The whole thing sounded completely crazy.

But she believed it.

"Who called?" Benjamin asked, a tinge of worry creeping into his voice.

She pulled him to the side of the walkway. "That was Paul," she explained, speaking quietly but intensely. "He said..." She shook her head, taking a deep breath. "He said he saw my dad again, and... He said my dad told him that he's going to kill you."

Benjamin laughed, a short sharp involuntary bark. "*What?*"

"That's what he said. He told us to get out of here because my dad's on his way and he's going to kill you."

"This is crazy!"

"I know, but—" *I believe him*, Gloria was about to say.

Then, over Benjamin's shoulder, she saw her father.

He was several yards away but making a beeline toward them, passing between pedestrians, cutting off a cyclist who had to swerve to miss him. Shirtless and wearing bright blue bathing trunks, he looked exactly as he had on that week they'd stayed in the house on Balboa Island. Their eyes met, and he grinned at her. In his right hand, Gloria saw, was a knife.

This couldn't be happening.

She grabbed Benjamin's hand, pulling him forward. "Run!" she yelled, not looking back to see if her dad was following them, assuming that if he had given chase with that knife in his hand, she would have heard people screaming or shouting or engaged in some type of startled commotion. Somewhere along the shore here was a police substation, Gloria knew, but she wasn't sure where it was located, and her mind desperately tried to think of someplace they could run where they might find protection or at least something with which to defend themselves, because she knew there was no way they could keep up this pace for long.

Benjamin, to his credit, did not plant his feet and stop, demanding to know what was going on. He went along with her, and even though Gloria was certain he did not believe he was in any danger, she was grateful that he was so devoted. With her in the lead, they continued running, past people and houses, until they reached a small side street that connected with Balboa Boulevard, the main road on the peninsula. Gloria dashed up the street, still pulling Benjamin with her. She was panting in ragged bursts that did not seem to provide enough air for her to breathe. Her mouth was so dry she wanted to throw up, and her lungs and throat hurt. Benjamin's breath was loud behind her, loud enough to hear above their flapping footsteps on the concrete and all of the chaotic ambient noise, and when they reached Balboa Boulevard, he said, "Stop."

Before stopping, Gloria looked over her shoulder behind them and was grateful to see that they were not being followed. Her dad was nowhere in sight.

She halted, inhaling and exhaling painfully. "I saw him," she got out between breaths. "My dad. He had a knife."

Benjamin, breathing heavily as well, looked at her, saying nothing, clearly not sure how to respond.

"I know how it sounds," Gloria told him. "But it's true."

He took out his phone. "Let's call the police."

"And tell them what? That we're being chased by my dead dad?" She was still catching her breath.

"No. That a man with a knife came after us and we managed to get away. We give them a description and let *them* find him."

Gloria wasn't sure Benjamin believed her entirely, but he obviously believed enough to take action, and she nodded her agreement.

Benjamin called 911, held the phone to his ear and, seconds later, calmly said, "I want to report an attempted assault."

They remained where they were after Benjamin provided the police with the pertinent information. She assumed the police had advised them to remain in place so that they could be shown the spot where it happened, which was just as well. She did not want to return to the rental house because she didn't want to lead her dad to the location where they were staying.

Although he no doubt knew already.

It was why he was here.

Gloria kept her eyes open as they waited, eyeing every approaching pedestrian suspiciously, trying to see the faces of passing drivers through their car windows. He might come at them any time from any angle, and she wanted to make sure she was ready. Paul called again as they awaited the arrival of the police, and he was only slightly calmer than he had been on the previous call. She assured him that they were all right, but she didn't sugarcoat the situation and spelled out exactly what had happened.

"Oh, God," he moaned. "Oh, God."

A police car was speeding up the street toward them, and Benjamin waved his arms to flag it down. "Don't worry," Gloria said. "I'll let you know what happens. They're here now. I have to go."

"I'm calling you every hour," Paul said. "Every *half* hour!"

"Maybe you should let Myra and Janine know..."

"No," he said. "They wouldn't believe me. Besides, Dad specifically said he's after Benjamin."

A cold chill passed through her. "I'll call," Gloria said and clicked off.

Two policemen arrived to take the report, and she and Benjamin backtracked their route and described everything, leaving out only her father's identity.

"And you have no idea where he went," the first policeman, an Officer Jackson, said.

"I told you," Gloria repeated for the third time. "We ran. We didn't look back."

"Uh huh." He sounded skeptical.

They were given business cards and phone numbers of the two cops, as well as assurances that a search would be conducted for the attempted assailant. Gloria was not convinced that would actually happen, and she suggested to Benjamin that they go back to the rental house, gather their belongings and head for home.

"And forfeit all that money?" He shook his head firmly. "No way. We're staying."

"But what if he finds us? What if he comes in at night and kills us in our sleep? Or kills *you* in your sleep, since Paul says you're the one he's after."

Benjamin allowed himself a small smile. "For defiling his daughter?"

She hit his shoulder. Hard. "*It's not funny*!"

"I know," he said apologetically. "I'm sorry. But if we seal up the house, make sure the windows are closed and the doors are locked, see if we can find a baseball bat or some type of weapon to put next to the bed, we should be fine." He put his hands on her shoulders, looked into her eyes. "I know he found us down here somehow, but I think it's way more likely that he would find us at our *real* house rather than a rental house because he already knows where we live." Benjamin shook his head. "I can't believe we're even talking about this. Your dad is dead."

"And yet he's here." Gloria returned his gaze. "*That's* why we need to be careful. We don't know what he can do."

Benjamin nodded. "And we will be."

Gloria sighed. "While we stay on vacation."

"For two days, yes." He kissed the top of her head. "I've been looking forward to this."

"I know you have. But...I'm scared."

"I won't let anything happen to you."

"It's you I'm worried about."

He smiled again. "Then I won't let anything happen to *me*."

Gloria hugged him, acting braver than she felt. "I won't, either."

Along with boogie boards, badminton rackets and a rolled-up volleyball net, they *did* find a baseball bat in the small standalone garage behind the house. Benjamin hefted it, swung it. "This should do."

Neither of them was in the mood to go in the water, but they dragged their folding chairs onto the sand, along with a small ice chest filled with drinks. Benjamin kept the bat handy. As much as possible under the circumstances, they enjoyed the rest of the afternoon.

Following an early dinner of takeout clam chowder from a randomly chosen local restaurant, Gloria insisted on closing up the house. It was not yet dark—the sun would not go down for at least another hour or two—but she wanted to be safely barricaded inside before that happened. Antsy, she kept getting up from the couch for various reasons, getting a drink of water from the kitchen, going to the bathroom, peeking out one of the windows, while Benjamin remained seated, calmly watching the weekend news.

Paul, true to his word, kept calling every half hour. Gloria had no idea what Danielle or the boys must be thinking. Her brother seemed hellbent on keeping their father's presence a secret from everyone except her, so his constant calls were no doubt worrying to his wife and kids. Gloria was grateful to hear from him, however, and it calmed her to be able to update reports every thirty minutes.

"Maybe you should take turns sleeping," Paul suggested when he called at eight. "That way one of you could keep watch."

It wasn't a bad suggestion, but when she mentioned it to Benjamin, he immediately shot down the idea. "I am *not* staying up half the night waiting for your dead dad to break into the house and kill me."

"I knew you didn't believe me!" Gloria said accusingly.

He sighed. "I believe you."

"But not enough to take precautions."

"We can't live like this."

"He had a knife!"

"So...what does that mean? We spend the rest of our lives on high alert?" Benjamin shook his head. "Look, I'll put cans or bottles or something noisy in front of each door and window. That way, if anyone tries to sneak in, we'll hear them."

She had to admit, it wasn't a bad idea, and though she was still on edge and would prefer taking far greater precautions, at this point it might be more prudent to go along with Benjamin.

So long as he kept the bat by his bedside.

The next time Paul called, Gloria told him to stop. She and Benjamin would be going to bed soon, and she didn't want his calls waking her up all night long. She'd call him in the morning when she woke up.

"*If* you wake up," Paul said.

"God damn it, Paul!"

"Sorry," he apologized. "But...he's out there. You know it and I know it. And he *said*—"

"I know what he said, and I don't want to hear it again."

"He had a knife when you saw him."

"I'm turning my phone off. I'll call you in the morning." Gloria terminated the call, then shut down her phone, not sure if she was more annoyed than frightened or more frightened than annoyed. Benjamin had gone into the bathroom, and she turned her attention back to the television, thinking that when he came out, she would surprise him with some oral sex. He deserved a treat after the day they'd had.

Only he didn't come out.

It took her several minutes to notice, and when she did, a cold fear accompanied the déjà vu. *Not again.* She was afraid to call out his name, afraid he wouldn't answer, and she remained on the couch, breathing heavily, her heart pounding, waiting. When he still didn't emerge and she turned off the television and heard no other sound in the house, Gloria forced herself to get up and investigate.

"Benjamin?" she said tentatively, approaching the closed bathroom door. She was glad the single-story rental house was so small—the last thing she wanted right now was to be alone in a large home with long hallways and an entire other floor—but at the same time, the cramped space was making her feel claustrophobic. "Are you all right in there?" She knocked once, then reached for the knob, turning it, pushing the door open.

As she'd known, the bathroom was empty. Benjamin was gone.

Why did this always happen while he was using the restroom?

A loud knock at the front door made her jump.

Her dad!

Gloria ran to the kitchenette, pulling out drawers until she found a knife. It was a steak knife rather than a carving or butcher knife, but it was better than nothing, and she approached the front door warily, weapon in hand. The knocking had stopped. "Who is it?" she called.

There was no answer.

Had the person left?

Carefully, she reached forward, unlocked the door, turned the knob, then jumped back, knife extended as the door opened.

It was not her dad. It was Benjamin. He stood there with a confused look on his face, and Gloria dropped the knife, grabbed his hand and pulled him in, closing and locking the door behind him.

"What?" he said groggily.

It was the last word he ever spoke. Eyelids fluttering, he fell forward, landing chin first on the floor. Gloria heard the cracking of bone, saw a pool of blood spread outward from beneath his head.

"Benjamin!" she cried, panicked. "Benjamin!" She tried to roll him over, but his body was heavy and unmoving—

dead weight

—and it was only with tremendous effort that she managed to get him on his side. His eyes were closed, and blood was seeping from his open mouth. She put her fingers to his neck, trying to check for a pulse. She felt nothing but wasn't sure she was even doing it right. Picking up his hand to check his wrist, she found that his entire arm was limp.

"Benjamin!" she screamed.

And pressed her face to his already cooling cheek.

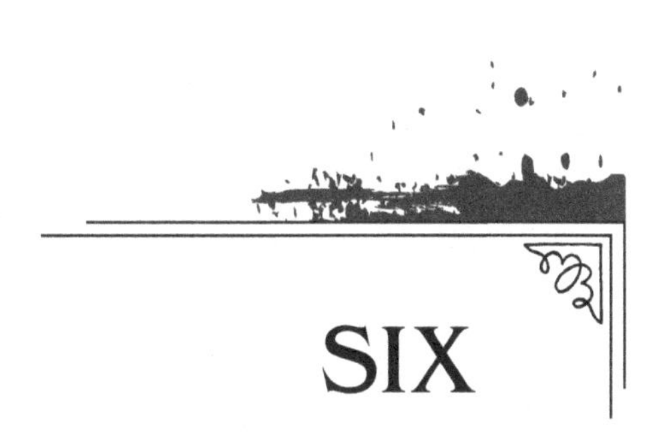

SIX

Gloria had not expected everything to be so complicated.

Maybe she had never really grown up, maybe she'd simply led a sheltered life, but she found herself woefully unprepared to deal with Benjamin's death. Forget about his unexplainable teleportation, forget about the specter of her dead dad hovering around the periphery of her life, it was the small bureaucratic details that seemed to have overwhelmed her, that had left her feeling inadequate, incompetent and hopelessly over her head.

She'd called 911 seconds after realizing Benjamin was dead, hoping the operator would talk her through the steps that would resuscitate him, restart his heart and bring him back to life, since she had never learned CPR, but the woman on the other end of the line took down her name and location, told her help was on the way, and abruptly hung up. Gloria called back, got a man this time, and immediately asked him how to perform emergency CPR, but even following his instructions, she was unable to revive Benjamin. Either whatever had killed him had done so instantly, with no possibility of reversal, or too much time had passed, because he remained limp beneath her, and even the paramedics with their equipment could not bring him back.

That was when the need for decisions started. Gloria had to arrange for someone to collect her husband's body, decide whether he was to be buried or cremated, as well as where and when, notify friends and relatives, hunt down Benjamin's life insurance policy, inform his employer, transfer everything from his name to hers... It was a never-ending parade of responsibilities and duties that could only be performed by her, and the sheer weight of them bogged her down. If Benjamin had had parents, or a brother or a sister, it would have helped. She wouldn't have felt so alone—

Gloria frowned.

Did Benjamin have a brother or sister?

And why *didn't* he have parents? Had they died?

She didn't know, Gloria realized. But *why* didn't she know? How could she *not* know? They'd been married for all these years, yet she remained completely ignorant of his background? How was that possible?

She tried to remember if his parents had come to their wedding, but found that she couldn't even remember the wedding.

And then...

She did.

She remembered all of it. Benjamin's parents had split when he was twelve, and he'd lived with his father, who had been granted sole custody of his only child and *had* been at the wedding, although he had died of emphysema three years later. His wife, Benjamin's mother, had abandoned both of them and no one had even known how to contact her to invite her to the wedding.

Where had *that* come from?

Gloria stood in the empty bedroom of her empty house, looking down at the open dresser drawer containing Benjamin's socks and underwear. Her brief mental blip aside, there was still a lot to do: a lot of belongings to sort through, a lot of household rearranging that needed to be done, a lot of paperwork that needed attention. She felt overwhelmed. Of course, she could always rope in her family to assist her, but her brother and sisters had their own children and spouses to tend to, and it didn't feel right to make them shoulder her burdens.

Oddly, it was only now that Benjamin was gone that Gloria wished the two of them had had children. Maybe the desire had been within her all along and she hadn't realized it, because now that the possibility had been permanently taken away from her, she felt a strange sense of loss. Would they have had kids eventually? Who knew? If they had, she thought, she would have preferred a boy to a girl. Maybe two boys. Somehow, she even knew the names she would have chosen: Bradley and Lucas.

But she had no children.

And her dad was still out there.

That was always at the back of her mind. He had disappeared, there'd been so sign of him since Benjamin's death—

had he caused it?

—and Gloria's hope was that he was gone for good, but she knew that was unlikely. However and whyever he had returned, it was doubtful that he would simply vanish, not when he'd been stalking Paul and lurking around the edges of her own life. Perhaps Janine and Myra were next on his list, and though neither Gloria nor Paul said anything to either of them, both she and her brother were constantly on the lookout for indications that anything was amiss in their sisters' lives.

Not wanting to be thought of as a charity case, Gloria had turned down repeated dinner invitations proffered by Myra, Janine, and Paul's wife Danielle. The result was that she had become more isolated. It occurred to her now that she would like to get out and see someone, but because she had declined so many times, the offers seemed to have dried up, and while she'd been assured she had a standing invitation to all of their homes, Gloria felt awkward about inviting herself. She thought about inviting *them* over, but that would entail more work than she wanted to do right now. She could call a friend, but wasn't in the mood to accept so much sympathy.

The phone rang, and she picked up the extension on Benjamin's nightstand. "Hello?"

There was silence on the other end, and a shiver caressed her spine. *Dad?* she wanted to say, but her mouth didn't seem to be working.

The man at the other end cleared his throat. "Uh, Gloria? This is Owen. Owen Portis?"

Relief flooded through her, relief accompanied by confusion. "Owen?"

He cleared his throat again. "I'm afraid I was a little... *brusque* with you the last time you called, and I just wanted to apologize for my behavior. It's just that it was such a shock to hear from you after all those years, and...and..." He didn't seem to know where to go from there.

"It's okay, Owen," she interjected smoothly, saving him. "I understand."

"Your father was in here yesterday, explaining..."

Gloria heard nothing after that.

Your father was in here yesterday.

Owen had seen him as well. Somehow that made it more real, and she wasn't sure what was more frightening: the idea that her dead dad was out and about and that other people could see him, or the fact that he was meeting with individuals she knew, lobbying on her behalf.

There was a pause in Owen's recounting, and while Gloria had no idea what he had just said, she decided that the best thing to do was to just be honest. "My dad's dead," she said. "He had a heart attack when...I...was...eighteen." She frowned. "But you knew that. You were there. I mean, you weren't there when he died, not at that moment, but you were there in my life, and we talked about it, and I think you might've even gone to the funeral."

Owen was silent for a moment. "I forgot," he said quietly. "You're right. I remember when your father died. I *didn't* go to the funeral, but I remember when it happened. You were off school for three or four days."

"That's right."

"So who was that man?"

"I don't know," she said. It would not have helped to be *that* honest. It would have only scared Owen away. "What did he look like?"

His description was of precisely the same version of her dad that she had seen by the beach, down to the blue swim trunks, although apparently he had put on a shirt. "I have to admit, I was a little suspicious at first," Owen said. "Even for a tourist, he looked a little too casual for someone walking into a gallery. But when he said he was your father... Not that he *looked* like the father of a museum P.R.O...." A trace of pomposity had crept into his voice.

God, she missed Benjamin.

"I was wondering if you would like to come by the gallery sometime and see what I've been up to. Your father...I mean, the man who claimed to be your father, well, he said you might... I just thought you might want to stop by, catch up."

"I thought I ruined your life."

Owen offered a strained, not very convincing chuckle. "I might have exaggerated just a bit."

Gloria smiled. "Drama queen."

Owen was silent.

"That wasn't a homophobic thing," she said quickly. "I didn't mean it like that. It's just—"

Owen laughed, and this time it was real. "I know," he said.

"I thought I might have offended you. You got quiet all of a sudden..."

"My throat was dry. I was getting a drink of water."

"Oh." She breathed out. "It's been awhile. Our rhythms are off. I guess we're not—"

"In sync," they said simultaneously.

Gloria smiled again. "Or maybe we are."

"Would you like to come by?" he asked.

"I would," she admitted.

"Just let me know—"

"How about this afternoon?"

"Today?"

"I could be there in an hour."

"Okay," he said slowly. "Sure."

"If you'd rather I come another time..."

"No, no. I was just thinking something. Today would be fine."

"Then I guess I'll see you in awhile." They both said their goodbyes and hung up, but immediately afterward, Gloria thought, *What am I doing?* Going back to the beach area? The beach was where she'd seen her dad. Not only that, but he had shown up at Owen's gallery! She picked up the phone again to call back and cancel, but at the last second, she dialed Paul.

He answered on the first ring. "What is it?"

Her name must have been displayed on his screen. "Owen Portis invited me to see his gallery in Laguna Beach. Remember Owen?"

"Yes," Paul said cautiously.

"Well, Dad showed up at Owen's gallery. Told him something about me, apparently. I was wondering if you'd be willing to go there with me."

"No way." He spoke quickly and firmly.

"But—"

"And you shouldn't go, either."

"Just listen for a minute!"

"I'm not listening to anything. I don't want to see him again. I *won't* see him again."

"Aren't you even curious?"

"No. And if *you're* curious about anything, call your friend on the phone and ask him what you want to ask him. There's no reason for you to go there." Paul took a deep breath. "He killed Benjamin, Glore."

"I'm not sure that's true."

"I am. And I'm not going."

"Then I'll call Myra or Janine. I'm not going by myself."

That gave him pause, as she'd hoped it would, but after several seconds he quickly said, "That's your decision," and hung up.

Gloria wasn't sure herself whether she wanted to drag either of her sisters into this. She definitely wasn't going by herself, and she almost called Owen to cancel, but then she thought that if her dad had appeared to her and Paul, it was probably only a matter of time before he showed up to see Myra and Janine. Maybe it was better to be preemptive.

Myra was at work, so Gloria called Janine. She gave her sister only the barebones outline of the situation. Judgmental as usual, Janine thought it was horrible of her to be looking up an old flame so soon after Benjamin's passing, but when Gloria explained that Owen was gay and happily married, she was all in.

"Owen? Gay? I never would've guessed it."

"I didn't," Gloria said drily.

"You want me to drive?" Janine asked.

"No. I'll pick you up. It's on the way."

"Let's do it."

On the ride over, travelling east on the southbound San Diego Freeway (one of the quirks of living in a county situated on the slanting coast of California), Gloria decided to come clean. Not knowing exactly where to start, she just blurted out, "I saw Dad at Balboa."

"Thank God!" It was almost an exhalation of breath. Gloria could hear the relief in her sister's voice. "I thought I was going crazy!"

A familiar chill crawled up Gloria's spine.

"I saw him, too! He was standing across the street, looking at my house. I saw him through the window, but when I went outside, he was gone."

"Why didn't you say anything?"

"I don't know. I guess because we gave you and Paul such a hard time..."

"Janine."

"I'm sorry."

"Were you scared?"

"I was, a little."

"All of us except Myra, then."

"Maybe it's a sign," Janine told her.

Gloria shook her head. "It's not a sign. First of all, that's exactly what Paul said you would say. Secondly..." She wasn't sure how to express what she felt. "I don't know what kind of sign it could possibly be. But you're older than me, so maybe your experience with Dad was different than mine..."

They were both silent for a moment.

"No," Janine said finally. Her voice was quiet. "I don't think it was."

Gloria looked at her.

"Dad wasn't a nice guy." She sighed. "Oh, you're right. It wouldn't really be much of a sign. Or at least I don't know what it would be a sign *of*. I guess I was just trying to make it seem...*not* scary. Because it's true; if Dad's ghost is appearing to us, it's probably not a good thing."

"I don't think it's a ghost," Gloria told her. "Neither does Paul."

"Then—"

"I think it's *him*."

Janine frowned. "I don't understand. You don't think he died?"

"I know he did. But somehow he's back. I don't think he's a zombie," she added quickly. "Or a vampire or any of those cartoon monsters. He's just...him. I have no idea how or why, but he's flesh and blood, he can think, he can talk to people."

"He's been resurrected."

"I guess that's the closest thing."

Janine rubbed her arms as though suddenly feeling cold. "So," she said slowly, piecing it together, "you invited me along in case you see him again."

"Paul wouldn't come," Gloria admitted. They'd reached Laguna Canyon Road, and she pulled off the freeway.

"You said you saw Dad at Balboa, not just at home. Was that when Benjamin..."

Gloria nodded. She felt the tears welling and angrily wiped her eyes with her right arm. She needed to see to be able to drive.

"Did he...?

"I don't know," Gloria admitted. She told her sister the entire story, starting from the beginning. She left nothing out, and as crazy as it all sounded, Janine did not make fun of her or express any skepticism. She merely listened and nodded.

"Jesus," Janine said when she finished.

"Yeah."

"What do you do when it's something like this? I mean, who do you call? In real life, there's no X-Files or Fringe division or top secret agency that investigates this stuff."

"We did call the police," Gloria pointed out.

"But you couldn't tell them who he really was."

"We gave an honest description, though."

"What happens if they catch him?" Janine wondered. "They run his prints, find out he's Dad. What comes next? I assume they call us, his family, but..." She let out a sigh of frustration. "The whole thing's so *crazy*."

"I know," Gloria said. "Believe me, I know."

Driving through the canyon into Laguna, they went over possible scenarios, planning what they would do if they ran into him. "Should we tell Myra?" Gloria asked as they drove past the site of the Sawdust Festival. Leaving her other sister out of the loop was starting to seem wrong to her. "Right now, she's the only one who doesn't know."

"I'm not sure," Janine admitted. "Maybe it would be better if she was prepared, just in case. But she's easily spooked, and I don't know if we want to freak her out and make her all paranoid."

"She feels differently about Dad than you do. Maybe that's not such a good thing right now."

"I'm sure it isn't."

There was something in her sister's voice that set off Gloria's alarm bells. She took a deep breath. "He didn't...I mean, he never..."

"No!" Janine exclaimed, shocked. "He was never like that! He was just—"

"Not a nice guy," Gloria finished for her.

"Yeah." There was a pause. "He didn't try...?"

"No," Gloria said quickly. "But it doesn't seem so farfetched now, does it?"

"No, it doesn't," her sister admitted.

They'd reached Pacific Coast Highway. Unsure whether Owen's gallery was to the left or right, Gloria turned left because she was already in that lane. She should have turned on her GPS or looked up directions ahead of time instead of winging it, but she hadn't, and she asked Janine to check the address on the piece of paper atop the cupholder between them, and let her know if they were headed in the right direction.

As it turned out, they were. In fact, the gallery was only three blocks away. They drove up and down side streets for several minutes, looking for a place to park, and finally saw a man in an anachronistic VW bug backing up. Gloria waited in the middle of the street for him to pull out, ignoring the horn honks behind her, and snagged the spot. Getting out of the car, they walked around the block to the gallery, where they paused outside and stood for several moments, looking at the rather impressive paintings displayed in the window.

"Aren't we going in?" Janine asked finally.

Gloria, who'd been gathering up her courage, didn't have time to answer because Owen was suddenly there, emerging from the doorway and heading straight over to her. He was indeed quite handsome, although she could tell that the photo she'd seen of him had been taken several years ago because in person he did appear older. He smiled at her, a not entirely natural smile, and her first thought was, *He's had his teeth whitened.*

Then they were greeting each other, hugging awkwardly. Gloria introduced her sister, and Owen said, "I remember you!" His delight this time seemed genuine, probably because the two of them had never had any sort of emotional connection.

"Come in, come in!" Owen said. "I saw you standing out here and waited for a few minutes, but then I thought you might leave without coming in, so I decided to grab you before you could escape."

They followed him into the gallery, and Gloria looked around at his artwork. She'd seen a couple of examples online, but had not paid that close attention, and after their disastrous reintroduction had had no interest in viewing his work. Now that she was here, though, she was impressed. Although there were definitely some concessions to the market, it wasn't the usual Laguna tourist schlock, and overall Owen seemed to have held remarkably fast to his original course. She admired and envied that.

"So Glore says you saw our dad?" Janine said out of nowhere.

Owen looked at Gloria, confused. "Your dad's dead."

"Yes, but—"

"What'd he look like?" Before Owen could respond, Janine already had a photo out. She'd come prepared. "Was this him?"

"Yes!" Owen said.

Gloria could hear the surprise and confusion in his voice, and she examined the picture herself. It was a variation of the one she'd found in her photo album, taken in front of the same Yosemite waterfall, only in this one her mom was missing, obviously taking the picture, her dad standing between Janine and Paul, with Gloria and Myra off to the sides. Once again, her dad's smile seemed too large and too intense, unnervingly unwavering.

"How's that possible?" Owen asked. He was looking at her expectantly.

Gloria had no idea what to say. She shot her sister a look of reproach, then simply stated the truth. "We don't know."

"Is he dead or isn't he? Is this some imposter?"

"We don't know," Gloria repeated. Janine, thankfully, remained quiet. "But I'm very impressed with your work," Gloria said, changing the subject and making a show of glancing around the gallery.

As she'd known, the appeal to his vanity drew Owen away from the topic she wanted to avoid. "Yes, I'm very proud of what I've been able to accomplish. I think when we were...well, when I knew you, I was heavily into abstraction. But that proved to be a dead end for me, so I branched out."

"But you've kept that aesthetic, even when your subject matter's more realistic. I like it." She glanced over at Janine, who rolled her eyes.

A phone rang, and Owen walked over to an old oak desk in the middle of the gallery. "Look around," he told the two of them. "Tell me what you think." He gestured toward the artwork on the walls before picking up the phone. "Good afternoon," he said to the caller, "Nightshade Gallery."

Gloria strode over to the rear of the gallery, admiring an over-sized brightly colored canvas that depicted a deconstructed nude male body. Janine sidled next to her. "Dad was here," she whispered. "He saw him."

"I know," Gloria whispered back.

"Shouldn't we quiz him? Find out what Dad said?"

"I know what he said. He told Owen to call me and reconnect."

Janine stiffened. "So he wanted you to come here." She looked quickly about. "He's probably been waiting for you to show up."

"Calm down," Gloria said softly.

"Calm down?" Janine's voice had risen.

"We're perfectly safe."

"It's Dad!" Janine said, as if that explained everything.

Owen got off the phone. "A customer," he explained.

Gloria was looking at a small framed drawing sandwiched between two large canvases. It was a pencil sketch, different from almost everything else in the gallery, but something about it spoke to her. She moved closer, peering at the image. The subject was a small shack, barely bigger than an outhouse, with a line of tall pine trees behind it. "What's this?" she asked, intrigued.

"Oh, that." Owen smiled. "We were vacationing in Northern California a few years ago, travelling through wine country and gold rush country, and we stopped for lunch at this little town. I'd brought along my sketchbook, and I just saw that building and drew it. Charles really liked it for some reason, so I framed it and gave it to him as a present, but he wanted me to hang it here instead of at home. Obviously it's not for sale."

Gloria nodded. What made the sketch interesting to her was not how Owen had come to draw it, but the fact that it seemed familiar to her. It was remotely possible that she had seen the building on her family's trip to Yosemite, but it didn't sound as though that was the area in which Owen and his husband had encountered the structure. Besides, even if she *had* seen it, she would have gotten only a glimpse in passing—back when she was in elementary school. Nothing in that scenario would account for the strange affinity she seemed to have for the building.

"Does this look familiar to you?" she asked Janine.

Her sister shook her head, and Gloria could tell that she wanted to leave. She kept glancing toward the door as if expecting their father to walk in at any second.

Moving away from the sketch, Gloria examined the larger paintings displayed in the gallery. An awkward silence seemed to have settled over the room, and Gloria realized that neither she nor Janine had much to say to Owen, nor he to them. If she'd thought this reunion would be a happy meeting where they relived old times and caught up on the intervening years, she had clearly been mistaken.

But of course that was not what she'd expected.

She'd expected to see her dad.

She wasn't quite sure why the prospect of seeing him did not frighten her this time, but it didn't. In fact, with Janine and Owen as witnesses, she'd hoped to interrogate her father and see if she could get some of her questions answered. Like, what *was* he? Why was he stalking them? How had he and Benjamin switched places that first time? Had he had anything to do with Benjamin's death?

But as it became increasingly clear that that wasn't going to happen, Gloria realized that there was no real reason for her to be here. She could quiz Owen about the encounter, but it was obvious he knew nothing. Besides, she could have done that over the phone. As for the two of them restarting some sort of new relationship...well, that wasn't going to happen. She didn't like this new Owen—she wasn't sure she'd liked the old Owen—and while he was definitely a talented artist, and she admired that, their lives had forked long ago, and despite their shared background and interests, deep down they had very little in common.

Janine made a show of looking at her watch.

"You're right," Gloria said. "We ought to get going. I have a lot of work to do, and it's a long drive back."

"But you just got here!" Owen said.

"I know," she told him. She almost lied and told him that something had come up or that they needed to beat the traffic, but she left it there, and she could see from the hardening expression on his face that he understood. Gloria gave him her biggest smile. "It really was nice to see you again, Owen."

"I should've known," he said.

"Maybe we can—"

"Just get out," he told her. "Bitch."

"Well fuck you. Your paintings suck. Drop dead and die." Janine grabbed her arm. "Come on, Glore."

Her sister led her out, and by the time they reached the car, Gloria was smiling. "'Drop dead and die?'"

"Best I could come up with under pressure."

"It was perfect," Gloria told her.

Janine smiled. "Really?"

"Really."

By the time they were once again heading north on Laguna Canyon Road, they were both laughing hysterically, and Gloria pretended not to notice that one of the men standing on the shuttle stop bench in front of the Pageant of the Masters was wearing blue swim trunks and bore a strong resemblance to her dad.

SEVEN

Gloria had assumed that the pain of losing Benjamin would lessen as time took her further away from the day of his death, but the opposite seemed to be the case. The hard immediate shock might have worn off, but new wounds that cut deep continued to accumulate, with each trivial reminder that he was gone leaving her feeling alone and bereft. Like the time she was brushing her teeth after taking a hot shower and saw in the fogged up mirror the happy face that he had once drawn on the glass. Or the time she found one of his old banana popsicles at the back of the freezer after she'd taken out two packages of frozen ground turkey.

In the middle of the night, she still sometimes reached over to put her arm around him, but encountered only empty flat bed instead of the soft hill of his body. In the morning, when the alarm rang, it continued to surprise her sleepy disoriented brain that *she* was the one who had to get up and turn it off because Benjamin was no longer here.

Would she ever stop feeling his loss?

She hoped so.

She hoped not.

Janine, as Gloria probably should have guessed, had told Myra everything. And, as Paul had predicted, Myra thought they were all crazy. Her doubt was stronger than Janine's belief, so Janine was soon won over to her side, and she and her husband began making a concerted effort to convince Gloria that she had not seen what she'd seen, that what had happened had not really happened.

She stopped picking up when either of her sisters called, letting their messages go to voicemail.

At least she had work. Although Ray, her supervisor, had urged her to take extra time off, Gloria had cancelled her vacation, forfeiting the hotel deposit Benjamin had made for their Yosemite trip, and had thrown herself into promoting the museum's newest exhibit. The last thing she needed right now was time off—she would only sit alone in her empty house and think about things she didn't want to think about—and she was grateful to be able to lose herself in her job. She arrived early, stayed late, and as soon as she arrived home at night, she ate a quick dinner and immediately went to bed. Gloria knew she was depressed, but as long as she didn't allow herself to dwell on it, kept to her routine, kept moving forward, nothing stuck.

It was mid-Saturday morning when Gloria got the call. She was still in bed—she hadn't gone to sleep late, had gone to sleep early, in fact, but twelve-hour nights were all too common these days—and it wasn't until the fourth or fifth ring that she managed to pick up the phone. "Hello?"

It was Paul.

"I know where he is," her brother said.

Gloria sat up. "Who?" she asked, although she already knew the answer. They had neither seen nor spoken of their dad since the Laguna Beach excursion, but he had never been far from either of their minds. "How?" she asked, not waiting for his response.

"The wonders of the internet," Paul told her. "He owns property in a town called, believe it or not, Hicksville."

"Hicksville? That's a real place?"

"It's a real place."

"Where is it?" Her assumption was Alabama or Arkansas, some Southern state, so she was surprised when Paul said, "Northern California."

"California? Huh. I've never even heard of it."

"Who has? But that's where he lives. Or owns property, at least. I can't find a street view, but Google Earth has an overhead shot of the house and the lot. Want me to give you the address so you can check it out?"

She was already out of bed, scrambling for a piece of paper and a pen. "Shoot."

He spoke slowly and clearly. "One-twenty-one Granite Dells Road. Take a look at it."

"I just got out of bed—"

"It's ten-fifteen!"

"I know, but I just got up, and it'll take me a few minutes. I'll call you back."

"I'll be here."

He hung up, and Gloria pulled on the robe hanging over the hope chest at the foot of her bed. She had to pee but decided she could hold it. Walking across the hall to Benjamin's office—

her office now

—she turned on the laptop, waited until it booted up, then went to Google Earth and put in the address Paul had given her.

Hicksville was indeed in northern California, a micro-community nestled in a wooded mountainous area, well off the beaten path and far away from any major city. Looking down from a satellite view, Gloria saw a main street with a handful of intersecting side roads, most of them dirt. Granite Dells was one of them, and the property that Paul claimed was owned by their father appeared to be a vacant lot bordered in the front by the street and at the rear by a copse of trees.

In front of the trees stood a small shack.

Gloria clicked on the picture, zooming in. There was something familiar about its extraordinarily small roof, although she didn't know how that was possible. A roof was a roof, and while she could not remember ever actually looking at one from above, either the size, shape or color of this one jogged some sort of memory within her, even if it was one she could not immediately place. Gloria looked carefully at the image, feeling sure that she had seen it before. She tried to zoom in even further but was already at maximum magnification, so instead she slowly zoomed out.

And suddenly knew *why* what she was looking at seemed familiar.

It was the roof of the shack in Owen Portis' pencil drawing.

A shiver passed through her. What she would have once considered a coincidence, now seemed more deliberately intersectional and decidedly more sinister.

Sinister?

Yes. Gloria had a bad feeling about that shack, and she stared uneasily at the rectangular image of its roof on the screen as she called her brother back and told him she'd found the property.

"So," he said, "Can you see Dad living there?"

"I'm looking at it right now, and I can't imagine *anyone* living there."

"Me either. Maybe he bought it for an investment?"

"Is that what you think?"

"I don't know what I think."

Gloria decided to just come right out and say what she was thinking. "That shack's creepy. I don't like it."

"I know what you mean," Paul mused. "You can't really see anything except the roof, but there's still something off about it."

He was agreeing with her, but in a passive, intellectual way, and Gloria didn't get the sense that he'd experienced the same visceral reaction she had. Looking at the screen caused goosebumps to pop up on her arms, and she didn't think her brother was responding on the same gut emotional level.

She was afraid of the shack.

Yet she knew she was going to go there.

An admission only to herself, it nonetheless surprised her. The notion seemed to come out of nowhere, but once lodged in her brain, it seemed the only natural course of action.

What did she expect to find? Her dad? Maybe. Gloria wasn't really sure. But she *was* sure that she had to get to the location and was filled with an increasingly urgent, almost physical need to leave for Hicksville as soon as possible.

Paul was still talking to her, and although she was answering, her brain was on autopilot, her conscious mind engaged not in the conversation but in planning how she could take a couple of those vacation days her supervisor had been urging her to use and, once she got her car checked out to make sure it was in good enough shape for such a trip, drive up north.

"I gotta go," she said abruptly to Paul, and hung up.

What was she doing? This wasn't like her. And wouldn't it make more sense to have Paul come along? What if she *did* run into their dad? What was her plan?

Everything about this was half-cocked, but she was still dead set on following through with it, and impulsively decided that she was going to leave today. Rather than take her own car, she was going to rent one, and she called and arranged for someone to pick her up and take her over to the closest Enterprise office. Two hours later, she was on the Golden State Freeway, heading north, a hastily packed suitcase lying on the back seat of her rented Nissan Sentra. She'd told no one she was leaving, but planned to give Paul a call later to let him know what was going on. Monday morning, if she still wasn't back, she'd call Ray at the museum and let him know she was using her vacation time.

Gloria had fully intended to stop when it got dark and look for a Motel 6 or some other bargain lodging. She wasn't used to driving at night, and Benjamin had always been the one to take the wheel on long trips. But she was motivated to get there as quickly as possible and surprised herself by continuing to drive straight through, not even stopping to eat, getting off the highway only to buy gas. She was not at all tired and felt as though she could drive for days. She remembered hearing a story from an acquaintance in college who claimed to have driven across country nonstop in a gonzo effort to make it back to California from Virginia in order to register for classes. She'd never believed the story, but thought now that it could be true.

It was technically Sunday morning, although the sky was still dark and several hours away from dawn, when Gloria reached Hicksville. On the ground, the town was almost comically small, and she twice drove past Granite Dells Road before spotting the small street and turning onto it.

She had never once questioned Paul's assertion that their dad owned property here, and she still didn't. Her brother knew how to mine information, and his research was seldom if ever incorrect. Besides, she *knew* he was right. She felt it in her bones.

So how in the world had their dad found this place?

How had Owen?

She pulled to a stop in front of what her GPS told her was 121 Granite Dells Road. From the front, it looked almost like a vacant lot, although at the rear of the lot was a line of tall trees, and in front of the trees stood the shack, or, more accurately, the shed. Strong moonlight and illumination from a security lamp on the front of the tire shop next door revealed that the shed was of wood construction. It looked almost homemade, assembled from mismatched boards and coated with flaking red and white paint. There was no window. A dark open doorway took up at least half of the structure's unadorned front. The path that led to the doorway was little more than a dirt trail between tall dried weeds.

If Gloria had thought the Google Earth view of the shed's roof was creepy, this small dilapidated building beneath the full moon seemed the very definition of "haunted." Ordinarily, she would have immediately made sure that the car's doors were locked, quickly driven away, and not returned until the sun was high in the sky and there were plenty of other people around. But whatever had come over her and impelled her to drive through the night to reach this place now caused her to dig through the car's glove compartment looking for a flashlight. There was none, only the rental agreement. Gloria recalled that her phone had a flashlight feature, and though she'd never used it before, she switched it on and was happy to find it satisfyingly bright.

Frightened but determined, she got out of the car and walked around the front of the vehicle, stepping onto her father's property, using her phone's flashlight to illuminate the path in front of her. Gloria saw no one else on the street, and the only noises she heard were her own. Indeed, the entire town seemed abandoned, and it was not until she was halfway to the shed that she realized she was not even hearing any nature sounds: no birds or animals or insects. Only her own footsteps and ragged breathing. While that should have given her pause, it didn't, and she continued up the path until she reached the open doorway.

She shone her light inside. The interior of the building was narrow but extended back surprisingly far, almost like a hallway. In the middle of the long single room was a raised section of flooring, and, as Gloria shone her light around, she noted with a combination of horror and incomprehension that the side walls were decorated with dozens of drawings and photos of herself. A giant framed portrait of her, wearing some sort of white tunic, was mounted on the back wall. There were no pictures of Paul or Janine or Myra, and an instinctive sense of self-preservation told her to get the hell out of here. *Now.* If this was her dad's place, her *dead* dad's place, he was clearly obsessed with her, and it was dangerous for her to remain a second longer. What if he showed up? What if—

A series of rustling noises behind her caused Gloria to turn around.

She was no longer alone. There was a line of men walking slowly up the pathway toward the shed, each of them holding a candle in his clasped hands. Seeing her in the doorway, they stopped. "She has arrived!" one of them said, reverent awe in his voice. Others took up the refrain, a whisper passing from one man to the next. "She has arrived...She has arrived...She has arrived..."

They were fanning out in front of her, blocking her path back to the street and her car. Was her dad among them? Gloria didn't see him, but the soft yellow light of the candles wasn't exactly making it easy to differentiate faces.

"She has arrived...She has arrived...She has arrived..."

The men were advancing, and Gloria instinctively backed into the shed, realizing only after she did so that she might very well have trapped herself. *Maybe there's a back door*, she thought.

Ignoring all the pictures of herself on the side walls, hurrying toward the large portrait in the rear, hoping to find a door that her light might not have illuminated, she quickly stepped onto the raised section of flooring—

"No!" someone called behind her.

FOUR

ONE

Smiling, Gloria sat on the folding beach chair, looking out at her family playing in the waves. Myron was holding Jean, lifting her high each time a wave broke. Benny, a year older and more independent, stood next to them, jumping over the waves himself, occasionally being knocked over but always popping right back up. Both children were laughing and screaming loudly enough for Gloria to hear them from all the way up here on the sand.

Myron looked back and waved at her, and Gloria waved back. Apparently, their earlier disagreement was forgotten, although it was quite possible that they each had differing opinions as to its outcome and the argument would start up again once the three of them came back to towel off.

It was as they were carrying the chairs, blanket, towels, umbrella and ice chest down the long winding path which led to the beach at Corona del Mar that Benny had said, "Can we eat at Baja Fresh for lunch? Last time we ate at Baja Fresh I had a burrito!"

"That sounds good," Myron responded. He looked over at Gloria. "How about it, hon?"

Gloria stopped walking and looked at him. The night before, they had specifically discussed bringing a picnic lunch, and she had sped over to the grocery store this morning for bread and luncheon meat, making sandwiches for all of them and cutting up apple slices for Benny and Jean.

"I packed us a lunch," she said. "We already talked about it."

"Oh, we can just save that for later."

"Which later is that?" she asked him pointedly. "We're having burgers for dinner—I've already marinated the ground turkey—and tomorrow for lunch we're going to Ron and Vivian's barbecue."

"Baja Fresh!" Benny chanted. "Baja Fresh!"

"See?" Myron said. "He has his heart set on it."

Gloria had started walking again, her flipflops sliding on the sand as she moved downhill. "We don't always get what we want."

She'd hated herself for saying that, for being so callous and dismissive, especially to a child. *Her* child.

This was not her.

It was a thought that had occurred to her often lately. Somehow, it seemed that over the years she had turned into someone different than the person she really was. But how was that possible? There was a mental condition of some kind, Body Dysmorphia or something like that, where a person's perception of her appearance didn't match the reality others saw. Could there be a similar thing for a person's mind or spirit? Because Gloria honestly did not feel that the person she was *was* the real her.

She was nicer than she acted, kinder than she came across. The things she said were not the things she really thought. Well, she *did* think them, but they weren't the things she *wanted* to think, weren't the things she was *supposed* to think.

This was not her.

But it was.

And she knew it.

Gloria leaned back in her chair, closing her eyes, but instead of the darkness she craved, there was only a fuzzy reddishness caused by the sun shining down on her eyelids. Around her, the sounds of the beach blended together, the rhythmic susurration of the surf merging with the cries of children, the conversations of adults, and the Mexican music blaring from someone's radio. Overhead, the growling of an airplane engine, the only noise strong enough to stand out on its own, moved from the left side of the sky to the right.

She wondered what her life would be like if she had never gotten married, if she had never had kids. It was a familiar fantasy, and one in which Gloria had often indulged lately. She imagined that she would have a job that required a lot of travel. She'd always wanted to travel but had not really had much of an opportunity to do so. Because she would be home so seldom, she'd probably have an apartment rather than a house. Maybe she would have apartments in different cities: New York, London, Paris, Rome. But what would her job consist of? Not flight attendant, definitely. Too cliché. Maybe some sort of translator. Or an advance person for a big company with offices all over the world.

"*Mommy*!"

Gloria felt a sprinkle of cold water on her legs and opened her eyes to see Jean standing in front of her.

"I need a towel!"

Gloria reached into the beach bag at her feet and unfolded a towel, draping it over her daughter.

"Dry me! I'm cold!"

Gloria laughed at Jean's exaggerated shivering and chattering teeth. "Come here." She used the towel to dry the girl's hair and face, then her shoulders and back, then her arms and legs and front, before draping the towel around her again. Behind Jean, Myron was walking up. He put one hand on his daughter's head and held out his other hand for a towel.

Gloria frowned. "Where's Benny?"

Myron looked surprised. "Right behind—" He turned, then saw that Benny was not following him as he'd obviously expected.

Gloria stood. Benny was running back into the water at the same spot where the three of them had been previously playing. He stopped, turned, then waved at her, grinning.

A wave broke over his head.

Benny went under the water.

And did not come back up.

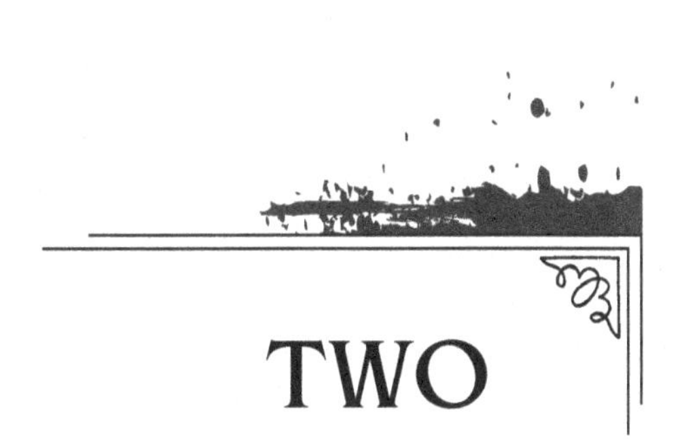

TWO

Gloria looked at the Caller ID.

Myron.

How *dare* he?

She left the phone alone. It would go to voicemail after five rings, and she prayed that Myron would hang up before that point, but when the fifth ring came and it was clear he intended to leave a message, she quickly picked up and then instantly terminated the call. The last thing she wanted right now was to hear his voice.

It had been exactly five years since they'd lost Benny, and not only had the pain not gone away, it had not even lessened. There was not a day, an hour, a moment that went by when she did not think of her son. If he were alive, he would be ten years old today, a tween. She tried to imagine what he would look like, how he would act, where his interests would lie, but quickly backed away from that pointless projection, knowing it would only make her feel more depressed.

Gloria blamed Myron for what had happened—and it *was* his fault—but always at the back of her mind was the knowledge that just before Jean had run up asking for a towel, just before Myron had strolled up behind her, just before Benny had gone into the water for the last time, she had been fantasizing about what it would be like not to have children. Of *course* her thoughts didn't cause the tragedy and had had absolutely no effect on anything, but the connection was there nonetheless—in her own mind at least—and it was that sense of guilt which had led her not to contest Myron's petition for sole custody of Jean. That was a decision she regretted every single day, even though she knew deep down that Myron would be able to provide a more emotionally stable life, a point driven home each time Jean was dropped off for a visit. Gloria loved her daughter, but the truth was that she always experienced a feeling of relief the moment she was returned to her dad.

It was Myron who had stayed in the house, to make the transition easier for Jean, while Gloria had moved to an apartment. Not wanting to remain in Brea, both because of the painful memories of the past it engendered and because she wanted to get far away from Myron, she transferred from the local Office Depot to one forty miles away in Riverside, where she found a one-bedroom unit just down the street from work. Local newscasts referred to this area as the "Inland Empire." It was indeed inland—and she was glad, happy to be away from the coast—but she had no idea how it could be considered an "empire." It was merely another county.

There was a knock at the door. Gloria frowned. Who could it be at this early hour? Who could it be, period? She knew none of her neighbors, didn't socialize with anyone from work and hadn't given her address to any of her old friends from Orange County.

The knock came again and, curious, Gloria got up to open the door. Standing on her apartment's doorstep was a cleancut young man who appeared to be in his mid-twenties. He looked vaguely familiar, and she was sure she had seen him somewhere before but couldn't remember where.

"May I help you?" she asked.

His mouth broke into a smile, and his smile seemed *very* familiar.

"Hi, Mommy," the young man said.

THREE

If this had been a movie, Gloria would have fainted or blacked out, opening her eyes to see her mysteriously grown son dutifully patting her hand as he tried to awaken her after carrying her to the couch. But this wasn't a movie, and she stood there dumbly for a few seconds before awkwardly inviting the young man inside. Afraid he might try and hug her, Gloria moved quickly away and invited him to sit on the couch, taking a seat directly across from him on a high-backed chair. She was not yet convinced of his identity, but she also did not discount the possibility, which was why she had allowed him inside rather than making him stand on the apartment's doorstep.

"Who are you?" she asked. "Who are you really?" The question came out more confrontational than she intended, a demand rather than a query, and she softened it by saying in a quieter voice. "You're too old."

The young man was still smiling, happiness beaming from his face. "It's me, Mommy. Benny."

"But—" Unexpectedly, the breath caught in her throat. "H-how can that be?" She believed it, Gloria realized, as impossible as it seemed.

The smile faded a little. "I'm not sure," Benny said.

It really *was* Benny.

She moved from the chair and sat next to him on the couch, allowing herself to touch his cheek. The skin was soft, just as it had been when he was little. "Five years ago," Gloria said softly, speaking as much to remind herself as explain to him, "you drowned at Corona del Mar. I was watching you when it happened."

"I remember. I was waving to you."

"Yes, and a wave hit you, and you went under. Your father was supposed to be watching you, but he was up by me with Jean—"

"Where is Daddy? Where's Jean?"

"At home." Something just occurred to her. "You didn't try going home? You came...*here*? How did you even know where I was?"

Benny shrugged.

"And how old are you? You would've been ten. You're supposed to be ten."

"I'm twenty-five."

"How's that possible?"

He shrugged again and, suddenly, she remembered that shrug, remembered him responding in exactly that way when she asked him what had happened to Jean's Dora the Explorer doll, which he had thrown in the garbage in retaliation for her stepping on one of his Hot Wheels. Gloria took his hands in hers. They were bigger, but they still felt like Benny's hands, still felt soft, like a child's. "What do you remember?" she asked. "Tell it to me from the beginning. From the second the wave hit you."

"There's not much to tell. It pushed me under the water, and I panicked and tried to scream, but my mouth filled up with water, and I choked, but I couldn't cough it out, because when I coughed more water came in, *salt* water, and it seems like I must've blacked out."

"You *died*," she told him. "The lifeguard found your body and did CPR, but it didn't work. They cleared the beach and kicked everyone out of the water. An ambulance came onto the sand. We buried you.

In the cemetery off Central in Brea. We put your Elmo in the casket with you so you wouldn't be lonely."

"That's not what I remember."

"What *do* you remember?"

Benny frowned, thinking. "Not much. I blacked out, and then when I woke up, I was standing in front of your door."

"How...how is that *possible*? Five years have passed! And you haven't aged just five years, you're twenty years older! And you talk and act like a regular adult, not like someone who's been in a coma or something since he was a *child*." Gloria shook her head. "I don't understand."

"Maybe we don't need to understand. I'm back, I'm here, and maybe that's all we need to know." He took his hands from hers, leaned forward, reached around and hugged her. "I love you, Mommy."

"I love you, too, Benny," she said, hugging him back.

And started crying.

How to tell Myron. *What* to tell Myron.

And Jean.

Benny wanted to visit them immediately, unaware of how strange and distant things had gotten between his parents. Gloria tried to think of a valid reason to delay the meeting but finally came to the conclusion that Benny was right. They should go straight to Brea. Sometimes just ripping the Band-Aid off was the best way to do it.

The Riverside Freeway was crowded, as usual, so it took twice as long as it should have to reach Orange County. Even with stoplights and a lower speed limit, driving on the streets was still faster than the freeway, so she got off early at the Imperial Highway exit and drove through Yorba Linda and Placentia to Brea. A sense of dread built within her as she passed through familiar intersections on the way to their old home, but Benny was increasingly excited. "I recognize that store!" he called out. "You used to take me to that park!"

And then they were there.

Gloria pulled to a stop in front of the house. The grass was paler than it should have been, she noticed, and while the lawn had been mowed, it had not been edged, and tendrils of grass crept onto the sidewalk and driveway. Most of the flowers she had planted along the front of the house had turned brown from lack of water.

"Daddy really let this place go," Benny said.

They had not discussed why she and Myron were living apart, in separate counties, but Benny seemed to have somehow intuited the situation. What did he know and how did he know it? Gloria wondered. She looked at him. He was her son. but she didn't really know him at all.

He frightened her a little bit.

Benny opened the car door and got out.

She probably should have called first, Gloria reflected. But she hadn't wanted to talk to Myron and still didn't want to see him. She also would not have known what to say. *Our son's back from the dead? Benny showed up on my doorstep and he's twenty-five years old?* Gloria got out of the car as well and walked around the hood, catching up to Benny. The two of them strode up the driveway to the front door.

Would Myron be home? Would either of them? It was a hot summer day. They might be at the mall or the library or some other air conditioned place. Myron could be dropping Jean and a friend off at a movie theater. He could be taking her to a friend's house. There was no car in the driveway, so it was quite likely they were out.

Could they have possibly gone to the beach?

Gloria didn't think so, but who could tell. Although the thought of them returning to the beach on this of all days made her feel sick to her stomach.

To her surprise, the door opened before she even had a chance to knock. She and Benny had no doubt been spotted as they were walking up. Myron was probably parking his car in the garage these days, she reasoned. Before, the garage had been too filled with junk to fit a car inside.

He may have attempted to call her earlier in the day, but the fact that she'd refused to talk to him must have made Myron mad because he scowled at her. "What do *you* want?" His hair was too long, she saw, and he didn't appear to have shaved today.

"I thought you might want to see your son."

"Daddy!" Benny said.

Gloria was looking over Myron's shoulder, into the house. "Where's Jean?"

Myron was clearly confused. He glanced from Gloria to Benny and back again. "What the hell's going on here?"

She pushed past him. "Jean!" she called. "Are you home?"

None of the furnishings had changed since she'd last seen the place, but everything looked a little shabbier. There was a framed photo of her late parents on the small table to the right of the front door, and Gloria wondered why she had not taken it with her—and why Myron still had it displayed.

"Jean!"

"What's going on here?" Myron said again.

"Is Jean home?" Gloria asked him.

"Who is this guy?"

"It's Benny," she said. "He's come back."

"I remember this house!" Benny exclaimed.

Myron's expression hardened. "I don't know what you think you're doing," he told Gloria, "but I want you out of here. Now."

Jean emerged from the kitchen. Gloria had just seen her a month ago—well, maybe two months ago. Okay, maybe three—but she seemed to have grown a foot and looked far more mature than Gloria was expecting. She squinted at her daughter. Was Jean wearing makeup?

"Mom?" Jean said, looking from her mother to her father. "What are you doing here?"

"Jean!" Benny cried, rushing forward. He threw his arms around her.

His sister screamed like a victim in a horror movie. Desperately trying to get out of his grasp, she kicked at him, curving her fingers into claws and attempting to rake his face.

"It's your brother," Gloria told her.

"Don't touch her!" Myron shouted, rushing forward.

Smiling, Benny pulled back from Jean, held her head in his hands and twisted.

Her life stopped. She dropped heavily to the floor, eyes wide and staring, blood seeping from her open mouth. Gloria heard the crack as her head hit the hardwood. Myron plowed into him at precisely that moment, bellowing like a wild animal, but rather than being knocked over by the weight and momentum of his father's body, Benny easily stood his ground. Possessed of seemingly supernatural strength, he wheeled around, picked his dad up—and snapped him in half. Gloria would not have believed it had she not been watching the incident herself, but she saw Benny lift Myron and, with one arm around his father's chest and the other holding his legs, *bend* his body in the middle until she heard a loud *crack* and both halves of his body went limp. Benny dropped his father on the ground, the dead body remaining in a U-shaped position.

Benny smiled at her.

Gloria was in shock. It had all occurred so quickly. Her mind had barely had time to register *what* had happened; she had absolutely no idea *why* it had happened. Seconds ago, Benny had been excited to see his dad again and was hugging his sister.

Now they were both dead.

Benny had killed them.

It made a kind of sense, though. It was Myron's fault that he had died in the first place. If his father had watched him properly, in the way a responsible parent was supposed to, Benny would not have drowned.

And Jean was the one Myron had been caring for at Benny's expense, the ultimate reason he had died.

Gloria preferred to forget about the fact that she'd been annoyed with Benny on that day, that it was his insistence on going out for lunch instead of eating the sandwiches she'd made—and Myron's weighing in on his side—that had caused her to start fantasizing about life without a family.

There was fault enough to go around, and she would not have blamed Benny if he took her life as well.

But he didn't.

He smiled happily at her and said, "Can we live here now?"

She marveled at the way his mind worked. Did he have a child's brain? she wondered. Was he slow or impaired in some way? Or was there a cunning craftiness behind the seeming innocence? Because, now that Gloria thought about it, the house was probably still half in her name; although she'd abandoned it for the "Inland Empire," she did not recall ever signing any papers to divest herself of their shared property.

Gloria looked at the two bodies on the floor, feeling strangely detached from both her daughter and her husband, her mind calculating. If she hid Benny somewhere, then called the police, telling them she had stumbled upon this scene on a routine family visit, the wheels would be set in motion. As long as Benny kept out of sight for the duration of the investigation, they should be safe. There was obviously no way *she* had the strength to do what had been done to Myron—and she certainly wouldn't murder her own daughter. And even if they found Benny's fingerprints all over everything, they weren't on file anywhere. Unless they were somehow matched with the prints of her long-dead son, which would confuse everyone because it made absolutely no sense whatsoever.

She turned back toward Benny and smiled. "Yes," she told him. "I think we can live here."

FOUR

What *was* Benny?

It was a question for which there appeared to be no answer, a question Gloria was not even sure she should be asking.

She had indeed inherited the house. In fact, she'd inherited everything, since the will they had both set up when Benny was born had never been amended. Afraid some neighbor might grow suspicious, or an overzealous police investigator might try to be helpful and keep tabs on her long after Myron and Jean's murders had chilled into a cold case, Gloria had sold the house and almost everything in it. The two of them were now renting an apartment near the beach.

Benny liked the beach.

He spent an inordinate amount of time standing on the sand, looking out at the sea. He seemed unnaturally drawn to the waves, an impulse that Gloria found strange and more than a little unnerving.

There were quite a few things about Benny that were strange and a little unnerving. Like the fact that, although he spoke like a simpleton, he sometimes referenced things that theoretically he should know nothing about, things that had happened during his absence.

Or the fact that he wanted a burrito for every meal, and if she tried to serve him something else, he wouldn't eat it. Or the fact that Gloria had never seen him sleep. She put him to bed each night in the same way she had when he was a little boy, but his eyes were always open when she left his room, and he was always up before her in the morning. A couple of times, she had peeked in on him in the middle of the night when she'd gotten up to go to the bathroom, and each of those times he had been awake, smiling at her when she peeked her head in the doorway and telling her, "Goodnight, Mommy."

There was definitely something off about Benny.

Did she love him?

Gloria wasn't sure. She believed—she *knew*—that he really was her son, so of course she was *supposed* to love him. But her actual feelings were more complicated than that. She cared about him, was concerned for him, but she was also a little afraid of him, and that fear kept her at something of a distance.

At the Office Depot in Riverside, she'd been in line for a promotion. The manager was leaving, the assistant manager had been tapped to take over, and Gloria was scheduled to move into the assistant manager position. But after transferring to the Costa Mesa store, she was back at the end of the line when it came to promotions. No matter. She still had the same amount of accumulated vacation time, and the sale of the house, plus Myron's life insurance, had given her money to play with. She planned to take Benny on a vacation to one of the national parks this summer. The Grand Canyon, maybe. Or Yellowstone. Or Yosemite.

Yes, Yosemite.

In the meantime, while she was at work, he was supposed to stay home, inside, away from prying eyes. He could go out with her when she returned, but otherwise she wanted him to remain indoors. He could watch TV if he wanted, and Gloria had given him a stack of books from the library that she thought would make him seem more age appropriate intellectually if he read them.

Only...

Gloria was not sure that's what was happening. Sometimes, she would arrive home to find dirt and small bits of leaves on the floor, as if Benny had gone outside and tracked them in. Other times, the door would be unlocked when she returned, even though she was sure she had locked it before leaving. Questioning Benny failed to clear anything up because he always claimed that he'd never gone anywhere or done anything.

In bed at night, trying to sleep after a long day at work and a confusing dinner with Benny, Gloria found herself thinking that this life was not hers, that the person she was at Office Depot, and even the person she was with Benny, was not the real her. She remembered that she'd had similar thoughts on the day Benny drowned, and, superstitiously, she got out of bed to check on him and make sure he was all right.

As usual, he was wide awake, and he smiled at Gloria as she poked her head into his room.

Her son, she reflected, quite literally was not the person he was supposed to be. He was years older than his actual age, and he was...alive.

How was any of that possible?

What *was* Benny?

It was only at times like this, alone late at night, that she even considered such questions. During the day, when she was acting like the Gloria everyone believed her to be, she just accepted the world as it was and acted appropriately. But at night, she could feel that something was off, not quite right, and though she was never able to figure out what it was, thinking about the possibilities kept her from sleeping.

Maybe no one, she thought, ever revealed who they really were on the inside.

FIVE

Gloria awoke late since Benny had not barged in, begging for breakfast the way he usually did, and when she checked on him after going to the bathroom, intending to wake him up, she found him lying on his bed, covers kicked down to his feet, eyes wide open. His eyes were *always* open when she walked into his room, but he was usually awake and smiling at her. This time, however, his face was frozen, his mouth slack, and the breath caught in her throat as she realized with a sudden flash of horrified comprehension that Benny had died sometime during the night.

The scream that escaped her lips was loud enough to wake the entire neighborhood. She fell upon him, wailing. It was an instinctive reaction, a primal cry from her shattered heart. She had lost her son again, and the feeling of his cold skin against her cheek burned a bottomless hole through the center of her being. She took his hand in hers, held it, squeezed it.

At some point, she sat up, wiping the tears from her stinging eyes. Practicality took over from emotion, and as guilty as she felt for thinking it, Gloria wondered how she was going to report his death. As far as the world was concerned, he didn't exist, and if she called

911 and explained what had happened, he would suddenly be on the authorities' radar. Gloria knew nothing about autopsy protocol, but she assumed that when a medical examiner attempted to find out why and how he had died, fingerprints would be taken for identification purposes. Once those fingerprints were on file, they would probably be automatically matched with those of the killer who had murdered Myron and Jean. And since it would be clear that Benny had been living with her, *she* would be implicated in their deaths.

The whole thing was a nightmare, and Gloria was just starting to think through possible scenarios, when she heard a knock at the door. Her instinctive reaction was to pretend she wasn't home, but she knew that her screaming must have frightened the neighbors. One or more of them had probably called the police, and it was probably either a cop or a concerned citizen who was trying to check up on her and make sure she was okay.

The knocking continued.

She was going to have to answer the door.

"Mommy!" a girl's voice called.

Jean?

Numbly, Gloria made her way through the living room. She wanted to believe that she'd misidentified the voice and imagined what it had said, but she knew it was Jean, and she opened the door, and it was.

Except that Jean was four years old, the same age she had been when Benny drowned. She was even wearing the same bathing suit she'd had on that day. And she was holding the hand of a much older woman.

Gloria's grandmother.

Who had been dead for twenty years.

"Grandma?" Gloria said.

Her grandmother fixed her with a disdainful look that cut straight to her core and that she remembered perfectly, though it had not been turned upon her since she was a junior in high school. "Are we going to have to stand here forever," she said archly, "or are you going to let us in?"

Gloria felt like Alice, either in Wonderland or Through the Looking Glass, stuck in a crazy world where nothing made sense. She was shocked and surprised to find her long dead grandmother and a younger version of her deceased daughter on her doorstep, but was neither incredulous nor disbelieving because she had been through this before, and her resurrected son was lying dead in a room down the hall.

Only he wasn't.

When she left her grandma and Jean in the living room to check on him, his body was gone, as were his clothes. The bedroom looked as though no one had lived in it for years.

Gloria's head hurt, and she could feel blood pumping through her temples in time to the accelerated beating of her heart. She stared for a moment at Benny's empty bed, then stormed back out to the living room. "What's going on here?" she demanded.

She'd addressed the question to her grandmother, but it was Jean who answered. "We're going to live with you."

There was another knock at the door, louder this time, more forceful. The police *had* arrived. Someone had clearly called the cops after hearing her scream, and while Gloria hadn't heard any sirens, two uniformed officers were standing on her front porch when she opened the front door. They were both fairly young, her own age, she guessed, both Hispanic, though it was the taller and heavier of the two who did the talking. He met her gaze, his eyes flat and unreadable. "Is everything all right here, ma'am? We've had a report of screams coming from this residence."

"Everything's fine," she told him.

"So there were no screams?"

"That was me. I was just...surprised," Gloria said. "I haven't seen my grandma in years—"

"Decades," the old lady said.

"—and it was a shock to find her on my front porch when I opened the door."

The officers looked at each other skeptically. "Do you mind if we come in, ma'am?"

Gloria stepped aside. "Not at all."

She led them through the house and even into the garage, until they were finally convinced that she was not hiding anything and nothing untoward was going on. "Sorry to bother you," the bigger man said.

She couldn't resist. "Well, next time I rediscover a long lost family member, I'll do so quietly and try not to show any emotion so my neighbors won't have to call the cops on me."

Both officers looked embarrassed.

This time, the shorter officer spoke up. "We're sorry," he said. "Have a nice day." His apology seemed more real, less obligatory, and he nodded toward her grandma and Jean. "You too."

Gloria waited until they had walked back down the driveway and gotten into their patrol car before closing the door.

"So what are you two doing here?" she asked, turning to face her visitors. This might be her grandmother and her daughter, but she felt completely disassociated from both of them. It was as if the familial connection they had once shared had been severed and they were now strangers meeting for the first time.

"You tell us," her grandma said.

"That makes no sense," Gloria told her.

Jean shrugged. "We've come here to live with you."

"But where did you come *from*? How did you *get* here? You're both...You're supposed to be...You're dead."

"Not anymore," Jean said. She smiled, and that smile made Gloria shiver. She remembered clearly her daughter standing in front of her on the beach looking just like this, wearing the same exact bathing suit, while in the water behind her, Benny was knocked over by a wave and drowned.

Her grandma stepped forward and put a bony hand over Gloria's shoulder. She remembered the parchment feeling of that wrinkled skin, the overstrong smell of Tabu perfume. "It'll all make sense in the morning."

"I'm not going to bed until I find out what's happening. I need to know what's going on here."

"You need to get some rest." Gently, her grandmother led her out of the living room toward her bedroom. The old woman seemed to already know the layout of the house.

"I'm tired, too," Jean said, yawning.

"I'll fix up a bed in the guestroom," Gloria's grandmother told her. "You can sleep with me."

Although she had not acquiesced, Gloria was no longer putting up any resistance. She *was* tired, she realized, and a small logical part of her mind was hoping that this was either a dream or the product of an overtired mind, and that if she went to sleep, everything would be back to normal in the morning. Allowing herself to be guided to her bedroom, she thought that there was something nice about having her grandma back again, something comforting about having an older person in the house.

It was nice having her daughter back, too.

Her grandma kissed her forehead. "Sweet dreams," she said. It was what she had always said when Gloria stayed overnight at her house. "Now kiss your mommy goodnight," she told Jean.

The little girl stood on her tiptoes, lips puckered, and, smiling, Gloria leaned down and presented her cheek. Her daughter kissed it, and then she kissed her daughter back. "Night night," she said.

"I'll put her to bed," her grandma offered. She put an arm around Jean and steered her toward the door. "We'll see you in the morning."

Gloria sat down on the edge of the mattress, feeling exhausted. She usually took her shoes off in the living room and left them under the coffee table, but she wasn't about to expend the energy to go all the way back out there. She pulled off her shoes and socks, pushing them under the bed with her foot, then stood and took off her pants and shirt, throwing them over the nearby chair. It was a warm night, and rather than going over to the dresser for her pajamas, she pulled down the comforter and lay on the bed in her underwear. The sheet felt cool against her skin, and she closed her eyes.

Before she knew it, she had fallen asleep.

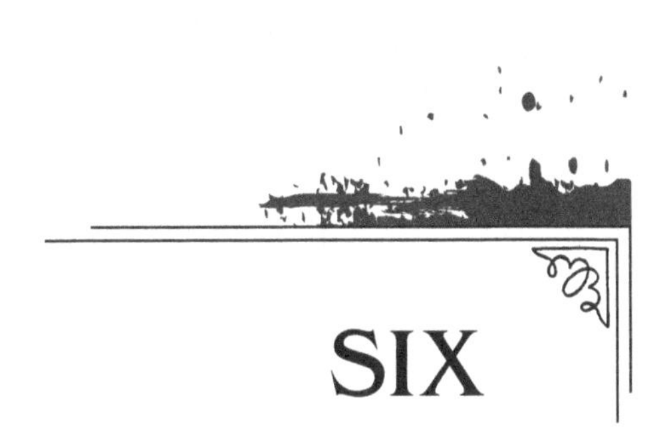

SIX

"Rise and shine, sleepyheads!"

Gloria opened her eyes to see her grandma standing in the bedroom doorway. "You'd better get ready. I let you and Jeannie both sleep in, but she needs to get to school and you need to get to work, so chop chop!" She started to walk away, then turned back. "I made waffles again. I probably should've asked, but you were dead asleep, and Jeannie loves them so."

"That's fine," Gloria said. "Thanks, Grandma."

The old woman moved down the hall. "Jeannie! Time to get up!"

Gloria pushed off the covers and stood, putting on the bathrobe she'd laid on top of the hope chest at the foot of the bed. Although it felt as though she'd been asleep for days, she was still tired. Rubbing her eyes, she padded wearily out to the kitchen. Grateful to see that her grandmother had made coffee, she poured herself a cup. She wasn't that hungry—she definitely wasn't in the mood for waffles—so she simply sat down at the kitchen table, sipping her coffee and trying to wake up.

Jeannie dashed in, followed seconds later by her great-grandma. She gave Gloria a kiss, then sat down in the chair next to her mother.

"Do we have syrup?" she asked. "Last time we ran out of syrup and my waffle was dry."

"I bought some yesterday. There's plenty."

"That's okay. I want jam anyway." She looked up at Gloria. "Can I have some milk?"

Gloria smiled. "What's the magic word?"

"Please!"

Standing, Gloria picked up her daughter's glass, carrying it to the counter. She took the milk carton from the refrigerator and filled the glass half-full (Jeannie had a tendency to spill if her glass was filled too high).

"Oh, could you get the jelly out while you're there?" her grandma asked.

"Jam!" Jeannie said. "Not jelly!"

"Jam."

Gloria put the milk carton away, grabbed a jar of strawberry preserves from its place on the shelf of the refrigerator door, and brought both the milk glass and the jar of preserves back to the table. Jeannie took a big drink. "Oh, yeah. I'm supposed to bring something for show-and-tell today."

"I wish you'd told me earlier," Gloria said.

"I forgot."

"Well, what do you want to bring? Last time, you showed off your cat doll, right?"

"But this time Ms. Druiff said I was supposed to bring something educational, like a shell or a rock or a wasp nest or something."

"We have that red leaf you found in the backyard."

"My fall leaf? That's perfect!" Jeannie said. She scrambled out of her chair. "I'm going to go get it!"

"Oh, no you're not," Gloria told her, taking hold of her arm and swinging her back toward the table. Her grandma had just pulled up the top of the steaming waffle iron. "Gram-Gram has your waffle ready."

"But—"

"No buts," Gloria said firmly.

"No butts?" Jeannie giggled. "Then what am I supposed to sit on?"

"Eat your breakfast." Gloria took the proffered plate from her grandmother and placed it down in front of her daughter. "Thank you, Gram-Gram," she prodded.

"Thank you, Gram-Gram," Jeannie said.

"What about you?" her grandmother asked Gloria.

"I'm not hungry."

The old lady shrugged. "Suit yourself. More for the rest of us."

"Suit yourself!" Jeannie said, pouring syrup over her waffle.

"I thought you wanted jam."

"I changed my mind."

Jeannie ended up eating two waffles—one with syrup, one with jam—before jumping up again. "I have to go to the bathroom!" she announced, and ran out.

Finished with her coffee but still not hungry, Gloria picked up the carton and poured herself a glass of orange juice. Her grandmother had bought the store brand again, after Gloria had specifically told her to get Minute Maid or Tropicana or another real brand. She took a sip and grimaced. How could this have even come from actual oranges?

"Now that Jeannie's gone, we need to have a quick little talk about that Benjamin," her grandma said.

Gloria frowned. "Benjamin?"

"I don't like you dating him. You have a daughter, remember, and it's not healthy for her to see her mommy traipsing about with strange men."

Benjamin.

For a second, she couldn't put a face to the name.

Benny.

She could put a face to *that* name, but...

But Benny wasn't a man she was dating. He was more like...a relative?

A son.

She didn't have a son, though.

"Are you listening to me?"

Gloria felt dopey, and she took another sip of the bad orange juice, trying to clear her head. "Yes, I'm listening."

"The most important thing for children is stability. Jeannie's used to it being just the two of you. If you start gallivanting around, it's going to cause problems."

"I'm not 'gallivanting around.'"

Her grandmother's mouth tightened.

"Do you not like Benny...uh, Benjamin, for some reason?" Gloria still could not put a face to the name.

"I just don't think he's right for you."

The toilet flushed down the hall, and Jeannie came running back into the room a moment later, holding her red leaf. The two of them dropped the subject. "Tell me what to say!" Jeannie pleaded, holding out her leaf. "I don't know what to say about it except it's red. Ms. Druiff is going to want me to say what kind of tree it's from and everything."

"Don't worry," Gloria reassured her, getting up from the table. "We'll practice on the way to school."

Gloria walked back to her bedroom to get dressed for work. *Benny? Benjamin?* She didn't know either of them, but the name that seemed more familiar was apparently the person who didn't even exist.

Something was wrong, something was off, and a deep, hypochondriacal part of her mind nagged that it could be the result of a brain tumor, but she chose to attribute the discrepancies to lack of sleep, inwardly assuring herself that if she ignored the current confusion it would go away of its own accord.

And it did.

“You know,” Benjamin said, “I don’t think your grandma likes me.”

Gloria laughed. They were at lunch, a fast casual restaurant that offered healthy dining options. She was having a salad of organic micro-greens, while he’d ordered a veggie burrito. “What makes you say that?” she asked.

He shrugged. “Just a vibe I get. You have to admit, she’s not the most welcoming person in the world. At least not to me.”

“She’ll get used to you,” Gloria promised, though she was not at all sure that was true. Leaning across the small table, she kissed his nose. “*I* like you, anyway.”

She did like him. In fact, she loved him, and it was hard to believe that only this morning she had not been able to recall his face. She’d even gotten him confused with someone she thought was a relative. *How had that happened?* Gloria wondered.

The brain tumor possibility refused to entirely go away.

A bushy-haired young man in a tie-dyed T-shirt passed by their table, sipping a smoothie.

Benjamin watched him, a reflective expression on his face. “You change as you get older,” he told Gloria, “and I’m not so sure that’s a bad thing.”

“Okay.”

“When you’re young, you see adults as sellouts, while you’re pure and idealistic, but that’s not always the case.”

“What brought this on?”

Benjamin chuckled. “I don’t know. That guy, I guess. And I was thinking about this old movie, *A Thousand Clowns*, where Jason Robards is this sort of anti-establishment character who refuses to get a job. It came out in the late 1950s or early 1960s, between the beatniks and the hippies, but it still spoke to me, as a child growing up in the nineties. I thought Jason Robards was so cool when I was a teenager. But you know what? Times change. And when I saw it again on TCM the other day, I realized he was a loser. A narcissistic, self-absorbed loser."

Gloria looked at him quizzically. "And you're bringing this up because...?"

"I was offered a promotion this morning, and I took it, but I felt guilty about it."

She punched his arm. "Why didn't you tell me?"

"I *am* telling you. But...like I said, I felt a little guilty. It's not the type of job I ever wanted to do, and I might've even turned it down when I was younger, but then I thought of you, thought of *us*, and I realized that in addition to more money, I'd get an extra week's vacation a year, and, to me, that made it worth it."

"We should celebrate," she told him.

He glanced around at the restaurant's lunch crowd. "Aren't we?"

Gloria laughed. "I mean a real celebration."

He leaned forward, lowering his voice. "One where we take our pants off?"

She smiled. "That wasn't exactly what I was thinking, but, yes, that would be nice."

"A romantic dinner at the Summit House, maybe?"

"That would be wonderful. And you can afford it now."

"Then afterward, we can take our pants off."

"I love you," she told him.

Touched, his voice softened, and he put his hand over hers. "I love you, too."

Gloria looked at him, paused for a second. "Did anyone ever call you Benny?" she asked. "When you were growing up, maybe? When you were a kid?"

Benjamin looked at her oddly. "That's a weird question."

"It just occurred to me. Did anyone ever call you that?"

He shook his head slowly. "No. No one ever did."

Gloria nodded. "Yeah, you don't seem like a Benny. You're definitely more of a Benjamin."

"Is that good or bad?"

"Good," she said, leaning forward to kiss him. "Definitely good."

And it was.

SEVEN

They were married in a church, although neither of them were believers. It was her grandmother and Benjamin's parents who'd insisted on the traditional formality, and the two of them went along with it in order to maintain peace in the families. Even though they weren't parishioners, they were required to meet with the minister for counseling prior to the nuptials, and while the man seemed nice, Gloria resented the fact that she was forced to participate in this charade. Still, she put on her best face, because she didn't know how this whole thing worked and was worried that if she didn't pass her audition, the minister wouldn't perform the ceremony.

For their honeymoon, she and Benjamin drove up to Monterey, where they spent several days exploring the Central Coast. Gloria had never been away from Jeannie for more than one night, and she missed her daughter terribly, but they spoke each evening on the phone, and Jeannie assured her that she was having fun with Gram-Gram.

"So how did Jeannie's dad die?" Benjamin asked on the second night, once Gloria had gotten off the phone.

"I told you that."

"I never did get it straight. And I think I should probably know the details since I'm going to be her dad from now on."

Gloria shifted her position on the bed, facing him. She started to say something, then stopped.

"What?" Benjamin asked.

She paused for a second. "I'm just trying to figure out where to start."

"Start at the beginning."

"Okay." Gloria nodded. "It's just..."

"Just what?"

"The beginning," she said, taking a deep breath. "Okay. I met Lucas in college. We dated for two years, and after we graduated, we moved in together, and later married."

"Did your grandmother approve of him?"

Gloria smiled. "No, she did not."

"Good. So I'm not the only one." He smiled back at her. "Go on."

"We both worked for Automated Interface in Irvine. He was a programmer, I was in HR. Everything was fine. About six months in, I got pregnant..." Her voice trailed off.

"And?" he prodded gently.

Gloria licked her lips. "I met a man. Or, rather, I ran into a man. In the women's restroom at work."

Benjamin sat up straight. "Jesus."

"Yeah. He was an older guy, and he looked a little like my dad. Or at least what I remember my dad looking like. Or maybe just the image of my dad I had from photos my grandma had shown me. He was standing there, in the middle of the restroom, in front of the sinks, and it was like he was waiting for me. 'Gloria,' he said, and the fact that he knew my name freaked me out. I turned to run away, but he said, 'Your husband is going to die.'" She sucked in her breath, as if even the memory of it was too much to handle. "That made me stop, of course, and I yelled at him. I can't remember exactly what I said—'Who are you?' 'Get out of here!' 'I'm calling security!' 'What the hell are you talking about?'—something like that. But I remember exactly what he said to me. He said, 'Lucas is going to have an aneurysm here at work. Tomorrow at his desk.'

"I didn't know how to react. I assumed he was crazy since he was in the women's restroom predicting the future, but..." Gloria looked down at the bedspread.

"It's okay," Benjamin told her. "I understand if you don't—"

She leaned forward, kissing him. "No," she said. "We're not going to have any secrets."

"Are you sure?"

"I'm sure."

"So..."

"So I believed him. I thought he was crazy, and he scared the hell out of me, and I even thought he might rape me or assault me, but he knew my name, he knew Lucas' name, and I believed him. I ran out of the bathroom and went straight upstairs to Lucas' office. I probably should've called security first, because by the time they finally went there to check things out, the man was long gone, but I didn't. I ran to Lucas, I told him what happened, and *he* called security. We had a big fight after that, because I didn't want him to go to work the next day, but he laughed it off—or didn't *laugh* it off, really, was more just skeptical, *scoffing* maybe—and we fought over it all that night and even the next morning, but I couldn't get him to take the day off. He went into work. We both went in." Her voice grew quiet. "And the man was right. Lucas had an aneurysm and died at his desk." She held up a hand. "I know it sounds crazy, and I'm not sure I'd believe it if someone was telling that story to me, but, honest to God, that's exactly what happened."

"Did you—?"

"Ever see the man again? No. And I have no idea who he is. Security couldn't find footage of him on any of their cameras, no one else saw him, and nothing like that has ever happened to me since." She ran a hand through her hair. "Sometimes it's even hard to believe it happened at all." She met his eyes. "But it did. And that's how Jeannie's dad died. Or her *biological* dad." Gloria scooted forward and snuggled next to Benjamin. "You're her dad now."

"Yes I am," he said, and kissed her forehead.

Gloria said nothing, but she felt cold all of a sudden.

And shivered.

Home from the honeymoon, life settled into a routine. Both Gloria and Benjamin lived in nice houses in nice parts of northern Orange County, and while they had never expressly discussed after-the-wedding living arrangements, Gloria did not want Jeannie to have to change schools. Also, she didn't think her grandma wanted to move.

Benjamin was not thrilled to have her grandmother living with them, but Gloria had made it clear at the outset that that was one of her pre-conditions to accepting his marriage proposal. It would probably be awkward at first, but they would figure things out, and she had no doubt that everything would be fine. Eventually.

The only thing that slightly concerned her was that Benjamin seemed to have no intention of selling his house. When she brought up the idea, he deflected, and Gloria wondered if he was keeping it as a backup.

Just in case the marriage didn't work out.

She hated having that thought, even if it was only a faint half-formed notion in the back of her mind, but she didn't bring it up to him, and it occurred to her that this reluctance to speak honestly on both of their parts was probably not the best way to start off on a new life.

Still, the transition was much smoother than Gloria had expected. Neither her grandmother's nor Jeannie's schedules were at all affected, and none of them had to change any of their daily habits. Benjamin slid easily into their lives, adapting to their family rhythms, and while some small adjustments had to be made, Gloria found that she enjoyed them. She liked taking a shower in the morning while Benjamin shaved at the sink, liked the two of them getting dressed together, liked carpooling to work.

And the sex was amazing.

Sometimes, life seemed almost too good to be true, and it was in those moments that she flashed back to the man in the women's room.

Your husband is going to die.

She told herself she was being foolish and paranoid. There was no way the same thing could happen again. But it shouldn't have been able to happen in the first place. It was a crazy, impossible occurrence to begin with, and in a weird way that made it seem more likely to her that it *would* happen again.

After Lucas' death, she had quit her job at Automated Interface. It was too tough, emotionally, to return to work every day at the place where her husband had died. And the thought of even passing by that restroom...

Besides, A.I. offered only two-weeks maternity leave. As if the hour-long commute each way wasn't bad enough, she would have had to return to work almost immediately after giving birth. Lucas' life insurance provided her with a little bit of freedom, and she took off the first year, moving her grandma in as full-time babysitter when she finally got a job working for a small tech firm in nearby Placentia.

Which is how she'd met Benjamin.

Jeannie, it turned out, *loved* Benjamin. Gloria had been careful to ease him into her daughter's life, not wanting a big disruption, but she was not even sure such an effort had been necessary. Jeannie seemed so happy to have a man around the house, a father-figure, a *dad*, and while Gloria wasn't an I-told-you-so type of person, she had to admit that she experienced a feeling of satisfaction whenever Jeannie displayed affection for Benjamin in front of her grandma.

"We're a family now," Jeannie said one night during dinner. She glanced happily around the table at all of them.

"We've always been a family," Gram-Gram told her with only a slight hint of correction.

"But now we're a real family," Jeannie said.

Gloria smiled at her. "Yes, we are," she said. Yes, we are."

EIGHT

Gloria awoke in the middle of the night with the feeling that something was wrong.

Next to her, Benjamin was dead to the world after a long tiring day. She'd been sleeping on her back, but he was on his side, one arm thrown around her midsection, a strong erection pressing against her thigh, though they'd had sex earlier and she thought she'd drained him dry. The house was silent, and she carefully extricated herself from his embrace without waking him, pulled on the panties she'd left on the floor and pushed down her nightie. She wanted to check on Jeannie to make sure she was okay, and she tiptoed across the floor and opened the door, sneaking into the hall.

The feeling that something was wrong had grown stronger.

Jeannie's door, as always, was wide open, and Gloria saw with relief that her daughter was sleeping peacefully. She had kicked off all her blankets and had somehow twisted herself around so that she was sleeping sideways on the bed. It was cute, and Gloria was tempted to get her phone and take a picture, so she could show it to Jeannie in the morning, but she was still filled with the nagging sense that something was amiss.

Could it be her grandma?

The worry solidified into a certainty as she continued down the hall toward her grandmother's room. Knocking softly and receiving no answer, Gloria pushed open the bedroom door, expecting, *hoping*, to see the old lady fast asleep in her bed.

But the bed was still made.

And her grandmother, wearing an old-fashioned white shift, was standing before the dresser mirror, staring at herself. The room was too dark for Gloria to see any facial expressions, so she reached for the switch on the wall and turned on the ceiling light. She expected that to break the trance or at least generate some sort of reaction, but her grandmother remained exactly where she was, and the light allowed Gloria to see that the old woman was not staring blankly at herself in the mirror, as she had assumed, but was actively frowning, glaring at her own image, her face twisted into a mask of anger and disgust.

"Grandma!" Gloria said, startled.

The old lady turned to face her. "You shouldn't have married him. He shouldn't even be here. Now..."

Gloria did not even have a chance to respond. Her grandma turned, strode purposefully across the room, opened the window, then pushed her way through the screen, squirming headfirst over the sill and onto the front lawn. Shocked, Gloria remained in place for a beat too long, unsure of whether to run to the window, hurry outside through the front door, or call for Benjamin. Finally dashing over to the window and looking through the woman-sized hole in the screen, she saw her grandmother stand, then race out to the sidewalk.

Panicked and frightened, Gloria rushed down the hall and through the living room, quickly unlocking and opening the front door, running into the night, leaving the door open behind her. Though she looked up and down the sidewalk in both directions, there was no sign of her grandmother. Acutely aware that she was barefoot and in her nightie, Gloria reluctantly returned to the house. Where could her grandma have gone? And why? Apparently it had something to do with Benjamin?

She had no idea what to do next, whether she should wake her husband (quietly, so as not to disturb Jeannie) and tell him what had happened, call the police and let them know a mentally unstable woman was roaming the streets of Brea, or just wait and see if her grandmother came back of her own accord. Unable to make a decision, Gloria opted for the latter, preferring to believe that her grandma had not suffered a mental breakdown but was just experiencing something similar to sleepwalking, a temporary incident that would soon be over. She left the front door unlocked and parked herself in the chair her grandma usually sat in.

Although Gloria had intended to stay awake all night, she must have dozed off, because she was awakened by a kiss on the forehead from Benjamin. "What are you doing out here?" he asked.

She opened her eyes. "Couldn't sleep," she lied.

He looked worried. "Is anything wrong?"

She stood, giving him a quick hug. "No," she told him. "Everything's fine."

Outside, the sun was up, and she both heard and smelled her grandma making French toast in the kitchen.

For a moment, Gloria thought that she'd dreamed the whole thing, but when she walked into her grandmother's bedroom and saw the open window with the torn screen, she knew that it had really happened. It was Saturday, so Jeannie was sleeping in. Benjamin had just gone into the bathroom, which gave Gloria a chance to confront her grandma directly.

Except...

She was afraid to do so. She stood outside the kitchen door, listening to her grandma hum an old Elvis ballad while placing a piece of French toast into a sizzling frying pan, and realized that she did not want to be alone with the woman. Of course, she wanted to know what had happened, but how could she bring it up? What would she say? *Why did you crawl out the window last night? Where did you go? What did you mean when you said Benjamin shouldn't be here?*

She imagined walking into the kitchen and seeing her grandmother turn toward her with that angry expression on her face.

Luckily, Jeannie emerged from her bedroom at just that moment. She saw Gloria and ran up to give her a hug. "Mommy!"

Gloria kissed the top of her head. "Good morning, sleepyhead."

"I smelled breakfast. That's why I woke up."

"Want to go in and see what Gram-Gram's making?"

"Yeah!"

The two of them walked into the kitchen and everything seemed normal. Her grandmother looked up from the stove and smiled. "Pour yourselves some orange juice." She flipped over the piece of French toast in the pan. "Who's ready for the first one?"

"I am!" Jeannie called, and hurried over to get a plate.

"Where's Benjamin? Isn't he up yet?"

Gloria stared at her grandmother, unsure of how to respond. Should she just pretend everything was normal and move on? Or should she demand to know what the hell had happened last night? Not wanting to get into a confrontation in front of her daughter, Gloria opted for the latter. "Bathroom."

Her grandma was wearing her bathrobe, and Gloria wondered if she still had the shift on under it. From the way she'd gone out the window onto the lawn, the white material had to be stained with dirt. If the old lady attempted to deny what had happened, that would be proof. That and the torn screen.

Gloria had a sudden inspiration. "What happened to the screen in your room, Grandma?"

Her question was met with a confused frown of seeming sincerity. "What?"

"I was walking by your room and saw a big hole in your screen. A hole big enough for a person to crawl through."

"Like a burglar?" Jeannie asked, eyes wide.

Her grandmother dismissed their concerns. "Oh, I noticed that, too. It's nothing." She popped a piece of French toast onto Jeannie's plate and smiled brightly. "Do you want another one or should I give it to your mom?" She dipped a piece of bread into a bowl of egg wash.

"Mommy can have it. I'll take the next one."

Benjamin entered the kitchen, scratching his head. "Smells good. What're we having? Pancakes?"

"French toast!" Jeannie said.

"Mmmmm!"

Gloria knew she'd lost her chance, so when her grandmother jokingly told Benjamin to pour himself some coffee and wait his turn, she reluctantly sat down next to him. She'd talk to her grandma later, in private.

After breakfast, Benjamin went off to take his shower while Jeannie moved over to the living room to watch TV. Gloria was left alone with her grandmother, and though she wanted to bring up last night, she remained where she was, at the table, drinking coffee in silence. She felt ill at ease around the old lady now. They both knew what had happened, but Gloria was not sure if her grandma would admit to it even when they were alone.

And if she did admit it...?

Gloria could think of no rational explanation for what she had seen and had no idea how her grandma could possibly explain her bizarre behavior. She watched as the old lady picked up Jeannie's dish and cup and put them in the sink, the back of her neck prickling. Gathering her courage, Gloria cleared her throat.

The doorbell rang.

Her grandmother looked at her pointedly. The expression on her face was hard, with none of the kindliness or affability she had exhibited when Jeannie and Benjamin were in the kitchen. "Are you going to get that?"

Gloria rose without replying. Jeannie was sitting on the living room floor in front of the television, watching the most recent iteration of Scooby Doo, and she walked past her daughter, opening the front door just as the bell rang again. Sadeen and Myla, their next door neighbors, were both standing on the porch. Ordinarily, the couple was cheerful and friendly, but today they seemed serious, *overly* serious, almost angry. "Good morning," Gloria said warily.

"Not really," Myla said.

"Could we speak to you alone?" Sadeen asked. He was looking over her shoulder at Jeannie on the floor.

Gloria stepped outside, unlocking the door before closing it behind her. Feeling uneasy, she addressed them both. "What's wrong?"

Sadeen had taken out his phone.

"Benny was killed last night," Myla said.

Benny

"Our cat?" she prodded when Gloria clearly couldn't place the name. There was a note of angry annoyance in her voice.

"I know," Gloria lied.

Benny

Myla and Sadeen looked at each other. "The thing is," Sadeen said, holding out his phone for her to see, "our doorbell cam caught it."

He played the video, and Gloria's heart sank as she saw her grandmother crawl out of the bushes to the left of the Lhasas' front porch on her hands and knees. She was wearing the white shift, and though the background of the video was dark, the foreground was well-lit by porch-light, and her face was clearly visible. The timestamp said: *2:46 a.m.*

From the right side of the porch, Myla and Sadeen's cat—

Benny

—strolled over. The fluffy orange tabby sidled affectionately up to her grandmother, who promptly shifted to a sitting position, picked up the animal with both hands and twisted off its head. Blood spurted onto the corner of the welcome mat visible to the camera and the cement of the stoop. Her grandma tossed the body into the bushes from which she had crawled, rolled the head in the opposite direction, then stood, smiling crazily, and ran into the darkness toward the street.

Gloria felt sick to her stomach, and her arms were covered with goosebumps.

"We're going to show this to the police," Sadeen said. "But we thought you ought to see it first."

"She's sick!" Myla said, and there was fear beneath her anger. "There's something wrong with her!"

Gloria glanced back at the closed door behind her. "I know."

"She needs to be put away!"

"You're right," Gloria said. "Take that to the police. Show them."

Myla and Sadeen looked at each other.

"There *is* something wrong with her," she told them. "And it's not something I can handle myself. Show that to the police." Gloria suddenly realized that, with Benjamin in the shower, Jeannie was alone with her grandmother. "I have to go," she said, turning to open the door. "And I'm sorry about Benny. Really."

Once inside, Gloria smiled at Jeannie, seated on the floor. "Stay there, sweetie. I need to talk to Gram-Gram."

Jeannie didn't even look up. "Okay."

Gloria walked into the kitchen. There was a *thunk* beneath her feet as Benjamin shut the shower off in the bathroom and water stopped flowing through the pipes. Her grandmother, putting butter, orange juice, jam and milk back into the refrigerator had her back to the door. "The Lhasas showed me footage from their security camera. You killed their cat."

"Did I?" Her grandmother still did not turn around, and Gloria was suddenly filled with the certainty that when she did, her face would be that of a monster.

"Look at me when I'm talking to you!"

The old lady closed the refrigerator door and turned to face her. She looked the same as she always did. "I told you not to marry him," she said calmly.

"Benjamin, Jeannie and I are going to move into Benjamin's house," Gloria said, pointing her finger. "You can stay here. But you are not to have any contact with Jeannie, do you understand me? No contact. If you so much as call our phone, I'm going to get a restraining order against you, and I'll have you kicked out onto the street."

"Your own grandma?" She smiled.

"And, by the way, the Lhasas are showing their footage to the police. So you'll be lucky if you don't end up in jail."

The smile grew wider. "Or a mental hospital?"

"That's where you really belong."

"I'm going to kill him. You know that, don't you?"

Gloria's breath caught in her throat.

Her grandmother stroked her chin in perfect parody of a person thinking. "I just haven't figured out how, yet. Should I get it over with quickly or make him suffer?"

Gloria backed slowly away. "You're crazy."

"Maybe so," her grandma admitted. "Maybe so. But that doesn't change the fact that your loving hubby is not going to last the month." She leaned forward, her expression one of sudden intensity. "He's supposed to be dead! He needs to die!"

Gloria turned and strode purposefully out of the kitchen. "Jeannie!" she shouted. "Get out of your PJs and put your clothes on!"

"But I'm watching—"

"Now!"

She ushered her daughter down the hall and closed the bedroom door once Jeannie was inside. "I'll be back in a minute to help you pack. Don't let Gram-Gram in."

"Where are we going?" Jeannie called from behind the closed door.

"We're moving."

"Is Gram-Gram really crazy?"

Little pitchers, Gloria thought. "Yes she is," she said. "That's why we're leaving." She pushed open the door of the bathroom across the hall. Benjamin was in his underwear and shaving. Leftover steam from the shower still fogged up the small space. Their eyes met in the distorting wetness of the medicine cabinet mirror. "We need to go," Gloria said quietly. "I'll tell you why on the way. Just hurry up and get dressed so we can get out of here."

"On the way where?" Benjamin asked, wiping shaving cream off his face with a washcloth.

"Your house. We're moving there."

He lowered his voice. "Is it your grandma?"

"I'll tell you later. Just get dressed and get packed so we can go. I'm going to help Jeannie with her suitcase."

Fifteen minutes later, they were packed and ready to leave. They were taking only the basic necessities—she and Benjamin would come back for the rest of their things at a later time, hopefully when Jeannie was in school and Gram-Gram was locked up—and they loaded their suitcases in the car without saying goodbye. She assumed her grandmother was still in the kitchen, but Gloria was not about to check; she did not want to see the woman.

Benjamin's house was dirty and musty, but it felt instantly welcoming. Upon arrival, Gloria immediately felt as though she'd come home. Her own house was strange to her now, and she never wanted to go back.

In her mind, she saw her grandmother squirming over the bedroom windowsill in her shift, saw her in the security footage twisting off the tabby cat's head and smiling crazily as she bowled it off the Lhasas' stoop.

Gloria shivered.

She had no idea what was going on here. Except...on some level, it felt like she did. Or, rather, that she *should*. Beneath the worry, horror and incomprehension, there was, for some reason, a lack of surprise. What she'd seen had shocked her, but it was not as unbelievable as it should have been, and Gloria understood that she was reacting far more calmly than the situation called for or than a person would ordinarily.

The three of them spent the rest of the morning opening up the house and terraforming it to the needs of their family. Gloria could tell that Benjamin wanted a more complete description of what was going on than she'd been able to give him, but he also knew that she could not give him that description with Jeannie around, and she loved him for his understanding. Finally, just before lunch, Jeannie announced that she had to go to the bathroom, and Benjamin told her to use the one off the master bedroom, it was cleaner. As soon as Jeannie was gone, he turned to look at Gloria, eyebrow raised quizzically.

"You'd better sit down," she said. "You're not going to believe this."

NINE

Her grandmother was gone by the time the police arrived.

Gloria found this out from Myla and Sadeen when she returned the next day with Benjamin to pick up more of their stuff. She had taken Jeannie to her friend Susan's house, not wanting her daughter to be exposed to...whatever might happen.

But nothing did happen. Her grandma was gone, and from what Gloria could tell, the old woman had taken nothing with her. How she had left and where she had disappeared to was a mystery. Her grandmother had no car, no nearby relatives and, as far as Gloria knew, all of her old friends were dead. She had taken off somewhere, though, and Gloria assumed the police were looking for her whereabouts, although finding her was probably a low priority. No doubt they had much more urgent crimes to deal with.

It made Gloria uneasy, however, knowing her grandma was out there somewhere. She imagined the old lady hiding in some small space all day long, like a nocturnal animal, then emerging at night, crawling through the city wearing only her bloody shift, twisting the heads off various pets.

Did her grandmother know the location of Benjamin's house?

Gloria didn't think so, and for that she was grateful.

"I'm going to kill him. You know that, don't you?"

Her biggest concern was that Benjamin didn't seem to be taking the threat seriously enough. Oh, he believed that her grandma was crazy. And he had always known that she didn't like him. But, considering what she'd done to the Lhasas' cat, he should have been more worried.

"We'll be fine," he assured her.

Gloria was not quite so confident.

But as the days passed and there was no sign of her grandmother, she began to relax a little. Not a lot, but a little. She would still not let Jeannie out of her sight, walking her all the way to her classroom each morning, arriving early to pick her up after school, though "Gram-Gram" had made no threats against the girl. And she still made Benjamin call her from work during his breaks and at lunch, while also keeping her apprised of his whereabouts at all times. But she started to allow herself to hope that her grandmother was gone for good.

The best case scenario? The old lady was dead.

Gloria felt awful for even considering such a thought, but it was the truth.

On the fourth Saturday after they'd moved out, exactly a month after her grandma had disappeared, Gloria awoke feeling good. The feeling of oppression that usually settled over her upon wakening did not arrive, and the sense of contentment engendered by last night's lovemaking still held sway. The delicious smell of waffles wafting in from the kitchen made her feel—

Smell of waffles?

Gloria sat up, wide awake, realizing only at that moment that Benjamin was not in the bed next to her. She saw instantly that he was not in the bathroom either, and without bothering to dress or put on a robe, Gloria rushed over to Jeannie's room.

It was empty.

"Jeannie!" she cried.

"I'm in the kitchen with Gram-Gram!"

Gram-Gram

Gloria's stomach dropped. "Benjamin!" she called. "Benjamin!" She was not strong enough to face her grandmother alone, and she ran through the house looking for Benjamin, but he was nowhere to be found.

"Mommy!"

Was that fear in her daughter's voice? Gloria ran into the kitchen, where her grandmother had opened the waffle iron and was placing a waffle on Jeannie's plate. She smiled at Gloria. "Tough time waking up, sleepyhead?"

"Where's Benjamin?" Gloria asked with barely controlled emotion. It hadn't been fear in her daughter's voice, she realized. The girl thought everything was normal.

Jeannie looked puzzled. "Who's Benjamin?" She turned to her Gram-Gram, and the old lady shrugged to indicate her confusion.

But Gloria met her grandmother's eyes and knew that she knew.

"We're living in his house," Gloria told her daughter.

"But this is *our* house!"

She felt strangely off balance, as though the world was shifting around her.

Again.

Benny

Gloria tried to clear her head. "Yes," she told Jeannie, "but this used to be Benjamin's house. Remember? We lived with Gram-Gram over on Putnam Street? Then me and you and Benjamin moved here?"

Jeannie was genuinely confused. "I don't *know* Benjamin. I never *met* anyone named Benjamin!"

"Maybe you just had a bad dream," her grandmother told Gloria. "Why don't you sit down? I'll make you some waffles."

"I don't *want* any damn waffles! I want *you* out of here!"

Jeannie burst into tears.

Her grandma smiled. "There's no problem that waffles can't solve."

Gloria's first instinct was to comfort her daughter, but she refused to let herself get distracted. She pointed at her grandmother. "I'm calling the police."

"Whatever for?" the old lady asked innocently.

And somehow, it turned out, the police *weren't* looking for her grandma. When Gloria called the Lhasas immediately afterward, they too seemed confused and had no idea what she was talking about, claiming they had never had a cat.

What in the world was going on here? Gloria's head hurt, and she felt completely overwhelmed. She knew she wasn't going crazy, and knew that her grandmother was aware of everything, but, somehow, the entire rest of the world had changed around them.

And Benjamin didn't exist. All of her pictures of him, in frames around the house and even on her phone, were gone. All of his entries in their shared address book had disappeared as well, and when Gloria tried to call his parents, the phone emitted a sequence of high jarring tones, and a pre-recorded voice informed her that the number she had dialed was out of service. A quick internet search brought up no names that matched those of either Benjamin or his parents.

Maybe she had a brain tumor, Gloria thought, and though she could not remember any details, she realized that this was not the first time such a notion had occurred to her.

Maybe she *did* have a brain tumor.

Despite her strong memories and even stronger feelings, empirical evidence was telling Gloria that fears of her grandmother were unfounded, but even if what she thought had happened had not really occurred, Gloria still felt it necessary to take Jeannie away from Gram-Gram. Although that was easier said than done. Jeannie had school tomorrow, and math homework that she needed to finish. Gloria herself had to go to work. Not to mention the fact that if she and her daughter took off somewhere, tried to get away, her grandmother would call the police and claim that she was unstable and endangering Jeannie, a claim that would probably seem both convincing and credible.

She took a deep breath...

and it was summer. Jeannie did not have to go to school, and Gloria was at the beginning of her usual two-week vacation.

Her grandmother would not be able to call the police simply because Gloria had taken her daughter on a trip—that's what single mothers did on holidays.

Gloria had no idea how the world had *shifted*, but she recognized that it had...and accepted it. This new reality was hers as well as everyone else's, and while she understood that it had not been this way only seconds before, it was now, and she was determined to take advantage of the situation.

Where was her grandmother right now? Gloria thought for a moment. It was after lunch, so she was in her room, taking an early afternoon nap. And Jeannie? At her friend Susan's house.

Moving swiftly and quietly, Gloria took a single suitcase from her closet, filled it with clothes for herself and Jeannie, grabbed some snacks and bottled water, some books to read, checked the wallet in her purse to make sure she had all of her credit cards as well as some spending money, wrote a quick note explaining that the two of them were going on a short trip, and left the house.

Benjamin's house

She closed the door quietly behind her, not bothering to lock it, and took the car over to Susan's, where she picked up Jeannie. It was not until they were on the freeway heading north that she told her daughter they were going on a vacation.

"We have to pick up Gram-Gram!" Jeannie exclaimed.

"Gram-Gram's not going with us. She's going to stay home and take care of things while we're gone."

"But—"

"She's old and tired. She doesn't want to go on a trip."

"But we can call her!"

"Sure, sure," Gloria said, and surreptitiously reached into her purse on the seat next to her to make sure her phone was turned off. She didn't want her grandmother to call and try to figure out where they'd gone.

Where *were* they going?

She didn't know herself, but some inner navigator was urging her north, so that was the direction she drove.

Thankfully, the car had a satellite radio, so their stations didn't die out past the Grapevine, and the constant stream of kids' music kept Jeannie entertained. After awhile, tiring of the scenery, Jeannie asked if she could use her mom's phone to play a game, but Gloria told her that they needed to keep the phone turned off and charged up in case they had car problems. They did have books, however, and Jeannie rummaged through the book bag in the space between them, happy to find not only the second Harry Potter book, which she was currently reading, but all of the others as well.

They stopped for the evening at a Holiday Inn off the side of the freeway in Fresno. In the room, while Jeannie lay on one of the two beds, flipping channels on the television, Gloria turned on her phone for the first time since they'd left. As she suspected, her grandmother had left numerous messages—twelve to be exact—and Gloria turned the phone off without listening to any of them.

What was her plan for tomorrow? She didn't know, and she didn't care, and not knowing and not caring somehow made her feel happy. She tickled Jeannie's toes. "Come on, lazybones. Let's get something to eat."

There was a pizza place across the street from the hotel, and they ordered two Cokes and a pizza with olives, but when a girl's soccer team burst into the pizza parlor, commandeered three tables and began boisterously shouting at each other, Gloria asked if they could get their food to go. They ate in the room, watching *Willy Wonka and the Chocolate Factory,* a movie they'd both seen a million times but never tired of, on a local station with far too many commercials.

In the morning, they woke late, ate a leisurely breakfast, then continued on.

"Where are we going?" Jeannie asked.

"You'll see," Gloria said mysteriously, but the truth was that she didn't know. Although she had no destination in mind, it seemed to her that she was headed *someplace*, and rather than follow her usual anal-retentive instincts and go online to get specific directions to a specific location, she simply drove north, turning off the highway when it seemed she should, taking increasingly smaller roads that felt as though they led to the sort of place where she would like to be.

In the late afternoon, after passing through a series of small foothill towns, many little more than a wide spot in the road, as her grandma would say, they entered the improbably named Hicksville. While still small, Hicksville at least had gas stations and grocery stores, a shopping center and a motel, as well as several restaurants.

"Are we staying here tonight?" Jeannie asked dubiously. She hadn't spoken much on the trip today; in fact, Gloria wasn't sure either of them had said a word since lunch.

"Maybe." Gloria slowed the car and looked around. It had not occurred to her that they might spend the night in this town, but now that her daughter had mentioned it, this did seem like an appropriate place to stop for the day. "Why don't we get out and stretch our legs," she suggested.

Gloria parked in the lot of the small shopping center, which contained a Dollar Tree, a donut shop, a closed real estate office and a hardware store. After being in the car for so long, her legs were cramped, and it felt good to be able to walk again. Jeannie, too, was moving slowly, acting as though she was not used to being on her feet.

Ordinarily, Gloria supposed, the two of them would have checked out one of the stores or gone into a restaurant to get something to eat, but her gaze turned away from what passed for Hicksville's downtown and toward an exposed section of granite cliff on the otherwise wooded hillside at the far end of Main Street. She had seen this view before, although whether in dream or reality she could not say. It felt familiar, though. The whole town felt familiar, and Gloria realized that she felt comfortable here, at home in these environs.

Taking Jeannie's hand, she walked past a Mexican restaurant (also familiar) and up to an intersection, where she turned left on a narrow barely paved road. There was not much to the town—it was barely wider than its Main Street—and what there was seemed exactly like what a person would expect from a place called Hicksville, but that was merely superficial overlay on land of an underlying beauty. Walking past a tire yard where a shirtless bald man sat in a broken lawn chair facing the road, Gloria felt like a woman contemplating buying a house, looking beyond its shallow exterior to the bones of the structure underneath. And Hicksville had good bones. She knew it. She could feel it.

They had passed the tire yard and were now in front of a vacant lot. At the rear of the lot was a line of tall trees, and in front of the trees stood a small wooden shed only slightly larger than an outhouse. A feeling of contentment washed over her as she stared at the lot. Odd, disjointed thoughts floated through her mind: *There should be six more trees. I want to take off my shoes and feel the grass on my feet. There used to be a pond where the tire yard is. It doesn't work when it rains.*

As if in a daze, Gloria walked up a narrow dirt path through the gently sloping lot toward the shed. She was still holding Jeannie's hand, but neither of them had said a word to each other since leaving the main street, and for some reason there didn't seem anything unusual about that.

A man emerged from the open doorway of the small building, an elderly man with salt-and-pepper hair and a bushy gray mustache dressed in a blue business suit. "Are you Gloria Jaymes?" he called out.

Her first instinct was to run, but she stopped herself, suddenly overcome by the odd and disorienting sensation that she had done this before, that this was not the first time she had been here nor the first time she had attempted to flee from this man.

These *men.*

For other men in suits were following the first one out the door of the shed.

Gloria looked down at Jeannie...and her daughter was gone. Her right hand was a fist stretched out and holding nothing. She should have been panicking, but instead felt strangely calm. Even Jeannie's disappearance seemed an echo of something that had previously occurred.

She stood in place, facing the man.

The men.

"Who are you?" she demanded.

"Are you Gloria Jaymes?" The man with the mustache—*Russell,* she thought. *His name is Russell*—squinted at her. "Your hair looks different."

"Who are you?" she demanded again.

"We're the ones who believe in you," he said.

Something told her she didn't want to hear any more. She turned away from them, and in her peripheral vision something shimmered.

"No!" Russell cried.

FIVE

ONE

Benjamin.

Gloria was filled with an almost unbearable joy as she looked upon his face. It was as if she hadn't seen him in years, though she knew it had been less than a half-hour since he'd gone to the store to pick up extra snacks for the party. Throwing her arms about his neck, she gave him a kiss, a big open-mouthed newlywed kiss, not the perfunctory sort of peck that had become their custom.

"Hey," he said, laughing. "What's that all about?"

She adored his laugh.

"Nothing. I just wanted to show how much I love you."

"You're acting weird," he said.

The doorbell rang, their first guests beginning to arrive, and Benjamin went out to greet them. It was Lucas and Jean, bearing a bottle of cheap wine that was unopened even though both of them were already slightly tipsy, and they were quickly followed by Paul and Myka, whose contribution to the potluck was a single small can of Planter's peanuts. Thank God Benjamin had gone out for extra snacks.

Fortunately, the remainder of their guests brought the main dishes they'd been assigned, and once everyone had arrived, Gloria set all of the food and drink on the dining room table. "Help yourselves," she told them.

She watched as their friends piled chips, tamales, and macaroni and cheese on their paper plates. This world was new to her. It felt as though she had lived here all her life, as though she'd known these people for years, as though this house had been her family's since childhood, but Gloria understood that was not the case. She had a half-memory of other houses, other people, brothers and sisters, sons and daughters, parents and grandparents. Some of the impressions were not so nice, but others were, and in her mind everything was jumbled up into one chaotic mishmash. Only Benjamin remained clear, and she looked at him now and realized that he was the reason she was here.

She needed to save him.

In this life, Gloria thought that she and Benjamin had been going through a rough patch—had he cheated on her? Had *she* cheated on *him*?—but something told her that that was a misleading memory. She was *supposed* to think that the two of them were on the outs, even though it wasn't necessarily true. Why that was the case, she had no idea, but the fact that she could see through it gave Gloria hope.

Benjamin passed by with a drink in hand, touching her shoulder, the silent shorthand reminding her to mingle with their guests in order to make sure everyone had a good time. He headed off toward a raucous group of men hanging out in the kitchen, so Gloria went in the opposite direction, into the living room.

Jean, who was going through some sort of new-agey phase, was talking to Myka about *convergences*.

"For example, the world's first two amusement parks—Knott's Berry Farm and Disneyland—were both built here in Orange County by two men both named Walter. Isn't that amazing? It's why I don't believe in coincidences, why I think fate, God, the universe, whatever you want to call it, comes together in certain places at certain points in time to make sure that what is supposed to happen happens."

Gloria didn't believe in coincidences, either. But she didn't want to talk about it with Jean. Caught listening in, she smiled politely when the two women glanced over at her, and moved on.

Next to the piano, a group of three men were listening to Benjamin's pompous friend Ron hold forth. "I saw *Lawrence of Arabia* when I was ten, and I think that's the perfect age. I knew nothing of geopolitics, had no idea where Arabia was or anything about the Middle East. The whole thing was as exotic as an alien planet to me. Even the British culture at the beginning that was supposed to keep me grounded was exotic, and that's the best way to see a film like that, with no moorings, no preconceptions."

No moorings, no preconceptions. That was exactly how she felt, and the fact that each conversation she encountered seemed to have import in regard to her, specific connections to her life, made Gloria wonder if this entire party was an artificial construct put on for her benefit.

But by whom?

A conversation on her right between a man and woman Gloria didn't know grabbed her attention.

"I went to the Orange antique circle on my lunch hour," the woman was saying, "and you know what they were selling in one of the stores?"

"What?"

"Bob Hope's poop basket."

The man laughed. "What the hell's a 'poop basket?'"

"I don't know, but that's what the sign said. I assume it was something he used when he was old, maybe he was incontinent..."

"You really think it belonged to Bob Hope? He lived in Palm Springs. How would it end up in Orange?" The man shook his head. "Sounds like a scam to me. What did it look like?"

"It was just a regular plastic bucket. I don't think it was even that old."

"And they were pawning it off as Bob Hope's poop basket?" He couldn't stop laughing.

Finally, a conversation that had no significance whatsoever and no relation at all to her. Gloria breathed a sigh of relief. Maybe *none* of the conversations had anything to do with her and she had only imagined that there were correlations. It was possible. More than possible. She was navigating a world that was both new and old, familiar and unfamiliar at the same time. There were bound to be moments of disassociation.

She was sure about her purpose, however. She needed to protect her husband. Someone somewhere sometime was going to go after Benjamin and try to kill him, and while she didn't think it was one of their guests, she didn't *not* think it was one of their guests. The threat could come from anyone, and it was her job to be vigilant and make sure her husband was not killed.

The way he had been before.

What made her think that? Gloria wasn't sure, but she believed it utterly. He *had* been killed, and she had been there, and while she recalled none of the specifics, the emotional memory of losing him was a permanent part of her.

Suddenly, she didn't want to be at the party anymore. She felt claustrophobic, and the thought of making idle chitchat for the next several hours with these people she did/did not know filled her with dismay. Excusing herself from a couple who had just walked up to speak with her—Tish and Jose Ramirez—Gloria went into the master bathroom and locked herself in. Their bedroom and bathroom were off limits to their guests, so as long as she stayed, she wouldn't be disturbed.

Sitting on the closed lid of the toilet, she slumped down, breathing deeply. The party was just getting started, and she couldn't hide in here forever, but, at least for the moment, it felt good to be out of the maelstrom. She had a brief flash of rooms in previous homes: a well-appointed yuppie kitchen with a center island, a small narrow bathroom, a children's bedroom with two boys' beds. She recognized and remembered them all, although she wasn't sure if any were from the same house.

Gloria looked up at the ceiling. She should have brought a book or magazine or her phone. As it was, she eventually began to grow restless, and when she looked at her watch, expecting at least forty-five minutes to have passed, she found that it had only been ten. Putting up with unwanted guests no longer seemed quite so onerous, and Gloria checked her face in the mirror, patted down her hair and rejoined the party, where she ended up actually enjoying herself. By the time the last guests left—Lucas and Jean, as it turned out—that weird feeling of discomfiture seemed to have passed.

It was nice to have Benjamin all to herself, and while he was a little standoffish at first—

Had he cheated on her? Had she cheated on him?

—he quickly loosened up, and they were soon at ease with each other, laughing and joking the way they used to as they cleaned the after-party mess left behind by their friends.

"Did you notice anything weird tonight?" Benjamin asked after taking a Hefty bag filled with recyclables out to the garage.

"Like what?"

"No one talked about their kids. Usually, everyone talks about their kids. But it was like they'd all decided ahead of time not to even bring up the subject."

"Huh," Gloria said.

"Not just that, but there was no real *personal* talk. Did you notice? I picked up on it after about the first hour. I mean, it was a party not a therapy session, and I didn't expect everyone to go all Morris Albert, but it was weird, you know? Like it was a fake party and people were just acting out the roles they were supposed to play instead of being who they really are. Not that I didn't have fun," he added quickly. "I didn't mean that. It was a great party. It was just...weird."

What was weird, Gloria thought, was the Morris Albert reference. Benjamin was born in 1982. Albert had been an easy-listening one-hit wonder in the early 1970s with the song "Feelings." How would her husband even know about that? It wasn't as though he was a big music aficionado. Why would he mention that so obliquely in such a casual conversation? Why would he assume *she* knew who Morris Albert was?

Why *did* she know who Morris Albert was?

She was born in 1984.

She felt off-balance again. Maybe the party *had* been fake. Maybe all of this was fake. Maybe...

"Gloria?"

She looked over at him. "Yes?"

He seemed hesitant. "Do you think...? I mean...what if they were just being polite, you know? We've been trying, and I know we haven't advertised it, but you've probably told your friends, and I might've mentioned it to Paul... Could be they just didn't want to, I don't know, hurt our feelings or make us feel bad or rub it in or whatever..."

Had they been trying to have a baby?

They had, Gloria realized, and had not been successful so far, a state of affairs that weighed heavily upon Benjamin's mind. A wave of sympathy and compassion swept over her, an emotionally protective feeling toward her husband, and she shoved the used napkins she'd been gathering into the trash bag at her side and threw her arms around him, hugging him as hard as she could. The solidity of his body felt warm and comforting, and once again she was filled with an almost overpowering love for him. She reached between his legs, cupping him, and was gratified to feel a stirring. "Why don't we try again?"

"Now?" He looked around the still messy kitchen.

"Now," she said, and pulled him down onto the dirty floor.

They worked for different employers in different cities, although she knew that in other places, other times, that had not been the case. He was Computer Operations Supervisor for a firm that made rubber floor mats and was headquartered in Irvine. She taught Nursing at UC Brea.

Benjamin was already up and eating breakfast by the time she awoke—it was their usual routine; he had to wake up earlier because he had farther to drive, while she craved that little bit of extra sleep—and Gloria quickly pulled on her underwear and slipped into a robe, wanting to see him before he left. He looked up in surprise as she entered the kitchen. "Thought you were going to sleep in a little longer." He smiled, almost shyly. "After last night."

Laughing, she threw her arms around him. "I just wanted to see you before you go."

"It's my late night again. David's still out, so I have to run all the backups myself. I won't be home until eleven or so."

"I'll wait up," she said.

"I was hoping you'd say that." He glanced at the wall clock above the stove. "Whoa. I'd better brush and get dressed." He quickly finished his coffee, gave her a quick kiss, then hurried back to the bedroom.

Gloria moved over to the sink and stared out the window at the Chins' house next door. The Chinese family had moved in only a month ago, but already they'd had the house repainted and both the front and back yards landscaped. They had to have money. Benjamin's hand touched her shoulder, and she jumped, startled. "Gotta go," he said.

What? He was fully dressed, face shaved and hair combed, and his briefcase was in his hand. She could have sworn that she had been looking outside for only a few seconds, but when she glanced over at the clock, she saw that fifteen minutes had passed. How was that possible?

Benjamin kissed her on the lips, then on the forehead. "See you tonight," he said. "Remember, I'll be late."

"I'll be here." She walked with him to the door, waving goodbye, and didn't close it until he'd backed out of the driveway and was gone. Gloria still had an hour before she had to leave, plenty of time to eat breakfast, shower and get ready—as long as she didn't drift off into a fugue state.

What the hell had that been?

She was pretty sure she'd never experienced anything like it before, and walking back into the kitchen, she was almost afraid to look out the window for fear it might happen again. She did look out the window, however, as a test, and was relieved when she peered out at the Chins' house, then turned back to glance at the clock and saw that only a few seconds had passed.

Relaxing a little, she made herself some toast and orange juice, checking her phone for news while she ate. There was a nagging thought in the back of her mind that something was different about the house this morning, that something within it had changed during the night. She had no idea what had put such an idea in her head or what aspect of their home could possibly have been altered, but the notion made her uneasy, and, leaving her unfinished orange juice on the kitchen table, she moved slowly from room to room, looking for anything that seemed odd or out of place.

She found it in the hallway, between the guest room and the den.

A closet.

That was strange. Gloria could not remember seeing the closet before, but here it was, and even as her eyes remained locked on the closed door, she found herself backing away from it. She didn't like that door. She found the wooden rectangle unsettling, its brass knob too shiny, its hinges too dingy. Even the size of the door was off, thinner than seemed proportionally correct, and Gloria wondered what such a narrow closet could have been designed for and why it should be situated in the middle of the hallway. She found herself overcome by the conviction that she had not noticed it before because it had not *been* here before.

How did she even know there was a closet behind that door?

Because she did.

The house seemed abnormally quiet. She wished she'd turned on the radio in the kitchen or the television in the living room. She wished Benjamin was here. The silence reinforced the fact that she was all alone, and Gloria considered simply getting dressed and going to work, but she needed to take a shower, and even though she could lock the bathroom, there was no way she was going to place herself in such a state of vulnerability without first looking behind that awful door.

The sound of Mr. Chin saying goodbye to his wife next door, their voices faint but clear, made her feel not so alone and gave Gloria the courage she needed. Steeling herself, she sucked in her breath, moved forward, took the too-shiny knob in her hand and turned.

Behind the door there was indeed a closet, empty, but unpleasantly so, as though whatever wretched thing had been stored in the small space had been absorbed into it, *eaten* by the little room. There was no overhead light, no light at all, but the enclosed area was so small that Gloria could see everything clearly. Not that there was anything to see: three narrow off-white walls and a strangely sloping ceiling that made it appear as though the closet had been built under a stairwell.

Gloria closed the door, stepping back. She didn't like the closet, didn't like the way it looked, didn't like where it was located, didn't like the fact that it existed at all. She was curious to know if Benjamin was aware of it and was almost tempted to call him, but was suddenly filled with the certainty that that's what the closet *wanted* her to do. She imagined Benjamin answering the phone while speeding along the freeway, then getting into an accident and dying horrifically in an explosive car crash.

Gloria returned to the kitchen, took one of the chairs from the table and carried it out to the hall. She tilted the chair under the closet's doorknob to keep the door closed. There wasn't anything in there, but if there had been, it would not be able to get out, and the small unnecessary precaution made Gloria feel a little safer. She took a quick shower (in the master bathroom, locking both the bedroom door and the bathroom door), got ready as quickly as she could, and was on her way ten minutes early. Getting into the car, she realized that not only had she forgotten to bring a lunch, but she had also forgotten to clean the breakfast crumbs off the kitchen table. There'd probably be ants when she returned, but at the moment that seemed preferable to going back into the house, and she backed out of the driveway onto the street, deciding she would buy lunch today in the university's food court.

This was not a good night for Benjamin to be coming home late. After her classes, Gloria remained on campus for office hours, then hit Whole Foods on her way home since they were having a sale on kale and mangoes, but when she arrived back at the house, it was dark. Something had gone wrong with the timer, so all of the lights were off. She really didn't want to go inside alone, but none of her close friends lived nearby, and she didn't feel comfortable imposing on any of the neighbors. She wished Benjamin were here (ironic, as she was the one who was supposed to be protecting *him*). Since he wasn't, however, she forced herself to open the door and step inside.

The first thing she did, after turning on all the lights, was to check the closet. It was still there, still unsettling in its appearance and dimensions, still completely empty in that *voracious* way she found so disturbing. Her fear of the space seemed to have abated, however. She didn't *like* it, but she wasn't *frightened* of it. She could coexist with it. Relieved by this reaction, she went to the bathroom, then passed back through the hall without incident on her way to the kitchen, where she heated herself up a Lean Cuisine.

Following dinner, Gloria went out to the living room. There were actually tests she needed to grade, but she wasn't in the mood and scrolled through the DVR list to see if they'd recorded anything she wanted to watch. The room around her was familiar and unfamiliar at the same time. She remembered going to Lamps Plus and picking out the standing lamp, buying the sofa and loveseat at Ikea, finding the rest of the furnishings at different stores and bringing them home, but this definitely wasn't her favorite living room. It was her taste, but a *version* of her taste, and not the one she preferred.

Her eye was drawn to the wall above the television. Next to an antique wall-hanging they'd found on their honeymoon in Monterey was a framed pencil sketch of a small shack with a line of tall pine trees behind it. They'd bought it at a gallery in Laguna Beach, she recalled, but...there seemed something different about it now. Moving forward and squinting, she peered more closely at the picture.

There was a small figure standing just to the right of the little shack.

There'd never been any figure in the drawing before.

It was almost too small to see, and Gloria went into the next room, digging through the middle drawer of her desk, pushing aside pencils, pens and paperclips until she found the magnifying glass she sometimes used to read the fine print on coupons. Holding it up to the picture and moving it until the figure was in focus, she was finally able to see the surprisingly detailed particulars of the tiny form. It was a man, a man with long uncombed hair dressed in a business suit and staring out at her. His eyes were wild, showing too much white, and he was smiling, a too-wide grin that seemed predatory, gleeful and crazy all at the same time.

Shocked, Gloria pulled back.

And saw two other figures standing on the other side of the shack. Two women.

Even without using the magnifying glass, she knew that they, too, were grinning in the same horrible way, and in her head she heard the harsh mad chortle that would accompany those terrible smiles.

A rattling of the lock on the front door made Gloria jump. The door opened, and Benjamin walked in, looking tired. She threw her arms around him, grateful for his return.

"What's this all about?" he asked.

Between the closet and the drawing, it had been a stressful day, and though she didn't want to tell Benjamin about any of it, Gloria decided the best thing was to be open and honest. She told him everything, from the beginning, and when she was through, he laughed. "That closet?" he said. "It's always been there. I was going to turn it into a darkroom when I got into photography and was still using film and thought I was going to make my own prints, remember?"

And, suddenly, she did.

How could she have forgotten?

"Then why haven't we used it for anything? We have all that crap in the garage. We could've stored some of it in the closet."

Benjamin shrugged. "I don't know. Now let me see that picture." He walked over to the wall, putting his face close to the frame. "I don't see anything."

"To either side of that shack."

"There's nothing there," he told her. "You imagined it."

She hadn't imagined it, there *had* been something there, but Gloria knew that when she looked at the drawing, the figures would be gone. And they were. She had no idea why it had happened or what it meant, but the experience had made her wary, and while she pretended for Benjamin's sake that it was probably the result of tiredness, she knew it was not.

"You're right," she lied.

"Told you." He gave her a quick kiss. "Is there anything to eat? I'm starving."

TWO

There were so many ways a person could die.

Gloria found herself living in a constant state of stress, worrying about what might happen to Benjamin. Many of her fears—*most* of them—were irrational and overwrought, ridiculous improbabilities that would never happen in a hundred years.

But they were still possible.

And if this turned out to be that hundred-and-first year...

When Benjamin walked outside to pick up the newspaper in the morning, he could trip over the hose, fall flat on his face and split his head open on the sidewalk, dying instantly. Driving to work, he might get into an accident, slam into the vehicle in front of him and be speared through by his car's steering column. He could be decapitated by an insufficiently fastened pipe flying off the back of a flatbed truck on the freeway. At work, a disgruntled co-worker might shoot up the entire office. He could be waiting in traffic beneath a bridge when an earthquake hit, and the bridge could collapse, squishing him. A mentally ill homeless man might hit him with a length of pipe while Benjamin was giving him a dollar for food. His McDonald's lunch could be the final straw that caused him to have a heart attack.

There was nothing she could do about any of that, which left her feeling useless and hopeless. But there were other, more obvious and identifiable threats that she *could* thwart, and Gloria concentrated her energies on stopping those.

So when Paul and Myka invited them out one Friday evening to a trendy new Asian fusion restaurant located in Little Saigon across the street from where a Vietnamese gang shooting had occurred the previous weekend, Gloria declined for both of them. And when they were about to walk across an intersection after their light turned green, and a red Porsche speeding up the street did not look like it was slowing down, she grabbed his hand and held him in place, even though he said, "Don't worry. They'll stop." The car did not stop, and Benjamin looked at her, eyes wide. "That asshole would've killed us."

"I know," she said.

There were no more creepy pictures, though, no more mysterious closets or doors. Life went on normally, and if they'd been going through a rough patch in that time before the party, a time that seemed oddly distant, as though she'd read about it rather than experienced it, they were experiencing a new golden age now, and she could not recall the two of them spending so much time together since the first idyllic year of their marriage.

Gloria was off for Arbor Day, a holiday that no employer save her school seemed to celebrate, and was curled up on the couch, catching up on the last Stephen King book, which she'd bought several weeks ago but hadn't yet had the time to crack open, when Benjamin called from work. "Just a heads up," he told her.

"What is it?"

He needed to go to Seattle for a weekend conference.

A trip? On an airplane? The very thought of it raised a red flag.

"You can't," Gloria told him.

She was overcome by a feeling extremely close to panic, and he must have sensed it because he said, "It's just me, Lucas and Brady.

And it's only two days, really. We'd be leaving Friday around noon and getting back Sunday around one or two. This is strictly business. We wouldn't even have time to get into trouble."

He must have thought she was worried about him seeing another woman, but that wasn't it at all.

The plane's going to go down.

She knew it as certainly as she knew her own name. It had happened before and was going to happen again unless she did something to stop it. "Listen to me," she said carefully. "Remember when I told you that Ron's dad was going to die? That I had a dream about it and he was going to have acid reflux and choke to death in his sleep?"

Had that happened this time or in a previous life?

"Of course," Benjamin said, and she breathed a sigh of relief.

"Well, I had a dream about this." She spoke as levelly as possible, making sure her voice reflected the seriousness of her concern. "That plane is going to crash. Everyone on board is going to die. If you are on it, you will die."

He started to laugh it off. "Glore—"

"You. Will. Die. Do you understand? I do *not* want you to get on that plane. I do *not* want you to go on that trip. Do I make myself clear?"

He definitely believed that she believed, and that, no doubt, was the reason he did not respond. Gloria could only hope that the intensity of her reaction was able to convince him not only of her sincerity but of the validity of her fears.

"Call in sick," she told him. "Claim a prior engagement. Do what you have to do. Say your sister's getting married, say my mom died. But do not get on that plane."

"It's just a seminar," he said weakly.

"I don't care."

They continued the discussion, but she had already won, and by the end of the call he had promised her that he would get out of the trip.

Gloria hung up the phone, her hands shaking. Benjamin was senior enough in the company and had an important enough position that missing a seminar, even a required one, was not going to affect his career. So he'd be able to get out of it this time. But what about next time? And the time after that? Other things were going to come up, other chances for him to die, and she had to be vigilant in making sure that her husband was not led into temptation but was delivered from evil. As anxiety-producing as it might be, Gloria knew that she was going to have to spend the rest of her life protecting him.

Benjamin never did tell her what excuse he used to get out of the trip, but he was safely home with her all weekend, and Sunday afternoon, the first thing he did was text Lucas to ask how the seminar had gone. Although that was not the real reason for the text. The real reason was to find out if he and Brady had survived the flight—and they both had. Neither the plane going to or coming from Seattle had crashed.

He pointed this out to her with only a slightly patronizing attitude, but she knew, with the same certainty that she had known the flight would go down, that the plane *would* have crashed had Benjamin been on it. That was something she would never be able to prove, but she knew it was true, and the fact that she had managed to change the outcome gave her a renewed sense of hope.

Benjamin was alive.

They had not been able to kill him.

But who were *they*?

She didn't know.

She made him a special dinner that night, then submitted to something in bed that he liked and she didn't, to let him know how much she appreciated his sacrifice. Although, it wasn't really a sacrifice. *Compliance.* She appreciated his compliance.

Another plane did go down the day after, en route from Tacoma to San Francisco, killing all 175 people on board, and the parallels were close enough to her warning that Gloria was pretty sure she had regained the credibility for Benjamin to listen to her the next time.

Because there would definitely be a next time.

Of that she was certain.

Life continued on in its weirdly dichotomous way, as though she'd been dropped into this life from somewhere else, knowing everything about her existence here while retaining only occasional flashes of memory from other times and other places. At work, she gave lectures on nursing, assigned readings and answered questions, but she didn't feel as though she should actually know anything about nursing. She was supposed to be someone else, she thought, with different skills, different interests, different knowledge. Even in her own home, while she was familiar with everything, it felt awkward, as though this was not really her house and not really her life.

Only her times with Benjamin felt right, and the happiness she experienced while being with him made all of the other discomfort worth it.

Gloria was still trying, without luck, to get pregnant, and they decided to throw away the ovulation schedule and just do it every night rather than stick to the rut they'd fallen into. The increased sex improved both of their moods—what was it that Big Momma said in *Cat on a Hot Tin Roof*? When a marriage was rocky, those rocks were usually in the marriage bed?—and it was a euphoria that Gloria hoped would never end.

But the following Monday, they ate dinner while watching the evening news, the way they always did, and she sensed an odd tension in the air. She put down her fork and studied him while he ate his lasagna. "Okay, what's wrong?" Gloria asked finally.

He looked up at her. "Nothing. Why?"

"Come on," she said. "I know you."

He hesitated.

"Benjamin," she prodded.

"It's probably nothing. I'm probably just tired." He laughed ruefully. "Hopefully, I don't have a brain tumor."

"What is it?"

"I saw my parents today."

Neither of them said anything for a moment. Gloria felt a cold shiver run down her spine.

"They were standing on a corner, waiting to cross a street."

"Maybe it was two people who looked like your parents."

"It probably was," he conceded.

"But you don't think so."

Benjamin was silent.

"I believe you," Gloria said quietly.

"It couldn't've been them, though. They're dead."

"It was. You know it was." She paused. "I know it, too."

They looked at each other across the table.

"What's going on here?" Benjamin asked. "That plane you didn't want me to go on. Your thing with that drawing and the hall closet. This. It's your turn to come clean."

"There's nothing to come clean about."

"You know something."

"I don't," she promised. "I wish I did."

"So your behavior lately has been totally normal."

Gloria sighed. "No. And, yes, I think there's something weird going on, but I don't know what it is. I just know it when I encounter it."

"And you really believe I saw my dead parents?"

She looked him in the eye. "I do."

"So..." He raised his hands in a gesture of helplessness. "What do I do? Look for them? Pretend it didn't happen?"

"Keep your eyes open and see if it happens again."

Benjamin met her eyes. "You really did see figures in that drawing, didn't you?"

She nodded.

"Anything since?"

"I've been afraid to look."

"But you'd tell me if you did see something?"

Gloria smiled. "Always."

He reached out and took her hand.

Shutting off the television, they sat at the table and talked as they finished their dinner, about Benjamin's parents mostly. His father had died before they met, but she'd known his mother a little before she, too, passed away shortly after Gloria and Benjamin were married. She'd seemed a nice, simple old lady, but the picture Benjamin painted was of a cold, self-absorbed witch. Gloria realized that while she knew *of* her husband's parents, she didn't really *know* them, because Benjamin's stories about his family had always been glancing and superficial. She was familiar with quite a few incidents from his childhood, but they were individual standalone episodes, and it turned out that they did not provide a true or comprehensive picture of what he'd gone through. With no siblings to deflect attention, he had been the sole focus of his bitter angry father, who'd moved to California to work in the high-paying aerospace industry but had ended up clerking for a hardware store. Danny Jaymes had bullied and emotionally manipulated his artistically inclined son into going into the fields he had once aspired to join himself, steering Benjamin into math and science courses in high school, making sure he majored in computer science in college, withholding approval unless his boy followed in those footsteps he'd originally intended to walk.

His mother, meanwhile, spent more time letting people *know* she was a good parent than actually *being* a parent. A shameless social climber, she had very little time for her only child and showed very little interest in Benjamin. She made sure he was fed and clothed, took care of him when he was sick, but other than that, he was on his own.

"I don't believe in ghosts or an afterlife," Benjamin admitted. "But, you're right, I *do* think I saw my parents, and I'll be damned if I know how that's possible." He looked at her. "I know you're not superstitious either, but..."

"There are things we don't understand," she said softly. "Things maybe we *can't* understand. And I believe in them."

Benjamin sighed. "I guess I do, too."

They went to bed early, both of them exhausted.

And woke up to the sounds of people rummaging through their belongings in another room of the house.

Gloria almost screamed, but Benjamin had awakened a few seconds ahead of her, and he put his finger to her lips. She heeded his warning "Shhh," as he gently pulled off the covers and sat up in bed.

Gloria grabbed his arm, squeezing it tight. "No you don't!" she whispered. "You stay right here!"

He was going to be killed by home invaders.

Benjamin easily pulled out of her grasp, standing. "Call 911," he said quietly. "I'm just going to go out and see what's what. Don't worry. I'm not going to do anything stupid."

Gloria picked up the cordless phone from its stand on the small table next to the bed, following him as she punched in the three numbers. The phone's beeps sounded extraordinarily loud to her, but the commotion in the living room obviously covered up the noise because whoever was out there did not even pause.

"Nine-one-one," the female operator said. "What's your emergency?"

Her voice seemed outrageously amplified, and Gloria pressed the phone hard to her ear in an attempt to muffle it. "Someone's broken into our house," she whispered. "They're here right now!"

"I'll send out some officers. Is your location one-eleven—?"

It was, and Gloria hung up, knowing her address had automatically appeared on the dispatcher's screen when she called and not wanting the intruders to hear them coming.

What if the dispatcher called back?

There was a mute button somewhere on the phone, but Gloria couldn't see it in the darkness, so she shoved the phone between the mattress and the box springs at the foot of the bed before following Benjamin into the hall. The noises here were louder and clearly coming from the living room. It sounded as though someone was overturning furniture.

She pulled on the back of Benjamin's T-shirt. "Stop!" she ordered him, her voice almost too low for him to hear. "This is crazy!"

He waved her away, moving quietly, stopping when he reached the end of the hallway and flattening against the wall before peeking around the edge of the doorway. Gloria did the same. Between the blue light on the satellite TV box and the refracted porch light shining through the square of frosted glass on the front door, there was enough illumination for them to see what was going on. A man and a woman, working in tandem, were trashing the room, knocking over tables, smashing lamps.

Benjamin's parents.

He gasped as he recognized them, and *that* they heard. Both stopped what they were doing and turned toward the hallway, his father letting go of the throw pillow he'd been attempting to rend, his mother dropping the framed photo in her hand. They were thin and old, but it was clear from the destruction they'd caused that they were far from frail. Without a word, Benjamin's dad started toward the hall doorway, crouching low in a fighting stance, hands clenched into fists. His mother stood in place, cackling.

Gloria screamed, grabbing Benjamin's arm and pulling him back toward the bedroom. He was pliable, almost limp, stunned no doubt by what he'd seen. She was filled with an instinctual bone-deep terror, certain that this time he would be killed and she would not be able to save him, but beneath her fear, her brain was working rationally. Already, her mind was cataloguing objects, attempting to pick out one that could be used as a weapon.

How could this be happening? And *why*? Even if his parents *had* come back to life (an occurrence not as unbelievable as it should have been), why would they trash their son's house and try to attack him? None of it made any sense, but she was used to things not making sense, and as soon as they made it to the bedroom, Gloria closed and locked the door, still desperately looking around for something they could use to defend themselves. Could they hit his parents on the head with one of the lamps? Do the old car-keys-in-the-fist routine? Throw perfume bottles?

Alternating red and blue lights strobed through the slats of the shades covering the window, and she realized with relief that the police had arrived. There was no noise coming from the hall, and for a brief second she allowed herself to believe that his parents had left, disappeared, or whatever resurrected dead people did, but then fists were pounding on the bedroom door as his mom and dad sought a way in.

"Go away!" she yelled.

Benjamin seemed to have recovered from his shock, because he was pounding on *their* side of the door. "Get out of our house! Now!"

How were the police going to get in? Gloria tried to recall whether or not the front door had been open.

Suddenly, the pounding stopped. Benjamin, emboldened, unlocked and opened the door, ready to confront his parents, but the hallway was empty.

"Police!" a man called from the front of the house.

Gloria followed Benjamin down the hall, expecting to be jumped at any time. But no one attacked them, and they reached the front door—which *was* closed and locked—and let in the officers.

How had Benjamin's parents gotten in? Through the kitchen door? She checked. No, that was closed, too.

Maybe they'd just appeared. Then disappeared.

It didn't matter. There was plenty of proof that they'd been here. The damage they'd caused was real, and Gloria was hoping that the police would be able to lift some prints that would confirm their identities.

Neither of them were stupid enough to tell the police that the intruders had been Benjamin's dead parents, but other than that, they relayed the events exactly as they had happened, even giving accurate descriptions of the man and woman who'd been vandalizing their home. They spent the next hour standing around, watching the two officers search for clues and answering occasional questions.

It was nearly four o'clock by the time the police left, and Gloria and Benjamin stood in the middle of their wrecked living room, looking at each other. They usually woke up at six to get ready for work, which meant that even if they went back to bed right now they would get only two more hours of sleep. Neither of them were tired, however, and without a word to each other, they both started to clean up the mess.

THREE

How had his parents gotten in?

How had they gotten out?

The questions consumed Gloria, because as long as they remained unanswered, as long as she was convinced Benjamin's mom and dad could appear or disappear anywhere at any time, she did not feel safe. What if they showed up while she and Benjamin were asleep, and stabbed them in their bed? What if they attacked Benjamin in his car or at his work? She would never forget the hateful expression on Benjamin's father's face as the old man approached them, crouching low, his hands clenched into fists. Or the terrible sound his mother made as she stood in the center of their dark trashed living room, cackling like a madwoman.

Gloria found it hard to concentrate on her job and even harder to sleep. Every aspect of her life suffered, and who knew how long it would have gone on had she not found his parents less than a week later.

And killed them.

It had been an accident of circumstance that she had encountered his mother and father once again. One of her best students, Rosario

Diaz, had stayed after class to discuss the midterm project and because of that had missed her bus. Though the young woman lived only about five miles away, that was a long way to walk, and when, ten minutes later, on her way home, Gloria saw Rosario striding down the sidewalk on a crowded street and nearly run over by a zigzagging electric scooter, she pulled over to offer her student a ride.

Dropping a grateful Rosario off at the apartment she shared with her mother and brother, Gloria said goodbye and drove off. She was waiting at a stoplight, returning to her usual route home, when, in the crosswalk in front of her, she saw Benjamin's mom and dad, shoving their way between a rail-thin homeless man pushing his belongings before him in a stroller, and a woman who bore an uncanny and disturbing resemblance to Tom Waits. Luckily, they didn't see her, and after the light changed, Gloria drove through the intersection, turned around in a 7-11 parking lot, and pulled onto the cross street where they were walking.

They were the only ones on the sidewalk, the other two pedestrians having gone off in a different direction, and she parked by the curb so as not to arouse suspicion, watching through the windshield as they went to the end of the block, crossed the next street and continued on. When they were far enough away, she drove up to the next block, parking on the side of the street once again, a routine repeated twice more on that street, then three more times on a side street. By this time, they were in a rather rundown industrial area. Many of the businesses were either closed for the day or permanently shuttered. She saw no cars other than her own and no pedestrians save Benjamin's parents.

Where could they be headed?

A cold voice in the back of her mind told her that they were *luring* her out here, that they knew who she was and what she was doing and were intentionally attempting to get her alone.

The smart thing to do would be to call the cops and tell them that she'd found the people who'd broken into their house and was now tailing them, letting the police know where she was so they could pick the couple up.

But she didn't do that.

Unsure of exactly why, Gloria continued to follow Benjamin's parents, not bothering to hide and pretend to park but simply rolling along slowly a block or so behind them. Maybe they'd seen her, maybe they hadn't. Maybe they knew who she was, maybe they didn't. At this point, she didn't really care, and when they started to cross the street in front of her, Gloria accelerated.

This was why she hadn't called the police.

Her car hit the old couple at fifty miles an hour. She felt the impact, but the airbags didn't deploy. Benjamin's dad flew sideways, crashing headfirst into the pavement, while Benjamin's mom went down and under; Gloria felt two harsh bumps as the car rolled over her.

Heart pounding crazily, she braked to a halt and looked in her rearview mirror and then her side mirror. The two bodies lay broken and unmoving in the street. She glanced quickly around to see if there were any witnesses, but there were still no other vehicles on the road, no pedestrians, and no one was coming out of any of the industrial buildings that lined the street.

No way in hell was Gloria going to get out of the car and check to make sure they were dead—she was afraid they'd leap back to life and attack her—so she simply turned the car around in an empty parking lot, then drove slowly past the site, steering around the bodies which were most definitely dead.

Good, she thought.

She wasn't sure how she was going to explain the damage to the car, but as it happened, Benjamin had arrived home before her and parked in the driveway, forcing Gloria to park on the street. Her plan was to say nothing, to "discover" the severely dented front end when she went out to the car in the morning, and as spur-of-the-moment as it was, the plan worked. She and Benjamin both blamed it on some drunk or incompetent driver who'd attempted to park there sometime in the middle of the night and fled once he'd hit their vehicle.

"We should get one of those security cameras," Benjamin said.

Gloria nodded. "We should," she agreed.

She hoped there'd been no security cameras on the street where she'd run over his parents.

What was going to happen? Gloria wondered. Once the identities of the bodies were established, and once it was learned that both victims had died years ago, how were the police going to handle it? Would they notify Benjamin that his parents had died *again*?

Protecting Benjamin had become almost the sole focus of her existence, and Gloria found herself wondering exactly how that had happened. Theirs had always been a marriage of equals, and she had never needed anyone else to complete her or give her a sense of meaning. She certainly wasn't the type to subvert her own desires and interests to those of someone else. Yet somewhere along the line, her primary purpose had become keeping him safe, keeping him *alive*, as though she had become his bodyguard. Such single-mindedness made no logical sense, but it felt right, and Gloria thought that maybe it was a holdover from some other place, some other time, some other life.

She still hadn't solved *that* mystery, either.

After learning of the damage, Benjamin called in sick to work, and the two of them switched cars for the day, since he was better at dealing with the bureaucracy of insurance companies. It had been several days since they'd talked about either the home invasion or his parents (Benjamin's method of dealing with adversity had always been to ignore it and wait for it to go away), and Gloria was hoping to keep it like that, but later in the afternoon he called and asked her to pick him up at the dealer, where he'd dropped her car off for repairs, and as soon as he got in, he sighed. "This has not been a great month. My parents come back to life, break into our house and try to kill us, and now someone hit your car." He laughed shortly, obviously aware of how ludicrous it sounded.

Gloria smiled sympathetically. "It can only get better from here, right?"

"How do you think...?" He paused, took a deep breath. "That was *them*, my mom and dad. They weren't ghosts, they were really there."

"I know," she said.

"How can that be?"

"I have no idea."

"Shouldn't we be researching this? Finding out how such a thing is even possible? What if it's happening to other people? What if it's happening all over and we're just not hearing about it? If everyone who died starts coming back to life—"

"I don't think that's what's happening," Gloria told him.

"Then what *do* you think is happening?"

She met his gaze. "Remember when I warned you about the plane crash?"

He frowned. "The one I cancelled my trip for? The one that didn't happen?"

"It *would've* happened. And I think it's connected to this. I think there's something...I think something wants you dead. Or some*one*. Or...I don't know."

Benjamin smiled tiredly. "This is a joke, right?"

"Was it a joke that your resurrected parents broke into our house? No. I'm totally serious. Something weird is going on, and it's connected to you, and I'm just...I just want to make sure that nothing happens to you." She touched his cheek. "I love you."

He softened. "I love you, too."

They hugged, staying like that for a minute. She felt the warmth of his body, his solidity, and she wished they could stay like this forever, but he eventually pulled away, holding her shoulders and smiling slightly. "Don't worry. It can't get any worse than this. It's bound to get better, right?"

"It *will* get better," she promised.

They were both wrong.

The construction worker attacked Benjamin with a two-by-four as he and Gloria were walking past a Walgreen's drugstore that was being renovated. The parking lot was crowded, so they'd parked in front of the AMC theaters and were walking over to Twin Dragon, the Chinese restaurant where they planned to order takeout. The construction worker came out of nowhere, rushing at them from within the gutted building, wielding his board like a sword. He slammed Benjamin in the stomach, whacked his back with a blow that sent him sprawling, and was about to smash the two-by-four down on his head when two of his co-workers who'd run out to stop him managed to grab the assailant from behind and throw him to the ground. One man sat on his chest while the other took the board out of his hand.

Gloria was screaming, crouching next to Benjamin to make sure he was still alive, and it was another onlooker who called 911.

She followed the ambulance to the hospital. Benjamin was unconscious when they wheeled him into Emergency, but by the time they allowed her to see him ten minutes later, he was awake. He'd suffered a concussion, and X-rays showed that he had two broken ribs and a chipped elbow but, miraculously, there'd been no spinal damage, despite the hard blow to his back. He needed stitches, however, where the two-by-four had split open his skin, a procedure they were prepping for even as she walked in. They were keeping him overnight for observation because of the concussion, but if there were no problems, the doctor told her he would probably be released tomorrow before noon.

Thank God.

The construction worker's name, she learned from the police when she gave her statement in the hospital lobby, was Charles Wister. The name sounded familiar, though she could not for the life of her figure out why. It seemed to be connected in her mind to the city of Laguna Beach, but while she had gone there often with her parents as a child, she could remember going there with her husband only a handful of times.

Her parents.

Where *were* her parents? Gloria wondered.

She frowned. How could she not know that? Gloria realized that she didn't even know if they were dead or alive. She could not recall the last time she had thought of them at all. She tried to remember what they looked like but couldn't and spent forty-five minutes searching through the house for a photo of either of them, without luck.

Sitting down on the couch in defeat, her mind conjured up the image of a woman wearing thick red lipstick, high purple eyeshadow and highly teased blonde hair, dressed in a bright blue, big-shouldered 1980s jacket—

Nora, her name was Nora

—and a middle-aged man with a too-wide smile that hinted at violence...and maybe something else. They were overlapping images, not necessarily connected and with an implication of other existences, other lives, other people. Once again, Gloria's memories felt jumbled and competing, like a crowd of reporters all shouting questions at the same time, and it was only the thought of Benjamin that remained solid and clear in her mind.

She had no idea what was going on, and her attempts to reason through it only made everything seem more complicated. The one thing she did know was that Benjamin's life was in danger.

What if a crazed orderly was injecting him with an overdose of something right now? What if a nurse was smothering him with a pillow?

She should not have come home, despite what Benjamin and the doctor had told her. She should be there with him right now.

She should...but, honestly, she was too tired. Her eyes kept fluttering closed, though she willed them not to, and it was all she could do to sit up and stumble down the hall to the bedroom, where she fell fully dressed onto the welcome bed.

If something happened to him, Gloria thought, she would do a better job saving him next time.

Next time?

What did that mean?

She didn't know, but there was no time to reflect upon it because, against her will, she was already falling asleep.

Gloria awoke in darkness to hear tapping and thumping and knocking, as though somewhere in the house boxes were being packed and moved about. Sitting up, she looked toward the open bedroom doorway as she listened, trying to pinpoint the origin of the sounds. Too near to be coming from the living room or the kitchen, yet not loud enough to be from within the hallway itself, they had to be coming from the guest room, the den or the bathroom.

Or the small closet in the hall.

Gloria knew, without getting up to check, that that was precisely the source of the sounds. She had never become fully accustomed to that too-narrow door, despite what she had told Benjamin, and though she'd accepted his explanation for the space's odd emptiness, fear and suspicion had always lain just below the surface in her mind. Now, hearing the thumps and thuds, she visualized something moving into that small closet, something she didn't even *try* to imagine.

She was not sure what to do. With Benjamin in the hospital, her options were limited to locking herself in the bedroom and waiting for morning, calling the police to tell them there was a burglar in her house, or going out into the hall to investigate. The third option was by far the scariest and stupidest, but she opted for it nonetheless, slipping quietly out of bed, pulling on a robe and putting on her slippers. The noises continued—it really *did* sound like someone was unpacking boxes and rearranging objects—and Gloria moved silently across the bedroom floor, stopping in the doorway and peeking out into the hall.

The closet was open.

And a light inside was on.

Now was the time to close and lock the door, dial 911 and hide under the covers until the police arrived, but even though she didn't have a weapon, something made her step forward and continue on. She was trying to be quiet and hoped against hope that the frantic panicked pulsing of her blood she heard thundering in her ears could not be detected by whoever—

whatever

—was in there. Before her, the sounds of movement did not abate, if anything grew more purposeful, and she sidled next to the wall opposite the closet, remaining in the shadows, and carefully peered around the corner of the open door.

The closet was empty.

Sounds were still issuing from the unoccupied space, as though being made by an invisible man, but no one was there, and Gloria reached forward and slammed the door shut, letting out a small involuntary cry as she did so. The sounds stopped immediately. She backed against the wall, waiting to see if the door was going to open again, ready to run if anything like that happened, but nothing occurred, and the house remained silent. She had not turned off the closet light—

How was there a closet light?

—and she kept an eye on the line of illumination beneath the strange narrow door, expecting it to shut off at any second, but the light remained on.

Whatever had been happening in there was over.

Something still felt off, though. She saw nothing, heard nothing, but there was an uncomfortable feeling in the air, a sense that she was not alone. It was probably just her imagination, but she was too keyed up to return to bed anyway and decided to check the rest of the house.

The guestroom: empty. Hall bathroom: empty. Office: empty. Kitchen and laundry room: empty. Dining room: empty. Living room...

Something was wrong.

She hadn't turned the hall light on when sneaking up on the open closet, not wanting to alert whatever was in there to her presence, but Gloria wasn't like one of those moronic characters in a horror movie. Rather than walk from dark room to dark room, she'd turned on every light she encountered until the whole house was flooded with illumination. The living room lights were on, too, but they were floor lamps and, in the middle of the night like this, some segments of the room were left darker than others. Her gaze was drawn to one of these areas, the wall above the television, where a shaft of moonlight from a crack in the drapes fell onto the framed drawing of the shack.

She advanced slowly, knowing what she would see, afraid of what she would see, but unable to look away. Indeed, the figures were back, and they were moving, penciled people leisurely bending to pick a well-drawn twig off the ground or strolling behind the meticulously rendered walls of the shack. Gloria knew she was not dreaming but could think of no other explanation for what she was witnessing. She stood there, staring, until all of the figures had walked around the sides of the small building. There were chills on her arms as she waited in place to see if they would come again, but the drawing was once again still, the show apparently over.

They'd bought that framed sketch in Laguna Beach, and for some reason it made her think of Charles Wister, the construction worker who'd attacked Benjamin. In her mind, there was some association between the two, but she could not quite connect the dots. She concentrated hard, trying to figure out the link, but whatever it might be eluded her.

The uneasy feeling she'd had was gone, the house seemed normal again, and Gloria checked the locks on all of the doors before going back to bed.

She left the lights on.

In the morning, she was dressed and showered by six, in Benjamin's room at the hospital by six-thirty. He was sitting up in bed, wide awake, waiting for the breakfast he'd ordered and for the doctor to stop by and check on him. Gloria hadn't had breakfast yet herself, but she wasn't hungry, so she waited with him as they talked about what had happened.

"Who *was* that guy?" Benjamin wondered.

Gloria shrugged. "Just a construction worker. His name's Charles Wister. The police have him in custody, and he's going away for a long time. There were plenty of witnesses and they're all willing to talk. Why he attacked you specifically is a mystery. Did the police talk to you about it?"

"They interviewed me, but I was all doped up. I think I'm supposed to talk to them again today. Tell them what I remember."

"What do you remember?"

"Everything."

His breakfast arrived just then, the orderly pulling out a metal tray on an arm attached to the side of his bed, and adjusting it so that it sat at chest level in front of him, before placing his breakfast on the top. Gloria inspected his meal: omelet, turkey sausage, fruit cup and orange juice. "Not bad," she said.

"Tastes great to me," he told her, digging in. "I'm starving. I don't think I had dinner last night."

"He did," the orderly said before leaving. "He just doesn't remember it."

Gloria waited until the man was out of the room. "About the attack. Remember I said something wanted you dead? I think this is another example of it."

"That guy?" he said between bites. "It was just random."

"I don't think so."

"Come on! You think he picked on me personally? You think he was waiting for me to come by? How could he even know I'd be there? *I* didn't even know. We decided to stop off and get Chinese food literally seconds before we pulled into the parking lot."

"I don't know how he knew," Gloria admitted. "I just know that he did. Listen to me: there are attempts being made on your life. I don't know how or why, I just know that they are, and I need you to know it, too. You need to be alert."

Benjamin sipped his orange juice. "Gloria..." he said in the patronizing tone of voice an adult would use to reassure a frightened child.

"Last night, I saw those figures in the drawing again, okay? And there was something in the hall closet!"

If she was hoping to sway him, that was not the tack to take. Now he looked even more skeptical.

Gloria took a deep breath. "You know the thing that happened with your parents is real. You saw them. So why won't you believe me on this?"

He didn't answer, but she didn't press him. She let him finish his breakfast in peace. Immediately after, the doctor came in to check on him, not the Asian man she'd met last night but a young African American woman. The doctor drew a curtain around the bed so as to block its view from the doorway, then proceeded to check on his stitches, press lightly on his bandaged chest, look at his readouts, and ask him a few questions about how he'd slept and how he felt. "I think he should be cleared to leave this morning," she said, speaking to Gloria. "I'd like to take another X-ray and do another MRI. I don't think we're too stacked up in radiology, so if we can get him in by ten, he should be able to check out before noon. If we can't, it'll be sometime this afternoon." She turned to Benjamin. "I want to see you once more before you go home, and I'll give you a prescription for painkillers and antibiotics. The painkillers take as needed, the antibiotics for a week." She addressed both of them. "You're very lucky. It could've been much, much worse."

"We're lucky," Benjamin said with a hint of a smile.

Gloria looked at him. "Yeah."

FOUR

Benjamin had enough sick time and comp time saved up that he could remain home for more than the week that the doctor suggested, but he was too conscientious to do that. They assured him at work that everything was covered, but he went in anyway after two days, still in pain but frustrated and bored by his convalescence, or, as he put it, his "house arrest."

Gloria had taken a day off herself, but even after she'd gone back to work, she checked in with him between classes and during her office hours to make sure he was okay.

She had a feeling this wasn't the end of it.

A month passed without incident. Nothing weird happened in the house, and no one tried to attack either of them. Benjamin was never contacted by the authorities about his parents dying for a second time, and Gloria assumed that either their bodies had resisted identification (maybe they didn't have fingerprints!) or had dematerialized before being found.

Still, she knew enough not to let down her guard, a strategy validated when, one Thursday after her last class, she returned to her office to drop off some books and found the door wide open.

Stepping out of the elevator on the third floor, the empty hallway before her dark due to energy-efficient lights that had not been activated by the motion of anyone passing by, Gloria saw yellowish illumination spilling out from the open doorway of her office halfway down the passage. She took a step forward, the motion detectors sensing her presence and turning on the corridor's lights. Brightness did not dissipate the feeling of dread that had settled upon her, and she turned, planning to re-enter the elevator and notify campus security once she was down on the ground floor, but the metal doors had closed with a sprightly *ding*, and lighted numbers indicated that the elevator was already on its way to the floor above.

"Gloria!" a woman's singsongy voice called out. "I'm waiting!"

The fact that it was a woman rather than a man made her feel a little braver, and anger pushed past fear as she strode down the hallway to see who the hell had broken into her office. Her footsteps were loud on the newly waxed floor. Too loud. She kept her ears open as she passed by the closed office doors of other instructors, hoping to hear sounds of occupation from within, but the only noises she heard were her own, and her bravery had dissipated somewhat by the time she reached her office. She put on her most fearless face and prepared to confront the intruder, stepping into the doorway.

"Gloria."

She did not know the older woman sitting behind her desk and smiling at her...but at the same time, she did.

Maxine.

The woman's name was Maxine. She had been her mother's best friend, and she had lived across the street from Gloria when Gloria was growing up.

Only she hadn't.

Staring at the old woman, Gloria recognized her, knew her name, but could not recall what her house or yard looked like, or a single detail about the neighborhood where they both had lived. Like too many things lately, Maxine seemed to have come from a world that might have been, not the world that was, and knowledge and memory twisted together in a confusing unexplainable tangle.

Gloria chose to act as though this were a normal situation and Maxine merely a woman who had entered her office without permission. “Get out of my office,” she said levelly, dropping the books she’d been carrying on top of the desk.

They landed with a sound more crack than thud, but Maxine did not flinch. Her smile grew broader. “How’s Benjamin? How are his parents?”

“If you don’t leave now, I’m calling security.” Gloria reached for the phone on the desk, but Maxine knocked it onto the floor.

“The hell you are,” the old lady said. Her smile was gone, and Gloria took an involuntary step back, intimidated by the fierceness of her gaze. Maxine stood. “You can’t put it off forever,” she said.

“Put off what?” Gloria asked, though she already knew the answer.

“He has to die. It’s his time. And no one can stop that, not even you.”

Gloria turned without responding, closed the door with as close to a slam as the slow hinges could muster, and used her key to lock the door from the outside. There was an emergency phone in an alcove halfway down the corridor for situations just such as this, and she pressed 1 for campus security, telling the man who answered who she was, where she was and what had happened.

“Someone will be right there,” the man promised.

Gloria leaned against the wall, keeping an eye on her office door to make sure Maxine did not escape. A campus security officer arrived less than five minutes later, and Gloria explained again that a woman had broken into her office as she used her key to open the door.

Maxine, of course, was gone.

She’d halfway expected it, but it still surprised her because she could think of no possible explanation for how the other woman had gotten out. The security officer looked confused. "I thought you said she was still in here."

"I thought she was."

"Could she have left while you were calling us?"

"Maybe," Gloria lied, though that was not possible because she'd been watching the door the entire time. "Are there security cameras here on this floor?"

The officer chuckled. "I know a few professors who definitely would *not* want that, so no. No there aren't." He took down a report of what had occurred and her description of the trespasser, advising Gloria to call campus security if she saw the woman again. There was no mention made of calling the real police or dusting for fingerprints—apparently, this wasn't important enough—and as the officer waited while she got what she needed out of the office and the two of them rode down in the elevator together, Gloria did not even bother asking him to find the woman, mostly because she didn't think it could be done.

He has to die. It's his time.

She said nothing to Benjamin about what had happened, pretending it had been a normal day at work, but she made desperate frantic love to him that night, and lay awake long after he'd nodded off, unable to fall asleep.

Saturday night, they were supposed to attend a get-together at Lucas and Jean's house in Anaheim Hills. Jean had just received a long-overdue promotion at the nonprofit where she worked, and the couple had decided to celebrate with friends. Still feeling uneasy after her encounter at school, Gloria did not want to go. "There'll be plenty of people there," she argued. "We won't even be missed."

They would definitely be missed, Benjamin assured her.

He was Lucas' oldest friend.

"We're going," he said.

The vibe was weird from the moment they arrived. They were a little late because of traffic on the Riverside Freeway, and when they stepped into the large home's high-ceilinged vestibule, they could hear laughter and conversation from the patio out back. There was splashing as well, from the pool, and Gloria looked at Benjamin. Should they have brought bathing suits? He shrugged, obviously knowing nothing about it being a swim party.

They'd let themselves in, and since there was no one on hand to greet them, they made their way into the sitting room and toward the sliding glass door that opened onto the patio. All laughter and conversation stopped as they stepped onto the cement. A premonitory chill passed through her as she saw their friends' stony faces. In the pool behind them, instead of the swimmers that she'd expected to see, a throw pillow, a book, a milk carton and a hand mirror were floating in the water. Between them, a puppy, a cat and a rabbit were either drowning or desperately paddling around trying to reach safety.

The splashing they'd heard was someone throwing Jean's pets and a bunch of random household items into the pool.

Gloria reached for Benjamin's hand, holding it tight.

"We told you the party was at seven," Lucas said. Around him, everyone was silent.

Benjamin smiled. "Well, you know that Riverside Freeway."

"You were supposed to be here at seven."

Benjamin looked at his watch. "It's only seven-twenty."

Jean threw up her hands. "What did I tell you? That's exactly what I said about your so-called *friend*. No respect for other people's time and effort. None at all!"

"Now wait a minute—" Gloria began.

"And who the hell do you think *you* are? Who died and made you queen?"

This had to be a joke. There was no other explanation. But the stony faces did not break into smiles, no one said "Gotcha!" or "Psyche!" Everyone remained rooted in place, staring at them, until Gloria began to feel extremely uncomfortable.

"Let's just leave," she whispered.

But Benjamin did not buy in to the reality before them. He could not seem to believe that what was happening was actually happening. Moving forward and pulling her along with him, he approached the covered picnic table and reached for a plastic champagne glass, still smiling.

Myka threw a piece of bacon-wrapped shrimp at his head.

It hit his cheek with a wet *splat!* before bouncing off his shirt and falling to the ground, leaving a shiny smear on his face and a greasy spot on the white material of his shirt. His smile starting to fade, Benjamin reached for a cocktail napkin to wipe off his cheek.

A man Gloria didn't know poked him in the stomach with a serving spoon.

Benjamin grabbed the utensil out of the man's hand and put it firmly on the table. The man reached for the spoon again, but Gloria got there first and threw it into the pool.

The partygoers were still eerily quiet. No one was saying anything, and Gloria pulled on Benjamin's hand. "Come on," she said. "Let's go."

"Oh, you're not going anywhere," Jean promised, and Gloria saw that the configuration of people was changing. Men and women were moving around, off to the sides, in what was clearly an effort to encircle them. She counted ten people altogether, but who knew if there were others inside or in the section of back yard hidden by the edge of the house.

She and Benjamin knew all of these people, counted most of them as friends. Why were they behaving this way? She didn't know, and wondered if they even knew themselves. She had the idea that they'd been swept up in something bigger, the force or whatever it was that wanted Benjamin dead. They'd stepped into the wave and were now being carried along with it. Maybe they wouldn't even remember it in the morning.

He has to die. It's his time.

Instinctively, she looked around for Maxine, but there was no sign of the old lady.

Jean had picked up a glass punch ladle, Lucas a frighteningly large knife meant to carve the congratulation cake. Paul grabbed a loose brick from the planter at the edge of the patio, Myka was gripping an empty champagne bottle, Rosalita was holding a spatula dripping with sauce and cheese that she'd pulled from a tray of enchiladas. Everyone seemed to be choosing a weapon.

Benjamin, unwilling or unable to completely give up on the hope of rationality, appealed to Lucas. "Dude," he said. "What the fuck?"

Knife held in front of him, Lucas lunged, and Gloria, expecting the attack, upended the table. The punchbowl, plates, food and serving dishes, as well as the table itself, toppled over and blocked his way, glass shattering on the concrete.

"How dare you?" Jean screamed crazily. Spittle was flying from her lips. She swung her ladle, but Gloria feinted to the left and it swished the air to the right of her face. Jean, she noted with shock and disgust, appeared to have wet her pants. She kicked her friend in the knee, and Jean collapsed, her chin hitting the edge of the overturned table with an audible crack.

But Jean was the only one with her sights on Gloria. Everyone else was converging on Benjamin, next to her. He dodged Lucas' knife, now thrown at him, and was hit in the face by a fist, in the chest by a stick, in the arm by Paul's brick. He kicked out at his attackers, punched one of them, then, dazed, bent to pick up the knife before being kicked in the side by Jean's friend Keiko, wearing sharp high heels. Standing, swinging the knife to repel all comers, Benjamin retreated toward the house, Gloria holding on to the back of his shirt and guiding him. A plastic glass half-filled with Everclear was lit and thrown like a Molotov cocktail, the flaming liquid landing on a corner of the tablecloth and setting it ablaze. Once inside, they shut the sliding glass door, locking it. A rock hit the glass, causing it to crack, and the two of them turned tail and sped through the house and out to their car, parked on the street.

Unable to get into the house, the partygoers had apparently decided to go around it, and they streamed out from both sides of the home, shouting wildly and wielding household objects and party supplies repurposed as weapons.

Benjamin threw the car into gear, stomped his foot down on the gas pedal and sped away, tires screeching the way they did in movies. The first stoplight they reached was turning yellow as they approached, and he accelerated even more, speeding through the intersection as the light changed to red.

"What was *that*?" Benjamin breathed when they were finally stopped by a red light several blocks down. "It's like...like they wanted to kill us. To kill *me*."

"I told you," Gloria said quietly.

He glanced over at her. "I can't believe I'm saying this, but you're right."

It gave her no satisfaction to hear those words, but the fact that he was now aware of the situation and finally believed it, gave Gloria hope. "Are you hurt?" she asked. "Do we need to go to Emergency?"

"No," he said. "I mean, yes, it hurts, but I don't think anything's broken. I don't need a doctor." The light changed, and he drove through the intersection, switching lanes to get on the freeway. "Jesus," he said, and he sounded overwhelmed. "What the hell is going on?"

Something wants you dead, was the only answer she had, but she knew no more than that and didn't even want to speculate about the other questions that answer brought up.

So she didn't reply.

FIVE

He didn't become paranoid, but he did grow more cautious.

Benjamin still had contact with Lucas at work, but luckily the two of them were in separate departments and only encountered each other at meetings, where neither of them brought up what had happened at the party. Now, he was careful to check in with her when he went someplace alone, even if it was only the grocery store. He made certain to tell Gloria where he was going, to call or text when he got there, and to call her again when he was about to return. He locked the doors of the house when he was home, even in the middle of the day, which was something he'd never done before, and he made a concerted effort to avoid sketchy areas or people who looked like they might be trouble. Nothing could be done about acts of God—he could still be hit by lightning or washed away in a flash flood—but Benjamin took every possible precaution to stay away from situations that could turn dangerous. Or deadly.

Gloria *was* becoming paranoid. Naturally more of a worrier than Benjamin, she saw peril around every corner, was afraid each time they parted that it would be the last time she saw him. And the worst thing was that she could see no way to escape this mindset. She was doomed to spend the rest of her life in a state of constant agitation. Or the rest of *his* life. Because the only possible end to this that she could envision was his death.

The fact that nothing more happened, that for days, then weeks, everything was pleasant and nice and on an even keel, only drew out the suspense and made her feel increasingly anxious.

Then, one Sunday morning, she woke up with a son and a daughter.

Gloria got up before Benjamin to make the kids their breakfast, fully aware that she made their breakfast each morning, even though she knew she had had no children when she went to sleep the night before. The knowledge of both realities coexisted simultaneously in her head, but Benjamin, when he awoke, believed that they had always had kids. She knew this because she asked him about it, when Bradley and Ruth were in the other room watching cartoons, and he could not even understand her question. He looked at her askance the rest of the morning, and she wondered fearfully if things had changed so much overnight that he was no longer aware of the danger he faced.

Apparently not, because later, when the kids were outside playing in the back yard, he told her that he was going to have to meet one-on-one with Lucas tomorrow morning about a project that was going to require an update to their servers. "I'm wondering if I should bring it up," he said. "It's the first time we'll be alone together since the party, and I'm thinking of confronting him and asking, 'What the hell?' Or maybe just kicking his ass."

"No!" Gloria said.

Benjamin smiled wryly. "You don't think I can take him?"

She hit his shoulder. "It's not funny."

"Don't worry," he assured her, and she could tell by his voice that he *knew* it wasn't funny.

"You really have to meet with him alone?"

"I could take Inessa with me."

"Do that."

"In case I need a witness?"

"Among other reasons."

"I would like to confront him, though."

She understood that impulse, but she understood as well that it was dangerous. Whatever was coming after Benjamin wasn't screwing around, and they would be foolish to underestimate it or provide it with an easy opportunity to have at him. "You're at work," Gloria said, "and you're discussing a project. Just...be professional. Don't bring anything personal into it. You're safe that way."

"Oh, they won't fire or even reprimand me for..." He suddenly got it. "Oh."

She nodded. "*That* kind of safe."

"I guess you're right."

"I am right. You don't just have you to think about, you know. You have me."

"And the kids," he added.

"And the kids," she agreed.

But she hadn't been thinking about Bradley or Ruth. Even now that she *was* thinking about them, they still didn't seem important enough to influence him in that way.

They didn't seem real.

That was the truth of it. They were, of course, but in another way, they weren't, not to her at least, and while it was clear that Benjamin felt differently, Gloria could not seem to find within herself the parental instincts she should have possessed.

Ruth had somehow re-entered the house without her noticing, and Gloria was surprised to hear the little girl's voice behind her. "Mommy?"

Gloria turned around. "Yes, sweetie?"

"I'm thirsty. Could you get me a drink?"

Gloria smiled at her daughter. "Of course. What would you like?"

Over the next week, she grew no closer to her children. If anything, she felt increasingly distant from them the more time they spent together. While she had been with them every day since their births, had *given* birth to them, Bradley first, then Ruth a year later, she was at the same time aware of a life without them, and it was these memories that felt more emotionally true.

They were nice kids. Their teachers thought so, the woman running their daycare program thought so, their friends' parents thought so, the neighbors thought so, but Gloria thought she detected a sneakiness in Bradley's demeanor, a subtle yet noticeable tendency to almost imperceptibly undermine his parents' authority. When Benjamin would tell him it was time for bed, Bradley might pretend not to hear him or feign a misunderstanding, acting as though he'd heard a word incorrectly and didn't understand the direction. When Gloria told him to do something, he would do it, but she would catch him rolling his eyes, at Ruth if she was there, at no one at all if he was alone. He was not exactly rebellious. In fact, his behavior would barely qualify as mischievous. But he wasn't quite the polite little boy he pretended to be, and Gloria noticed it.

And it worried her.

It concerned her even more when she recognized that most of his small acts of defiance were directed at his father. Trusting soul that he was, Benjamin seemed completely clueless. He loved both of their children so much that Gloria doubted he would notice any fault with either of them. But on a Saturday soon after, she was watering the ficus in the living room when all of a sudden there came crashing sounds from the kitchen and Benjamin cried out in pain. Flooded immediately with a sense of panicked terror, Gloria dashed through the living room and into the kitchen, where she saw her husband lying on the floor, bleeding amidst a jumble of knives and broken plates.

"Oh, God!" she said, rushing forward.

He was already trying to sit up, but there was a long cut on the palm of his right hand, and putting pressure on it as he tried to push himself off the floor caused him to cry out in agony. Her feet slid on the floor—it was coated with something slippery—but she righted herself by holding a hand against the counter. Grabbing his upper arm, she helped pull him to his feet, turning on the cold water in the sink and placing his hand beneath the stream. "Hold it there," she told him. "I'll get an ice pack out of the freezer."

There was no ice pack, but there was a bag of frozen edamame, and she took his hand out of the water and pressed the bag against it to stem the bleeding.

He had other cuts as well, further up on the same arm, on his other arm, even on his cheek and chin, but they were minor compared to the gash on his palm, and she hoped he wouldn't have to go to Emergency and get stitches.

Gloria looked down at the floor, put her hand to the slippery tiles and smelled her fingers. Olive oil. She saw no broken bottle amidst the mess and wondered how the olive oil had gotten on the floor. Who could have put the knives on the counter, for that matter? The plates had been near the sink because she had placed them there after breakfast, intending to rinse them off before putting them into the dishwasher. Benjamin had probably walked in, slipped on the oily tiles, grabbed the counter and knocked the plates to the floor as he fell. But the knives? She counted five of them, her entire collection. How had they gotten there?

From the corner of her eye, she noticed Bradley standing next to the refrigerator. Turning, she saw him calmly watching the scene with a complete lack of expression. He could have been in shock, but Gloria knew that was not the case. There was a sly cast to his purposefully blank countenance, an indication that perhaps *he* knew how this had happened, and she felt a cold tingle slide down her spine, causing peachfuzz hair all over her body to bristle.

"I think it's okay," Benjamin said, taking the frozen bag off his wound. "It's still bleeding, but not as bad. I don't think it's that deep."

"Keep it cold," Gloria told him. "And press that bag down. I'll get some Neosporin."

Bradley had already left the kitchen. She saw him in his room as she rushed by on her way to get Band-Aids and the tube of Neosporin out of the bathroom. He was climbing on his bed, and she thought she heard him laugh.

She began watching Bradley after that. Oh, she made his meals and read him bedtime stories and did all the things a mother was supposed to do, but she kept a close eye on him at the same time, trying to see if he exhibited any behavior that was...suspicious. She hated herself for even having such thoughts, and, more often than not, suspected that she was overreacting, wrongly reading import into random observations, or even just plain crazy. For all of her close observation, she caught Bradley doing nothing out of the ordinary, nothing even remotely unusual—but there was always the chance that he might.

So she kept it up. She couldn't help herself.

While Gloria and Benjamin were supposed to take turns picking up the kids from daycare, the responsibility usually fell to her because she worked closer to home and her hours were more flexible. Benjamin was scheduled to pick them up on the day she went for her annual mammogram, but after leaving the medical center and turning on her phone as she walked to her car, Gloria discovered that he'd left her a frantic message. An emergency at work required him to remain after hours, so there was no way he could get there on time. He'd called the Montessori school that acted as the children's afternoon daycare and let them know that Bradley and Ruth might need to stay a little longer. Could she pick them up?

Of course she could, and she called to tell him that, hearing both guilt and relief in his voice. "I'm sorry," he said. "I had no choice. I was *ordered* to stay."

"Don't worry," she told him, but a nagging voice in the back of her mind told her that this was intentional, that he was being forced to stay late so that...what? He could be in the office when a disgruntled ex-employee went on a shooting rampage? He could be killed in an accident on the way home?

"Be careful," she told him.

He took her meaning, and she heard the sincerity in his voice when he said, "I will."

She was not the only parent late to pick up her children, and Gloria sat in a line of idling cars in the horseshoe-shaped driveway of the school. When it was her turn, she pulled up to the pickup station and waited while one of the aides opened the car's rear door and helped the children in, buckling their shoulder harnesses.

"Thank you," Gloria told the woman. "Sorry I'm late. I appreciate all your help."

The aide smiled. "No problem. They're good kids. Goodbye, Ruth," she said. "Goodbye, Bradley."

"Goodbye, Miss Robin!" they shouted.

The door was closed, and Gloria pulled onto the street. "How was your day?" she asked.

For the next few minutes, they excitedly talked over each other, telling her about the games they'd played, the snacks and lunch they'd had, and the fingerpainting they'd done, which was drying and would be sent home with them tomorrow. "That's great," she said encouragingly.

There was a moment of silence.

"Mommy?" Bradley said.

"Yes?"

"If Daddy died, would you get married again?"

Gloria looked at him in her rearview mirror, shocked. "Why would you even ask such a question?"

He shrugged innocently. "Hugh Ngo's daddy died, and his mommy said that she was never going to get married again."

Why would a mother discuss that with her son? Gloria wondered. And how could it possibly come up in a conversation between preschool children at daycare?

"Cindy Valles said that if her daddy died, her mommy would marry her uncle!"

Gloria did not believe any of it. Stopping at a red light, she made a point of studying Bradley's face in the mirror. Was that a smirk she saw there? Glancing over at Ruth, she saw that her daughter was looking distractedly out the side window, not paying attention.

"What would you do if Daddy died?" Bradley asked.

"Daddy's not going to die."

"He might," Ruth said, still staring out the window.

The light changed, and Gloria drove through the intersection. What she wanted to do was pull over and call Benjamin to make sure he was okay. She didn't like the fact that he was staying late at work. But she forced herself to remain calm and drive carefully. "Let's talk about something else," she said firmly.

The kids seemed to have run out of things to say, however, and after several moments of silence, she turned on the radio, and the rest of the way home they listened to music.

That night in bed, after Bradley and Ruth were asleep, Gloria tried to convey to Benjamin how unnerving it was to hear the children talk about his death. He laughed it off, saying it was perfectly natural for little kids to wonder about such things, it was all a part of growing up. "Pretty soon they'll be asking where babies come from," he said. "You'd better brace yourself for that."

But it had been more than natural curiosity, and she was unable to make him understand the weird mood in the car, and the vibes she'd been getting from Bradley not just today but...

Since the day he'd shown up.

That was something she couldn't possibly make him understand and had no intention of even trying to explain: her dichotomous life, the leeching in of an another reality into this existence. She herself had no idea what it was or why it happened, but something within her accepted it, even as she acknowledged its impossibility.

Maybe she *was* going crazy.

In the morning, Gloria awoke before Benjamin because she wanted to wash her hair. She usually did so at night, but she'd put it off after attempting to share with her husband the unnerving death discussion she'd had with the kids in the car. She'd set the alarm fifteen minutes earlier than usual and quickly shut it off when it rang so as not to wake him. They were out of shampoo in the master bathroom (how in the world had *that* happened?), so she went out to get another bottle from the bathroom down the hall.

And almost tripped over a line of Hot Wheel cars centered in the middle of the hallway floor.

It was only because she was barefoot rather than in slippers, and her big toe had touched cold metal before instantly pulling back, that she avoided landing flat on her face. The bathroom light was on as always, in case one of the kids needed to use it in the middle of the night, but the line of Hot Wheels started just *past* the illuminated rectangle that fell upon the floor, which she noticed only after turning on the hall light.

In fact, the small cars were positioned only in front of their bedroom.

There was a familiar sound of tapping and knocking coming from behind the small closet door on the other side of the hall. Goosebumps popped up on her arms, and she almost fled back into the bedroom to wake up Benjamin, but something about the knocking seemed off. These weren't the same unexplainable sounds she'd heard last time. They seemed more...normal. Curiosity overcoming fear, Gloria strode over to the narrow door and pulled it open.

Bradley sat in the center of the small, otherwise empty room. He had changed from his pajamas into day clothes, and in his hands was an orange length of Hot Wheels track.

How long have you been up? Do you know what time it is? Why are you dressed? What are you doing in the closet? were some of the questions she wanted to ask, but the overriding takeaway was that Bradley had purposely lined up those Hot Wheels in front of their doorway. He *knew* that one of them could have tripped over those cars, and yet he had intentionally placed them there.

Bradley looked up at her, and she knew he knew that she knew.

He smiled at her.

"Pick them up," she ordered, and, still smiling, Bradley stood, dropped his length of orange track and walked out into the hall to do just that.

"Now get back in bed," she told him when he had finished putting the toys away.

Benjamin was already up, awakened either by the commotion or his own internal alarm clock, and he stood in the bedroom doorway in his underwear, yawning. "What's going on?"

"I need to wash my hair," she said. "Everyone go back to bed. I'll wake you up when I'm done." She needed time alone to think, and once she had made sure that Bradley was in his room and Benjamin had happily returned to catch a few extra winks, she got a shampoo bottle from the hall bathroom and carried it back with her into the master bath, closing the door.

What now?

It seemed to Gloria that her son had actively attempted to harm his parents, most likely his father—

What would you do if Daddy died?

—and she wondered if she should confront the boy, or tell Benjamin what had happened so that both of them could sit down and discuss it with him. Would it make any difference?

She had no proof, Gloria realized, only an interpretation of events that could be very easily explained in another way.

She turned on the water in the sink, pushed down the stopper on the drain and put her head under the faucet, grateful to have something else to focus on, if even for a moment.

She did end up telling Benjamin, when the kids were out of earshot, but he didn't buy it. "Bradley?" he said skeptically. "That's a little paranoid even for you." He was still with her on the idea that *something* was after him, but he refused to believe it could be his own son, so she didn't press it.

Over the next several days, she kept a close eye on Bradley. He didn't actually *do* anything, but his questions to both her and Benjamin seemed pointed, the topics he chose to discuss weighted with far more meaning than their surface subject matter would suggest. Once, picking him up at school, she heard the tail end of a conversation he was having with his friend Raul. "Would you be sadder if your daddy died or your mommy?" Bradley asked.

Raul, shocked, didn't have time to answer because Gloria was telling Bradley, "Get in the car."

"What were you two talking about?" she asked after he was buckled in.

"Homework," he lied.

Another time, she caught him explaining to Ruth how the rake prank worked. They were in the back yard and had just finished watching cartoons, so most likely they'd seen one character do it to another, but as he put the rake down on the ground and gently pressed his foot against the prongs, causing the wooden handle to raise up, Gloria imagined him setting up a rake in front of their doorstep so Benjamin would step on it and hit himself in the head.

He seemed to be hanging out more often with his sister lately, and several times Gloria caught them whispering together and then quickly pulling apart the second they saw her. It made her suspicious not just of Bradley but of Ruth as well. They were partners, and while he was undoubtedly the leader, she seemed a willing follower.

Unless it was all just in Gloria's head.

That possibility refused to go away, and it was doubt and uncertainty that haunted her, the prospect that nothing out of the ordinary was occurring and she was jumping at shadows that weren't even there.

Then they most definitely were.

Gloria had to stay late after her last class, proctoring a midterm for her friend Hong, who'd had a family emergency, and she'd called Benjamin to tell him to pick up the kids. Daylight Savings Time had ended the week before, so it was now getting dark early, and night had fallen by the time she arrived home. Benjamin's car was parked in the driveway when she pulled in.

But there were no lights on in the house.

Gloria's heart skipped a beat. Panic welling within her, she scrambled to get out of the car, leaving her book bag on the passenger seat and only grabbing her purse because it had her keys in it. The keys were out and in her hand by the time she reached the front door, but it turned out that she didn't need them. The door was not only unlocked but ajar.

Suddenly wary, she pushed the door open. "Benjamin?" she called. "Bradley! Ruth!"

She was *hoping* Benjamin would shout out that they were home and explain to her when he walked out that there'd been a blackout or a fuse had blown. She was *expecting* to hear no response, to have her call met with silence. What she was not prepared for was what she actually got: a familiar thumping that sounded incredibly loud in the silence of the house and that she knew was coming from the weird little closet.

Taking her phone out of her purse, she remained where she was and called 911. A dispatcher came immediately on the line, and Gloria told the man her name and address and said that someone had broken into her house and was still inside.

"Do not go in. Stay outside," the dispatcher told her. "Someone will be there in three-and-a-half minutes."

That "three-and-a-half" was reassuringly specific, and Gloria had no intention of going inside, fully intending to wait on the doorstep where she was, but suddenly the thumping noise stopped, replaced by the voices of Bradley and Ruth calling out, "Mommy! Mommy!"

Whatever suspicions she might have about them, they were still her children, and in their cries she heard fear and alarm and a desperate desire for their mother. Instinctively, she dashed into the darkened house, calling out their names—"Bradley! Ruth!"—praying that the police arrival estimate was accurate. She flipped the switch to the side of the door as she hurried in, but, as expected, no lights came on. All of the drapes were still open, and illumination from the street lamp by the sidewalk leavened the darkness by outlining in silhouette the furnishings of the front room.

Gloria was heading directly toward the inky gloom of the pitch-black hallway when she sensed movement out of the corner of her eye. Swiveling her head and holding her phone out in front of her to use the brightness of its screen as a flashlight, she saw, in the center of the living room, two small barely distinguishable forms: Bradley and Ruth. They were facing the television or, more accurately, based on the upward tilt of their heads, the framed sketch above the television.

The sketch of the shack in which Gloria had seen penciled figures moving.

"Bradley!" she said, hurrying over to them. "Ruth!"

They turned toward her, and this close she could see that both of them were grinning. Feeling suddenly cold, she said, "Where's Daddy?" Not *Are you all right?* or *What are you doing in the dark?* but *Where's Daddy?* There was a sick terrified feeling in the pit of her stomach.

As if in answer, the thumping started again. It was definitely coming from the hall closet, and Gloria left the kids, running into the darkness, phone out in front of her. She found the narrow door and immediately turned the knob, pulling it open. Her lighted screen shining into the small space illuminated Benjamin's body. For he was just a body now. Bloody and lifeless, he lay crumpled in the center of the unpleasant little room, blotches of spattered crimson dotting areas of the floor and the strangely sloping ceiling, as though a very small, very strong man had held him by the feet and swung his body up and down, smashing his head against the upper and lower perimeters of the closet.

There was no one in the space with him.

Benjamin's head flopped to the side, facing her, and within the bloody pulp of his face, Gloria saw a staring white eye.

Her screams blended with the wail of the arriving police siren.

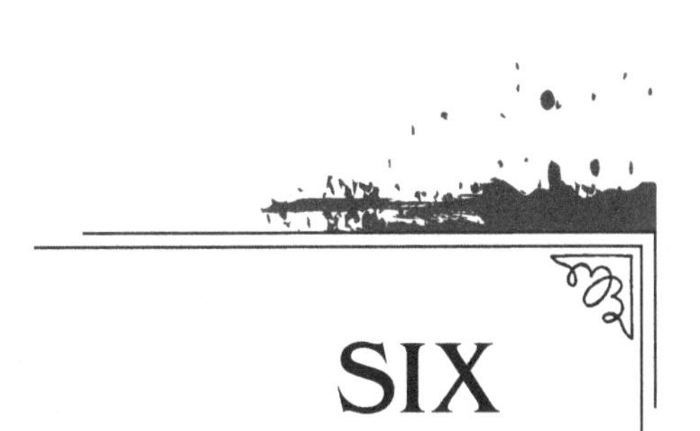

SIX

Benjamin's funeral was well-attended. Lucas, Paul and their other ex-friends were not invited and didn't show, but Benjamin had been well-liked and well-respected, and a host of individuals from both his work and private life came to pay their respects.

Bradley and Ruth were gone, and it was as though they had never existed. No one at the funeral made any mention of them, their bedrooms were once again office and guestroom, respectively, and all of their toys and artwork had vanished from the house.

Numbly, Gloria went through the motions of living. She got up each day, did what she needed to do, ate breakfast, lunch and dinner, went to sleep each night.

The days passed, the weeks, the months.

She continued to teach, occasionally saw friends who invited her out because they were worried about her mental state, but it was as though the purpose of her existence had been taken away. She'd invested so much time and effort in keeping Benjamin safe, it was as if, now that he was gone, her life had no meaning and there was no reason for her to still be here. Endless hours were spent in a completely silent house—no music, no radio, no television—going over each and every thing that she could have done differently in order to save Benjamin's life. An equal amount of time was spent wondering exactly *how* he had died and who had done it. The police, it seemed to her, had given up on solving his murder far too quickly, as if the unexplainable strangeness of the killing had scared them away.

Her money was on Bradley, although he had never seemed that strong and Gloria had absolutely no idea how he could have done it.

The fact that no one else knew the boy had ever existed made it impossible for her to share her theory with anyone else.

Suddenly it was summer, and three full months stretched in front of her, empty months she had no idea how to fill. In her mind, Gloria had gone over everything she could remember about Benjamin with obsessive scrutiny, trying to determine who, or more accurately, *what* wanted him dead and why. She had never arrived at an answer, and part of the reason was the stumbling block of her jumbled memory. For she seemed to recall other times, other lives, where she and Benjamin had had different friends and relatives, worked different jobs, lived in different houses. It was only after the potluck they'd hosted, where the marital problems that had for some reason been building suddenly dissipated, that her memories seemed to solidify. Everything from then on was clear, and it seemed to her that that was when she had realized the danger her husband was in.

But how could that be?

Gloria knew who *would* know what was happening: those people who tended the shack in Northern California, the one depicted in her living room drawing. She was not sure when she'd become aware of the real shack's location—maybe she'd always known where it was—but as she stood in front of the television, staring at the framed sketch above it, remembering the last time she'd seen Bradley and Ruth, at this exact same spot—

grinning

—she couldn't help thinking that those people, the ones she'd seen in penciled representation moving about the small structure, would be able to tell her what she wanted to know. It seemed to her that she had met them somewhere at some time, but it was more an impression than a memory, a feeling that it may have happened even though she had no recollection of the experience.

She stared at the drawing, hoping to see movement, though none occurred. She needed to go there, she decided.

Hicksville.

The town was named Hicksville.

There were no pictures of the town on Google Earth, but MapQuest had directions to it, and she printed them out. Gloria had the feeling that she might not need them, that instinct or something like it would lead her to that spot, but it was better to be prepared. In the back of her mind, she thought that there *had* been a satellite photo on Google Earth once, that she had previously looked it up and found the shack, but the memory was hazy and fuzzy and might have been a wish rather than a reality. So many memories these days were vague, and once again she found herself wondering if there was actually nothing out of the usual here, and her brain was merely complicating reality because she could not face the harsh truths of her life.

Like her husband being killed by having his head slammed against the roof of a creepy little closet while the police made no effort to find the murderer.

No, she wasn't burying her head in the sand with fantasy scenarios. Peculiar things *were* going on, and while it might be a long shot, Gloria had a feeling that the people connected to the shack might know something about it.

She told no one she was leaving. She didn't have to notify the university because the semester was over and she wasn't teaching any summer classes. She didn't tell any of her friends because the follow-up questions would be too difficult to answer, and she wasn't close enough to any of them to tell the truth. She had no family to inform, and the neighbors didn't need to know.

So she had her car checked by the dealer to make sure it would be able to make the trip, packed enough clothes in her suitcase for a week, bought some snacks and drinks to keep her awake as she drove, and early Sunday morning took off.

She'd chosen Sunday figuring there would be less traffic, but while there might be fewer cars on the road, there were enough freeway-widening projects that it still took over two hours to pass through metropolitan Los Angeles. Finally, she was out of the city and passing through the Tehachapi mountains, heading north.

Driving through the San Joaquin Valley, Gloria felt lonely. She was pretty sure that when she'd come through here previously, she'd had children with her, although she could not remember whether those children had been her own or someone else's. Above her, the sky was hazy, and around her the land was ugly, the blue skies and green rolling hills of cinematic farmland nowhere in evidence. She passed an abandoned gas station and a peeling billboard graffitied with racist epithets.

Noon came and went, but she didn't feel like eating lunch, so she kept on driving. Eventually, she did stop to gas up the car and go to the bathroom, but then she was on the road again, trying not to get hit by the massive semi-trucks that sped up the two-lane highway and seemed to switch lanes indiscriminately.

She passed the turnoff to Yosemite sometime in mid-afternoon, continuing north. Gloria *was* getting hungry when dinnertime rolled around and she stopped in Sacramento to grab a bite. Feeling tired and not trusting herself to drive in the dark, she decided to spend the night at a Day's Inn and then start off fresh in the morning.

Which she did.

It was supposed to be summer, but there was snow on the ground as Gloria drove along the increasingly narrow roads that led to Hicksville. She saw a couple frozen in the snow by the side of the road, next to a pickup truck with its doors open. The woman was dressed in shorts and a halter top, curled in a fetal position behind the vehicle. The man was sitting atop the hood, hands in his lap, facing the road as though he'd been flash-frozen in place.

Gloria drove past without stopping.

Further on, two women dressed entirely in black were kneeling before a homemade cross posted by the side of the road that probably marked the location of a fatal accident. There was no vehicle nearby, and Gloria wondered if the women had walked.

The road began winding down through sloping foothills. The elevation dropped, the snow disappeared, and less than half an hour later, it was so warm outside that she had to turn on the air conditioning.

Finally, she reached the town of Hicksville and sensed almost immediately that there was something off about the place. It was a small town and picturesque, but for a community of this size, there seemed a noticeable lack of people. It was practically a ghost town. Gloria saw no cars on the road, no one walking along the sidewalk, no indication that any of the small downtown's businesses were open. There were three cars parked in front of a Mexican restaurant that for some reason seemed familiar, and she was tempted to stop there just to prove to herself that she was not the only person left alive, but something suddenly clicked in her head, and she knew that the shack for which she'd been searching was down a side road up ahead.

She turned onto the narrow lane and, just past a dirt lot on which stacks of used tires were piled, saw the shack.

Gloria had known it was small, but it seemed even tinier than she'd been expecting, more like a shed than a shack and barely bigger than an outhouse, although the trees behind it were taller than she thought they'd be. She pulled over to the side of the road. Several cars were parked on both sides of the lane in front of her. A group of men dressed incongruously in business suits sat in a loosely knit circle on the lightly sloping ground in front of the small building. One of them saw her and hastily stood.

"Stop!" he shouted. He hurried down the dirt path that led through the weedy lot from the doorway of the shack to the road. "Don't go!" She could see that he was older with a big thick mustache.

"I'm not going anywhere," she said as he approached.

The man breathed a sigh of relief. "Thank God." He caught his breath, looked into her face. "Are you Gloria Jaymes?"

For some reason, she was not surprised when he asked that. She nodded. "Yes. And I'm here for some answers."

He nodded back. "Let's talk," he said and started back up the path to where the other men had risen from their circle and were standing in front of the shack. He looked over his shoulder at her. "Are you still there?"

Gloria nodded.

"Don't leave."

"I wasn't planning on it."

Russell, she thought, *his name is Russell*, although she was not sure how she knew that.

The two of them passed through the lot, stopping before the other men who were milling about in front of the shack. They were all looking at her, but Gloria found it impossible to read their expressions. Was it curiosity she saw on the face of that one, or fear? Was the one next to him hopeful or anxious?

"She's here," Russell announced, although surely they could see that for themselves.

"Is she ready?" another man asked. *Jimmy*, she thought.

"Ready for what?" Gloria wanted to know.

The men looked at each other. Russell held up a hand, indicating that the others should be quiet and let him talk. "You don't remember," he told Gloria. It was a statement not a question, and before she could respond, he motioned toward the ground in front of the shack where they had all been sitting in a circle. "Have a seat."

"I'm not sitting on the ground," she told him.

"This may take awhile."

"I'm *not* sitting on the ground."

"Would you like to go inside?"

She would, Gloria realized. She knew she should probably be afraid, going alone into a little shed in a weird town in the middle of nowhere with a bunch of strange men, but for some reason, she wasn't. Russell led her through the open doorway, the others following behind. Inside, the shed was larger than it had seemed from the front, stretching back. The walls were covered with paintings, drawings and photos of herself. A giant framed portrait was mounted on the rear wall. In the center of the narrow room was a raised section of flooring that made her think of a stage.

She had been here before, Gloria realized.

Russell sat down on the raised platform and motioned for her to sit next to him, but like the other men behind her, she remained standing.

He nodded. "Okay. So...I'm not sure where to start."

"Start at the beginning."

"Do you know where you've been? What you've been doing?"

Again, she didn't understand.

The confusion must have shown in her face. "You find people," Russell told her. "People who have died. And you bring them back."

"To life?

"From the dead."

This made no sense whatsoever. "So you think I'm what? Some sort of faith healer?"

"That's not what I'm saying." He took a deep breath. "Somehow, for some reason, you're able to *go* to places where people who have died are still living."

It was crazytalk. She was aware of that. But...somewhere in the back of her mind, she thought there was something to it.

"I don't know what you mean," Gloria said. Her hands were trembling.

"From what we understand, from what you've told us, you go to a place that's just like here, only the people who have died aren't dead there. Sometimes they're different—they're older or younger, have different jobs or different families—but you find them." He met her eyes. "I don't know if you actually create this place yourself or if you just go there, but somehow you bring people back." He shrugged. "Maybe they're not even the same people, not *exactly*—who knows?—but they seem like they are, they act like they are, they *feel* like they are."

"Bobby Perez," Jimmy said. "You brought him back."

Russell nodded. "And many others."

"What do you have to do with this?" she asked. "How are you involved?"

"We're sort of facilitators, I guess. People come to us, people whose loved ones have died, and we come to you, tell you who they are and somehow you find them."

"So you profit off this?"

"Not profit, no. But we *are* the ones who know what you can do. And we help people get their loved ones back."

"But you don't know *how* I do...whatever I do?"

Russell shook his head. "We have no idea. One moment you're there, the next you're gone, and sometime later, maybe a day, maybe a week, maybe a month, maybe a year, you come back, usually wandering in from someplace else like you'd been here in this world all along."

"But I haven't been."

"No. We don't think so."

"You're a goddess," another man said, a tall heavy man with a receding hairline. She did not know his name. "That is why we worship you."

Worship?

That creeped her out, and she glanced around at the pictures. "I'm not a goddess," Gloria insisted. "Even if I *do* have this ability, and that's a *big* if—"

"You brought back my wife Nora!"

The other men nodded.

She looked from one face to the next, took a deep breath. "How long have I been doing this?"

"Since you were a child."

"I don't remember it."

"You will. It takes a little time."

"So we've had this conversation before."

Russell smiled. "More than once." His smile faded a little. "More than usual lately."

"Then why did you ask if I was Gloria Jaymes?" She gestured toward the portraits and pictures on the wall. "Obviously I am."

Russell and Jimmy shared a glance.

"What?"

"You don't always know who you are. When you make your way back here. Sometimes you're confused. Once, you thought your name was Selma. And recently…it's gotten worse."

"Why?"

"We don't know. All we know is that you've been trying to get Benjamin. And, apparently, it's been a lot harder than usual."

"Benjamin is—?"

"Benjamin *was* your husband," Russell said.

Jimmy nodded. "He died last year."

She glanced from one to the other. "So I have a normal life. I don't do this all the time. I actually got married and…probably went to school and…" Gloria frowned, suddenly aware that she'd had no reaction when they'd mentioned the death of her husband. "Benjamin… Benjamin… I don't remember him." And she didn't. She remembered that his death was the reason she had driven here from Southern California, that despair at his passing had led her to Hicksville looking for answers, but try as she might, she could not conjure an image of what he looked like, could remember nothing of his personality or who he was.

"You met in college," Russell prodded. "You've been married for fifteen years. He's into computer science."

That rang a bell. "Wait a minute," Gloria said. She thought hard.

Benjamin.

She remembered him now. The specifics of his appearance were not entirely clear, but she knew he had brown hair and a warm smile. He liked The Beatles. He was patient. Kind.

And she loved him dearly.

Tears welled in Gloria's eyes, her vision growing blurry. "How did he die?"

"Cancer."

"I haven't been able to bring him back?"

"Not so far."

"But if I can resurrect people, why can't—?"

"We don't know," Russell said.

She saw the worry on his face. "What?" she asked.

"It's occurred to us...I mean, we've talked about..."

"We think something might be working against you," Jimmy said.

Gloria frowned. "Like what?"

Russell shook his head. "Fate? God? Someone else like you? Maybe a different version of yourself floating around out there from some other time?" He leaned forward. "The thing is, none of us knows anything. As far as we're aware, you're the only person on earth who can do this, and what little we do know is from the bits and pieces you've told us over the years, because even *you* don't know how you do what you do. Sometimes you come out and you remember things, sometimes your memory's been wiped clean."

"I'm starting to remember," she said.

"That's good," he told her, but he still looked worried.

"How long was I gone this time? How long has it been since you saw me?"

"About ten minutes."

Ten minutes! That was impossible. She could not recall much, but she definitely remembered driving up here, a journey that had taken over a day and a half, and before that, she had lived with Benjamin (and their children?) in Brea for...some time.

Certainly more than ten minutes.

Obviously, time worked differently wherever she sought out the dead.

Cancer. Gloria wiped the tears from her eyes. Benjamin had died from cancer. In the fogginess of her memories, she thought he had been murdered. She could almost see him in her mind, though details remained unclear. Her heart, however, ached from his loss, and she felt empty inside, as though an important part of her had been removed.

Gloria glanced at the large portrait on the rear wall of the room—

She was blonde in real life. Why in the portrait was she brunette?

—then pushed her way through the gathered men toward the door. "Excuse me," she said. Once outside, she breathed deeply, unaware until that moment of how claustrophobic she had felt inside the shack.

The shrine.

"I'm going back," she told Russell when he followed her outside. "To get him."

"How? What are you going to—?"

"I don't know. But I feel it. It's happening. Are you going to be here when I return?" There were still a million questions she wanted to ask.

"We always are."

And—

SIX

ONE

They were living in wartime. Gloria had no idea who was fighting or how long it had been going on, but the streets of Brea were cratered by bomb blasts, and what used to be the university was little more than massive heaps of steel, glass and concrete rubble. There was no freeway anymore, only crumbling cement pylons indicating where the raised highway had once bisected the eastern half of the city. Their house—if it could be called a house anymore—was missing a section of roof, which was now covered by blue tarp, and there was a huge hole in the outside wall of the living room, also covered by tarp. They had no electricity or running water.

She found Benjamin and their four children sitting on a stained saggy couch, Benjamin reading a Dr. Seuss book to the kids. The two older boys were long past the Dr. Seuss stage, but with no radio, TV or internet to entertain them, they were listening as raptly to *If I Ran the Zoo* as their younger sisters.

Gloria had gone next door for water. Somehow the Yangs' outside faucet was still working, although the water that came out of it was rust-colored and undrinkable. They used it to flush the toilet, and drank only what they could find in sealed bottles or cans. She walked back to the bathroom, emptied the two gallon jugs she was carrying into the toilet's tank and walked back out to the living room. "Your turn," she told Benjamin. "We need enough for tonight and tomorrow morning."

"As soon as we finish here, I'm on it."

He had placed his rifle on the listing table in front of the couch, though he knew she didn't like having the weapon so close to the children. He must have seen or heard something when he'd gone out on reconnaissance earlier, and her muscles tensed up as she thought about the last time a squad had come down their street, taking out the Lhasas before a drone had assisted the neighborhood militia in taking them out.

They switched duties. Gloria read the kids *The Sleep Book* while Benjamin went next door for more water. From overhead, she heard the buzzing of a drone—one of theirs, she hoped—and from somewhere not too close yet not too far, the tinny garbled sound of an official announcement broadcast through the speakers of an armored vehicle. She hoped they weren't going to be evacuated again. This time, they might return to find their house completely destroyed.

Water needs taken care of, Benjamin gave her a high sign as he locked and barricaded the front door. "Mommy and I need to talk for a minute," he said. "Bradley, watch Luke and your sisters."

The boy nodded, and Benjamin led her into the bathroom, acting as though they were about to have an important conversation, but as soon as he had locked the door behind him, he pulled his pants down and sat on the closed lid of the toilet. He was already erect, and she took off her own dirty pants and panties and straddled him. A minute or two of deep quick thrusts and they were done, silently dressing before unlocking the door. They shared a smile, and that smile nearly broke her heart. Here in this impossible situation, in this hellish locale, tenderness still bloomed, and Gloria began to tear up, not for herself or even their children, but for Benjamin, who deserved a better, happier existence.

She heard the sound of far-off gunfire, followed by a disconcertingly loud explosion. On the couch, the kids were huddled together, all of them except Bradley closing their eyes and covering their ears. He had his arms around them, trying to be strong, and her heart went out to him as she and Benjamin sat reassuringly on opposite sides of the couch, like sentries protecting the young charges between them.

She tried to remember who was fighting and why, but the war had been going on for so long that she couldn't recall.

Only that wasn't quite true, was it? Because she actually hadn't been here that long. Despite possessing memories of this place, she had only just arrived, and she had arrived for a purpose. She glanced over the kids' heads at Benjamin, who appeared lost in thought. For once, somehow, her *real* memories were intact, if not all of them at least most of them, which meant that Gloria knew what was going on. She might not know exactly what was happening in terms of the war and this existence, but she knew the truth *behind* this existence, understood the real reason why she was here. While she was by no means an expert, she had a layman's headline knowledge of string theory and the concept of a multiverse. Whether that was applicable or not, Gloria knew that this world was this world only because certain decisions had been made, certain words spoken, certain actions taken. If another decision had been made here, a substitute word spoken or an alternative action taken there, everything would be different, in small ways, or perhaps even larger ones. There were pivot points in life, in time, and given who she was and what she could do, if she was able to find one of those points and zigged instead of zagged...

She could change the narrative.

How she would do that, Gloria had no idea.

But she intended to figure it out.

The next morning, after a cold breakfast of stale bread and dusty-tasting bottled water, the same thing they'd had for dinner, the family went out searching for food. On Imperial Highway, women were weeping in the street. An old man was wailing for the family members he had lost. Others were wandering, as they were, trying to find basic necessities. It seemed to Gloria that she should begin looking for a way to escape this existence and change this reality. She recalled, in another place, another time, attending a celebration where she and Benjamin had been suddenly and inexplicably attacked by their friends. She needed to find something like that now, an occasion where the unexpected could occur, where *she* could be the one to move events in another direction.

Gloria felt a tug on her hand, and glanced over to see Jenny looking up at her. "I have to go to the bathroom."

Luke shook his head. "You were supposed to go at home before we left," he told his sister.

"But I like the bathroom at the store better! It still works like it's s'posed to!"

They had not intended to go into Albertson's. The grocery store had long since been looted of everything, but Jenny was right: the last time they'd gone in, the restroom had still had running water. It might be a good idea for *all* of them to go to the bathroom, Gloria reasoned. It would save her and Benjamin from having to carry jugs over to the Yangs' faucet, which, realistically, could go out at any time, leaving them high and dry.

The minute they walked into the darkened supermarket, Gloria could feel that something was off. They seemed to be the only ones in the building, for one thing, which was odd because it was not only a perfect place for squatters but it *did* have a working bathroom, which should have generated a huge line. They were all alone, though, and the air felt strangely heavy, almost liquid as they moved forward.

She glanced over at Benjamin to see if he felt it, too. Gloria could tell from his expression that he did, and she was about to tell everyone that they needed to leave, when Jenny let go of her hand, broke away, and ran down the first aisle toward the restrooms at the far end.

"Jenny!" she called, but her voice did not travel far through the thick air, and she hurried after her daughter, exhorting the others behind her, "Come on!"

It was much darker back here than it was toward the front of the store where the windows were, and she was surprised her daughter was brave enough to run through the gloom by herself.

She followed Jenny into the bathroom, which fortunately had an opaque skylight that allowed them to see inside the enclosed space. Jenny was already in the closest of the two stalls, and Gloria was ready to yell at her and give her a lecture for running off, when she was suddenly hit by the acrid stench of the bathroom air. The sink faucet was running, she saw, and bug poison flowed from the tap, its harsh chemical odor nearly overwhelming in the confined area.

Gloria opened the bathroom door and told Benjamin, "Hold it there," while she told Jenny, "Get out of here, now!"

"I'm almost done!"

"*Now*! And don't flush! Can't you smell that poison?"

At the word "poison," Jenny screamed and dashed out of the stall, pulling up her pants.

Gloria hustled her out of the restroom, and Benjamin closed the door behind them. "Jesus," Gloria breathed.

From the other side of the building, somewhere beyond the farthest aisle, came a high-pitched keening. It was not constant but ebbed and flowed. The six of them stood there, looking at each other. Gloria had no idea what could possibly be making that sound, and she didn't want to find out. All she wanted to do was get her family safely back outside, and, as they did in all hazardous situations, they moved without speaking swiftly and in single file up the aisle toward the exit, Gloria in the front, Benjamin in the rear, the kids safely in-between.

It occurred to her as they emerged into daylight that whatever was going on in that supermarket was aimed at Benjamin, was trying to take him out. It also occurred to her that this was one of those pivot points, that if she went in there and confronted whatever was making that terrifying noise, she might be able to *shift* things.

But she wasn't going back in there. She would have other, less dangerous opportunities to do what she needed to do, and there was no reason for her to put herself in harm's way.

A contingent of uniformed soldiers was marching down the center of Imperial Highway behind two armored vehicles. Everyone on the street moved aside to let them pass, many of them cheering. Gloria did not recognize the uniforms, but she knew that the soldiers were on their side in the war.

Whichever side that was.

Her family watched the parade from the Albertson's parking lot before walking out to the sidewalk. The fact that she knew almost nothing about this war seemed strange. Ordinarily, she would be fully immersed in her life. It would be previous lives, *real* life, that she would have forgotten. The details of this existence would be a part of her, as though she'd dwelt in this realm since birth. The fact that the usual norms had been upended set off alarm bells within her, and made Gloria realize that she might not have all the knowledge she needed.

She knew enough, however, to pick up a battered battery from the ground when she saw it, aware that batteries were used as currency in those few places that still accepted such tokens rather than bartering for goods. With this Double-A, they'd be able to get a couple of apples, carrots or potatoes, fresh fruit or vegetables that the kids' growing bodies desperately needed.

"Hide it," Benjamin said quickly, blocking her from the view of people passing by on the street.

She put the battery in her pocket.

"Let's go," he urged.

With the stores all looted, it was in the park that vendors sold their wares from carts and wagons. An armed guard stood at the fenced entrance to the park, making sure that all who entered had the means to pay, and when Gloria showed the stoic man her dented battery, he let her family pass.

In any other place at any other time, the offerings available would have been rejected even for zoo animals, but to their desperate eyes, the wrinkled vegetables and soggy fruit looked like manna from heaven. She was able to buy a brown banana, a soft zucchini and *three* potatoes with her battery, and Benjamin put them in his shoulder bag with his knife for the trip home.

They went to bed that night with stomachs that were fuller and happier than they had been in a long time.

They were awakened in the morning by a knock at the door.

Benjamin instantly grabbed his rifle. The Yangs and their other neighbors knew to identify themselves as friends by knocking twice, slowly, then pausing before knocking three times in rapid succession. This was just a random series of raps on the door, indicating a stranger.

"Let me handle it," Benjamin said.

Gloria moved in front of him. "Let *me* handle it." She didn't want him to be killed before she figured out a way to save him, and with the children huddling in their rooms and Benjamin right behind her, she peeked through the peephole to see who was out there.

It was her sister Mila.

Her first impulse was to open the door and immediately let Mila in, but she stopped herself. Whatever was trying to keep Benjamin from returning to life always took the form of people close to her: her mother, her father, her children. It was the same here. This wasn't her sister, she realized. In fact, she had never had a sister. She recognized the person in front of her as a woman who'd been killed by her husband and whose brother had wanted Gloria to bring her back to life.

Why had that woman's appearance been chosen to represent her sister?

"It's Mila!" Benjamin said, peering through the peephole and putting his gun aside. Before Gloria could stop him, he had opened the door and let her in.

Gloria tensed, but nothing out of the ordinary happened. Mila gave her a hug, kissed Benjamin on the cheek and remarked on how the children, who had come out of hiding upon hearing her voice, had grown so big that she barely recognized them. It was a regular family reunion, and Gloria even recalled their last meeting and the tearful goodbye, though she was acutely aware that those events had not happened to *her*.

Who *had* they happened to, though? What happened before she arrived and after she left? Was there another Gloria?

Or did this entire universe spring into being when she arrived and collapse when she left?

She had no answers for any of these questions, and wasn't even sure it mattered. She was here for only one reason: to protect her husband and bring him back into what she now thought of as the *real* world.

Unless it wasn't.

She didn't even want to start down that path.

"I was on my way to see Mom, and I thought I'd stop by in case I can't get across The Gap," Mila said.

Gloria nodded as though she understood, but no part of what her sister said made any sense to her. Amidst the shattered landscape and personal privations of wartime, Mila's breezy nonchalance seemed jarringly out of place, and the gaps in her own knowledge meant that Gloria had no idea what "The Gap" was or what would happen if it could not be crossed.

"When's the last time you saw Mom?" Mila asked.

Benjamin answered for her. "She came over for Jenny's birthday last month."

Mila bent down. "Oh, was it your birthday?"

Jenny nodded.

"How old are you now?"

"Ten thousand."

"That's a good age."

Gloria felt uneasy. There was no attempt on her sister's part to elicit a correct answer, and no one laughed at what Jenny had said or made any effort to correct her.

"I have late birthday presents for *all* of you," Mila promised. "They're in my car. I'll show you once I get unpacked." She straightened, addressing Gloria and Benjamin again. "How did Mom look?"

"Not good," Benjamin answered for them.

"That's what I was afraid of."

Gloria looked outside. Mila *did* have a car, although how she was able to drive it over the cratered, rubble-strewn streets, Gloria had no idea. Leaving the kids inside, she and Benjamin walked out in their underwear, helping Mila unpack for what her sister insisted was merely a one-day stay.

"Have you guys had breakfast yet?" Mila looked at them in their pajamas and underclothes. "I assume not. Get dressed and I'll have something ready."

"We don't—" *have anything except potato water*, Gloria was about to say, but her sister cut her off. "I brought bagels and oranges."

The children cheered, jumping up and down excitedly, and even Benjamin had a huge grin on his face. This was like a wish come true, and everyone hurried back down the hallway to change.

Gloria made sure she was out first, slipping on a worn T-shirt and pulling dirty jeans over her torn panties before heading into the kitchen.

"My legs have gotten so hairy," Mila said as she walked in, and Gloria gasped as her sister hiked up her pants.

Mila had an animal's legs.

Gloria stared. *Goat? Ape? Kangaroo?* It was impossible to tell what type of legs were ensconced in those fashionable boots, but they were definitely not human, and she experienced an involuntary shiver as her gaze moved from those hairy sinewy shins to that soft womanly face and back again.

Mila lowered her pantlegs seconds before Jenny and Paula ran into the kitchen. They were followed immediately afterward by Bradley and Luke, all four of them excited at the prospect of having a proper breakfast. "What kind do you want?" Mila asked. "I have blueberry and cinnamon raisin." She placed a plate of sliced bagels on the tilting table. "I'm going to squeeze us some fresh orange juice."

"Blueberry!"

"Cinnamon!"

"Raisin and blueberry!"

"Cinnamon!"

Gloria's mouth was watering, and she temporarily pushed aside all thoughts of her sister's legs as she herded her children over to the table. Benjamin walked into the kitchen, reaching over their heads and grabbing the top bagel half. "Mmmm," he said, biting into it.

Gloria allowed the kids to take what they wanted before picking up one of the leftovers. It was cold and untoasted, but when she bit into the sliced bagel, it was delicious. Blueberry.

They all sat down on the mismatched chairs and stools that ringed the breakfast table, talking excitedly. Mila, at the counter, had sliced her oranges and was juicing them. Feeling happy, Gloria turned to Benjamin.

Whose face was turning blue.

He was choking on his bagel.

Gloria screamed, knocking over her chair, causing the children to scream. Benjamin was clutching his throat, and not a sound was issuing from his wide open mouth. His airway was completely blocked. Somewhere, sometime, she'd had CPR training, and she got behind him, threw her arms around his stomach and pulled in as hard as she could. There was no change, and she jerked harder, practically punching his stomach, then immediately repositioning her arms, pointing her joined hands upward then downward as she yanked, trying to find the right angle.

"*No!*" she screamed.

Was she supposed to put her fingers in his mouth to try to clear the air passage, or was that only for babies and small children? Could the chewed bagel be too doughy to be dislodged in such a manner? Was she supposed to do something else?

She was about to throw him over the back of one of the smaller chairs—it seemed she recalled that being one of the options for larger people—when a high breathy whistle escaped from his open mouth, and he spit an ill-defined lump of bagel onto the floor. He pulled away from her, mouth open, looking upward at the ceiling as he alternated between coughing and loudly sucking in gigantic gulps of air. Gradually, his color returned, and his breathing approached something approximating normal.

Hands shaking, her heart pounding, Gloria hazarded a look at her sister, not surprised to find Mila exhibiting a complete lack of concern for Benjamin's condition. A flash of anger coursed through her, and Gloria vowed that as soon as they finished eating, she was sending Mila on her merry way. Benjamin had avoided choking to death only by the purest luck, and she wasn't about to tempt fate by allowing this woman to remain in their house. It was more than possible that this entire breakfast had been arranged in order to kill Benjamin, and Gloria was determined to cut off any chance of a reenactment.

She glanced over at her husband to make sure he was recovering from the incident—

—and he collapsed without uttering a sound as a stray shot from a hail of gunfire that had just erupted in the street, shattered the kitchen window and ripped through his chest.

The wordless cry that escaped from her lips bore no resemblance to human speech and its piercing volume did not abate as she swiftly crossed the five feet between them and instinctively pressed her palm against the gushing wound in the center of his chest. Blood flowed out between her fingers and around the sides of her hand in an unstoppable surge, and though she could feel the pumping of his heart, she could also sense it weakening, the muscles beneath her palm relaxing into death.

"Don't..." she managed to get out, but could not follow it with another word as she choked on a sob. She had no idea what the kids were doing, or Mila, but she could not afford to take her eyes off Benjamin. *Call 911*, she wanted to say, but there was no 911 in this world, and at that second, she knew that he was going to die. She looked into his face, and though his eyelids were fluttering, his gaze remained focused on her. "Don't die," she said, and her voice was barely audible even to herself. "Don't die..."

Through his pain, Benjamin managed to smile at her, but the smile instantly began fraying around the edges as he started to fade away. Outside, shots were still being fired. Another window shattered.

Maybe *this* was a pivot moment, she told herself.

She took her hands off the wound, which was no longer gushing as his heart was too weak to pump, and she lay down on the floor, holding Benjamin close, hugging his bloody body. Her lips brushed his ear. "This war is over," Gloria whispered.

TWO

They broke their embrace and rolled over to their respective sides of the bed. Through the curtainless open window came a clattering sound as a bevy of birds perched on different levels of the feeders and messily attempted to eat, excess seeds noisily raining onto the dry leaves below. The morning had dawned unusually clear and bright, and Gloria could see blue sky above the fall colors of the changing trees.

Their home was in Colorado, just outside of town, close enough that a fire truck or ambulance could get here quickly in an emergency, but with enough of a buffer zone that they had some privacy and did not have to look out their windows at neighbors' houses. Their own home was large, two stories with a screened-in porch and a small guest house in the back, by far the best and biggest place she had ever lived.

She did not know who she was in this life. Were her parents alive? Did she have brothers and sisters? Who were her friends? Did she have a job, and if so, what was it?

It would come to her. It always did. And she lay on her back, staring up at the ceiling, enjoying the moment, feeling not just content but genuinely happy.

"I guess I'd better get up," Benjamin said reluctantly, and she understood that he ran a tech support business where he helped local companies and individuals maintain their computers. It was a peculiarly old-fashioned trade for such a modern field, but in a small town like theirs, where even the biggest businesses could not afford an IT department, his services were not only welcome but necessary.

And she was...?

It would come to her.

In the meantime, she remembered clearly what had happened before this, retaining not only memories of her last life but the ones before that. How many times could Benjamin die, Gloria wondered, before he actually ceased to exist and could never be brought back? The question did not seem to have occurred to her before, but it loomed large in her thoughts now as she watched him get out of bed and pad off to the bathroom.

She was an oncologist's nurse.

Or she had been, until Dr. Lee had retired. At the moment, she, like the rest of the doctor's office staff, was unemployed. Or "between jobs," as her friend Lupe liked to say. Apparently, Gloria had not been in much of a hurry to find another position, because Dr. Lee had shut down his practice at the beginning of September, and it was already mid-October and she hadn't so much as applied anywhere else.

"Must be nice not to have a regular schedule," Benjamin said, emerging from the bathroom, and while that could have been a shot, it wasn't. He was joking with her, and Gloria understood that he didn't care if she ever went back to work. He was making enough to support them both, and if she eventually became pregnant, as they were hoping, it would be better for the baby if at least one parent remained at home.

"Want an omelet?" Gloria asked, getting out of bed herself.

He shook his head, opening the closet door and taking out a pair of black jeans and a casual long-sleeved shirt, his usual attire. "That's okay. I'll just stop by Dunkin' Donuts and get some coffee."

"Coffee! You need something to *eat*. Breakfast is—"

"—the most important meal of the day," he finished for her. "I know. But I had all I could eat last night." He wiggled his eyebrows in a parody of lasciviousness, and she suddenly remembered what had happened. Which explained why her panties were on the floor.

She picked them up and put them on. "Well, *I'm* hungry."

"More power to you. I'm taking a shower."

"There'll be breakfast when you get out."

"But—"

"There'll be breakfast when you get out."

They did end up eating together—it turned out that he was hungrier than he thought—and after Benjamin left, Gloria cleaned both the breakfast and leftover dinner dishes before taking her own leisurely shower. At nine o'clock, Lupe came over. Since Dr. Lee had retired and Gloria lost her job, the two of them had taken to walking each morning for exercise. Lupe's two kids were in elementary school, so, like Gloria, her friend had the rest of the day free, at least until three-thirty, when school got out.

More often than not, their so-called "exercise" was an unhurried stroll as the two of them chatted and gossiped about other neighbors. Today, Lupe was furious because Helen Stewart, the old lady who lived across the street, had called the city to complain about Lupe's husband Rick parking his car on the street overnight in front of their house, which he did so that their boys could play basketball in the driveway. "That stupid old biddy spends all day every day just staring out her picture window and looking for things to complain about. She made it seem like some homeless guy was camping out in his car or some criminal was casing the neighborhood, because the cop who actually came to my door asked me if I knew anything about a mysterious gray Jeep Cherokee that had been parked all night in front of my house. He actually used the word 'mysterious'!"

"That's crazy," Gloria said, but she knew exactly what Lupe was talking about. The mailman had told her that Helen had complained to him one time about their yard, telling him that Gloria and Benjamin should hire a gardener since Benjamin was obviously too lazy to mow the lawn as often as he should.

"Of course, I told him the Jeep was ours, and we had a perfect right to park in front of our own house, and Helen Stewart was a meddling old bitch."

Gloria laughed. "You told him that?"

"Well, not in so many words. But you could tell he thought so, too."

They moved on to other topics: their husbands' job stress, Lupe's mother-in-law problems, their divorced friend Leslie's new boyfriend. At the park where they turned around to walk back, several mothers were there with their toddlers, a couple of them sitting on a bench chatting while their children played in the sandbox in front of them, several more helping their kids up the slide or pushing them on the swings. Lupe sighed. "I miss that age. Don't get me wrong; I love my boys and love where they're at right now, but, selfishly, it's a lot more fun to take them to the park and spend all day with them than help them do math homework when they get home from school."

Gloria knew exactly what Lupe was talking about...only in this life, she didn't. So she remained silent and merely nodded.

Returning home in plenty of time for lunch, she reflected on the curious fact that she was not as concerned for Benjamin's safety as she probably should be and was nowhere near as stressed out as she had been previously. Upon waking, she'd worried that if he died again he might not be able to come back, but since then, the fear that that might happen seemed to have dissipated. Moreover, the certainty had grown that, should something happen, she would be able to put it right. She felt inexplicably confident, a feeling that provided her with a welcome sense of security.

Walking through its rooms, Gloria recognized elements of previous houses in the furnishings of her home. The patterned couch in the living room, for instance. The dining room table and the hanging lamp above it. The headboard of their bed. However this world had come to be, it was a variation on others that she'd visited previously. Places and things had been recycled. People, too, perhaps. Or, if not exactly recycled, then reworked into deviations, however slight, of those that had come before.

Her sister Celia called as she was preparing to fix lunch, and that name was familiar to her, although Gloria did not think it had ever before been the name of one of her sisters.

"Hey," Celia said, "can you talk?"

"I was just about to make lunch, but..."

"Luke's back."

"Back in Colorado?"

"Back in *Pyrite*."

Gloria was startled. Not just startled. Outraged. The last she'd heard, their brother was in Utah, working on some sort of federal highway construction crew, after dropping out of ASU for the third time, which was par for the course. He'd been causing problems in their family since he was a child, and Gloria remembered how, when he was in high school, he had frightened their parents half to death when he skipped graduation and, without telling anyone, used the money he'd received from his grandma and grandpa to buy a bus ticket to Aspen, leaving the entire unwitting family to sit in the audience with every other senior's relatives, having no clue why he didn't walk up to the stage when his name was called.

Now Luke had returned to Colorado—not just Colorado but *Pyrite*—and he hadn't even bothered to let anyone know?

"How long's he been back?" Gloria asked.

"Six months."

"*Six months*!"

"I could've kicked his ass when I found out."

"I wonder why he called you and not me." Gloria had always been closer to her brother than Celia had.

"Oh, he didn't call me. I was at the grocery store, waiting in line, and I looked over at the next checkstand and there he was. I almost didn't recognize him at first—he's shaved off his beard—but then he saw me and got this kind of embarrassed look on his face, and I knew it was him. I got out of line, parked my cart and just went over to where he was. You know what Luke's like. He very well could have paid for his groceries and escaped without saying word one to me."

"So you talked to him?"

"Oh, yeah. I made him talk to me. He wasn't very forthcoming, as usual, so it was mostly me asking questions and him answering, but I tried to pin him down."

"And?"

"That Utah thing lasted about a month. You know he's not cut out for manual labor. So he moved to New Mexico, get this, giving tours of Indian ruins. Some friend of his would drive the van, and Luke would tell stories about the history of the sites. He must've lied through his teeth on that one. Then I thought he said that he'd gotten married, but I found out he'd *almost* gotten married. To some girl he met in a bus station in Albuquerque, for God's sake. Maybe he'd gotten her knocked up, or *thought* he'd gotten her knocked up, and, once he found out he was free and clear, bailed."

"Is that what he said?"

"He didn't say anything. That's what I'm guessing. It sounds like him, though."

"It does," Gloria admitted.

"I honestly didn't get much out of him. I don't even know where he lives! But I got his latest cell phone number. So if you want to take it down..."

Gloria fumbled for a pen and a notepad. After she'd written down their brother's number, she said, "Did you invite him for dinner or anything? Suggest we all get together?"

"Of course." Celia seemed offended she would even have to ask. "He said he's busy. What do you think? I made him promise to call—me *and* you—but you know how likely *that* is."

"I'll call him," Gloria said.

"Do it quick. Before he changes his number." Celia was joking, but not really, and as soon as she hung up, Gloria did try to call Luke, but the call went directly to voicemail and she was forced to leave a message. It was driving her crazy that Celia hadn't learned his address—*she* would've gotten it—and Gloria spent the afternoon alternately pacing, working on the computer, reading a book and trying to figure out whether her brother would actually return her call.

She still hadn't heard from him by the time Benjamin got home, and she told him about her brother before he'd even had time to close the front door. "Luke's back," she said. "Celia ran into him at the store. He's living right here in Pyrite, and he came back half a year ago but didn't bother to tell anyone."

"Is that so?" Benjamin said mildly.

"'Is that so?' *That's* what you have to say?"

"I'm sorry. What did you want me to say?"

"I didn't *want* you to say anything. I just thought you might have an opinion on the subject. I haven't heard from my brother in a year, haven't seen him in two, and now he's living practically right next door but hasn't contacted anyone. Celia happens to spot him at the grocery store, confronts him, and all you can say is 'Is that so?'"

"Sorry," Benjamin said, and this time he actually did sound apologetic. "It's been a long day, and I just walked through the door and you sprung this on me. I need a little time. You know I'm not exactly spontaneous."

Wasn't that the truth. As long as she'd known Benjamin, she could not recall him having an immediate reaction to anything. He was always circumspect, always having to think through and logically support whatever opinion he eventually came to hold. She, on the other hand, was impulsive, often rash and hasty in her decisions, forming permanent opinions based on first impressions, blurting things out and not considering the consequences. It was why they tended to get on one another's nerves, why they were probably not as compatible as they should be.

It had not always been this way, not in every life, but this was definitely not an aberration, and she realized that in at least one of the times before he had died, she'd considered leaving him.

The thought sobered her.

What was happening? Benjamin was the entire reason she was here. She existed in this place because she wanted to bring him back. Why was she contemplating the ways in which they were not well-suited?

"Gloria? Hon?"

She looked over at Benjamin, aware that she'd drifted off for a moment.

"Are you going to get that?"

The phone was ringing! How long had that been going on? She sped over to the nearest phone, the one in the den to the side of the entryway, picking up the receiver in mid-ring. "Hello?"

It was Luke.

THREE

"Do you think he'll stick around this time?"

Luke had just left, and Gloria and Celia were talking.

Celia shrugged. "Who the hell knows? I doubt it."

"You heard him. He says he missed us, and missed Colorado. He definitely seems glad to be back."

"How long do you think that's going to last? Face it, Glore. He's a flake. Always has been, always will be. He doesn't care about anyone but himself. If I hadn't accidentally found him, there's no way he would have called us. And once he screws up and loses his job or gets bored, he'll be off again."

She was probably right, but Gloria couldn't help thinking—well, hoping, really—that this time their brother had changed. Maybe she was being too optimistic, but he genuinely seemed more mature than she remembered him being, and more responsible. He had a real job, was putting money aside in a bank account, and was apparently dating a woman who was educated, financially stable and his own age.

"I think he actually might have grown up," Gloria said.

"We'll see," Celia told her.

Benjamin could have probably offered a more clearheaded perspective, but he hadn't been there for the lunch. The two of them had had a fight this morning, and he had stormed off, which wasn't like him at all. Neither of them, in fact, had been acting like themselves the past few days. They'd been testy with each other, at odds for some reason, though she could not figure out why. Everything she did seemed to irritate him, and everything he did seemed to irritate her, and they'd spent most of their time staying out of each other's way.

She hadn't discussed it with her sister, though. Or anyone else. Her problems with Benjamin were not exactly *outside* this life—in fact, they seemed specifically tied to it—but Gloria knew she needed to find a way to get past this on her own.

By the time Benjamin returned, Celia was long gone. If he was still pouting, she was prepared to sit him down and pull the we-need-to-talk routine, but he walked into the house apologetic, chastened even, and they hugged and made up. "I don't know what got into me," he said. "I'm sorry."

"I'm sorry, too. We've both been on edge lately," Gloria admitted, "although I have no idea why."

He smiled. "The wind? The old Raymond Chandler thing?"

"I guarantee I haven't been looking at either knives or your neck."

He laughed, a real laugh, and she realized how much she missed that sound. It had been awhile since either of them had found anything the other person said funny, and she hoped this was a sign that they could start anew.

It actually had been unseasonably windy lately, and the fires this year had been bad enough to make the national news. She had no idea how anyone who'd lived in Colorado for any length of time could deny that the weather patterns had altered, and she tried to recall if climate change had been this noticeable in every iteration she'd gone through or if some version of the world had somehow managed to stave it off.

By dinnertime, they were each back in their corners, although Gloria wasn't sure how that had happened. Even though it was Sunday and his business was supposed to be closed, Benjamin had spent most of the afternoon on the computer, walking through solutions to technical problems with a couple of his clients, while she had worked briefly in her garden, gone grocery shopping and planned the coming week's meals. They came together to eat the shrimp gumbo that Gloria had prepared, and for some reason found themselves acting irritable and impatient with each other. It was probably her fault as much as his, but they both bristled at innocent questions, became defensive and took offense at subsequent answers and soon lapsed into a prolonged silence as they ate their food.

Looking at him across the table, watching him methodically chew his food and take a small sip of milk after every fourth bite, she began to be irritated by his very existence. He was so rigid, so set in his predictable routines. Sometimes, Gloria had to remind herself of why they were even married. It wasn't as though they were natural soulmates. Both her friends and his friends had expressed surprise when the two of them had gotten together. But she had honestly fallen in love with him, and it was that moment that she tended to revisit when she started feeling like this. For, as corny as it sounded, it *had* been a specific moment, a quickflash realization that he was The One. She had been a college sophomore, a scholarship student at UC Brea in Southern California, and she'd been dragged to a party she didn't want to attend by Nina, a friend who had her eye on a senior she knew was going to be there. Gloria was quickly left alone after Nina zeroed in on her target. Not knowing anyone, she parked herself by the punchbowl, realizing unhappily that her increasingly debauched fellow partygoers were *not* people she would ordinarily want to socialize with.

Then Benjamin walked up.

He seemed as out of place as she felt, and after getting himself a cup of spiked punch, he stood awkwardly next to her. Neither of them spoke at first, but eventually he made some cleverly disparaging remark about the party which made her laugh, and the two of them began talking. It turned out that he had been dragged here as well, by his roommate, and when she found out that he had his own car and was the one who had driven here, she asked him if he'd be willing to take her home.

They both happily left the party, but instead of following her directions and driving her back, he drove to the Disneyland Hotel. They parked in a side lot, and, without telling her where they were going, he led her between the two multi-story hotel buildings to a tiered series of ponds in a corner of the central area. "What's this?" she asked.

He looked at his watch and said, "Nine o'clock. Dancing Waters."

As if on cue, music began playing, and a sequence of fountains sprayed upward from the ponds, lights beneath the water turning the fountains different colors. The water jetted up in various configurations, swaying and jumping in time to the music as the colors changed. It was getting chilly, and as a Disney tune segued into the kitschy theme from "Happy Days," he put his arm around her to keep her warm.

That was when she knew.

Her friends tried to warn her away. He was a dork, they said. She deserved better. But she didn't want better, she wanted him, and they began spending more and more time together, *all* of their available time, and after graduation they became engaged.

It surprised her to realize now that they had met this way more than once, and from behind the fog of experiences and layers of lives, she had the impression that this was how they'd *really* met.

She continued to look at him across the table, her attitude softening. Maybe he *was* a little stodgy, but deep down so was she. And, at heart, he was a good person, a nice person.

She loved him.

She found herself smiling. "Want to do it tonight?" she asked.

And calmly, as if she had merely asked him to pass the salt, he said, "Always."

"Told you," Celia said with a subtle note of triumph in her voice.

Gloria had to admit that her sister was right. Luke seemed to have disappeared into thin air. She had tried calling her brother several times during the week, but with each instance the phone on the other end just rang and rang, with no one picking up and no voicemail answering. She'd finally driven over to his apartment this morning, only to find it abandoned. The door was closed and locked, but the front window's shades were up, and she could clearly see that there was no furniture inside; the apartment was completely empty.

"Do you remember the name of that girlfriend?" Gloria asked. "Maybe—"

"Oh, give it up," Celia told her. "He's gone, he's husking, he's history."

"Husking?"

"I heard it somewhere. Don't badger me."

Gloria smiled. She was glad her sister was here. But she felt genuinely sad that Luke had lost touch with them again. Celia was right, they should have expected it, but hope sprang eternal, and Gloria had thought that this time things might be different.

Why had he turned out this way? she wondered. It must have something to do with their upbringing, but while their childhoods hadn't been ideal, they were no worse than what most people went through. Sure, their father had left when she was two, Celia was three and Luke was a baby, and maybe that had been harder on their brother because he was a boy, but their uncle and grandfather had always been around, so it wasn't as though he'd had no male role models. And their mother had done a pretty good job of taking care of them, keeping them fed and clothed and housed and happy.

Or had she?

For some reason, Gloria thought that maybe that memory wasn't quite correct, although she could not come up with anything else to supersede it.

Benjamin's parents, she recalled, had died in a hit-and-run accident in Orange County, where he had been born and raised. She had never actually known them—they'd been killed before she and Benjamin met—but there'd always seemed something suspicious to her about their deaths. Why had they been walking in an industrial area, far away from where they lived and nowhere near where either of them worked? Had the police ever caught the driver of the vehicle that had hit them? Had he been drunk or had he...intentionally run them over? Over the years, Gloria had tried asking Benjamin for more details about what had happened, not just for the sake of her own curiosity, but because she thought it would be good for him to talk about it rather than keep everything bottled up. True to form, however, he'd exhibited very little interest. She wanted to believe it was because the memories were so painful, but that was probably just wishful thinking on her part. In his dispassionate reciting of the facts of their killing, he might as well have been talking about two strangers he'd seen on the news.

"Ceelie," she said, "what do you remember about Dad? Anything?"

Her sister sighed. "This again?"

"I was just wondering."

"Not much. I told you before, a million times."

"But Mom... She did a good job, right? With us?"

Celia snorted. "She did a great job with Luke, can't you tell?"

"Overall, though, we had a pretty good childhood, didn't we?"

"Yeah, I guess. What's all this about?"

"I don't know," Gloria admitted. "I was just thinking."

"Think about something more cheerful, why don't you?" Celia glanced down at her watch. "Look, I gotta go. Danny's going to be wondering where I am."

"You didn't tell him?"

"No, and my phone battery's low, so I can't call."

"You could—"

"I think we've had enough family time for now. I'll see you later." She held up the bottle of water Gloria had given her as she walked out of the kitchen. "Thanks for the drink."

And she was gone.

It *had* to be their upbringing, Gloria thought. Because their familial bonds were almost nonexistent. Luke had been absent for most of his adult life, and while she and Celia lived in the same city and talked on the phone once a week or so, there was a superficial quality to their relationship, as though they were acquaintances rather than sisters.

She considered Benjamin her real family now, but even here there were problems, since the two of them often seemed to be moving forward not together but apart, on diverging tracks.

Maybe it was her. Maybe she was the one who couldn't connect with people. She wondered if their kids would end up turning out the same way.

Kids?

Yes, they had kids. Teenagers. Two boys and a girl. That had not been the case only seconds before, but it was true now, and Gloria knew that Paul, their oldest, was at band camp this weekend, while the twins, Liz and Brady, were in their bedrooms. Liz entered the kitchen just at that moment, carrying an empty can of V8 that she tossed into the recycling bin. She opened the refrigerator and took out another. "Did Uncle Luke really disappear again?" she asked.

Gloria nodded. "I'm afraid so."

Liz laughed. "What is with this family? They're all so crazy!"

"Present company included," Gloria said.

"Come on, Mom. You know what I mean. I've seen him, like, twice since I was two. And Aunt Ceelie won't acknowledge my existence because she's a religious fanatic and thinks I'm a lesbian."

Was Celia a religious fanatic?

Apparently so.

Was Liz a lesbian?

"*Are* you a lesbian?" Gloria asked.

"Oh, Mom!" Liz popped the top of her V8 can and went back to her room.

That wasn't an answer, and Gloria realized that there was a lot she didn't know about her children. Not just because they had suddenly appeared in her life but because they were typical teenagers. She actually remembered their entire histories, had sense memory of the twins' births, recalled when Paul had broken his arm playing stuntman on the school playground, recollected thousands of minute details of their childhoods. But, again, there was a distance, and once more Gloria wondered if it was something within herself that bred detachment.

Paul returned from band camp late Sunday afternoon, and he returned with an attitude. Two days away from the family had given him a self-confidence that bordered on arrogance, and what started out as condescension toward his brother and sister blossomed into self-righteousness in his interactions with his parents, so much so that halfway through dinner, he and Benjamin got into a heated argument over nothing, and Paul stormed off to his room, leaving most of his food on his plate. There were ripple effects over the next week as Paul remained apart from the rest of the family, claiming that he had band practice or had to study at the library or invented other reasons to be home as little as possible. The twins complained that Paul got to go to band camp and do fun activities while their requests for subsidized pursuits were always rejected.

The thing was, her kids had always been this way. There'd been no major personality shifts when they hit puberty. The teenage years were perhaps cementing their characters and temperaments, but those traits had been there all along. Paul had always been self-centered, Liz heedlessly outspoken, Brady secretive.

It was tiring being a mother, Gloria realized, and tiring being a wife. If she'd still had her job, the drudgery of it all might not seem so obvious, but with nothing else to focus on, domestic responsibilities seemed nearly overwhelming. Of necessity, family minutiae became the center of her life.

"Maybe it's time for me to start looking for work," she suggested to Benjamin as they were getting into bed.

"If you think so," he said noncommittally.

She felt suddenly annoyed. "If *I* think so? Well, what do *you* think? Have you ever thought of expressing an actual opinion?"

He looked over at her, surprised. "What?"

"Maybe you could *engage* a little more?"

"You always say you don't want me to dictate what you should do."

"I don't want you to treat me like one of the kids, but it would be nice if we could have a normal discussion and, you know, actually be involved in each others' lives. Like a real couple?"

"Can't win with you," he muttered, crawling under the covers.

She slept that night with her back to him.

The next morning, Benjamin left early for work without eating breakfast, although he did give her a quick perfunctory kiss goodbye. Paul tried to sneak away without eating breakfast, too, but since he'd be at band practice this evening and wouldn't be here for dinner with the family, she made him stay and have cereal with his brother and sister. All three were silent and sullen for some reason, and she made their lunches while they got ready for school, sending them off with exhortations to have a nice day, which they ignored.

Lupe stopped by later to see if she wanted to walk, but Gloria told her friend that she couldn't today. Instead, after closing the front door, Gloria went to look at her children's rooms. She knew every detail of them intimately yet still felt distanced. Standing next to Paul's bed, looking at the pile of clothes on the floor, the posters on the walls, she could still see what the room had looked like *before*.

Something had changed her life while she was in the middle of living it, giving her children she had not previously had. Well, she could change her life, too, and on impulse, Gloria packed some underwear, socks and a couple of changes of clothes into a suitcase, then drove herself to the bus station. She could have gone anywhere, but the next bus out of town was heading southwest to Tucson, Arizona, and she used her Visa card to buy a ticket, humming "By the Time I Get to Phoenix" to herself, trying to remember at what point in the lyrics, in what city, the woman in the song had finally noticed that the man was gone. Phoenix? Albuquerque? Houston?

When would Benjamin and the kids notice that she was gone?

Probably when dinnertime rolled around and there was no food, Gloria assumed.

Would she even be missed?

That was a hard question to answer. From a practical standpoint, she definitely would be. She did almost everything around the house. But emotionally? Perhaps not.

That wasn't fair. And it wasn't entirely true. Benjamin would miss her. As different from each other as they might be, as much as they got on each others' nerves, deep down they loved one another. Even on the surface they loved one another.

So why was she leaving?

It had been a spur-of-the-moment thing with no real reason behind it, but it occurred to her now that while, in this life, she was supposed to be watching Benjamin and her ultimate goal was to bring him back to their *real* life, it might be safer for him if she were not around. Her previous attempts to safeguard him had all been for naught. Perhaps if they were apart, whatever forces were working against them would be divided and diffused.

Or was she just rationalizing?

The bus wasn't leaving for another hour, so she waited around the transportation center, avoiding eye contact with the homeless people sleeping on the benches. As soon as the doors to the bus opened, she got on, choosing a seat in the back. Gradually, the bus filled with passengers, and, finally, with a pneumatic hiss, the accordion doors closed. Seconds later, they were rolling smoothly out of the transportation center and onto the street, headed for the highway. Not wanting to speak to the seedy-looking man in the seat next to her, Gloria leaned back against the cushion, closed her eyes and pretended to sleep. It was broad daylight and she had awakened from a full-night's rest only a few hours ago, but somehow, she actually did manage to fall asleep (although it took more than a half-hour), and when she finally opened her eyes again, there was no sign of any trees, and the only thing she could see outside the window was desert.

She began mentally tallying everything she had: a suitcase with clothes enough for several days, a cell phone, thirty dollars or so, and her Visa card, which she could probably use for only a day or two, since once Benjamin had determined that she'd left, he would probably close the account. *If* he determined that she left. Because she hadn't left a note or called anyone, and if she maintained phone silence and didn't answer when her husband or sister tried to call her, he would most likely determine that she had been kidnapped or was the victim of some other type of foul play.

Was she planning to call?

Of course she was. But only to let everyone know she was all right, not to provide them with her whereabouts. She had no plans beyond that, however. Vaguely, she thought she might try to get a job—wasn't that what Ellen Burstyn did in *Alice Doesn't Live Here Anymore*? Find a job in Tucson?—but if she wanted to be hired on as a nurse, she would need proof of her education and experience, references. Was she qualified to do anything else? Maybe. She would see.

It was a twelve-hour ride, with only two pit stops and a short half-hour in Gallup for lunch, and by the time they passed through Phoenix, the sun had already set. The land between Phoenix and Tucson was dark, with only the occasional twinkling lights of far off ranch houses pricking holes in the uniform blackness, but as they approached Tucson, deep jet brightened to what was almost a dark red as the lights of the city illuminated the sky ahead.

Gloria found herself slightly concerned. It was after ten, and bus stations weren't ordinarily in the nicest area of town. She needed to find someplace to sleep for the night, a motel that was hopefully safe and cheap.

She needn't have worried. The bus pulled into the terminal, and through the large window, she saw Benjamin standing on the sidewalk waiting for her.

How was that possible?

Feeling uneasy, she stood, getting in line behind the other passengers shuffling up the central aisle of the bus, keeping an eye on Benjamin through each window she passed. He broke into a huge grin as he saw her step through the doorway and start down the steps, almost as though he had not seen her for a long time. His hair was longer than it had been this morning, and he was wearing different clothes: torn faded Levis and a denim shirt.

Benjamin didn't even own a denim shirt!

Only...

He did. There were three of them hanging in the bedroom closet in their house, located less than three miles away on Rancho Road. And two more in the laundry.

Things had shifted around her again.

Gloria suddenly felt tired. This Benjamin was slightly older, and a little paunchier than she was used to. They were both older, she realized. She had aged on the bus ride over, and at the moment she wanted nothing more than to get back on that bus, return to Colorado and resume life with her family. But Paul and the twins no longer existed, and Gloria felt a sharp stab of loss when she thought about them. In this life, she and Benjamin had no children, and as soon as the bus driver unloaded the luggage compartment, she retrieved her suitcase and the two of them drove home.

FOUR

Would she have been happy living in Tucson if she had never known any other existence? Gloria thought she probably would have. They had a nice life, she and Benjamin. The problem was that she *did* remember other existences, and for her this one was too constrained. This was not who she was. It was not even who Benjamin was, although he'd always had those tendencies.

For the past week, since she'd arrived in/returned to Tucson, Gloria had been reflecting on her journey here. The shift must have occurred while she was sleeping, she decided, although that brought up the two questions that were behind everything: How? And why?

She was able to recall her last conversation with Russell and the Tenders of the Shrine, as she'd come to think of them, but everything from before the time she had set out to bring back Benjamin was a blank. Details of her real life and previous efforts to resurrect the dead had been wiped from her mind. It was only because of what Russell and the others had told her that she even knew why she was here now.

We think something might be working against you. That was what one of them had said, and it was the part of it all that she least understood. Was this some sort of cosmic joke? Had she been granted the power to bring back people who had died, only to be hamstrung when it came to people in her own life? Was it some rule of physics that she couldn't understand, like the "paradox" they always brought up in time travel movies where, for some reason, you were unable to meet another version of yourself without some major catastrophe occurring, like time ending or the world blowing up?

Gloria glanced around the kitchen. It was solid, but was it real? Where *was* this place, exactly? She was pretty sure it wasn't the Afterlife, whatever that might be. Her assumption had been that she went into alternate realities to bring back people who had died in her own, and she still thought that the most likely explanation. What was it Russell had said to her?

Maybe they're not even the same people, not exactly.

Maybe this wasn't Benjamin, not exactly. It seemed like him, she felt it was him, but he was different than any Benjamin that had come before, and it was possible that he was a *version* of her husband, Benjamin as he would be if they had...moved to Tucson.

But if she did go into other existences to bring back people who had died, wasn't it similar to that time travel paradox? Wouldn't those realities collapse around the holes formed by taking a person out of them? Did she doom those other worlds when she returned individuals to what she considered their real time and place? Maybe that's what was hampering her efforts to rescue Benjamin. Maybe her *own* world would crash if she altered its course.

Maybe.

But she didn't think so.

We think something might be working against you.

That's what she really believed; that's what it felt like to her. But who or what could be doing such a thing? And why?

Gloria wondered, as she had before, if she actually could change the world around her. Or if she could at least guide its trajectory by doing things that would push it in the direction she wanted. The jury was still out on that. She'd tried it in the past—sort of—but the results, to put it charitably, had not been conclusive.

Across the breakfast table from her, Benjamin cleared his throat, his signal to her that she had zoned out and was not paying attention. Had he been saying something? She looked up apologetically.

"Guess I'll head out to work," Benjamin said.

He was a plumber.

She was a teacher's aide.

"Do you want me to drop you off?" he asked.

"That's okay," she found herself saying. "Sarah's picking me up."

Sarah was the school nurse, and the high school at which they worked was in one of the city's lower income areas. Some of the teachers were burned out, and a couple of others were out-and-out bigots, but even after twenty years, Gloria still found her job rewarding and was continually surprised and inspired by the primarily Hispanic students she assisted. As an aide, her job was to support kids who had physical or learning disabilities. This year, one of her pupils was a foreign exchange student from Guatemala who was still learning English and needed help transitioning into an American classroom. The girl, Gabriella, a freshman, was incredibly smart, very ambitious and was moving along so quickly that Gloria would not be surprised if she ended up Valedictorian her senior year. At the very least, she would probably earn a scholarship to a major university.

It was students like Gabriella who made her job worthwhile, who made her feel a real sense of accomplishment.

In the staff lounge at lunch, two teachers were discussing Hector Lopez, a senior at the opposite end of the spectrum, who had just been suspended for fighting. Hector lived in a group home, and while most of his teachers seemed to have written him off as a lost cause and were simply shoving him through the system so he could graduate and get out of their lives, Gloria saw hope there. Hector would never be a Rhodes Scholar, but he was on track to graduate and he had a good work ethic. He would make someone a fine employee. He was also a nice kid, and despite what his teachers were saying, she knew that if he had gotten into a fight, he had not started it.

Gloria got off at two because the district would have had to pay benefits if she worked full-time. On the days she caught a ride with Sarah, she ordinarily waited around until her friend was through, going to the library to do research, or remaining to help students on a volunteer basis. But today, she looked up Hector's address on his school record, told Sarah where she was going and that she would be back before it was time to leave, and walked to the group home where the boy lived, which was only a few blocks away.

The group home was far less institutional than Gloria was expecting. It was an actual home for one thing, albeit a large one, with a broad green front lawn. She didn't get a chance to see what it looked like inside because just as she was starting up the walk, Hector came out to meet her. He must have seen her approach from his bedroom window. Gloria found herself scanning the front of the house, trying to figure out which window was his.

"Ms. Jaymes?" He seemed surprised to see her and not particularly pleased. There was an expression of mild confusion on his face. "What are you doing here?"

"I heard that you got suspended. For fighting!"

He shrugged.

"I thought maybe I could help you, talk to the principal, get him to lift the suspension. I know it can't be your fault."

"Yeah, well..." He wouldn't meet her eyes.

"It *was* your fault?"

"No. I mean...yes, maybe, kind of. I did throw the first punch, but that asshole was riding me, talking about...all kinds of stuff. He was *trying* to get me to hit him. He *wanted* to fight." Hector sighed. "Or he wanted to get me in trouble. Because he sure didn't get suspended. He's just the innocent victim."

"I'm sorry, who was this?"

"Mark DePozo."

Mark DePozo was not only an honors student but the high school's star quarterback. No wonder the teachers in the lounge were taking his side over Hector's. That was not a mistake Gloria would make. Behind their backs, she had already gotten a glimpse of the sneaky entitled Mark DePozo Hector was talking about, and now a sense of righteous outrage built within her. "I'll talk to the principal for you, if you want. Mr. Nicholson will listen to me."

Hector shook his head. "Don't bother."

"Let me at least talk to your—" *mom or dad*, she'd been about to say automatically, but obviously that didn't apply to someone living in a group home. "—your supervisor or guardian or whoever's in charge and let them know it's not your fault."

"You don't want to meet my guardian," Hector told her, and from the tone of his voice, Gloria knew that was true.

My guardian.

The phrase should have had a positive connotation, the idea of a person assigned to protect Hector. But it made her think of the word "guard," and in her mind she pictured a prison guard, a hulking brute whose job it was to keep Hector confined and in-check.

He looked back toward the doorway of the house, a nervous expression on his face. "Maybe you'd better just leave."

"But I can help you."

"I don't need any help. Besides, I'll be back to school on Monday."

"But—"

"Don't worry about it."

She thought he might thank her for making the effort, but instead he turned and walked back into the house without a word. She was surprised to find that she felt a little bit hurt, but then she thought about his worried expression and his troubled tone of voice—

You don't want to meet my guardian.

—and decided that it might be better for him if she did just butt out. He knew she was there for him if he needed her. For the moment, that would have to be enough.

She told Sarah what happened on the drive home, and her friend clucked sympathetically. "I know exactly how you feel," she said. "I've dealt with a lot of kids like Hector, and sometimes they end up falling through the cracks no matter what you do."

Benjamin shrugged when she told him about it. "You can't save everyone."

That might be true, but it didn't stop her from trying.

The school year ended, Hector graduated, and while she asked him to keep in touch, she knew he wouldn't, and he didn't. That was the way of things. Students came into her life and drifted out, and most of the time she never learned what happened to them.

At home, though, things had never been better. She and Benjamin were older in Tucson than they had been in Colorado, and they were more easygoing, more laissez faire about everything. What might have once irritated her about Benjamin, or annoyed him about her, no longer seemed so consequential, and arguments that otherwise would have broken out did not even register as minor disagreements.

Sometimes, she thought, you just got set in your ways, and the routines of ordinary life, the small everyday experiences, ended up being the things that were most important. It was drinking coffee with Benjamin in the morning, disagreeing about whether to watch a cooking show or a basketball game and compromising on a movie, reading aloud to each other interesting articles in the newspaper. It was the smell of his skin when she snuggled against his back in bed or the comforting sound of water rushing through the pipes beneath the floor when he was taking a shower. It was looking at his profile when he was driving in the car and she was sitting next to him or shopping together for groceries. All of these unremarkable occurrences made up their lives and while individually they might seem trivial or inconsequential, there was absolutely nothing more meaningful or significant to her.

The following year, enrollment at the high school was up, but while she had less time to spend with the students she assisted, they were, on the whole, more diligent and studious, and in June Gloria shed tears at graduation when several of them ascended the dais to receive their diplomas.

On the Monday after school let out, with Benjamin having already left for work, Gloria sat alone at the kitchen table, staring out at the deep blue sky and the white clouds massing over the Rincon range. The concern over how she was going to bring Benjamin back to what she thought of as "real life" was always simmering at the back of her mind, and occasionally, at times like this, it bubbled to the forefront. There was no magic spell for her to chant, no secret shimmery doorway to walk through, and she had no idea how the mechanics of it actually worked.

The big question was: did she still *want* to bring him back? She loved her life here in Tucson, her life here with Benjamin. She liked her job, liked their friends, liked everywhere they went and everything they did. There was literally nothing she would change, even if she could. Her knowledge of their "real life" was practically nil, but she had a hard time believing that it could be better than this. Besides, what if returning him didn't work? What if she ended up alone and Benjamin was gone for good? She did not think she could survive that.

It didn't seem as though she had to worry about that, though. Because if there *was* a way to return, she had no idea what it might be. That particular information, if she had ever known it, had been wiped from her mind. If there was something she was supposed to do, she had no clue as to what it might be. And if there was some sort of organic natural process, it probably should have happened by now.

Maybe *this* was where they would be spending the rest of their lives.

Gloria smiled to herself. That would be nice.

The summer passed quickly. She expanded her garden, started working on getting a teaching credential through an online university, took up painting. Benjamin was encouraging, surprising her by buying and bringing home art supplies one evening, and she spent several weeks working on two side-by-side canvases in the garage. The paintings weren't bad, but there seemed something familiar about them, and she was sure she had seen them before in some other place, some other time.

On the night before school started in August, she awoke in the middle of the night, overcome by the feeling that someone was standing beside the bed next to her. For some reason, she did not seem able to sit up, or even move her head to look, but the feeling quickly became a certainty, and though she could very well be dreaming, Gloria knew she was not.

This was real.

The figure radiated a powerful sense of malevolence, and Gloria was sure that he?...she?...it? meant her harm. She braced herself for a blow to the head or a knife to the heart, convinced that her time had come.

Then suddenly she *was* able to move her head, and when she looked to the left, there was no one there. Not the huge hooded figure her mind had begun to conjure or even a waif-like female drug addict who had broken into the house in order to steal loose change. She and Benjamin were all alone, and she let out her breath in a grateful woosh, aware that for the past few moments she had been holding it.

In the morning, she told Benjamin about the experience, and he dismissed it, telling her that she'd simply had a particularly vivid dream. She tried to argue that it wasn't just a dream, but that was pretty hard to do by the light of day, and even before she'd finished making breakfast, Gloria had convinced herself that it had not really happened.

The kids came home for Thanksgiving.

Her life slid away, replaced by a new one, and even as Gloria tried to hang on to this reality, she felt it slipping, supplanted by another correlated existence. Memories remained, but they were intellectual not emotional, and while she recalled how she had felt before, she did not actually feel that way anymore.

"Hello, Mica," she said, answering the door.

Her daughter, Gloria noticed, was starting to look a little frumpy. Heavier than she had been the last time they'd seen her on the Fourth of July, Mica was wearing a beige dress that was supposed to be nice but hung on her like a sack. Her hair, always limp and colorlessly brown, was cut into an unfortunate pageboy. Her husband and son were equally plain, and though Gloria knew it wasn't fair, she blamed their church. Mica had once been cute and fashionable, and Michael was not a bad looking man, but ever since the two of them had been "born again" and started attending that fundamentalist church, it seemed that they considered adherence to the standards of contemporary society somehow against their religion. She knelt down to say hello to her grandson Mark, smiling widely, but he stared at her uncommunicatively and muttered an obligatory "Hello."

Paula arrived next, alone, but busy and talkative enough for two. She'd discarded her latest boyfriend, a doctor, signed up for a belly dancing class in January ("It's the best exercise! Your whole body gets a workout!"), was in the middle of remodeling her beachfront condo in California, and was volunteering to be part of a youth mentoring program set up between the tech company at which she worked and a local school district.

With Paula's arrival, the house was suddenly more festive and filled with life, and Paula even managed to coax Mark out of his shell a little bit. Everyone chatted and caught up on each others' lives, snacking on chips as Gloria flitted in and out of the kitchen, seeing to preparation of the meal.

They were having a good time, happy to be together for the holiday, but Dan's loss was still there, like a hole in the center of the family. It was three years since he'd been killed in a training accident at Fort Hood, and Gloria would never forgive Benjamin for allowing him to join the military. She'd known something like this would happen—a mother's intuition—but she'd been ignored, her concerns discounted, and look what had happened. Their boy was dead. Dan, their firstborn. She felt his loss every day but always more acutely during holidays and family get-togethers. Of course she was glad to have her daughters here, and her grandson, but things would never, could never, be the same as they were, as they should be.

She glanced over at Benjamin, laughing at something Paula had said, and part of her hated him.

Was this the purpose of their children? Gloria wondered. Was this why they had been introduced? In order to create a rift between her and Benjamin?

She retreated into the kitchen, her head hurting.

Benjamin had made what he called his "famous pumpkin pie"—canned filling dumped into a store-bought crust—while Gloria was responsible for everything else, and the meal was ready shortly before one. They sat around the table, Mica forcing them to listen to her uncomfortably long prayer before they dug in. She wanted everyone to say one thing they were grateful for before they started eating, but Paula saved them by saying, "We can do that later, Mica. I'm starving! Let's eat!"

Gloria had just forked two slices of turkey onto her plate when there was a knock at the door. Since everyone else had already started eating, Gloria went to answer it, wondering who it could be. A neighbor looking for a missing dog? Someone who had accidentally bumped into one of the girls' cars parked on the street?

Dan was standing on the porch.

He was still in his military uniform, but there was no sign of the injury that had killed him. He was smiling, and that smile was at once heartbreakingly familiar and frighteningly alien. "Don't tell anyone I'm back," he said.

Behind her, she could hear Paula and Mica already into their predictable argument about religion.

"Hunger is human," Paula was saying.

"And what's that supposed to mean?"

"It's a line from Joni Mitchell."

"So what's it supposed to mean?"

Dan was still smiling at her. "May I come in?" he asked.

Gloria nodded dumbly, knowing she should throw her grateful arms around him and give him the biggest hug ever, but not feeling like doing anything of the sort.

He moved past her, through the living room into the dining room. Closing the front door, Gloria expected to hear shouts of surprise, squeals of delight, but the rest of the family's reaction was as muted as hers, and she realized when she saw the curious faces turned toward her that they did not recognize who Dan was.

How was that possible?

She didn't know, but it was, and when she glanced toward her son, the look on his face told her not to give it away.

Don't tell anyone I'm back.

She'd assumed he said it because he wanted to surprise his father and sisters by his reappearance, but Gloria understood now that he hadn't wanted her to reveal who he was. She was the only one who recognized him, and as the rest of the family looked at her with inquiring expressions, she thought fast and told them one of her ex-students had dropped by.

Paula seemed suspicious when Gloria pulled up a chair for Dan—this was not the type of thing their family did, invite strangers over to holiday meals—but Mica suddenly became all churchy and self-righteous and, as Jesus no doubt taught, started treating their new guest as though he was a member of the family.

Which he was.

Although nobody except Gloria knew it.

She had been through this before, in another time, another place, and rather than feeling happy that her dead son had returned, Gloria felt uneasy. Why? Why was this happening and why was she apprehensive about it?

Dan was Dan. Confident and assured, he reached across the table for the mashed potatoes without asking anyone's permission. He scooped a huge dollop onto his plate, used his fork to spear a couple of slices of breast meat, then spooned a large amount of gravy over everything. Gloria caught the look Paula exchanged with her father, but Mica was practically beaming at the opportunity to show off her goodness. "We've already said grace," she told Dan, "but if you would like to say a few words of thanks..."

Dan shook his head, lifting a forkful of food to his mouth. "Nah. That's all right."

Paula laughed, and Mica stiffened, turning away from Dan and shooting Gloria a look of reproach, a how-dare-you-invite-this-heathen-to-our-Thanksgiving glare. The meal was awkward, but they got through it, and afterward Gloria told the rest of her family that she wanted to talk privately with her old student and catch up on things. Grabbing Dan's arm, she led him out of the house and onto the back patio, closing the sliding glass door so they could not be heard.

She ushered him away from the house, toward the back fence. "Why are you here?" she demanded. "What do you want?"

"Mom..."

"Don't call me that. Why are you here?"

"I just wanted to see everyone. Dad. Paula." He smiled. "Even Mica."

"But you won't tell them who you are?"

"They don't recognize me anyway."

"Why *is* that?"

He shrugged.

She lowered her voice, though no one could hear them from this far away. "*How* are you here?" she asked. "How did this happen?"

"I don't know. I died...and then I was here."

Gloria frowned. Could someone else be bringing people back *here* the way she brought people back *there*?

Worlds within worlds.

Maybe this had been going on all along. Anything was possible. Since she didn't understand herself how she did what she did, it could even be the case that *she* was responsible for her son's resurrection. Gloria didn't think so, but her feelings toward Dan grew slightly more sympathetic, and she asked him, "Where are you going to stay? What are you going to do? Are you going to try and get a job?"

He shrugged. "I don't know yet."

"We have a guest room, But I don't think—"

"That's okay." He smiled, and something about that smile sent a chill shuddering through her. It was Dan's smile, but at the same time it *wasn't* Dan's smile, and she knew with a sudden certainty that she had had nothing to do with this.

She wanted him out of here, wanted him gone. Whatever he was, he was *wrong*, and she looked back toward the house and said, "I think it would probably be best if you left."

He nodded.

She'd been planning to escort him back through the house, but to her surprise, he turned around, grasped the horizontal board near the top of the wooden fence, pulled himself up and hopped over. There was no "thank you," no "goodbye." She heard him land on the worn and crumbling asphalt of the alley, then walk away, his footsteps crunching on the dirt and gravel.

Stunned and disconcerted, Gloria traversed the small section of lawn and walked back inside, sliding the door shut behind her.

"Where's your student?" Benjamin asked.

"Oh, he's gone. He had to leave."

"Where'd he go?" Benjamin frowned. "I didn't see him."

"That guy was rude," Mica said assuredly. "What do you expect? He wouldn't say grace, he leaves without saying goodbye." She turned toward her mother. "I don't understand why you invited him to eat with us in the first place."

"It was a mistake," Gloria admitted. "He used to be different."

Not wanting to answer more questions but prepared to do so for as long as necessary, she was happy when Mica changed the subject, telling her father, "I saw that you have one of those 'I Heart Tucson' bumper stickers on your truck."

Paula snorted. "You can't *heart* something. 'Heart' is not a verb."

Mica turned toward her sister and was about to argue, but Benjamin said, "She's right."

Mica shut her mouth.

"I knew one of the guys who worked on the 'I Love New York' campaign. He retired here in Tucson. That's where this whole heart thing started, you know. They were trying to change people's perception of New York, so they came up with the 'I Love New York' slogan and used a heart to represent the word 'love.'"

"That's great, Dad," Mica said, cutting him off. "But I was simply wondering where you got the bumper sticker."

"Oh, I don't know," he said vaguely. "Somewhere."

"They sell them at The Store, Wal-Mart, Target, any of those places," Gloria offered. "In the front, where they keep the postcards and tourist stuff."

"I'd like to get one. I do love Tucson."

"You could always move back here," Gloria suggested.

Mica shook her head. "Oh, Mom..."

Paula was staying with them until Saturday, in the guest room that had been her old bedroom. They had invited Mica and her family to stay in their house as well, but, as usual, they had booked a room at a hotel. The house was too crowded, Michael insisted, and there weren't enough bathrooms for everyone. This was just easier and more convenient. Mica apologized, as though the decision was out of her hands, but Gloria was pretty sure that she preferred to stay at a hotel as well. It might even have been her idea.

"We'll go out to lunch tomorrow," Mica proposed. "Our treat." She gave her sister a quick begrudging glance. "You, too."

"Go out?" Benjamin said. "When we have all these leftovers?"

"You can have leftovers for dinner," Mica told him. "We'll go out for lunch."

"You're expected for dinner, too," Gloria reminded her.

"I know, Mom."

Before everyone got even more touchy and permanently retreated into their respective corners, Mica and her family took their leave. Outside, Gloria promised her daughter that she'd get her father in line and they would all go out for lunch tomorrow. "We can come by and pick you up, if you want. Or you could come by here. Or we could meet at the restaurant." She waved her hands. "Just call and tell us what you want to do."

The next two days were pleasantly uneventful, everyone getting along much better than usual. Mica and Paula actually hugged each other when they said goodbye this time, and Gloria's were not the only eyes that were moist.

It happened exactly a week after Thanksgiving.

Gloria had gotten off work at two, and, since she hadn't car-pooled with Sarah, walked out to the faculty lot, turning on her phone and checking for messages as she headed toward her car. There were none, but when she arrived home, the blinking light on the answering machine indicated that 24 messages had been left. With a sinking feeling in the pit of her stomach, she pressed the button to play them back. All 24 messages were the same: urgent pleas from the Farmington Police Department asking either her or Benjamin to immediately call them back.

Mica and her family lived in Farmington.

Gloria could barely breathe. Her heart was pounding so hard it felt as though it would punch through her ribcage. Fingers trembling, she punched in the number the police had left, thinking even as she did so that she should have called Benjamin first.

Maybe it was some sort of mistake, she thought. Maybe it wouldn't be so bad.

It was bad.

Mica, Michael and Mark were dead. The entire family had been slaughtered in their home overnight by an intruder who had used what was either a sword, a machete or some sort of knife with an extremely long blade to slit their throats and slice up their bodies. All three of them had been found piled on top of each other in the bathtub, although blood and overturned furniture throughout the house indicated that they had not been killed in the bathroom.

The detective to whom she spoke had not volunteered this level of detail but had only provided it when she asked questions and demanded answers. By the end of the phone call, Gloria was lying on the floor, tears streaming down her face, unable to see anything but the bloody images her mind had conjured.

The police had no idea who could have done this. There were no leads and no suspects, although they were questioning neighbors and hoping to find doorbell or security camera footage.

Dan.

It was her first thought, although it made no logical sense. Would her resurrected son really have followed his sister all the way to New Mexico in order to slaughter her and her family? The idea seemed ridiculous on its face, but Gloria remembered with a chill the disquieting smile he had given her and the abrupt way he had hopped over the fence, and realized she could not completely rule it out.

Dan.

Not only could she not rule out the idea, she could easily see him doing such a thing. Not *her* Dan, the Dan who had died, but *this* Dan, the one who had come back.

Beneath her emotional devastation, a horrifying thought crept in. Panicked and suddenly terrified, she called Paula, but after five rings, the call went to voicemail, and her daughter's cheerful voice announced: "I'm not able to come to the phone right now. Please leave a message, and I'll get back to you as soon as I can!"

"This is Mom," Gloria said. "Call me as soon as you get this."

Immediately, she dialed Benjamin's cell, and when he didn't answer and the call went to *his* voicemail, she called the office, where Judy, the plumbing company's secretary, told Gloria that her husband was not in.

"Is he out on a job?" Gloria asked. "Because he's not answering his phone."

"Let me check," Judy said. "Nope. He hasn't been assigned anything this afternoon, and he finished his morning call before noon. I'm not exactly sure where he is. You want me to have him call you if he comes in?"

Gloria was having a hard time keeping her fear at bay. "Yes, please. Thank you." She hung up.

Where could he be?

She refused to acknowledge the thought lurking at the back of her mind.

Just when it seemed the weight of everything was about to crush her, Benjamin walked in, and Gloria could not remember ever having felt such relief.

"What is it?" he asked, seeing her face.

She was about to blurt it out, when her phone rang. The caller ID read: *Newport Beach Police Department.*

"No!" she screamed, all of her pent-up emotion exploding out of her in a single primal scream.

"What is it?" he demanded again. He took the phone from her, identifying himself to the caller, and she saw his face collapse as he heard what she had known he would hear.

"Paula's dead," he said numbly. "She's been murdered."

Tears were rolling down his face, but he remained on the line to hear all of the information the police had to give. Gloria was no longer screaming, but she could not stop sobbing, and visions of Paula, Mica and even Dan as little children flooded her brain.

Benjamin was still alive.

That was the main thing.

He looked so wrecked when he terminated the call—

terminated

—that Gloria was almost afraid to tell him about Mica, but she had no choice, and, as she'd originally planned, she just blurted it out. "Someone killed Mica, too. And Michael and Mark." They were the only words she managed to say before collapsing onto the couch.

She knew, in her mind, that Benjamin was the only person who really mattered. Sons, daughters, grandchildren, all changed depending on the exigencies of the reality in which she found herself. But Benjamin was constant.

It didn't feel like that, though. Intellectually, she might be aware that her kids had appeared in this life only recently, but emotionally, her heart had been ripped, dripping with blood, from her suddenly empty chest, and the loss was more profound than any she had previously experienced. She kept imagining her daughters' last moments, the pain and horror they must have suffered as their bodies were being hacked apart and they realized they were going to die.

Numbly, Gloria looked up at her husband.

He sat down next to her, held her tight. "We'll get through this," he said through his tears. She could tell he didn't believe it, but his words gave her comfort anyway, and she hugged him back.

As long as I have you, she thought. *As long as I have you.*

FIVE

It had been three years, and sometimes an entire week would go by without her thinking about Paula or Mica.

She could not remember the last time she had thought about her son-in-law or grandson.

Gloria felt guilty about that, but life moved on, as she knew better than most. Because she was still able to recall a life without children...and lives with different children. She'd hoped against hope that such a shift would happen again, taking Benjamin out of the pain he'd been in since the murders, but maybe that was the point of all this. Maybe the goal was to get Benjamin to kill himself.

Whose goal, though?

And what would happen if he did commit suicide? Gloria suspected it might mean the true end of him, but that was something she never wanted to find out, and she had spent every day of the past three years burying her own grief and attempting to keep her husband on an even keel, providing him with reasons to live.

Dan had disappeared.

He was not suspected by anyone other than herself in the murders. How could he be?

Officially, he was dead. She looked for him, though, in real life and online, searching for evidence of his existence, but he seemed to have vanished into the ether from which he'd come.

Maybe he was really gone this time.

She hoped so.

Neither Paula nor Mica showed any signs of returning. *Their* revival she would have welcomed—and resurrection would certainly have brought peace and joy to their father—but both of her daughters remained stubbornly dead.

More than once, Gloria awoke in the middle of the night, certain that she was being watched. A couple of times, she was frozen in place, unable even to turn her head and look, certain that a dark figure was standing by the side of the bed, looking down upon her. Other times, she awoke with the feeling that something had just departed after observing her asleep. Her reaction was the same one she had had years before to Hector Lopez's unseen guardian, a sense that the figure's purpose was to keep her in place, guarding against any attempt to leave.

You don't want to meet my guardian.

The figure even turned up in a few of her paintings, though Gloria was not sure how that happened. During the summers, she had continued pursuing her artistic interests, and while she tended to depict southwest landscapes and old western buildings, occasionally she found herself putting dark hooded forms in the backgrounds, amidst trees or rocks, behind broken windows.

When she discovered what she had done, she invariably painted over the scenes.

The years continued to pass. She and Benjamin could not call themselves happy, but neither were they miserable. They existed. They were together, though. They had each other. That was the most important thing. And if their lives consisted of one long string of repetitive routines, those patterns and habits were comforting.

All of that changed after a field trip to Saguaro National Park.

It was the middle of the fall semester, though temperatures were still summer hot. Mrs. Lee's sophomore biology class was scheduled to take a trip to the park's Tucson Mountain district to study the native plants and animals of the Sonora Desert, but there weren't enough chaperones for the number of students, so staff members had been asked to volunteer. Always glad for an opportunity to be outdoors, Gloria signed up. Two of her students were in Mrs. Lee's class anyway, and she sat next to them on the bus as it travelled the long way around Gate's Pass to Saguaro's entrance.

"Everyone make sure they go to the bathroom at the visitor's center!" Mrs. Lee announced as they got off the bus. "Once we're on the trail, you'll have to hold it!"

There was a chaotic rush to get to the restrooms, and by tacit agreement the teacher and chaperons spaced themselves out in order to herd the students into orderly lines.

Ten minutes later, the kids were starting out on the nature trail, pens and notebooks in hand. A ranger led the tour, with Mrs. Lee periodically chiming in about specific things that were going to be on an upcoming test.

The group stopped in front of a stand of ocotillos, one dead and bare, the rest covered in small green leaves, two of them with red flowers blooming on the tips of their branches. At the rear of the group, Gloria was unable to see the ocotillos up close, so she waited until the class began moving on to the next stop before stepping forward to get a better look at the red flowers.

"*Gloria.*"

It was a whisper of her name, and she swiveled around to see who was calling her, but there was no one close by. Unable to see how such a whisper could have carried farther than her sight line, she assumed she'd misheard or imagined it.

The whisper came again.

"*Gloria.*"

The voice seemed to originate from the other side of a large palo verde, and, curious, she stepped off the trail and moved around the green trunk of the tree. A woman was standing there, an older woman wearing oddly fashionable clothes.

Maxine.

Her mother.

Her *real* mother.

Gloria had no idea how she was able to recognize the woman's true identity, but somehow she knew the old lady instantly. In another life, another time, Maxine had been her "mother's" neighbor. When Gloria had taught nursing at a college, another version of Maxine had visited her to issue vague disturbing threats. But she understood now that in her *real* life, Maxine was her long-absent mom.

Long-absent?

How did she know that?

Gloria wasn't sure.

The woman smiled. Not a friendly smile but a cruel one, an expression of hostility and antagonism for which Gloria could think of no rationale.

There were questions she wanted to ask the woman. If her mother was here, that probably meant that she, too, had lived other lives. Did she have the capacity to exit and enter existences at will? Could she make changes to the world around her?

Did she know how to bring people back?

"We meet again," her mother said, the hard smile fixed on her face.

It was the sort of trite comic book dialogue Gloria might expect to hear in an old James Bond movie, but in this context it carried an element of real threat. There was no indication that her mother was happy to see her after all these years, all these lives. On the contrary, the implication was that the two of them were enemies on the verge of some sort of showdown.

"Mom?" Gloria said.

The woman's expression darkened. "Don't call me that."

"It's what you are."

"It's what I *was*."

"What do you want with me?" Gloria glanced around the side of the tree toward the path, aware even as she spoke that the students she was supposed to be chaperoning were moving further away.

"I want you to stop."

"Stop what?"

"I know what you're trying to do."

"I'm not trying to do anything. I'm just living my life."

"You're trying to resurrect Benjamin. You can't fool me."

A sex- and role-reversed lyric from the song "Cat's in the Cradle" repeated itself in Gloria's mind: She'd grown up just like her. Her mom was just like her.

Only it was the other way around. She was just like her mom.

"I told you before. Benjamin has to die. You can't save him."

We think something might be working against you.

Russell had said that, back in the shack, and in her mind she'd conjured up some vague dark force, a looming formless shadow. But it wasn't that at all. It was her mother. For some reason, it was her mother.

Even as she tried to make sense of that truth, the woman was stepping forward, out of the dappled shadows of the palo verde, and Gloria could see that her mother was older than she'd originally thought. The skin of her cheeks looked thin and papery, like brittle parchment, and deep lines on her thin lips were almost mummy-like.

How old was she?

"Get out of here," her mother said.

Gloria feigned ignorance. "Get out of where? The national park?"

"This life!"

"I don't know how."

"Yes, you do."

"I really don't." But in the back of her mind sprouted the germ of an idea.

"Get out and leave Benjamin where he is."

"I would never do that."

She could think of no possible reason why her mother would try to keep her from resurrecting her husband. Gloria had apparently returned plenty of other people with absolutely no pushback from her mother whatsoever. And Benjamin had been taken far too early. He deserved a full life. They both did.

"I've stopped you before, and I'll stop you again."

The sun suddenly seemed hotter. Gloria used a hand to wipe the sweat off her forehead. "Why are you doing this? What's it to you? You don't even know us."

"You don't know what I know."

"Well, I came here for Benjamin, and he's going back with me."

"Why? Even if you did manage to do it, you wouldn't remember who he was."

"That's only temporary—"

"Not this time." Her mother smiled, and Gloria's stomach sank as she saw the certainty in her expression. "You've been away too long now. And you've tried once too often."

Was that possible?

"Nice try." She pretended to think her mother was bluffing.

"You're not going to remember who he is."

"Why are you so against him? I don't understand. Why do you care *what* happens to him?"

"We can't save people. We're not supposed to."

Gloria took an angry step forward. "Who says?"

"It's something I know. And the fact that you don't..." She shrugged.

"Stay away from us," Gloria warned.

"I don't think so."

A whole host of childish retorts readied themselves in Gloria's mind, most of them addressing her mother's abandonment of her, all of them intended to hurt. She hadn't realized she was so angry, but she was. Instead of saying anything out loud, however, Gloria turned away and stepped back onto the trail. There was no call for her to stay, no final taunt or threat, and, hurrying to catch up with the class, she was afraid to look back, afraid her mother might not be there, afraid she might have *disappeared*, and she kept her eyes on the path ahead.

All the way back to school, sitting at the front of the bus, she thought about what had happened, her head filled with far too many questions. Chief among them was why her mother wanted Benjamin dead. Gloria could still think of no possible reason for such a prejudice, and she couldn't help feeling that there was something she was missing, something just beyond her grasp that would explain it.

She wondered, too, about the woman herself. How had her mother found her? She'd somehow known that Gloria would be on that specific trail at that specific time, so it stood to reason that her perceptions weren't as limited as Gloria's were, but what did that mean? Was her mother bound by the rules of this world? Was she living a normal life here, as Gloria herself was? Or could she pop in and out at will? Did she have...powers? Maybe she could transform into other people.

None of the implications were good, and though they returned to school in the middle of lunch and Gloria still had another hour to work, she told the office that she wasn't feeling well and went home early.

Alone in the house, she paced back and forth from the living room to the dining room to the kitchen and back again, feeling antsy and ill-at-ease. Periodically, she looked out one of the windows, expecting to see her mother standing in the yard like some wraith. Once, she even picked up the phone, though it hadn't rung, expecting to hear her mother's voice on the other end of the line. There was only a dial tone, but that did not put her mind at rest. Indeed, she felt even more nervous, certain that her mother would appear once again but having no idea when.

I've stopped you before, and I'll stop you again.

That was what scared her the most, the idea that her mother might be able to keep her from saving Benjamin and maybe even get rid of all...this. She glanced around the house, thinking about her paintings and her garden and her job and her life. Her gaze alighted on the dining room table, and a bleak sadness welled within her as she reflected on what had happened to Paula and Mica, and Mica's family. Dan was still out there somewhere, Gloria knew, and she wondered if he had any connection to her mother.

Maybe he was working with her.

Maybe he *was* her.

Benjamin arrived home from work shortly after five, and she told him immediately that they needed to move, get away, get out of Tucson. She didn't want to have to explain things to him, but she did, and to his credit, he did not immediately think her crazy. There might have even been a part of him that *understood*, but ultimately the totality of everything overwhelmed him, and he simply could not wrap his head around such a complicated and all-encompassing scenario.

He shook his head slowly. "You want us to sell our house because—"

"Not sell," she said. "Leave. Now. We don't have time to waste. She's out there, and she's coming."

"Your mother?"

"Yes! I told you!"

"And you think we've lived other places and had different children. Or no children."

She held his arms, closing her eyes as she pressed her forehead against his. "Just think about it. *Please.* Not logically, but...does it *feel* true to you? Does it feel like it's *possible*?"

He was silent for a moment. "Where would you want to go? And for how long?"

"I don't know," Gloria admitted. "I just know we need to get out of here as soon as we can."

Benjamin smiled tiredly. "I'm trying to follow this. I really am."

"You don't have to follow it. You just have to trust me."

He started toward the kitchen. "It's been a long day, Glore. Why don't we just sleep on it and—"

"Have you heard a word I've said?"

"Every single one." He took a glass from the rack next to the sink, turned on the faucet and filled it with water, taking a long drink.

"She. Wants. You. Dead. Do you understand? I'm trying to save your life!"

A flicker passed over his face, and she was afraid she'd said the wrong thing. Since they'd lost their children, she knew he had thought about it, and one of the ways she'd tried to keep him alive was to prevent him from considering suicide.

That would give her mother what she wanted without her having to do a thing.

"A vacation," Gloria said quickly. "Let's call it a vacation. How long has it been since we've had one of those? We'll pack and go, be spontaneous, like we used to be when we were younger."

"We were never spontaneous," Benjamin pointed out, but he didn't automatically dismiss the idea. He thought for a moment, finished his water. "Where would we go?" he asked, putting his glass in the sink. "Not Europe or something. Not a cruise, I hope?"

"We'll drive there," Gloria said. She knew he liked to drive.

"Where?"

Since coming back from the field trip, the idea at the back of her mind had continued to grow. *Hicksville*, she thought. They needed to get to Hicksville.

"Hicksville," she said. "It's in northern California."

Why had that not occurred to her before? Other than Benjamin and herself, it was the one constant throughout all incarnations of her life. Sisters and brothers came and went, sons and daughters, friends, but she and Benjamin were always there, and somehow she always ended up in Hicksville, and while she seemed to forget it over and over again, it always seemed to be her way out.

Except in that apocalyptic scenario.

Could there be a connection?

She didn't know, didn't care. All she wanted to do was return Benjamin to the life they were supposed to be living.

You're not going to remember who he is.

She was willing to take that chance.

"You want me to drive to California to some town called Hicksville? For a vacation? *Hicksville*? Really?"

Desperation was setting in. She'd thought she'd be able to just tell him what was happening, and the two of them would take off. She hadn't expected that convincing him would be so hard.

Behind Benjamin, through the window above the sink, Gloria detected movement. Not the usual bird or squirrel, but something bigger, and, stepping forward, she peered over his shoulder through the glass.

Her mother was standing on the lawn. To the sides of her were other men and women, people Gloria recognized from other places, other times. Neighbors, coworkers, store clerks, passersby. Background people.

And Dan.

Her son was staring straight at her, smiling the disconcerting smile that was simultaneously his and not his. In his right hand, he held a long curved knife.

Something ran over the grass and around the assembled group on all fours. A dog? No, a woman.

Her grandmother.

The one who hated Benjamin, who had twisted the head off the cat next door.

Gram-Gram

A feeling of panic engulfed her. “Turn around!” Gloria ordered, twisting Benjamin’s shoulders. “Look!”

He turned. “At what?” he asked, and Gloria saw instantly that the lawn was empty. In the few seconds she had looked away, all of them had disappeared.

“It doesn’t matter!” she said, her voice frantic. “We have to go!”

She realized that she sounded crazy and had no doubt that she would have thought her husband off his rocker were the shoe on the other foot. But she knew what was happening—she was the *only* one who knew what was happening—and if they didn’t leave immediately, there was a good chance that Benjamin, and maybe even she, would end up dead. Permanently.

Gloria pulled at his arm. “Come on!” She was crying, and it was that more than anything which gave her plea credence. He could see how frightened she was, and she could tell from his expression that he was wavering. “If you ever loved me, you have to—”

From the bedroom or bathroom at the back of the house came the sound of shattering glass.

Benjamin instantly turned toward the door.

He’d heard it, too!

“That’s her,” Gloria said.

Something in her voice must have convinced him, because he grabbed *her* hand, and without speaking, the two of them hurried through the dining room, through the living room and out the front door, which Benjamin locked behind them. To her relief, there was no sign of her mother, Dan or anyone else. The lawn, driveway, street and sidewalk were all empty. By tacit agreement, they headed straight to the car, separating when they reached the hood of the vehicle, Gloria going around to the passenger door, Benjamin taking the driver’s side since he had the keys.

“Get out your cell,” he said. “Call the police.”

"The police can't help with this."

"We could drive there. To the station."

"You don't seem to understand." They were falling back into the same argumentative rut. "We. Need. To. Leave."

"Well, even if we drive away now, we have to come back for our clothes and..."

"And what?"

"If we're going on a trip, we have to bring our bathroom stuff and make sure all the windows are closed and the house is—" He jerked backward in his seat. "*Jesus*!"

Gloria looked through the windshield. The old lady who had once been her grandmother—

Gram-Gram

—had sped around the corner of the house on all fours and was loping toward the car, grinning madly.

Benjamin threw the transmission into reverse, backed out of the driveway and skidded onto the street before immediately shifting into drive. They sped away at twice the posted limit.

"What the *hell*?" he shouted.

"I tried to tell you."

"*That* was your mother?"

"My grandmother. From another life."

"Jesus!"

"I told you."

"You were right. It's really real."

Gloria breathed a sigh of relief. He finally got it. He actually understood.

They had reached Speedway, and, slowing down, Benjamin turned left onto the thoroughfare, heading toward the center of town. "So what do we do?" He was gripping the steering wheel so tightly that his knuckles were white.

"We go to California."

"*Hicks*ville."

"Yes."

He nodded slowly. "All right, then. We'll get some gas, and we'll head out. We just need to find out how to get to this Hicksville."

"Just get us to California," Gloria said. "I'll be able to find it from there."

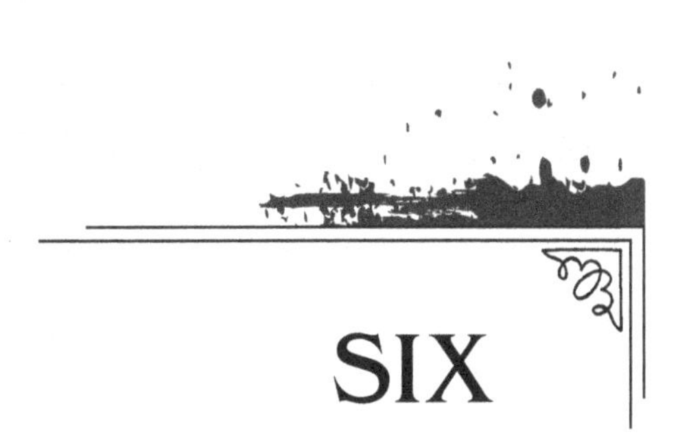

SIX

The night lasted longer than it was supposed to, and the desert was neverending.

Gloria didn't say anything at first. They were headed west, after all, so it made sense that the sun would come up later than it would back in Tucson. But when the dashboard clock said it was nearly eight o'clock in the morning, and they were still driving through desert with no sign of the dawn, she knew something was wrong.

"Benjamin?" she said softly. She must have said it too softly, because he was nodding his head to music from one of the jazz stations on the satellite radio and didn't seem to have heard her. "Benjamin?" she said, more loudly.

He glanced over at her. "What?"

"Shouldn't we have hit Quartzite by now? Or Blythe? Or at least a sign telling us how many miles until we get there?"

"I was just thinking the same thing," he told her.

"And it's still dark." She pointed to the clock. "At eight in the morning."

"Huh." That news seemed to surprise him, and she detected a note of concern in his voice.

Gloria cleared her throat, not quite sure how to convey what was going through her mind. "I'm not sure we are where we think we are," she said. "I'm not sure we are where we're supposed to be."

Benjamin glanced instinctively at the fuel gauge. Gloria did, too, and she saw that they had only a fourth of a tank left. Then they were coming around a bend and over a rise, and the sky was suddenly lighter. Not as bright as it should have been for this time of morning, but definitely on the way there. And below them, on the right side of the straight sloping highway, was Quartzite, the lights of the small town still visible in the fading darkness of the approaching dawn.

By the time they got gas at a Pilot station next to a McDonald's, the sun was up. Twenty minutes later they were crossing over the Colorado River into California. Neither of them spoke of the too-long night and the too-long desert, and though Gloria was hungry and she assumed Benjamin was, too, they did not stop anywhere for breakfast but continued on.

They reached Orange County shortly after noon, driving the Riverside Freeway through Anaheim Hills. Pulling into the right lane, Benjamin turned onto the 57 Freeway.

"What are you doing?" Gloria asked. "We need to go through Los Angeles."

He got off on the Imperial Highway exit.

"Where are you going?"

"Home," he said, as though puzzled by her question.

Home? Was he talking about the house in Brea? They were heading in that direction, so it seemed likely, but she wasn't sure how that was possible. That had been an entirely different life, one he did not know. Something had apparently changed during that endless drive through the dark desert, and while it made her uneasy, the idea that things had *shifted* again and Benjamin was still here, gave Gloria hope that her mother's dire warnings had been nothing more than idle threats.

Gloria was silent as they drove, her uneasiness cut with an unfamiliar optimism.

Sure enough, Benjamin drove through downtown Brea and into their old neighborhood. It was the same as it had been—yet different. The houses themselves were the structures she recognized, but some were painted in new colors, and many of them had unfamiliar landscaping. Making a wide swing, the way he always had, Benjamin pulled into the driveway of their house, which had not changed at all.

He shut off the car's engine. Now that they were here, he seemed confused. He stared through the windshield at the garage door for a moment, then turned toward her. "Why did I come here?" he asked. "We were supposed to be going up north. You should've said something."

"I did say something." She touched his arm, looked into his eyes. "Do you know where this is? Do you recognize where we are?"

He shook his head.

"We lived here. In one of those other lives. This was our home."

He stared through the windshield at the house, clearly willing himself to remember, but whatever memory had led him here was gone, and he shook his head.

On an impulse, she got out of the car.

"What are you doing?"

Gloria didn't reply. She walked up the three steps to the porch and knocked on the front door. She had a sudden crazy thought that *she* would answer the door, that she would be confronted with another version of herself. But no one came to the door, no one was home, and when she peeked through the narrow window to the side of the door, she saw that the furnishings were foreign to her. This was not their house.

Except...

She adjusted her angle of vision. *Yes*. There, on the wall above a large flat screen TV mounted on a low stand, was the antique wall-hanging they'd bought on their honeymoon in Monterey. And, next to it, the framed pencil sketch of the shack in Hicksville with a line of tall pine trees behind it.

Maybe this *was* their house.

Benjamin had gotten out of the car. She felt as confused as he looked, and she almost turned to leave, but something made her reach out and check the door. It was unlocked, and as her finger pressed down on the handle, the door opened.

"What are you doing?" Benjamin said, hurrying up the steps. His voice was low, as though he was afraid of being overheard.

"I just want to see something."

He pulled her away, closing the door. "That's breaking and entering. We could get arrested. Come on. Let's get out of here."

He was right, she knew. Already her fingerprints were on the door handle, and if anyone on the street had a porch security camera, they were on it. The smart thing to do would be—

The door opened.

"Mom? Dad?"

Gloria saw Benjamin's face before she saw their daughters, and though his expression was one of shock, there was an unbelievable joy in it as well, and she could not remember ever seeing him so happy.

Mica and Paula were teenagers, both of them cute and fresh-faced and completely unscarred by life. They were wearing clothes she did not recognize but hairstyles that she did.

Benjamin rushed forward, not bothering to stifle a sob, and wrapped his arms around both girls at the same time, hugging them close.

Gloria followed them into the house. She recognized the furnishings, now. They were not her own, not precisely, but seemed to be an amalgam of different styles familiar to her. She saw an end table she had had in Colorado beside a couch from her Aunt Ruth's sitting room, and a reclining chair that looked suspiciously like one that Maxine—

her mother

—had had in the house across the street from what she'd once thought was her childhood home.

The girls removed themselves from Benjamin's grasp as soon as his hug loosened. Both, Gloria saw, were staring at their parents with something like fear.

"What happened to you?" Paula asked. Her voice quavered. "You're so *old*."

Mica was backing away from them, frightened. "You're not really our parents."

"We are!" Benjamin insisted, still crying, obviously overwhelmed by the fact that his daughters were alive again and young.

This is not right, Gloria thought.

Things were breaking down, and whether that was her doing or her mother's, it did not bode well for what was to come. She felt helpless, trapped in a loop that seemed to be disintegrating around her.

"Dan!" Paula yelled, with Mica taking up the cry. "Dan!"

Their brother emerged from a hallway that was far too dark, wielding the long curved knife he'd held back in Tucson. Unlike his sisters, Dan was not younger. He was the same age he had been when she had seen him with the assembled crowd in the yard, the same age he'd been when he'd come to Thanksgiving dinner, the same age he'd been when he died.

Benjamin instinctively staggered backward even as his arms were reaching out. "Son?"

Gloria grabbed his wrist, her fingers digging in tightly. "She found us. We have to get out of here."

"But the kids—"

Dan, grinning, swung the knife through the air in front of him.

"They're not our kids," she lied.

She assumed Dan would continue advancing slowly. But real life didn't work that way. That was a technique used in movies to heighten suspense. Dan wanted to kill them, and he suddenly ran forward, knife raised, the girls cheering him on. He would have sliced open the top of Benjamin's head, but Gloria immediately grabbed the floor lamp next to her, right hand closing around the thin stem, and wielded it like a baseball bat, swinging the heavy base into Dan's midsection, striking the knife out of his hands and knocking him over as the plug was yanked out of the wall socket. Before he could get up, she used both hands to raise the lamp over her head and bashed in his face with the base.

The girls were screaming, and Gloria dropped her makeshift weapon, yanked on the stunned Benjamin's arm and pulled him outside. "Let's go!" she said. "Now!"

"You killed Dan," he said dazedly.

"That wasn't Dan. Dan's already dead. Besides, I don't think I killed him. That's why we have to get out of here."

Benjamin was fumbling with his keys, and Gloria took the keychain from him, pushing him toward the passenger side of the car as she moved quickly to the driver's side. From inside the house, Mica and Paula were still screaming.

Gloria started the car and without waiting for Benjamin to strap himself in, backed up and peeled out. She slowed her speed to the flow of traffic as soon as she pulled onto Brea Boulevard, not wanting to attract attention or get a ticket.

"That was our house?" Benjamin asked.

"It *was*. But not anymore."

"Because I think I do remember it now. There was a weird little closet, wasn't there? In the hallway?"

She nodded.

"I never liked that closet."

That wasn't true. He was the one who had told her there was nothing wrong with the small room after it suddenly appeared in their house, assuring her that it had always been there and was completely normal. But she remained silent.

"How...?" he began, and cleared his throat. "How did they get to be alive again?"

"I think they just *are*. Here, at least."

"So this is one of those...?"

She nodded. "I think it happened in the desert. Maybe that's why the night was so long."

"So can we go back to Tucson? That should be different, too, right?"

"We need to go to Hicksville."

He nodded as though he understood, but he didn't. She didn't either, not exactly, but she knew it was true.

They did not speak again until they were on the Santa Ana Freeway and headed toward Los Angeles. Traffic slowed, and Benjamin stared out the side window at a group of yellow-vested highway workers in a blocked-off lane. "So this isn't our real life?" he said.

Gloria shook her head.

"Then what's our real life like? Where do we live? What do we do for a living?"

"I'm not sure," she admitted. "I can't remember that far back. I only remember...these lives. These fake lives."

He smiled wryly. "It's been a pretty good fake life, though, hasn't it?"

She smiled back at him. "Yes, it has."

"Do we actually have children?"

"I don't know."

He gestured out the window. "So all of this...the freeway, the cars, the buildings, the cities...none of it's real?"

"Maybe. I'm not sure. I think, probably, it is, and it's just different from where we're supposed to be, different than the place we're from."

"Even though it looks exactly the same?"

"I think so."

"Will we remember this once we're back?"

"My mother says we won't." Gloria paused. "She said we won't even remember each other."

Benjamin glanced over at her. "Do you believe that?"

"I kind of do."

"Then maybe we should stay."

"We can't," Gloria said flatly. "She's trying to kill you. She wants you dead."

"What *is* she?"

"The same thing I am."

"What is that?"

Gloria spoke softly. "I don't know," she said. "I don't know."

The weather was wrong. Rain, hail, wind, sun. Too hot one minute, too cold the next. They traded off driving duties in Bakersfield when they stopped at a Subway (what meal was it? Breakfast? Lunch? Dinner?), and once back on the highway she saw a hitchhiker who looked like Dan, though she said nothing to Benjamin about it.

They took turns driving and sleeping. Gloria dozed off shortly after midnight, and when she awoke, it was three o'clock and bright outside. There was no way she could have slept for fifteen hours, but there was also no way it could look like afternoon at three in the morning. Things were breaking down, she thought again, and her sense of urgency increased. They needed to get to Hicksville as quickly as possible.

Gloria was once again in the driver's seat when something told her to get off the highway, and from that point on, she navigated by instinct, passing through a landscape of alternating farmland and forest that was unrecognizable yet somehow familiar, finally driving over a small hill and into the town of Hicksville.

Things had changed. On Main Street, where she recalled seeing a Mexican restaurant, there was now an art gallery. Next to it was a beach cottage, though the ocean was at least a hundred miles away. The shopping center across the street was abandoned, the empty supermarket's blank storefront eerily reminding her of a vacant Albertson's she remembered from elsewhere. Everywhere she looked, Gloria saw buildings she recognized that shouldn't be here.

There were no other people out, and no cars driving through town, though several were parked along the side of the street. That part seemed right, since she recalled Hicksville being underpopulated the previous times she'd been here. Slowing down, she pulled the car into a parking spot by the fast-casual restaurant Fresh Garden. The eating establishment was undoubtedly part of a chain, but this one looked *exactly* like one in east Brea. She was thrown off balance by this dizzying collision of lives.

"So what now?" Benjamin asked.

Gloria turned to her husband, seeing him in a way that she hadn't for quite some time, and her heart experienced an ache so deep it was almost physical.

As long as I have you.

There seemed a very real possibility that she might lose him, and the knowledge hit her like a punch to the stomach. It suddenly seemed harder to breathe, and the thought of living a life without him filled her with a looming despair. Gloria knew she had lost him before, and while she didn't actually remember it, his death had started her on this journey. She'd been so unable to live with his absence that she had gone after him in the same way she had gone after strangers, even as a part of her had known that such an effort was dangerous.

Her desire now was to postpone the inevitable for as long as possible.

"Aren't you hungry?" she said. "I'm starving."

"Is it lunchtime or breakfast?" he asked, his internal clock obviously as screwed up as her own. "I kind of dozed there for awhile."

They both knew that wasn't the reason for the confusion, but they pretended it was.

"Lunch," Gloria said, randomly picking a meal. "Let's see what they have."

Inside, there were no other customers, and the two employees behind the counter, an overweight older woman and a prim-looking younger woman, stared at her with hostility. She recognized them both. Aunt Ruth and Cousin Kate. In a life where Maxine had lived across the street, these two had been her nearest relations, although she had never liked either of them.

"What do you want?" Aunt Ruth demanded.

Gloria chose to ignore their identities and pretend they were merely Fresh Garden employees. "I'd like a spinach wrap and passion fruit iced tea."

Cousin Kate slammed a tray down on the counter in front of her. "You are not welcome here."

Gloria felt her anger rise. "What's that? What did you say?" An almost electrical charge passed between them, and Gloria knew from the way the other woman's eyes widened that she was afraid of her. On impulse, she leaned forward, over the edge of the counter, and Cousin Kate jumped back. "Take our order if you want to live," she said menacingly.

Suddenly servile, the uniformed woman bowed and backed away, moving into the kitchen, while Aunt Ruth, in a much more polite voice, said, "Spinach wrap and passion fruit iced tea." She turned to Benjamin. "And you, sir?"

Benjamin was looking at Gloria, stunned by her behavior, but he managed to turn his attention to ordering. "Veggie burger and, uh, iced tea," he said. "Regular, not passion fruit."

"Are these together?"

Benjamin nodded.

"Thirteen fifty-three," Aunt Ruth said, ringing it up on the register.

Benjamin paid, and, looking once again at Gloria, stepped aside.

"We don't want any trouble," Aunt Ruth said nervously.

"Then don't make any," Gloria said, holding her gaze.

The other woman nodded and hurried to pour the drinks as her daughter made haste in the kitchen. Moments later, the food was ready, and Benjamin carried their tray to the farthest table. The two women moved to the back of the kitchen, where they stood close together, whispering fearfully.

Benjamin spoke quietly. "What was that about?"

"I know them," she said.

"From...somewhere else?"

Gloria nodded.

"Do you think they know you?"

She mused on that as she sipped her iced tea, glancing over at the kitchen. "I'm not sure. Maybe, maybe not. But either way, they're doing my mother's bidding."

"It's almost over," he said. "Isn't it?"

"Yes."

"I don't know why I didn't believe you at first, back in Tucson. I should've—"

She put her hand on his. "I know why. Because it sounded crazy. It *is* crazy. But it's also true."

They ate for a moment in silence.

So this...multiverse," Benjamin said slowly. "You can travel it? You can go to these different existences?"

She shrugged.

"And this is what happens when people die? It's not heaven or hell or...nothing. It's other versions of their lives?"

"I don't know," Gloria said, which was the truth. She was still not sure that *she* wasn't creating these worlds. Her or her mother.

Because the elements in them all seemed to have some connection to her own life. Maybe it was all real, but maybe it was just an overlay she generated herself, a more familiar and understandable way to navigate something that was impossible to know or understand.

"And how exactly are you going to get us back where we're supposed to be?" Shaking his head, Benjamin let out a short laugh. "You're right. It *does* sound crazy. It *feels* crazy. Because this is the only life I've ever known. This is reality. I understand intellectually everything you told me and everything you said is going on, but..."

"We have to go to that shack. I'm not sure what I need to do after that—it's still a little hazy—but it'll probably come to me."

"So...we're going there after this?"

She squeezed his hand. "Let's just enjoy our lunch right now."

They ate slowly, not speaking again of why they were really here but pretending this was an ordinary meal, talking occasionally about nothing in particular, letting the silences fall naturally, enjoying being together.

For what Gloria feared might be the last time.

More than an hour later, after forcing Aunt Ruth to give them multiple refills on their drinks and then taking turns using the single unisex bathroom, they walked back outside. There were still no cars on the road or pedestrians on the intermittent sidewalk.

"So," Benjamin said, "do we walk or drive or what?"

"It's not far," Gloria responded, pointing. "Just around that corner, in fact. We can walk."

At the end of Main Street loomed the familiar section of exposed granite cliff on an otherwise wooded hillside, and holding Benjamin's hand, she led him up the short section of sidewalk to the next intersection. As before, Hicksville lived up to its name once they were off Main. There *were* people here, rough-looking individuals in white trash yards, staring hostilely, although where the tire yard should have been was a tire *fire*, noxious black smoke billowing from a pile of...

Not tires.

Bodies.

Gloria felt sick. It was not a tire fire after all but a funeral pyre, a mass cremation. In the flames, burning slowly, she saw people she recognized: Ricardo, the owner of Hicksville's missing Mexican restaurant; the Yang family, their onetime next door neighbors; Guyla, her former employer Dr. Gorshin's old nurse; her college friend Nina.

Her mother had to be nearby.

It occurred to her that they should have seen the rising smoke when they drove into town, or at least when they had turned onto this street, but they hadn't. Gloria glanced around, saw local residents glaring at her. There was an energy in the air that seemed to presage danger. She tightened her grip on Benjamin's hand.

"Are those…people?" he asked incredulously, staring at the blaze.

She didn't answer but pulled him forward, walking.

Then they were standing in front of the empty lot that was home to the shack.

The small building stood before a line of tall trees, at once a part of the landscape and completely out of place. Without a door, the entrance opened onto blackness, as though the interior was not a single room but a vast empty space. There was movement on the right side of the shack, and emerging from the trees Gloria saw a shirtless man with long wild hair, holding a long curved knife and smiling a predatory, too-wide grin.

Dan.

Two other figures stood on the other side of the shack.

Paula and Mica.

They, too, were grinning crazily. For some reason, they were wearing business suits.

Afraid that Benjamin would be deceived by this tableau, she turned to him, but he was no longer next to her.

When had she let go of his hand?

She turned to see him several steps behind, frozen in place. Not blinking, apparently unable to move, he stood in the center of the street. Next to him, her arm through his, was her mother.

The crude men and coarse women who populated this part of town were stepping off their properties onto the street, approaching slowly.

"So you made it here," her mother said.

"Let him go," Gloria ordered.

"He's not leaving."

"He's coming with me."

She said what Gloria knew she was going to say, what she didn't want her to say: "He needs to die."

"He's already dead!"

"And you don't bring people back when they die."

"Why not?"

"That's not what we do. That's not our purpose."

"Then what *do* we do? What *is* our purpose?"

Her mother's voice was almost tender. Almost. "We do what we have always done. What my mother did, what her mother did, what her mother did."

"And what is that, exactly?"

"*Survive.*" The faux tenderness was lined with steel.

"But we can *help* people! That gives us a responsibility. We can return people's loved ones! Don't you understand how wonderful that is?"

"Oh, we can do a lot more than that." Her mother leaned forward. "It is why we were once thought gods."

Gloria took a step toward her—

And somehow their positions were reversed.

With the shack behind her, she had been facing her mother, who'd been standing in the center of the street holding Benjamin while rough-looking locals coalesced around her. But now her mother was standing halfway up the dirt path that led to the shack, and Gloria found herself facing that direction. Glancing over her shoulder, she saw that the residents of Hicksville stood in a line at the edge of the street, blocking any escape.

Her mother smiled.

"Give him back to me!" Gloria demanded.

"Do you even remember how he died?"

She thought about what Russell had told her the last time she'd been here. "Cancer."

Her mother was taken aback. "You can't possibly remember that."

Gloria stared at her defiantly. "But I do."

"Well, he's going to wish he had cancer." She let go of Benjamin's arm, and before Gloria could react, Paula and Mica ran down from their side of the shack and pulled him away. He half-staggered and was half-dragged to the opposite side of the building, where Dan, still grinning crazily, shoved him to the ground and stood over him, knife in hand.

"Stop!" Gloria cried. By this time, she had sprinted halfway up the lot, but her mother was moving to block her way. "Don't you touch him!"

There was an expression of bewildered anger on her mother's face. "Why are you doing this?"

"I love him."

"We don't *fall* in love!" her mother screamed. "That's not the way things are supposed to be!"

"But it's the way things are."

"He. Has. To. Die."

Gloria looked into her mother's distorted angry face, at once familiar and unfamiliar, and came to a sudden hard realization: she would have to kill her.

The idea was not as shocking or foreign to her as it should have been or as she wanted it to be. Something had shifted, both within and without her, and Gloria experienced an odd sense of liberation when she thought of doing away with her mother once and for all.

The force that had been pushing against her, the thing that had prevented her from making any progress would be gone, and she had no doubt that her muddled conception of who she was would clear up as soon as the obstacle before her was removed.

Her mother was obviously entertaining similar thoughts.

"Go back now, and I'll let you live," the old woman said.

"Not without Benjamin."

What was the look that crossed her mother's face? Envy? Incomprehension? Whatever it was, it cemented Gloria's feelings, and she was overcome with rage and hate unlike any she had experienced before. In a fury, she reached down and picked a rock up off the ground. Her mother laughed mockingly. "What are you going to do with that? Throw it at me?"

"I'm going to bash your brains in."

"I'm afraid that won't help poor Benjamin," her mother said, making an exaggerated sad face. "He died."

And Gloria turned to see Dan pulling his long curved knife out of her husband's body.

It was impossible to breathe. Every last bit of oxygen seemed to have been sucked out of her lungs. It was over. All of her time and effort had been for nothing. Everything she had done had failed. Benjamin was gone. As she'd argued with her mother, her husband had been killed, and now he lay there in the dirt, his shiny blood dripping from the blade, and gushing in weakening spurts from the gaping wound in his chest. Dan was still grinning crazily, and he wiped first one side of the blade and then the other on his shirt, painting a crimson X on the pale material.

Gloria rushed her mother, rock raised, screaming like a wildcat. She would kill the bitch. And then kill Dan. He was her son, but she wanted him dead, and she was filled with fury as she—

—sat on a white stone bench in a white stone room. She was no longer herself, her mother was not her mother, and the two of them stared silently at each other across the empty space between them. Her mother had no mouth, Gloria saw, and neither did she. Both of their bodies were covered with fur.

Was this what they really were?

They were no longer in Hicksville or anywhere remotely recognizable. Benjamin was there, too, or rather his body was, but it had been reshaped and formed into a conveyance of some sort. Wooden wheels were attached to his downward-pointing arms and legs, dowels pushed through holes in his hands and feet, and upon his perfectly straight back was a carriage seat that had been strapped around his midsection. She could see his face from where she sat, and it was blank, expressionless, wiped clean of all trace of who he was.

But it was still him.

Rage overwhelmed the grief she felt, and Gloria stood—

—and was on a wide metal bridge whose surface had been overlayed with what looked and smelled like tar. Beneath the bridge, a red river ran, and in the water floated a line of naked men, all of them Benjamin. She was shoved hard from behind, and only quick reflexes saved her from landing face first in the tar. Her hands broke the fall, sinking into the sticky black goo, while a hard kick between her splayed legs sent a bolt of excruciating pain shooting up through her body. Rolling over onto her side, knees and elbows adhering uncomfortably to the tar before wrenching away, she barely missed a second kick. Pushing against the resistance of the tar, Gloria continued rolling onto her back and looked up to see her mother glaring furiously down at her, ready to kick again.

Only her mother was a man, a long-haired young man far more beautiful than her mother had ever been.

Gloria pulled up her own legs and kicked out, hearing a satisfying crack as her heels connected with the man's kneecaps. The man staggered backward and fell, as Gloria awkwardly and painfully pushed herself to her feet. She could see into the red river down below, and the line of...

...of...

...of *men* that had been floating by was gone.

Men?

Her husband.

Billy? Bram? Benny? Bob?

You won't remember who he is.

That couldn't be true.

But she couldn't seem to recall his name. Benny was closest, but that wasn't quite right, and Gloria was filled with a growing sense of panic.

Benjamin!

That was right, and she repeated the name aloud as she faced off against the young man standing at the foot of the bridge. He had regained his footing and now held a stick in his hand, shorter than a staff and thinner than a bat but clearly intended to be used as a weapon. Gloria found herself clutching a baseball-sized rock, the outer area of which was covered with tar.

"Benjamin...Benjamin...Benjamin..." she said to herself.

The young man who was her mother jabbed the stick in front of him like a lance, then, smiling broadly, whipped it from side to side, making a whooshing sound in the air. Calmly, purposefully, keeping her pain and anger in check, Gloria walked forward, cocked her arm back and threw the rock as hard as she could, aiming straight at the young man's face. He tried to block the projectile with his stick but missed by a wide margin, and the rock found its target, smashing into the bridge of his nose, hitting the corner of his right eye, and—

They were in a world where the cloudless sky was a flat metallic gray, with no sign of either sun or moon, and the blighted landscape was flat and strewn with rubble. There was only herself and her mother, sitting once again on stone benches facing each other. Benjamin—

she remembered his name!

—was nowhere to be seen, and Gloria was filled with an ominous sense of dread. The air, she noticed, was heavy and warm and smelled of sulfur, and from somewhere far off sounded a constant high keening. A batlike creature the size of a bicycle flew overhead and promptly disappeared.

How had this world come to be? she wondered. At what point had the world she'd known forked off into this reality? What had caused it to become this way?

Her mother.

Her mother had to be behind all this, but how was it done? It seemed as though she had the ability to shift realities around them, shift even their own corporeal forms, and to do so instantly.

It is why we were once thought gods.

We.

Maybe Gloria could do the same.

Acting on instinct, she closed her eyes. While she had no idea how to go about effecting such a transformation of her surroundings, she forced herself to concentrate hard on Maxine's house, across the street from what, in her mind, still felt like her childhood home, trying to remember every detail about the old lady's front sitting room. She saw the flowered sofa with white crocheted doilies over the padded arms, the small lamp in the center of the round end table, the elaborately decorated bone china in the glass case next to the console television, and—

She was sitting on Maxine's couch, looking through the large picture window. She smelled mothballs and peppermint candy, heard a cheap cuckoo clock in another room announce that it was half-past something. Gloria was alone in the house, but across the street, a familiar older man wearing blue swim trunks was standing in the opposite driveway, glaring at her.

Her mother.

She knew it was true. She also knew that her mother had not expected to be here right now, had not expected to have this form, and Gloria closed her eyes, concentrating again, and—

She was back in Hicksville, in the weedy lot in front of the shack, still holding the rock in her hand. Not more than two feet in front of Gloria, her mother stood, glowering. Beyond her mother, on the right side of the shack, Benjamin's body lay on the ground. There was no sign of Dan, Paula or Mica.

Her mother leaped at her, hands clawed.

Gloria fell back, arms out for protection, and found herself enfolded by a crush of men and women who shifted in front of her and blocked her mother's attack. She recognized the surrounding faces as they passed: Celia, Susan, Janine, Paul, Lizzie, Linda, Sadeen...

This was *her* Hicksville, and the townspeople—not the hostile rustics of before but her friends, her brothers, her sisters, her children—had moved up from the street to back her. From outside the engulfing throng, she heard her mother's cries of wrath and frustration.

Gloria was pushed to the left and then to the right, jostled about, but not roughly or with intent to harm. It was the ripple effect of something happening that she could not see, but then a man's voice shouted "We have her!"

She recognized that voice. Luke. He had once been her brother.

The gathering parted, and Gloria saw that her mother was on the ground, being held by people who had never before known each other and perhaps had never existed. Her mother's capture had obviously been difficult; she had a black eye and there was blood on her teeth.

"You're learning," she said. "Maybe with Benjamin gone you can make something of yourself."

"Bring him back."

"No."

Gloria knelt down next to her. "Why?"

"I should have killed you *and* Benjamin. I never should have let you live." She smiled through bloody teeth, and the arms of the men holding her down jerked as she struggled unsuccessfully to break free.

Beneath them, the ground shifted to cement. Above them, the blue sky darkened and began to fade.

Gloria leaned forward and pressed down on her mother's neck. "Stop it! I know what you're trying to do!"

An expression of pain crossed the old lady's features, she began to gasp for air, and the ground was once again dirt, the sky blue.

Gloria let up on the pressure. "What do you want?"

"The same thing you want."

"What?"

"You know."

"I don't!"

The two of them stared into each other's eyes, and it was Gloria who looked away first. Something in the other woman's parchment face frightened her, something she almost recognized.

"What are we, Mother?" she asked.

"We are what we are."

"If I let you up—"

"I will kill you."

"Why?"

"You know why."

Once more, the sky darkened, blue becoming white becoming gray.

"Stop!"

"No."

"I told you to stop!"

The air in front of them thickened and began to consolidate, what appeared to be a wall taking form in the space between themselves and the shack.

Gloria grabbed her mother's neck and pressed her fingers into the flesh. "I don't want to do this."

Her mother gazed at her defiantly. "Yes, you do."

The wall continued to solidify, expanding outward, and Gloria squeezed as tightly as she could, pressing down on the dry wrinkled neck with the heels of her hands, putting all of her weight behind it.

Her mother's eyes bored unflinchingly into her own.

Then Gloria felt something give. There was a sharp *crack*, and the body beneath her went limp. The nascent wall winked out of existence and color instantly returned to the sky.

Breathing heavily, Gloria staggered to her feet, stepping away, the men who had been holding her mother down finally releasing the old woman's arms and legs as they stood themselves. On the ground, her mother began to change, her hair growing out then disappearing, her body shortening then lengthening, the features of her face merging then paring down—no mouth, no nose, one eye—until finally she was unrecognizable as anything human. The men moved back, and Gloria stood over the body, staring down at what her mother had become, at what she had always been.

She felt exhausted, angry, confused and, more than anything else, terribly, terribly sad.

The crowd from the street had either dispersed or disappeared. There was no one here but herself, and the bodies of her husband and what had once been her mother.

Around them, the world seemed to be getting gauzy around the edges...fuzzier.

Gloria hurried past her mother to the right side of the shack and dropped to her knees next to Benjamin, suddenly unable to stop sobbing. His eyes were closed. Looking into his face, she could almost pretend that he was asleep, but the blood still seeping from the hole in his chest belied that false narrative, and his utter lack of animation, the complete absence of life in his beloved features, was both obvious and undeniable. She bent over to touch him. His skin was cool against her fingers, and when she kissed his lips, they felt springy and fake and tasted of her own tears.

Straightening, Gloria saw that her surroundings had grown even more indistinct. For a brief second, she thought that it might be an optical illusion, but when she wiped the tears from her eyes, she knew that the world around her was becoming increasingly insubstantial, revealing a sharper solid identical world beneath.

Her gaze returned to Benjamin—

You won't remember who he is.

—and she was overcome by a grief and despair so complete that it rooted her in place and robbed her of any ability to act or even think. She stared at his unmoving form, engulfed by overwhelming sadness. Already, her memories were starting to fade. She could not remember where the two of them had lived or even whether they had had children. In her mind, she caught fleeting glimpses of past times together—breakfast around a kitchen table, a backyard barbecue, a small closet with a sloping ceiling, a creepy bathroom in an abandoned store, a house in Colorado, a field trip to see cactus—but none of it tied together.

The temperature changed as the light dimmed, increasing cold causing goosebumps to ripple over her skin. Softly, she touched his lips with her index finger. "Goodbye," she whispered.

And she was sitting flat on a raised section of floor within a long narrow room. On the wall opposite was a gigantic portrait of herself. Other, smaller pictures of her, some photographs, some sketches, were taped, tacked and plastered all around. The wood on which she sat was dusty, as was the rest of the room. Her head felt heavy, numb. She was not sure where she was, but, much more concerningly, was not sure *who* she was.

She sat there, trying to get her bearings, staring dully at her surroundings. Gradually, she realized that the room was not as strange to her as she'd originally thought. In fact, she was pretty sure she had been here before. At the far end of the narrow space, opposite the giant portrait, was an open doorway, and through it she saw sunlight. She squinted against the brightness. She felt sad for some reason, empty, and it seemed to her that she had lost something or someone very important to her.

She stood, wobbling for a moment on unsteady feet. She recognized the clothes she was wearing in the huge portrait, as well as some of the outfits depicted in the smaller drawings and photographs. Memories were starting to return, and she understood that the room she was in was the interior of a small building in a small town.

The location where she helped people recover those they had lost.

She remembered who she was.

Gloria looked about with fresh eyes. The structure seemed to have fallen into a state of disrepair since she had seen it last. Weeds poked through cracks in the dusty wooden floor, and from a hole in the ceiling a small sliver of sunlight streamed. She should have been greeted by a group of men—

Russell, the leader's name was Russell

—but she was the only one present. They had given up, perhaps. Or died off. How long had it been since she was last here?

She walked outside. The weather was warm, and the vegetation brown, indicating that it was probably summer. Standing before her, at the head of a dirt pathway that led to the street, was a middle-aged man. He appeared to have been waiting, and she frowned. *What do you want?* she felt like asking, but he was kind of cute in a sad puppy dog sort of way, and he was looking at her with an expression of anticipation that made her think she might once have known him, although she had no idea how or where.

An echo of a warning sounded somewhere in her brain.

You won't remember who he is.

Who had said that to her? And when? It had been more than a warning, she seemed to recall, closer to a threat, but she could not remember who had said it or to whom it had referred.

Could it be him?

He stepped forward, and she examined his features more closely. There was something almost familiar about him, but it was an indefinable association, an ambiguous feeling that they might once have met. He looked like a nice man, though, and just seeing him made her feel somehow lighter, lessened the sadness that continued to absorb her.

She met his eyes, and something in them jogged her memory.

She knew those eyes.

"Hello," he said.

She knew that voice.

She stepped forward. Hesitated. "Benjamin?"

He smiled widely. "Gloria."